2 nd floor

SUSPICION
OF
BETRAYAL

Also by Barbara Parker

BARBARA PARKER

SUSPICION OF BETRAYAL

A DUTTON BOOK

DUTTON
Published by the Penguin Group
Penguin Putnam Inc., 375 Hudson Street, New York, New York 10014, U.S.A.
Penguin Books Ltd, 27 Wrights Lane, London W8 5TZ, England
Penguin Books Australia Ltd, Ringwood, Victoria, Australia
Penguin Books Canada Ltd, 10 Alcorn Avenue, Toronto, Ontario, Canada M4V 3B2
Penguin Books (N.Z.) Ltd, 182–190 Wairau Road, Auckland 10, New Zealand

Penguin Books Ltd, Registered Offices:
Harmondsworth, Middlesex, England

First published by Dutton, a member of Penguin Putnam Inc.

First Printing, April, 1999
10 9 8 7 6 5 4 3 2 1

REGISTERED TRADEMARK—MARCA REGISTRADA

LIBRARY OF CONGRESS CATALOGING-IN-PUBLICATION DATA:
Parker, Barbara (Barbara J.)
   Suspicion of betrayal : a novel / by Barbara Parker.
      p.   cm.
   ISBN 0-525-94468-0
   I. Title.
PS3566.A67475S84   1999
813'.54—dc21   98–52080
                                CIP

Printed in the United States of America
Set in Stone Serif
Designed by Julian Hamer

PUBLISHER'S NOTE
This is a work of fiction. Names, characters, places, and incidents either are the products of the author's imagination or are used fictitiously, and any resemblance to actual persons, living or dead, events, or locales is entirely coincidental.

This book is printed on acid-free paper. ∞

CHAPTER

ONE

Like anyone else with a telephone, Gail Connor had received her share of crank calls, but none where the person on the other end had disguised his voice, called her a bitch, and said she was going to die. The night she received such a call, it was more annoying than frightening. At thirty-four, trained as a litigating attorney, she was not the sort of woman to be easily rattled. And she thought she knew who had done it—the kid across the street. He was fourteen, and earlier she had yelled at him to stay out of her backyard. He'd been smoking in the gazebo. Even worse, Karen and two of her friends had been out there with him, and Karen was still under eleven years old.

Later on that night, Gail wondered if her temper might have been the result of so many changes in so short a time. Divorcing one man, falling in love with another. Giving up a partnership to open her own practice. And moving into an old house that was making her crazy. She and Karen had lived in it less than a month. They were not used to high-beamed ceilings and heavy plaster walls, to narrow stairs that twisted to a second floor, or to an immense gas stove that hissed, then popped into flame. The toilets gurgled; the air conditioner wheezed. Warped windows stuck halfway open. Gail would have to go outside and shove while Karen jiggled the crank. During heavy rains they put towels on the sills. Gail told Karen they were having an adventure. Karen crossed her arms and rolled her eyes. Gail's mother had warned against uprooting the child so abruptly from her old neighborhood. Gail could see the point—in hindsight—but didn't know what could be done about it now. To make Karen feel better, she had allowed her to bring home a kitten from the animal shelter, a little black-and-white female named Missy. So far the creature had thrown up twice on Gail's bedroom rug and peed on one of Anthony's best jackets.

They had planned to move in after the wedding to a home freshly painted and patched, with a new kitchen and refinished oak floors. Karen would get to design her own bedroom. But the week after Gail put their old house on the market, expecting to have months till the closing, a Brazilian couple offered full price—if they could close right away. Not wanting to lose the deal, Gail called a moving company and had all her and Karen's belongings hauled from their modern three-two in South Miami to the 1927 coral rock and stucco relic in Coconut Grove, where air plants sprouted from the leaky tile roof and the bushes had not been pruned in decades.

She had assumed it would take only two or three weeks, with little disruption to her schedule. She had been wrong. The workers, few of whom spoke English, showed up when they showed up, and charged extortionate rates for off hours. The painting couldn't be done until the carpenter was finished and the carpenter had to wait for the plumber. The wedding was only two months away, and Gail imagined the worst: home from their honeymoon, Anthony sweeping her into his arms, stepping over the threshold. They plunge between the open floor joists.

The night Gail received the telephone call wishing her dead was a Thursday, the middle of June. Officially Anthony was still living in his town house on Key Biscayne, fifteen miles away, but he would often come by after work. On this particular night he had stopped by a gourmet grocery. He opened the aluminum takeout pan and showed it to Karen, who was sitting backward in a kitchen chair with her chin on crossed arms.

"Look. Lasagna."

"Yuck."

"*¿Qué pasa, mamita?*"

"I hate mushrooms."

"Karen!" Gail turned around with a hand on her hip. "If you can't be polite, then go upstairs until you can."

"Fine. I'll starve to death."

Gail called out to her retreating back. "And take a bath. I'll come check on you in a while."

"Don't bother. I'll be dead." Karen scooped up her kitten, which was playing with a toy lizard under the table. Heavy-soled sneakers thudded up the stairs, and a few seconds later a door slammed.

"Sorry about that," Gail said. She jerked on a drawer to free it, then scooped silverware out of the tray. The cabinets were fake walnut, and the appliances were avocado green. It would all go during remodeling—if they could ever decide what to put in its place. She gave the silverware to Anthony—three sets in case Karen repented.

He was still frowning at the empty archway that led to the hall, which seconds before had contained a skinny girl with long brown hair and jeans so baggy they dragged on the floor. "What's the matter with Karen? Is she mad at me for a reason that I fail to grasp?"

"No, it's me. I told her she couldn't go outside and play—excuse me, go hang out—with Jennifer and Lindsay."

"*Que va.* It's almost dark." He glanced at the ceiling. A stereo had come on, playing just below the volume at which someone might go upstairs and ask that it be turned down.

"Just ignore her," Gail said. "She's almost eleven, and I've heard that girls go through this when they hit puberty. It's a natural phase of development. Supposedly."

Half to himself, Anthony muttered, "Ah, yes. The obnoxious phase."

Gail made a little face at him, then put the lasagna in the oven to warm and went about making the salad. Rip open a plastic bag of mixed baby greens, throw in a few walnuts, some cherry tomatoes, and crumbled Gorgonzola. Toss with bottled vinaigrette—not the cheap kind, the five-dollar brand from Chef Alan. She and every woman lawyer she knew had a repertoire of recipes that could produce a meal in ten minutes flat. It helped if somebody else brought the main course.

Anthony had taken two glasses from the cabinet. "What would you like to drink?"

"Just wine. Anything stronger will put me to sleep, and I have a case to work on." Her wineglasses were lost in the boxes stacked in the living room. He poured white wine into one short glass and dark rum over ice into another.

"I would have gone over the file at my office, but the handyman called. It cost me a hundred dollars, but at least he fixed the sink. There was a cat toy stuck in the drain, don't ask me how."

Anthony touched the rim of his glass to hers. *"Salud."*

She gratefully took a swallow and leaned over to give him a quick kiss. "Thanks. And hello, *mi cielo*, whom I haven't seen in two days. I wonder. Is your secretary telling the truth when she says she can't reach you? Why am I always the one to let the repairmen in?"

"Well, you live here." Anthony leaned against the counter next to her, sipping his drink. He had gracefully masculine hands. There was a ring on his last finger—garnet set in gold.

"That is *not* the right answer." Gail pulled on his loosened tie. Patterned red silk, which matched the ring, which went with the monogrammed initials on the pocket of his custom-made shirt. "I bet you don't even know what a P-trap is, do you?"

"Of course. I keep them in my nightstand."

She narrowed her eyes. "Hopeless."

He set down his drink and kissed her. His soft, full mouth was cool from the ice, tangy-sweet from alcohol. Both hands went under her shirt to caress bare skin. She had not worn a bra. He quickly discovered that fact and pinned her against the counter.

Stopping to catch her breath, she said, "Stay tonight. Say yes." She left a trail of light kisses across his cheek. "Yes. Yes. I promise you many exotic delights . . ."

"Should we? If you have work to do, and with Karen in her phase—I'll stay if you want, but is it wise?"

"Probably not. You make me very *un*wise. I'm crazy about you. Absolutely wacko."

He curled her fingers over his hand and kissed them. The movement made her engagement ring sparkle, even in the kitchen's buzzing fluorescent light. The stone was perfect, a man's diamond he had worn on his own hand, reset for her. His eyes lifted to focus on hers. "Gail, are you going to tell me what happened in court today or not?"

Since morning that topic had been in and out of her consciousness like an intermittent toothache. She reached for her wine. "The judge is going to appoint a psychologist to interview Karen. I haven't told her about it yet."

"What do you mean, a psychologist? The motion was about visitation."

"Yes, well, they raised the issue anyway, after the judge said that Dave getting Karen five afternoons a week was a bit much. They said I've made Karen afraid to admit she wants to live with her father. Afraid? What in God's name do they think I do, beat her? What really galls me is that Dave doesn't consider how this is affecting Karen. Never mind what she's going through, he wants to get back at *me*. Our marriage failed, and it's all my fault, but I got the house and the kid. Well, excuse me. It was Dave who wanted out. Then he took off on his damned sailboat for six months. Lived with some girl in San Juan. He hardly ever wrote Karen. I can't tell you the times she cried over him and I had to make up some story. 'Yes, sweetie, of course your daddy loves you, but there's no post office on the islands.' And now he's back and I'm such a bad mother they need a psychologist to determine the extent of the damage." Gail let her arms fall to her sides. "Sorry for ranting."

She could feel the heat building from Anthony's direction. "Come on. This isn't about you. Dave is angry with *me*. You're just bonus points."

A lift of Anthony's brows said he doubted that. "Karen is old enough to decide where she wants to live, don't you think? Why doesn't the judge leave it up to her?"

"Karen won't make a decision. She doesn't want to hurt either of us, so she won't say anything."

"You haven't asked?"

"I'd rather not put pressure on her."

"Gail, she's not a baby. You should take another look. A girl is better off with a mother, who can tell her about—" Anthony looked for the word—"feminine things. She can visit her father when she likes, but her home is with you. Be as subtle as you need to, but make your point. You have more power with Karen than he does."

"Maybe you're right, but I really don't want to talk about it anymore."

Gail grabbed a towel to take the lasagna out of the oven. Maneuvering it past the door, she grazed her knuckle on the hot metal. "Ouch. Dammit!" The door slammed shut with a clatter of oven racks. She dropped the aluminum pan on the table and waved her hand to shake off the burn.

"Are you okay?"

"It's nothing." She looked down at the pan. "I should have put the lasagna in a nicer dish. As if I could find one in that chaos in the garage." Gail let out a long breath, then noticed the folder Anthony had laid on the end of the table when he'd come in. "What's in there? The architect's drawings?"

"I thought we could look at them over dinner," he said.

Away from the tourist-clogged section, streets in Coconut Grove curved around overhanging trees and dense tropical foliage— small streets with odd names like Ye Little Wood, Battersea, and

Kiaora. The land could rise and fall, as this part of Miami had some altitude—fifteen feet above sea level. One might see a starkly modern house of angled glass and concrete beside a run-down clapboard cottage. The next would be hidden behind a wood fence laden with hot pink bougainvillea. A rainbow flag might fly from one roof, Old Glory from another. At this time of year plants thrust upward and out, blocking the light, climbing over each other, bursting with buds, tendrils, fronds, and leaves the size of dinner plates.

Clematis Street was a cul-de-sac running along a canal that led to Biscayne Bay. The dozen or so homes were generally of a Mediterranean design, with a few tropical moderns and one white-columned colonial out of its latitude. Gail and Anthony's house was constructed of block and stucco, with a circular drive and covered terraces front and back, tiled to feel cool in the summer. There were two coral rock fireplaces, downstairs and in the master bedroom, for those days in winter when one might want the glow of a fire. The real estate saleslady had used the words *charming* and *cozy*.

As Anthony laid the drawings out on the table—pen and ink with washes of color—Gail wondered if the architect had looked at the right house. It was evident he had gone far beyond plans for a kitchen. The long, narrow living room had doubled in size. The side wall had been pushed out twenty feet, and a massive brass chandelier hung from the ceiling. The stairs, which had been torn out and moved across the room, curved to form a balcony that looked down from the second floor. Gail laid her fork carefully on her plate.

Anthony showed her a drawing of the new master bedroom. "Here's a view of the upper-floor terrace from our room. It's completely private. Karen's room and the other two bedrooms would have balconies. The guest house would be next to the pool, separate or connected to the main house, whatever we prefer."

"The pool?"

As if finally aware of what he was showing her, Anthony

shuffled through the sketches. "Well, the architect thought it would add value to the house. You don't want a pool?"

"But we were only going to redo the kitchen and make some minor repairs, not redesign the entire house. We don't have time for major renovation right now."

"That's what contractors are for."

"But *somebody* has to be here to deal with these people. Not *you*. I get to do it because I live here."

"I do not want to live in this house the way it is, and it is better—in my opinion—to do it now, to get it over with—"

"Anthony, let's just get the kitchen done."

"Why are you being so negative?"

"I'm not negative, this is insane!" Gail sat back in her chair. "How much would it cost? Ballpark figure."

He shrugged. "I don't know. Two-fifty. Three hundred."

"At least." She propped her chin in her palm. "I hate to tell you, but I've got that old Hawaiian disease—lackamoola." When Anthony went blank, she repeated, "Lackamoola. Lack of —"

"Okay, I get it."

"Miriam's been asking for a raise, the computers are costing a fortune, and I'm afraid to spend money right now."

He scooted his chair out and reached for her hand. "Sweetheart, listen to me. It was my decision to hire the architect, and the changes—those over our budget—I'll take care of them. You don't have to match every dollar I put into the house. I don't expect you to."

"But I *want* to."

"Why?"

"Because . . . I just do."

His laugh was an exhalation of disbelief. "What are you trying to prove?"

"I am not trying to *prove* anything. But when you blithely start talking about three hundred thousand dollars . . ."

He spun a drawing to the table. "Maybe we shouldn't have bought this house. Maybe we should find something else."

"Well, you know, I can't say it hasn't crossed my mind a few times as I waited around for someone to come fix the roof."

"Is that what you want? All right. Okay, *vamos a venderla.* I'll call a realtor tomorrow."

"Another of your typically extreme responses—"

Above the whir and hum of the air conditioner—always on this time of year—Gail heard a high-pitched noise. It took her a few seconds to realize it was a scream, and that it wasn't a sound effect on one of Karen's CDs. She leaped up.

"What was that?" Anthony asked.

"Karen!"

He automatically glanced upward, then raced for the stairs. Gail heard it again—closer, and coming from the backyard. She ran through the kitchen and onto the terrace, seeing nothing but tangled trees and through them a glimmer of light on the water.

Karen came hurtling out of the darkness, another girl closely behind, legs pounding. Gail ran across the terrace, nearly tripping on a broken tile.

A third girl followed more slowly. "Come on, guys. He was just kidding."

Fists clenched, Karen whirled around. The friend with her giggled, breathless with excitement. Gail reached for Karen to make sure she was all right, then moved to stand in front of her, guarding her from whatever might be out there. The gazebo was a crisscross of pale lines, and a small orange dot—a cigarette— flew into the shadows. "Who's there?"

The third girl slowed. "It's my brother. He didn't mean anything."

A boy sauntered down the steps. Gail could see only a slender frame and blond curls. His voice carried easily on the heavy, humid air. "My mom sent me to find Lindsay."

Gail glared at him, the same kid who had skidded over her freshly laid sod on his older brother's motorcycle. "Go home, Payton. Now. And stay off this property."

He shouted back at her, "I wasn't doing anything. Don't get so hyper."

"I said go home! Do you want me to call your parents?"

"Go ahead."

Karen screamed, "Payton, you asshole!"

Gail grabbed her upper arm. "Don't talk like that!"

"Owww!"

"I'm not hurting you." She came closer and sniffed Karen's hair. "What were you doing out there? Smoking?" She shook her. "Answer me."

The boy vanished into the bushes, and his sister fled after him.

"I wasn't!" Karen tried to twist out of Gail's grip, but slipped and fell on her backside. The girl beside her quickly moved away. This was a chubby little brunette whose tight shirt showed it was time for a bra. Karen started to wail.

"Oh, stop being so dramatic!"

The back door banged open, slamming against the wall. Anthony appeared. "*¿Qué en el demonio—?*"

"Jennifer!"

A woman stood at the edge of the house. Gail recognized her—Mrs. Cabrera, Jennifer's mother. They lived a few doors down. With some urgency she called out, "Jennifer, *ven aca*. Time to come home. Right now."

Gripping Karen's arm, Gail pulled her to her feet. With Mrs. Cabrera's accusatory eyes on her, she hurried to explain. "They were in the gazebo with friends. I don't know what was going on."

"Nothing!" yelled Karen. "Mom, let me *go*!"

Jennifer made a guilty little wave at Karen. "See ya." Mrs. Cabrera shot another look at the three of them, then bustled her daughter away with a terse "Good night."

Gail took Karen into the kitchen. "You. Go to your room and get ready for bed. I'll be there in a minute. We're going to talk." She turned Karen toward the stairs and gave her a little shove to send her off.

Anthony closed the back door and locked it. "What was that about?"

"You tell me. They were out there with Payton Cunningham, who was smoking. I'd like to know how many cigarette butts I find down there tomorrow, and God help them if I find anything else. Payton is fourteen, a budding juvenile delinquent who dug tire tracks in the yard last week." With a little moan Gail brushed her hair off her forehead. "Welcome to family life."

"I know. I have kids."

"Yes, but yours are comfortably away in New Jersey." Gail noticed the drawings on the table. "I need to see about Karen. Could we talk about the house later? Not tonight. I really have to get to work. You can stay if you want."

"No." As if trying to decide what to say, Anthony glanced toward the terrace, then back at Gail. "You let her get away with too much."

"Let her? I didn't *let* her go outside—"

"But she did, and why did she assume she could get away with it? When I'm living here, that behavior is going to change."

"Really. Well, good luck."

He was gone in less than five minutes. She watched his car pull out of the driveway. Red taillights flared, then grew smaller up the street. His kiss had been more polite than affectionate. Gail locked the door, then leaned on it. The lamp on her glass-topped table did little to illuminate the living room. Her furniture looked ridiculous, all modern white sofas and chairs and light wood.

In her head the words she had bit her tongue not to say were whirling around: *Yes, let's sell the damn thing. I'm sorry we bought it.*

Twenty-five-watt bulbs in pitted, brass-colored sconces lit her way up the stairs. She glared at them, vowing to rip them off with a crowbar at the earliest opportunity. No sound came from

Karen's room. Gail tried the door. "Karen? Let me in." When there was no response, Gail smacked her palm on the varnished wood panel. "Karen! Open this door."

The lock clicked. Karen was in her pajamas and the light was off. She yawned widely. "I was asleep."

"You were not." Gail flipped the switch, and the desk lamp went on. "Don't *ever* lock your door like that."

"You lock yours." Retreating to her bed, Karen drew up her legs and hugged them with thin arms. "When Anthony is here, you lock your door, so why can't I lock mine?"

Gail took a breath, then another. "What were you doing outside?"

"Nothing." The kitten mewed to get on the bed, and Karen picked it up, a handful of black-and-white fur.

"I have eyes, Karen. I saw Payton's cigarette."

"Mom!" She dropped her forehead onto her knees. "I wasn't smoking. Cigarettes stink." The cat batted a strand of her hair.

"I told you not to go outside, and you did it anyway. You're grounded for a week."

"Mom!"

"You go to day camp, you come home, and you stay inside. I intend to inform your father of this too."

"That is so unfair! I called Lindsay and said I couldn't go out, and she said she had to get her Beanie Baby back. I went to give it to her, that's all."

"You were in the gazebo with your friends and Payton Cunningham."

"He's the one that should be grounded. He's a spoiled brat idiot. I hate him! I hate everybody in this neighborhood. I hate this house. I hate you and I hate Anthony!"

"That's enough!"

Karen stared up at her with red-rimmed eyes, and her mouth trembled. There was more than rebellion in that reaction, Gail thought. Quietly she said, "Karen, what happened out there? Why did you scream?"

Karen wavered.

"Don't be afraid. Did Payton do something to you?" Gail sat beside her on the edge of the bed.

"He kissed me. I didn't want him to, Mom." Her eyes filled. "I didn't. Jennifer let him, but I didn't want to. He grabbed me. He was laughing."

Gail folded her in an embrace. "Oh, sweetie. It's okay. Good for you, saying no. Don't do anything with a boy—ever—that you don't want to." Gail kissed the top of her head. "You're a good, good girl. I'm proud of you."

"Mom, I'm sorry." Karen lifted her tear-blotched face. "I didn't mean to say all that. I don't hate you or Anthony, I swear."

"Well. You're still grounded."

"I know."

The summer sun had browned Karen's skin and streaked her hair. Her adventure in the backyard had tangled it. Gail combed it with her fingers. "Is it so bad here? You're making friends. You know, Anthony and I were talking about the house tonight. He wants to put a pool in the backyard. What do you think? You could have your friends over. Invite the girls from the old neighborhood."

"That would be fun."

"You loved this house when we first saw it. Remember? You and Anthony. I think I said yes because you both loved it so much." Gail sat quietly for a few moments, rocking Karen. "Are you hungry? You missed dinner."

"*Very* hungry."

"Okay. I'll bring you something."

Karen clung. "Can I sleep with you tonight? I'm scared. Please, Mommy?"

"Sweetie . . ." Gail extricated herself. "Nobody's going to get you."

"Yes! Me scared!"

"Oh, Karen!" Gail had noticed how she could take these turns, veering from mature to childish. Nothing used to frighten her, but now anything could. Gail was at a loss, not knowing what to do. If Anthony was here, he would not want a visitor in their bed. To start a precedent meant breaking it later. But now Karen needed her.

Finally she said, "Okay. Just for tonight."

Karen flung herself at Gail and wrapped her long legs around her waist. Her body was taut as a wire. "Carry me. Carry me, Mommy." Leaning back against the weight, Gail went across the hall, opened the door to her room, and dropped Karen on her side of the king-size bed, where she bounced, then burrowed under the sheet and light summer blanket. "Missy! I want Missy."

Gail went to Karen's room, found the kitten under a chair, and brought her back across the hall. "Don't you let her pee in my bed." She tucked Missy under the covers. "I'll be back in a few minutes."

"Where are you going?"

"To get something for you to eat. I won't be long."

"Tell me a story."

"Karen, I really can't tonight. I have some work to finish."

"Daddy always tells me a story."

"I doubt that." Gail turned on the ceiling fan. "I'll bring you a book, okay?"

She chose one quickly from Karen's collection and assured her again she'd be right back. Once around the corner, Gail almost broke into a run. There would be a hearing early in the morning, and earlier still she had to meet her client and go over the testimony. Gail berated herself for not having prepared her case earlier in the week, but so much had intervened to pick away at what little time she had. A divorce case, Wendell and Jamie Sweet.

The Sweets. A funny name for two people who detested each other so thoroughly. The judge would set an amount for temporary support and an award for attorney's fees. Gail was hopeful she could collect at least twenty thousand dollars. She had put in the hours to justify it. If the judge signed the order, she could take care of some past due bills at her office and pay overhead for the next month.

She made Karen a sandwich and some chocolate milk, then turned on the gas stove to boil water for coffee. While it was heating, she put away the leftovers and rinsed the dishes. Lightning flickered to the east, an ocean storm too far away for thunder. The palm trees were spiky silhouettes. Her own reflection looked back at her, a tall woman with tousled blond hair.

The phone rang just as she had started back up the stairs with a tray. Her watch said 9:52. At this hour it would be one of three people: her mother, a frantic client, or Anthony. She wanted it to be Anthony. They would talk for a little while, and everything would be all right again.

There was an extension on a table just around the corner in the living room. A streetlight shone weakly through the blinds, making jagged stripes across the floor.

She set the tray down. "Hello?"

The only reply was a faint buzz that said the line was open. She heard some background noises and thought it might be traffic. "Hello? Anthony?"

For a second she thought that something was wrong with the connection. There were low-pitched clicks and echoes. Then her mind registered a pattern resembling human speech.

It was speech. A robot. A computer. Something speaking in a metallic monotone. Then she recognized her name.

GailConnor.

Then she fixed on another word. *Die.*

Her breath stopped.

—*goingtodie, bitch. You'regoingtodie.*

As if the handset were a snake, she thrust it back into its cradle. Then she laughed. Laughed at her own fear. "You little shit." She marched across the living room to pull down a slat in the blinds. Lights from the Cunningham house shone in small patches through the high hedge that ran down the side of their property. She thought of calling his parents but without proof, what could she say?

She took the tray upstairs. Karen was already asleep, her book open on her stomach. "Thank God." Gail tiptoed to the phone by her bed to check the caller-ID box. A red light blinked, indicating a new call. She pressed a button. The display said PAY PHONE. She whispered, "Well, aren't you clever?" Gail hit the button to delete the entry, striking it out of her mind. She turned off the ringer. Bending low, she kissed Karen's cheek. "A story tomorrow. I promise."

Gail quietly unpacked the banker's box that held the files from her office. *Sweet, Jamie. Dissolution of Marriage.* She spread out the pleadings and exhibits on Anthony's side of the bed, careful not to disturb the little mound softly snoring on hers.

It was almost two o'clock in the morning when she turned off the light.

TWO

"**M**s. Connor—" The lawyer glanced down at his legal pad, which lay between his extended arms on the lectern. "Ms. Connor, do you consider that assisting Ms. Sweet to find household help is a legitimate use of your time as a lawyer? I see on page sixteen an entry for one hour. Did you expend two hundred and fifty dollars' worth of your time helping Ms. Sweet find someone to help her clean the house, when Ms. Sweet herself is not currently employed?"

The bill for services rendered—all thirty-some pages of it—lay on the railing of the witness box. Gail slowly turned to the page in question, although she could have spoken from memory. "Mr. Acker, if you will examine the entry more closely. I spent an hour reviewing my client's financial situation to determine whether she would be able to continue to afford help—and she cannot. As you know, the Sweets had employed a housekeeper during the marriage to assist with the children. Ms. Sweet had a job, but she lost it. She's looking for another. As the mortgage is seriously in arrears, she has no choice."

So one accusation that the wife was lazy had been countered by another that the husband was vindictive and cheap. This sparring between Gail and her opposite, Marvin Acker, had been going on for fifteen minutes. Claiming fees for her services, Gail had taken the stand to testify.

There was a squeaking of springs from Judge Ramirez's chair. His Honor was getting restless. Gail did not think this would go on much longer. She listened to the muffled sound of a car horn on Flagler Street twelve stories below while Acker adjusted his glasses, licked his thumb, and flipped through pages till he found what he wanted.

"You have reported . . . one-point-three hours for telephone calls to Jamie Sweet's brother in Pascagoula, Mississippi, *re* trip to Miami. Were you acting as a travel agent, Ms. Connor?"

"No, Mr. Acker." Gail spoke directly into the microphone. "We discussed whether he should attend the hearing on a restraining order. On other occasions he had seen Wendell strike her—"

"Ob-jection," Acker said tiredly. "Not relevant. I move that the response be stricken from the record."

The judge tapped a bongo rhythm on his desk. "You ask, you're stuck with the answer. Proceed, counselor."

Unruffled, Acker proceeded. Gail could tell his heart wasn't in it, which usually meant one of two things. Either he wasn't getting paid, or his client was a pain in the ass. Gail bet on the latter. Marv Acker had a reputation for charging high hourly rates and getting most of it up front. That meant Wendell Sweet was lying when he said he had no money.

Gail looked past him at Wendell, who was staring out the window, pretending not to give a damn. What she knew of him she had learned from Jamie. Thirty-eight, born in Brownsville, Texas, mother half Mexican. His father had been an oil rigger, and Wendell got into the business that way. With a degree from Texas A&M, he started doing geologic surveys. He had a string of good luck off the north coast of Venezuela, and people said he could find oil by the way the ocean rose and fell. He went into consulting, putting Americans into deals with the big Venezuelan oil companies. Five years ago the Sweets moved to

Miami, the center of commerce between the United States and Latin America.

His wife, Gail's client, sat stiffly on the edge of her chair, as she had earlier on the stand. Jamie Sweet was thirty-two, a freckle-faced natural redhead with wide hips and a heavy bosom. Sequins outlined the collar of a pink silk suit too fancy for court. She dressed like a woman who had come from nothing and sure as hell didn't want to go back.

Jamie Sue Johnson, the oldest of seven children, had dropped out of school at sixteen and hitched a ride to Atlanta with a long-haul trucker. She got pregnant and a month later found an envelope on the dresser with $500 cash and the address of a women's clinic. She moved to Nashville, to Memphis, to Dallas, living with a series of losers, then ended up dancing in New Orleans. She pronounced it *N'Awlins*. Got stoned and had a pink rose tattooed on her thigh. Wendell admired it. *Wendell. He was one black-haired, good-lookin', honey-mouthed boy. "Baby, I'mona treat you like a queen."*

Wendell Sweet was still good-looking, if one didn't mind eyes too close together and a chin like a shovel. He had the thick wrists and big shoulders of a man who had wrestled with drill bits and steel. His smile was slow, and his drawl was charming. He could wear a suit well, and his cuff links gleamed, but Gail thought that if she was around him long enough, she would start to see the crude oil under his fingernails.

After they married, Jamie had waited tables and sold Mary Kay cosmetics to pay Wendell's tuition. When he drank, he got mean, and Jamie learned to keep out of his way. Ten hard years went by before the money started coming in, and when it did, they spent it. In Miami they bought a two-story house with a pool. There was a Land Rover to take the children to school in and a Cadillac for when Jamie and Wendell went out. But Wendell was gone more often than not. For something to do, Jamie redecorated the house—three times. Took cooking lessons and put on weight. Lost thirty pounds on diet pills, was hospitalized for an overdose, then put it all back on. She caught Wendell cheating and forgave him. She forgave him the times he hit her because she had three kids, no education, and a firm belief that somehow he would stop if only she could do better. To keep herself from going completely crazy, Jamie went to work for a resort company.

One day Wendell said he was tired of being married to a redneck whose bad grammar and fat ass embarrassed him with his clients. Something clicked in Jamie's head, and she said she'd had all she could take. Jamie's boss spoke to Anthony Quintana, and Anthony sent Jamie to Gail.

It took a court order to get Wendell out of the house. He had sat outside in his car and called her on his cell phone, alternating between teary-eyed pleas for her to come back to him and vicious threats that he would kill her if she didn't. He followed her. She saw him behind her at the grocery store or the shopping mall. A restraining order was issued. Wendell hired a lawyer. Settlement negotiations failed. Finally, five months after Gail had taken the case, here they all were on a motion for temporary support and attorney's fees. Wendell was claiming poverty. His consulting business was way off, due to downturns in the industry and political instability in Venezuela. Gail's friend Charlene Marks, who specialized in family law, told her that apparently Wendell had come down with RAIDS—Recently Acquired Income Deficiency Syndrome. The moment a divorce is filed, the husband's income drops.

Judge Ramirez interrupted Wendell's lawyer in mid-question. "Mr. Acker, I think I've heard enough to make a ruling." Acker seemed almost relieved. A big man, he sighed, took off his glasses, and folded them into his breast pocket.

Wendell swung around from the window, waiting to hear what the judge had to say.

Gail closed her file and went back to her chair. As she sat down, she smiled at Jamie and gave her a subtle wink.

Ramirez gave a cursory glance through the pleadings. "Okey-doke. Are you ready, Ms. Court Reporter?" The fiftyish woman in front of his desk nodded and said she was ready for anything.

There were a few laughs, then Ramirez said, "The court is not satisfied that respondent, Wendell Sweet, has fully disclosed his assets. Testimony from the petitioner's accountant suggests that respondent has engaged in . . . well, let's say that he appears not to have accurately reported his income to the IRS. Therefore, imputing income to Mr. Sweet consistent with the demonstrated spending patterns of the parties, I am going to award temporary support as follows. The court finds that the petitioner, Jamie Sue Sweet, has a need for three thousand dollars per month as temporary alimony and five hundred dollars per month in temporary child support for each of the three children. The husband is to bring current and continue to pay the mortgage, the wife's car loan, and all medical and dental expenses. All said amounts are to be paid forthwith."

Under the table, Gail squeezed Jamie Sweet's icy hand. This was exactly what they had asked for.

The judge went on, "The wife has also alleged a need for temporary attorney's fees in the amount of twenty-two thousand, five hundred dollars. This case is set for report in thirty days, at which time I will make a ruling on fees and reconsider the amount of support awarded to Mrs. Sweet, based on the husband's ability to pay."

Gail kept her expression neutral, hiding her bewilderment.

Ramirez consulted his notes. "Additionally, the court grants the wife's motion for contempt. Although previously ordered to do so, Mr. Sweet has not produced copies of documents relating to any and all offshore corporate or personal transactions in which he has had, now has, or expects in the future to have an interest. You shall produce said documents within one week, or this court will consider jail time. Mr. Sweet, are you paying attention? You give Ms. Connor those documents by five o'clock next Friday, or you're going to jail. Are we clear on that?"

Acker nudged his client. Wendell Sweet shifted in his chair. He drawled, "Yes, Your Honor."

"Good." Ramirez looked at Gail and made a slight smile.

"You need to get busy if you expect the court to continue this level of support. Seek and find, Ms. Connor."

She stood up. "Judge, do I understand that this order of support will *expire* in thirty days?"

"No. The court will reconsider in thirty days. The amount might remain the same. It might not."

"Yes, Judge." A mixed victory. Jamie would get some immediate help, but Gail would get no fees. Not yet. And everything depended on what she could uncover about Wendell. She sent a cool glance his way. His dark eyes poured acid.

The judge banged his gavel. "That's it. See you folks for the final hearing in October. Sorry it can't be sooner. See if you can work out a settlement before then." Everyone rose as he left the courtroom.

Jamie seemed stunned. Her lips barely moved to whisper, "Oh, my God. Did we win?"

"More or less. We'll talk after they leave."

Gail went over to speak to Marv Acker. She felt no animosity. They were both doing their jobs.

Acker had his back to his client. Quietly he said, "I'm telling you, Gail, he can't pay what he ain't got. If there's something tucked away in a bank in Nassau or wherever, it's news to me."

"Well, clients aren't always forthcoming," she said.

"Take a look at the documents, but I think it's going to be blood from a stone. How's the office going, by the way? I should get over and see your new place."

"I love it," she said. "No one to answer to but the staff. It's tough, though, after eight years in a big firm."

"Tell me about it." When he turned away, the sour expression was back on his face. "Come on, Wendell, let's get out of here. We're going to discuss an appeal." That last remark was pitched loud enough for Gail to catch it, but she assumed it was more for his client than for her.

Jamie Sweet helped load the luggage cart that Gail had wheeled in two hours ago. They took their time, lingering to make sure that Wendell left first. They didn't want to ride down in the same elevator.

While his lawyer was packing up, Wendell Sweet walked casually across the courtroom. He had pouty red lips that reminded her of Elvis Presley. Jamie threw back her head and stared at him defiantly, but her face had gone so pale her freckles stood out like spatters of brown paint.

Gail said, "Mr. Sweet—"

He said to Jamie, "Quite a lawyer you have. She runs up the bill over twenty thousand bucks, and you expect me to pay for it."

"Wendell, the judge has spoke, and that's that."

"*Spoken*, my little Mississippi belle. The judge has spoken. Yes, he has. A fine example of judicial intellect."

"Mr. Sweet, don't talk to my client."

The close-set brown eyes—they seemed crossed at this range—shifted to Gail. "I recall a saying from where I come from, about women like you. A man fool enough to stick it in is gonna get it froze off."

His lawyer was pulling Sweet's arm. "Wendell. Shut up."

Gail said, "Mr. Acker, apparently your client didn't understand the term 'contempt of court.' The judge is in chambers. If I asked him, I'm sure he would explain it."

With a hand on Sweet's elbow, Acker escorted him out.

Jamie watched them go, then sank into her chair. She pushed her fluffy red bangs off her forehead, which shone with perspiration. "Oh, Lord."

Gail smiled at her. "It's okay. Wendell's manhood depends on making a remark like that. This is better than last time, right?" At his deposition he had come across the table, and Jamie had slid under it to get away, the court reporter's machine going over, everyone screaming.

"I guess so. At least I can sit in the same room as him and not start shakin'." She took Gail's hand in both of hers. "Thank you so much." Then Jamie Sweet gave a laugh that lit up her face.

"You know what? I'm startin' to feel like I might get through this."

"We still have a long way to go," Gail said. "The order is only temporary. The judge is going to reconsider in thirty days. Meanwhile, Wendell has to produce copies of every scrap of paper in his possession relating to offshore business, right down to his Kleenex. I'd like you to help me go through everything." Jamie said she would, then Gail asked if she had any questions.

"No, I pretty much got it all." She added, "Gail, I don't know what help I can be. Wendell handled the money. If he was cheatin' on the taxes, I never knew about it. He didn't talk much about his business. He could have accounts anywhere. Lord, how stupid I was, never put aside a nickle for myself or the kids."

"Most women don't. You weren't to blame." Gail dropped her dog-eared copy of the Rules of Civil Procedure into the box and put on the lid. "To be honest, Jamie, I'm not sure Wendell will give us everything, or if he does, what we'll find."

Jamie steadied the luggage cart while Gail dropped one box on it, then another. "You know what I think? We ought to talk to Harry Lasko."

Harry Lasko was Jamie's boss—her former boss. Jamie had lost her job as the receptionist at Premier Resorts Inc. after the U.S. attorney had indicted Lasko for money laundering. He was currently out on bond awaiting trial, represented by Anthony Quintana. It was Harry Lasko who, several months ago, had recommended that Jamie Sweet talk to a lawyer.

"What does Harry know about Wendell?" Gail asked.

"Well, him and Wendell were friends. Not *friends*, like buddies, but they knew the same people, and I do recall Wendell sayin' he went out on Harry's boat a few times. You know how men talk about stuff."

Gail nodded, visualizing Wendell Sweet and Harry Lasko on a cabin cruiser anchored in a crystalline little harbor, far out of American jurisdiction, reeling in grouper and comparing notes on tax havens. "We know that Harry is a financial felon, so why not Wendell?"

"Harry isn't like that! He made some mistakes, but he isn't a *criminal*. You should see all the pictures of his grandchildren in his office. He loves those babies. Harry has been good to me, Gail. He gave me the money to pay your retainer."

Gail backtracked. "Of course you know him better than I do."

Jamie reached across the luggage cart to take Gail's hand. "I didn't mean to jump on you like that. I just feel so bad for Harry. Maybe Mr. Quintana can help him. I pray every night that Harry won't have to go to prison. At his age he might never get out. You tell Mr. Quintana to do his very, very best, will you? Tell him I said so."

"I'll tell him." Gail tilted back the cart and gave it a shove with one foot to get it rolling while Jamie held open the door. "If Harry Lasko is as fond of you as I think, he'll help us out. You know, I should check with Anthony first, since this criminal matter is pending, but I don't forsee a problem."

Charlene Marks gave a deep-throated laugh that made her gold earrings shake. "Wait. If a man is fool enough to stick it in— Then what? Do the accent again. Do the accent."

Gail smiled. "He'll git it *frooooze* awf."

"God. That's priceless." She slapped her desk with an open palm. "Well. Congratulations. And good luck with round two."

"Thank you, Charlene. And I appreciate your help, your advice."

"Pooh. You know what you're doing in a courtroom. I've seen you eviscerating some poor schmuck on the other side."

"Never like this. Divorces are so *personal*. They're vicious. People kill each other over divorce."

"Love gone bad," Charlene said. With a push of one black stiletto heel on the edge of her desk, she swiveled her leather chair and leaned back to take from her credenza a little silver flask. "May I interest you?"

"What is that?"

"Russian potato water." She unscrewed the top.

"Vodka at eleven in the morning?"

"Not by itself, good God. Bleahhh." She pressed a button on her phone. "Ruth, would you bring me and Ms. Connor—" Gail was shaking her head and mouthing *nothing for me*. "Just me, then. Bring me a spicy V-8 and some ice, would you dear? And a nice piece of celery." She smiled at Gail. "I'm on a diet. Salad for lunch."

Listening closely, one could still hear the New York in Charlene Marks's husky voice. She had curly gray hair, a bad complexion she hid behind makeup, and incredible legs she showed off in slim skirts well above her knees. Charlene Marks had been a prosecutor, and defense lawyers had cheered when she quit to go into civil practice. She slept with a judge on the appeals court a week before arguing a multimillion-dollar divorce case, and appeared so surprised when she won that her opponent actually forgave her. For her fiftieth birthday she bought herself a screaming red Porsche Turbo-Carrera. At fifty-two she traded it in for a more sedate Jaguar sedan. *I'm too old for this shit.* Gail could never remember how many times Charlene had been married, divorced, and widowed. But that was before she went into marital law. *Now I know better,* she had said.

Charlene's secretary brought in her vegetable juice, dropped a few messages on her desk, then went out again while Gail gave an opinion as to why the judge had ruled so strongly in Jamie Sweet's favor.

"Basically he just didn't like Wendell. The judge thought he was lying. When I looked at Wendell, and knew we had him, what a grand feeling."

"You don't have him yet. First the evidence. Then the execution." Charlene drizzled vodka into her glass. "One word of caution. Keep your emotions out of it. Feel sorry for Jamie Sweet if you must, but don't let her know it. You have to keep a safe distance between you and the client. Don't be their lover, their mother, or their pal."

"I thought you and I were pals."

"We are. I should know better."

"Well, as my attorney, what's on your mind?"

When Gail had returned from court, Miriam had told her that Charlene Marks wanted to see her, so Gail had gotten back on the elevator and punched the button for the top floor. The view here was better than on the fourth, where Gail had her office.

Charlene stirred her drink with the celery. Her diamond-faced watch glittered. "The judge's assistant in your case called me with the name and phone number of the psychologist appointed for Karen. Sorry to give you the bad news."

"Which bad news is that?"

"The man is a putz. But aside from that, he's an ambitious little twerp by the name of Evan Fischman. He likes kids to call him Dr. Fish. Makes it all nicey-gooey with the little darlings. He's about five-four with lifts in his shoes, and compensating like mad." Charlene clipped off the end of the celery with a sharp crunch. "I think he hates women."

"Marvelous. What do I do, make an appointment for Karen?"

"At your convenience. He'll want to talk to you and Dave too, of course, and no doubt Anthony as well. Do the complete family portrait."

"Should I worry about this?"

"Not yet. If he goes against you, we can hire someone to rebut his opinion. I have a Rolodex full of shrinks."

Gail laughed wearily. "It's like . . . 'Take off all your clothes, put on this paper robe. The doctor will be with you in a moment.' "

Sympathy showed in the warm brown eyes. "I know this isn't pleasant for you. In fact, it sucks. And I would be lying, my darling, if I told you that you are guaranteed to retain custody of your daughter."

Gail involuntarily hugged her crossed arms close to her chest.

"We can make it hard. I could run up his legal expenses so high his ears would bleed. But here's what I think. You should talk to Dave. Find out where he's coming from."

"Talk to him? How?"

"Make some excuse. I don't want his lawyer calling me to whine. Listen. You're going to be hooked to that man as long as you live. Not only through Karen; there will be a son-in-law someday, God willing, and grandchildren, and they're all going to appreciate it if you and Dave aren't sniping at each other. It just ruins the holidays. You know I don't like to compromise, and if you want me to pound his ass into the ground I will do my damnedest. But what do you get from that in the long run? No, I think you should find out what he really wants, and if it doesn't make you puke, give it to him to make him go away."

"I think he wants Karen."

"Does he? A man thirty-six years old, running a bar, who gets to ride on boats and look at women in bathing suits all day? A guy with a nice tan, who can play tennis with the rich folks? Does he really want a child in the way? He may think he does, but no. Karen is a substitute for something else."

"What?"

"Jesus, I don't know. You were married to him. You find out." Charlene crossed her long legs and rotated one foot, the sharp point of her shoe making a slow circle. "Don't bother asking directly. Men are rarely introspective enough to understand their own motivation. It's either money or sex. Start from there."

THREE

Over the last week or so, coming home from work usually meant seeing the roofer's truck in the driveway. Or not. Gail couldn't decide which was worse. To see an empty driveway meant nothing was being done. To see the truck meant irritation of some kind. The smoky stench of tar. The incessant pop of a nail gun. Or those little plastic cuplets for Cuban coffee tossed into the bushes.

The truck was there, a rusty half-ton flatbed with a railing of two-by-fours around the back. Recio Roofing, blocking the garage. Pallets of Spanish barrel tiles had been offloaded into the yard. With nowhere else to put her car, Gail parked along the narrow, sun-dappled street.

Walking into the driveway, she saw how the rear truck tires, a double set, had left tracks over the newly laid sod. Then she noticed the little alamanda bush. It had come from her mother's yard, and now looked like a big boot had stomped it. She picked up one of the branches. The trumpet-shaped yellow flowers were limp. Gail muttered a low curse.

Karen looked at her. "Mom!"

The men were coming down off the roof, finished for the day. "Look at this." Gail pointed. They looked in the right direction, but none of them seemed to notice. "*Aquí.* Look at this. *Mira.*"

One of the men came to see what she was talking about. Gail assumed he was in charge, a big-bellied guy in a sweat-soaked T-shirt. His work boots were black with tar. "What's the problem?" he said.

"Were you driving the truck?" When he shrugged, she said, "Well, you ran over this bush! It was right there! Didn't you see it?"

"A bush . . ."

She waved the broken branch at him. "My mother planted it. And last week you—or somebody—broke two sprinkler heads. I asked you to stay off the lawn." She pointed toward the pallets. "And these weren't supposed to go there. We just had the sod laid down. They can't stay there all weekend, they'll kill the grass."

"I can't move them now. The forklift went to another job."

She heard a snicker behind her. The others might not know what they were saying, but they were enjoying the scene.

Gail turned around to give them a look and caught sight of a long-legged girl in shorts climbing onto the back of the truck. "Oh, my God! Karen, get down!" Karen held herself suspended by her fingers, then dropped, ponytail swinging. "Go inside, sweetie, and get cleaned up."

"The door is locked."

"You have a key in your backpack."

She turned back to the men and squinted in the glare. It was hot out here, and already she could feel sweat on her neck. These men had been up on the roof all day, baked red by the sun and splattered with tar, and now had to take shit from a woman lawyer who had just driven up in her little air-conditioned Mercedes.

Gail tossed the branch aside. "Never mind."

The men got into the truck, two in front and the others in back, hanging on. Salsa music blared through the open windows. Gail watched the rear tires just miss the grass; then the truck headed off with a grinding of gears and blast of smoke, ripping through the low-hanging limbs of a black olive tree.

When the racket of music and engine had subsided, Gail took out her keys to move her car. There was another sound. *Snik-snik-snik.* Across the street the bushes were moving, and sprays of red flowers bobbled. Someone was pruning behind a low coral rock wall. Through the big heart-shaped leaves she saw a white head band and sunglasses. And behind them a woman pretending not to have noticed her new neighbor fighting with the roofers.

Gail walked over and stood in the gravel next to the wall. There were no sidewalks. "Hi, Peggy."

A yellow-daisy garden glove waved at her, and Peggy Cunningham came farther into view. She had the golden tan of a woman who spent time by the pool. "Hi. Sure is hot and muggy today."

"Sure is. Listen, Peggy. Was your son home last night around ten o'clock?"

"Payton? Why?"

"Somebody phoned my house and made some rude remarks. I didn't recognize the voice. It was going through an electronic device of some kind. That's my guess."

Peggy Cunningham shifted closer. "An obscene phone call?"

"No, not obscene, just . . . rude. Anyway, Payton was in my backyard last night, with Karen, and she wasn't allowed out, and I told him to go home. Maybe he was mad at me—"

"Yes, he said you yelled at him for being on your property."

Gail forced herself to smile, not liking the way this was going. "I thought he might have been playing a little joke."

A chilly smile was returned to her. "No. Payton wouldn't play jokes like that."

"At that age, who knows? Kids can be unpredictable. If I could find out for sure, then I could stop worrying about it. Really, I'm not angry."

"I can't imagine Payton would do that."

"Well, was he home or not?"

Peggy Cunningham made a small laugh and waved a bug away from her face. "I feel like I'm being cross-examined."

"Would you mind if I ask him?"

"Yes, I do mind. I don't like your accusations. Payton would not harass anybody in any way. I know my son."

"Really. Then you know he smokes."

"He does not smoke."

"I saw him in my gazebo last night with a cigarette."

The sunglasses pointed directly at Gail. "If that is true, I'd call it youthful exploration. Payton does not *smoke*."

"Is it also youthful exploration to grab my daughter and kiss her?"

A silence was punctuated by a bird somewhere overhead. *Twip-twip-tweeee.* Then Peggy Cunningham said, "Is that what she told you? Well, I'm not sure that's the way it happened. Karen seems to be more advanced in that department than most girls her age."

"Who? Karen?"

"Oh, yes. Last week I overheard the girls in Lindsay's room, talking about sex. In detail. Karen was telling them what she hears going on when your fiancé is there. I went in and had a little chat with them, but I didn't want to bother you with it." She picked up her basket of gardening tools. "If I were you, before I accuse others, I would put my own house in order."

Gail could only stare at her.

Peggy Cunningham tilted her head to one side and smiled. "But I guess it's hard, having a career that takes up so much of your time." She started to leave, but turned back to say, "And if you wouldn't mind? Ask your roofers not to put their trash out before pickup day. We try to keep the street well maintained."

"I'm sure. And how fortunate we are to have you watching out for us."

But Peggy Cunningham was only a disappearing flicker of shorts and T-shirt in the swaying bushes.

"Bitch," Gail said under her breath. She spun around and went back across the street, heels clicking on the pavement.

She wondered what had happened in the gazebo. Maybe Karen had wanted to be kissed. And maybe she had teased Payton, never thinking he would *do* anything, or if he tried, she could push him away and laugh about it. But she had never been around boys of fourteen, with real muscles in their arms. And sex on their minds.

Gail thought of the other girl, Jennifer. The one with the guilty smile. More likely she had started it, then blamed it on Karen.

What bothered Gail was that Karen might have lied to her. Till now Gail had never doubted that she and Karen had a relationship that permitted them to be open about anything. Gail had never taught her daughter to regard sex as anything but natural and right—depending on the circumstances, of course. But maybe she had been too open. What had Karen overheard? A couple of times Anthony had put his hand over Gail's mouth when she had moaned too loudly. Maybe there had been some laughter. Gail cringed to think of Karen with her ear to the door.

Stop it, Gail told herself. A few words from Peggy Cunningham, and her mind had started churning. It didn't matter what Karen had heard. At least it was love. Poor Jamie Sweet's children had covered their ears not to hear the slaps and the cursing.

She got back into her car, parked it in the driveway, then went inside. Hurrying upstairs, she checked her watch: 5:15. When Dave had visitation with Karen, he usually picked her up, but today Gail had said never mind, she would drop Karen off at the marina. This would give her a chance to talk to him, but she didn't have much time. At seven she was expected at the home of Anthony's grandparents for dinner. There was a standing joke in Miami about Cuban time, which permitted one to arrive an hour or so late, but it didn't apply at the Pedrosa house. The old man's health was fragile, and his wife would wheel him off to bed by nine.

As she passed the hall bathroom, she could hear water running. Gail leaned inside. The shower door was steamed up, but she could see Karen's shiny pink body behind it, doing a dance routine from a Spice Girls video. "Karen, are you about finished?"

There was a shriek. "Mom, I don't have anything on!"

"I hope not, in the shower."

"Get out!"

"Sorry. Hurry up, will you?"

"All right!"

Gail closed the door, intending to speak to Karen about her tone of voice. In her room, she stripped off her clothes and turned on the water.

Where had Payton Cunningham been last night—home or popping change into a pay phone? His mother hadn't wanted to say. That could indicate guilt, or just that Peggy hadn't wanted her son grilled by a lawyer, a woman who would jump all over a simple workman for squashing a plant. If Payton hadn't made the call, then who? Wendell Sweet passed through Gail's mind. His hateful stare. He could have gotten her unlisted number somehow. But to call *before* the hearing went against him? That didn't make sense.

Gail remembered her mother's advice about such calls. Ignore them. If the guy on the other end doesn't get a reaction, he will bother somebody else.

She whipped off her shower cap, fluffed her hair, and dried herself with a towel, then stood on it while she put on a lacy pink bra and matching bikini panties. A gift from Anthony. He liked to leave little surprises in her underwear drawer. Gail dabbed perfume between her breasts, noticing how clearly they showed through the soft fabric. Then a touch of perfume under the lace that spanned her belly. The panties were just high enough to cover a silvery stretch mark. Anthony had said it was a mark of her motherhood, then kissed it, and she had melted.

She wiped the steam off the mirror and stared at herself. Too skinny and pale. She flattened her breasts with her hands. Her diamond sparkled. She studied her hip bones, how prominent. But he had kissed those too. And her bony knees. And everything between. *Mi girafa linda.* My pretty giraffe.

The water in the other bathroom had stopped. "Karen, are you getting dressed?"

The muffled response came back, an annoyed yes.

Gail found the right shade of eye shadow in the vanity and leaned close to the mirror. "Don't forget to pack your swimsuit! You brought it back from your dad's last time, and you'll probably need it this weekend."

Karen appeared in the doorway in white shorts and a little striped top. "Ta-daaaah. I'm ready first," she said. "You owe me a quarter, suckah!"

"You got me," Gail said, stroking on mascara, watching Karen at the same time. Skinny legs and size-eight tennis sneakers. Five-two already, and on the cusp of a growth spurt. "Come talk to me."

Karen sat on the closed toilet lid while Gail finished her makeup.

"I wish you could go with me tonight, sweetie."

"That's okay. I'd be bored with all those old people. Not you, Mom."

"Do you think Anthony's old?"

"Sort of medium." She sniffed in Gail's direction. "You smell nice."

"Thanks. Put some on if you want to. Not too much." Gail gave the bottle to Karen. "Mr. Pedrosa is eighty-four. That's old. His wife is eighty-one. They've been married over sixty years. Imagine." Karen was dragging the glass stopper from the Fabergé along her bare arm. "Married love is a beautiful thing, Karen."

"You're not married."

"You know what I'm talking about. It's also very private. Not something to be discussed among one's friends."

Karen glanced at her, then dabbed perfume behind her ear.

Gail brushed her hair, lifting it off her neck, curling it under with a deft sweep of the bristles. "If you ever have any questions, you can ask me. Okay?"

"I know."

With one eye closed she gave herself a light spritz with hair spray, then motioned for Karen to get up. "Come here." Gail undid her ponytail. "We'll just make it a little smoother on top."

Karen stared straight into the mirror, her head jerking slightly as Gail pulled through from behind with the brush. "Am I pretty? Don't lie, okay?"

"Of course you are. You have gorgeous blue eyes. A great smile—when you decide to let people see it." Except for her build, Karen looked like her father. She had his straight brows, square jaw, and big nose. A strong face for a girl. One to remember. "You're very pretty." She fluffed Karen's bangs out of her eyes. "See?"

"Not as pretty as you."

"Oh, sweetheart. Yes, you are. You're special and beautiful."

Karen's eyes shifted in the mirror to meet Gail's. "Excuse me for saying this, Mom, but you really shouldn't run around in your underwear."

Karen's father had bought and renovated a restaurant near the public marina in Coconut Grove. The distance from Clematis Street was under two miles, but not a fast trip this time of day, with the traffic.

On the way Gail told Karen about Dr. Fischman. The judge wanted him to talk to Karen—to all of them—and make a recommendation. Then the judge would decide where Karen should live. It was routine, Gail said. This was not exactly true, but she didn't want Karen to feel she was causing problems.

"Do you have any questions? Comments? Anything?"

"Nope." Karen concentrated on bouncing her tennis racquet on the toe of her sneaker. Her eyes were hidden by the bill of her turquoise Miami Hurricanes cap.

"Well, if you do, let me know."

The road was a narrow stretch of asphalt called Main Highway that curved northeast through a green tunnel of banyan trees. It led past a 1920s theater, a string of outdoor restaurants, and small shops. It was Friday, and by nightfall Coconut Grove would be jammed. Kids would be cruising up and down, lines would form outside the multiplex, and tourists would wander through Gap and Ralph Lauren and Hooters, some spending incredible amounts of cash, others settling for a carved wooden parrot and a seven-dollar hamburger at Planet Hollywood.

After a while, Karen said, "Did you ever wish for something you can't have, but you wish for it anyway?"

Gail glanced at her, then back at the road. "I guess everyone has done that. What do you wish for?"

"Promise you won't get mad," Karen said.

"I swear."

"I wish we could all be together again. You and me and Daddy. That's mostly what I wish." The hat turned toward the passenger window. "I know it isn't going to happen."

Several seconds passed while Gail picked through words, choosing them carefully. "No. It won't happen. But that's not the important thing . . . as long as we remember we're still a family. We have to try to care for each other."

"Do you care for Daddy?" The blue eyes were fixed on her.

Gail watched the road, then looked back at Karen. "I'm not . . . happy with him right now. You argue with your friends sometimes, don't you?"

Karen's look grew stern. "You're not friends. You hate him."

On a green light Gail waited for the pedestrians to clear so she could make the turn. "I don't hate him. We're both trying to do what's best for you, and it's hard to know what that is."

Karen turned away again.

"I love you very much." Gail hesitated, then said, "I love Anthony too. He adores you, Karen. He thinks you're great." A snort came through Karen's nose. Gail said, "Just try. For me? Please?"

"Okay."

Letting out her breath, Gail wheeled her car around the corner, then down a slight hill past the library and the grassy expanse of Peacock Park. The bay was just beyond, separated from the harbor by clusters of mangrove islands. Boats lay at anchor, and the sun sparkled on the water. The street took a left past an old sailing club Gail's family used to belong to before her father died. Gail had been thirteen.

For the first time it went through her mind to give in. If Karen wanted to live with Dave, then maybe it was for the best. He wouldn't put up a fight about visitation. He was basically— and Gail could still say this—a nice guy. According to Karen, he was perfect. He bought her a new Beanie Baby every time she came to see him, and she had her own TV. They had dinner early or late, as they pleased, and she could eat whatever she wanted. He saved the dishes for tomorrow, but the apartment was clean. He let her stay up late, but she got her rest. There was always a story at bedtime. She had lots of friends in the building. They played tennis. He took her out on boats. He was never in a bad mood. They had a great time.

Gail had met David Metzger at the University of Florida, probably attracted by the fit of his white tennis shorts. He had been a star on the team. Falling in love had not been a precipitous drop, as with Anthony, but a steady progress, and one day they found themselves engaged. After law school Gail took a job with a prestigious firm on Flagler Street. Dave managed a marine-supply store. When they were able, they bought a little marina, and he ran it. Not very well, unfortunately. She tried to help, but he resented her interference. He played tennis to fill his weekends, and she brought more and more work home. Until one day Dave said he wanted out.

They sold the business for only a few thousand more than they had paid for it. She took the house and Karen, and Dave took their forty-foot sloop, the *Princess*, and sailed away. For weeks she heard nothing, then postcards showed up in the mailbox with stamps from St. Thomas, Antigua, Grenada, Martinique, Curaçao—Karen charted his progress on a hurricane map. The cards came from resorts where he gave tennis lessons or offered the boat for charter excursions. Gail suspected that the message for her was: *See, Gail, how much fun I'm having without you?* He rarely called Karen, but when he did, the calls usually closed with Karen saying, "Love you too, Daddy. I miss you."

It was never clear to Gail what had happened, but Dave returned to Miami, leaving the *Princess* with a yacht broker in Puerto Rico. He had apparently made enough on the sale for a down payment on the restaurant. He had not offered any details, and Gail had not asked.

At first she had welcomed him back. It was better for Karen, having her father nearby. Gail had been generous with visitation, never a complaint. And then this demand for custody. Gail planned to take Charlene Marks's advice and find out what was really behind it.

She drove through the wide gate in a chain-link fence surrounding the boat yard, then parked under a palm tree. Gathering her purse, she told Karen she needed to talk to her father for a few minutes, and suggested she find some crackers in the kitchen to throw to the fish.

The Old Island Club faced the water, and they followed the landscaped path around the side. There was an indoor area with big windows, but most of the tables were outdoors. A new wood deck still smelled of pine resin, and two dozen striped umbrellas fluttered in the late afternoon breeze. Karen dropped her racquet and backpack on one of them and ran through a double set of screen doors. The kitchen was beyond, and Gail heard the clatter of dishes. She found a stool at the outdoor bar, which looked like a Disney version of a bar from the islands. The colors were hot pastel, ceiling fans spun overhead, and reggae played on speakers disguised as coconuts.

A waitress in a brightly flowered shirt came to ask what she would like.

"Thanks, but I won't be here long. Is Mr. Metzger around?"

"Yes, I saw him a few minutes ago." She leaned into a cooler to fill a glass with ice. Her eyes were on Gail. "You're Karen's mother, right?"

Gail said that she was, and made a polite smile in return. The woman was in her early twenties, athletic build, short brown hair without much style to it. Not Dave's type, Gail thought. Then she wondered what Dave had told people about his ex-wife. What a cold fish *she* is.

Gail scanned the menu, which listed conch fritters, pigeon peas, and rice. Jerk chicken and pork. Captain Dave's soup of the day, $3.95. The clock over the bar was set into the mouth of a leaping swordfish: 6:10. Gail tapped her nails on the counter, which was plastic resin poured over shells and sand and fake gold treasure coins. Cute, she decided.

Her companions were a mixed bag—a leathery old man in a yachting cap, reading the sports section. A group of office workers squeezing lime wedges into their Coronas. The table nearest the water was occupied by three darkly tanned men in shorts and T-shirts, wearing enough gold jewelry to make a thief or a DEA agent pay close attention. Gail guessed that they owned the monster speedboat tied to the dock.

Karen ran along the seawall, dropping crackers to whatever darted just under the surface. Farther along, a dog lay asleep in the grass under a newly planted coconut palm still propped up on stakes. A row of banana trees had been added for ambiance, and there was a turquoise picket fence draped with bougainvillea. Across the inlet, and behind city hall, the marina was slowing down for the evening. The sailboat rigging clanged softly against the masts.

When Gail looked back at Karen, she saw that Dave was there too. Karen said something, then Dave turned toward the bar. Even at this distance she could see the color of his eyes. He stood still for a moment, then wove his way through the umbrella tables, the light flickering on his Island Club shirt. The sun had browned his skin and turned the hair on his arms and legs golden. He had put on some weight, but his shorts still fit.

"Captain Dave."

"Hi," he said warily. "What's up? Karen said you had to talk to me."

"I have a phone number for you. Dr. Evan Fischman. The judge's choice." She reached into her purse and brought out a folded piece of paper.

"My lawyer told me," Dave said.

"Oh. Well, I thought it would be a good idea to coordinate Karen's appointment."

"Joe Erwin said to go through him on everything."

"Naturally. If you go through him, he can put it on his time sheet and bill you. That's how it works."

"You should know."

Gail dropped the paper back into her purse. "Dave, this is not an issue, it's a question. Who takes Karen to see Dr. Fischman? Do you want to take her? Should I? Should we go together?"

He let a few seconds pass. "I guess I could take her. Or you could. I'll think about it and let you know. All right?"

"Sure. Call me."

Dave looked her over. "You're dressed up. Got a big night planned?"

"Just a family dinner at Anthony's grandparents' house." Gail wore a slim black dress and gold earrings and necklace.

He put one canvas boat shoe on the foot rail and an elbow on the bar. "I was going to call you anyway. There's a tennis tournament next weekend on Key Biscayne. I'd like to take Karen."

"You mean keep her next weekend too?"

"Just one day. Saturday or Sunday, whichever. Unless you have plans."

"Nothing in particular. I'll leave it up to Karen."

"She should see the pros play," Dave said. "She has talent, and I'm not saying that because I'm her father. She's a natural athlete. But I'm not one of those parents who push a kid into doing nothing but tennis, day and night. I've seen too much of that. I'm trying to do what's right for her."

"So am I." Making some time to find her way into a conversation, Gail pretended just now to notice the bar. "My, this is interesting. You've done so much here. How's business?"

"Business is great."

"I hope so."

"You never had much faith in me, did you?"

"Oh, Dave. Come on. I didn't mean it like that. I want you to succeed."

He tapped a rhythm on the bar, making a final flourish by pointing at her. "This place is going to be a gold mine. On weekends, with the steel band, you can't find a parking place. I even had Jimmy Buffett drop in here last weekend."

"Fantastic." With a little jolt of surprise, Gail realized she was smiling. She looked away from him and picked up the menu again. "Old Island Club. Catchy."

Dave nodded toward the map of the Caribbean in a rope-trimmed frame on the back wall. "See that? The original Old Island Club is at Sapphire Beach on St. Thomas. It's got white sand beaches and a good harbor—the yachties love it. They've got a big-screen TV for sports, and they take coconuts right off the trees and make a rum drink called the Green Flash. People party all night. If you sail in that area, you've been there."

"How can you get away with using their name?" Gail asked.

Dave grinned. "I bought the name. I traded the *Princess* for it."

"That was a hundred-thousand-dollar boat!"

"It was a bargain, believe me."

The waitress reappeared. "Dave? Excuse me. Can I get you anything?" Her wing-shaped brows lifted in expectation.

"Gail, you still like Red Stripe? On the house, old times' sake."

"No, I really can't stay." She reached for the small black purse on the counter.

He laid his hand on her arm. "Five minutes. I can't stay either, I've got to take Karen for her tennis lesson. Vicki, one Red Stripe and two mugs from the freezer."

"Sure." The woman made a smile, standard waitress-friendly. She went away to find the mugs, but she glanced back at Dave before the screen door to the kitchen banged shut. She was not unattractive.

Gail reconsidered. "Is there something going on between you two?"

"Me and Vicki? Naah. Not really."

"Sort of?"

"Not anymore. We went out a few times, but I've got Karen to think of. It has to be the right person."

There might have been an accusation there, but Gail let it slide. "Dave . . ."

He had blue eyes with pale lashes. The sun had sketched lines at the corners.

"Can I ask you something? Why . . . do you think I'm such a terrible mother? Is that what you really think?"

He turned around and leaned against the bar. "I never said that." For a while he watched a little ketch with furled sails coming into the inlet, bumping gently against the dock. "Where is it written that the mother always gets the child? I've read books that say a girl can do just as well with her father. Look, you work fifty, sixty hours a week. You've got Karen at summer camp till late in the afternoon. I can pick her up at four—"

"And you're running a restaurant, Dave. This place closes at one a.m. on weekends."

"I have a manager. I live three blocks from here, and I know what my priorities are, okay? My daughter." He faced her. "I spent a lot of nights alone out there at sea, looking up at that empty sky. There was plenty of time to contemplate what's really important in life."

"Really. I thought you and your girlfriend were staying at the Caribe Hilton in San Juan in exchange for your services as a tennis pro."

The waitress—Vicki—arrived with the beer. No one spoke while she poured it into two frosted glass mugs. "Enjoy," she said, smiling again. She went to tend to a customer.

Gail dropped her forehead onto her palm. "I apologize. This is driving me crazy."

Dave pushed a mug toward her. "You're not the only one. I wish we *could* work it out." He laughed. "Goddamn lawyer's eating up all my profits. Cheers." He clinked his mug to hers.

They sat for a minute in silence. He said, "You really do look good, though. Money agrees with you."

"I'm not sure I should consider that a compliment," she said, "since you place so little value on it."

He smiled. "Relatively speaking, Gail."

"Of course."

Dave set down his mug and turned it on its coaster. "Money. Everybody's after the long green."

"But you're doing all right."

"Great." His smile deepened the lines around his eyes. "And better to come. In fact"—he leaned so close she could feel the warmth of his shoulder on her bare upper arm—"there's a company—very big—interested in a franchise. We're still working out the details, so I don't want to jinx it by saying too much."

"Be careful," she said. "Make sure they show you the money before you sign anything."

"Don't worry about that. This deal is golden." His forearms lay on the counter. His hands were blunt with muscular palms. The right was callused from holding a racquet. A dive watch was strapped to his left wrist. He wore no jewelry.

Gail hesitated, then said, "Dave, are you angry at me because we split up? Do you blame me?"

His smile faded. "You think I want Karen for revenge? That I'd put myself through this pain to even the score? No." Once again they were on opposite sides. "No, Gail. I love my daughter. Period. I want a way of life for her that she's not going to get living with you and"—it was as though Dave couldn't bring himself to say the name—"and that joker you're engaged to."

"Way of life? What—"

His forefinger hit the counter, accenting his words, which

came out in a heated whisper. "A basic, simple, decent American lifestyle. Hard to find these days. It's getting damn near impossible in Miami. But that's what I want for Karen, and I will do my best to make sure she has it. You want to marry Quintana, go ahead. But you're not taking Karen with you. No. He is too slick and too damned shady. Any guy who would make his living defending dope dealers and cold-blooded killers—"

"Oh, for God's sake."

"Ask yourself: Who's his family? Did you read that article in the *Herald* last month? They investigated city contracts and found Pedrosa Construction Company in bed with the head of building and zoning. The reporter nearly got shot!"

"That has nothing to do with Anthony!"

Dave looked at her, then shook his head. "You just don't see it, do you, Gail? You, Ms. Independent, marrying a Cuban? It won't last."

"You are so wrong," Gail said.

He glanced around. The quick thump of sneakers was approaching from behind them. He said to Gail, "Yeah, I wish I were, for *her* sake." Dave pivoted on the stool. "Hey, princess. What've you got there?"

"A shell. Vicki gave it to me. What kind is it?"

"Well, let's see." Dave drew Karen closer. The cone-shaped, brown-spotted shell had spines radiating out from the opening, which was tinted with delicate pink.

"Oh, these are all over the Caymans. The water is clear as glass. I'll take you some day, princess."

Gail glanced at her watch. "I have to go." She said to Karen, "Be good. See you Sunday. Give me a kiss."

"Bye, Mom." Karen tilted her face sideways to be kissed, then turned the shell over and wondered aloud what the spines were for.

Dave said, "I'll call you about the appointment." For a long moment their eyes were locked over Karen's head.

Gail nodded, then turned and walked out.

CHAPTER

FOUR

Shadows were lengthening by the time Gail arrived at the Pedrosa house, and the row of lamps along the wall had been lit. She drove through the open iron gates and spotted Anthony's Eldorado among the cars parked in the circular driveway. She pulled in behind it, then grabbed her purse and hurried toward the entrance, set back under a portico draped with bougainvillea. Water splashed in a fountain.

A few moments after she pressed the bell, the housekeeper swung back the heavy door. *"Buenas noches, señora."*

"Gracias." Gail gave the woman a smile as she came inside. There was a wide opening to her left, and the living room was beyond. She heard conversation and laughter.

Anthony stepped into the hall, saw who was there, and held out a hand to pull her close. His expression was a mix of relief and annoyance. "Why didn't you call? I was worried."

"Is everyone starving? I'm so sorry. My phone was in my other purse. I had to talk to Dave, and the traffic—"

He kissed her cheek. "It's all right. We're having appetizers. Relax."

Inside the living room there were more kisses and greetings for everyone, as if she had not seen most of them just last weekend for the christening of the newest great-grandson.

Family dinners were frequent, usually based on a special occasion. Tonight was somebody's birthday. A great-aunt, Gail thought. She had a moment of panic before remembering that Anthony had said he would take care of the gift.

The matriarch of the family, Digna Maria Betancourt de Pedrosa, in a chic silk dress and pearl earrings, reached up from the sofa when Gail bent to kiss her. From behind his thick glasses Anthony's grandfather gave her a wink. "Anthony, *ya ella está hecha una cubana.*" She's Cuban already—a reference to her tardiness. Gail winked back. This man was fluent in English, but spoke it less and less. In the 1940s he had ridden for the Cuban equestrian team. Now he sat in a wheelchair. He had fought against this indignity—being pushed through his own house like an invalid—but after one too many falls Digna had insisted.

When Señora Pedrosa grasped the handles of her husband's chair, everyone moved toward the dining room. Gail walked with the youngest granddaughter, Betty, who carried her new baby on her shoulder. Anthony escorted Aunt Graciela, his late mother's sister.

The double doors were open, and a chandelier cast a glow on the polished wood table and the marble floor beneath it. Twenty chairs had been squeezed around the table. Señora Pedrosa wheeled her husband to one end, then took her own seat at the other, host and hostess. Anthony touched Gail's waist. "Come sit here with me." He held a chair, and she sat between Anthony and his cousin Elena's husband. Pepe spoke to Anthony, and the men laughed, then went back and forth in Spanish too fast for her to follow.

Glancing around the table, Gail counted twelve people who managed one or another facet of a family empire worth close to three hundred million dollars. A bank, a construction company, rental properties, shopping centers. And it was all controlled by Ernesto Pedrosa—who was now over eighty. How much longer could he make decisions? Someone would have to take over.

There were three granddaughters and their husbands. There were grand-nephews and nieces. And Anthony.

But he and his grandfather had been at odds for years, on different sides of an issue that had torn their country apart. Pedrosa had taken his family out of Cuba after Castro seized power, but Anthony and a sister remained with their father, Luis Quintana, a decorated hero of the revolution. When Anthony was thirteen, Pedrosa arranged for him to come visit his mother in Miami, then refused to let him go home. Anthony was forced to go to school in enemy territory, forced to learn a new language. He refused to denounce his father. At twenty he was thrown out of this very house after a raging argument with Pedrosa. Brilliant and rebellious, he had gone north and made his own way through law school.

Relations between him and his grandfather gradually thawed, then grew to mutual respect. Anthony Quintana managed nothing belonging to Ernesto Pedrosa. Had been given nothing, had asked for nothing. He was Pedrosa's chief irritant and greatest hope. The favorite, and everyone knew it. But he had said no.

The courses were served, and plates were passed. *Puerco asado*—pork roasted with garlic and spices. *Moros*—black beans and rice cooked together. Fried plantains. Boiled yuca *con mojo*—oil and more garlic. Sometimes there would be chicken, beef, or delicately cooked fish. But always the garlic, the beans and rice, and then—the world would stop otherwise—tiny cups of espresso after dinner.

Someone told a joke, which was duly translated for Gail. They waited to see if she laughed, and when she did, the laughter went around the table again.

In Havana the Pedrosas had employed a French cook. Here they could have had whatever they wanted, but even the menu made a political statement: solidarity with the displaced exiles, rich and poor alike. Ernesto Jose Pedrosa Masvidal had decreed that only traditional Cuban food would be served in his house.

In Havana he had ordered his shirts from an English tailor, but here he stuck to his four-pocket *guayaberas*.

A nicely sun-browned hand with an onyx ring on it deftly poured wine into Gail's empty glass. Anthony. She smiled at him. "Trying to get me drunk?"

He said quietly, "I apologize for last night. I shouldn't have left you like that."

"It wasn't your fault," she said. "I was stressed out. Why do you put up with me?"

His lips parted just enough for her to see him smile. He leaned over as if to kiss her cheek. His breath was warm in her ear. *"Porque me gusta tu sabor."*

Her mind processed the words. *Because . . . I like . . . I like the way you taste.* Her skin tingled. She spoke with the wineglass in front of her mouth. "When we get home, I am going to tie you to the bed. Open the bottle of love potion. Unzip your pants . . ."

When she didn't go on, he prodded, "And . . ."

"Well, I don't know. If we stay as late, as we usually do, I might be too tired."

"We won't stay. As soon as the old man is asleep, Nena will come downstairs. We'll say good night to her, then leave."

"No cigars with the guys," Gail said.

"And you won't get into a long conversation with the women about the wedding," he returned.

At least the wedding had given her something to talk about. The Pedrosa women were polite. They embraced her and kissed her cheek, but she would always be *la americana*. Anthony's first wife, a Cuban woman, had fit in better, even though Rosa— they gossiped about her—had been out of his social class, the daughter of a meat packer in Union City, New Jersey. But she had been pretty, and Anthony had been so young. Gail had felt their eyes on her, appraising. She could imagine their thoughts: *She's American, but we can overlook that. Her family is prominent, and she will make a good wife.*

Gail pushed a piece of tomato around on her plate, nudging

the chunks of pork into a straight line. She had no appetite, and the thought of pork made her queasy.

"Anthony, I need to see a client of yours, Harry Lasko." Anthony's fork paused halfway to his mouth. "It's about the Sweet case you sent me. Wendell Sweet says he has no money, but he's lying. Harry Lasko knows him and might be able to tell us what he did with his cash. If I don't get some information, Jamie could be in real trouble. And my fees! I've got twenty-two thousand dollars' worth of time in this case. The judge won't rule on it until he knows what Wendell can afford. I've got to talk to Mr. Lasko."

Anthony shook his head as he finished chewing. "No."

"What do you mean, no?"

"N-o. I can't let Harry talk to anyone until I work out a plea with the prosecutors. They could tack on more charges if anything else comes up."

"Such as?"

He made a slight shrug. "One never knows."

Gail was still looking at him. "Give me something about Wendell. Come on."

Anthony didn't want to get into it, she could see that. Barely moving his lips, he said quietly, "Harry and Wendell had some business dealings on Aruba, and before you ask—yes, they were legitimate. However. Wendell knows some questionable people, and the DEA is interested in who they are. I don't want to open that can of worms, not while I'm trying to persuade the government that poor, bumbling Harry Lasko tripped on his shoelaces and fell over the line—"

"Wendell is a drug dealer?"

"Let's say . . . that Wendell has terrible taste in friends."

"I don't see what all this has to do with a divorce case," Gail said.

"It doesn't. But if Harry slips up and says more than he should, and you file a list of assets in the Sweet case that shows a connection in any way to Harry Lasko—"

"Who would see it?"

"No, Gail."

"I just want to *talk* to him. It would be confidential."

"Sorry."

"Well, I don't see why not."

"You don't practice criminal law, *bonboncita.*"

"Then I defer to your expertise—reluctantly."

"Thank you." Anthony leaned away to ask Alex for the beans and rice. *Alex, favor, los moros—* The only place Anthony ever ate Cuban food was here, she had noticed. Otherwise, he preferred pasta or steaks.

"Why is Harry pleading guilty?" Gail whispered.

"That often happens when a client thinks he'll do worse at trial."

"But you're too good a trial lawyer to give up so easily."

"Well, the situation is not so simple."

"What do you mean?"

Ignoring her question, Anthony tapped vinegar onto the *moros.* "This is what we'll do. After I work out a plea, you can talk to him. He'll be around for a while. All right?"

"When are you going to do this?"

"Probably next week."

"I don't want to wait too long," Gail said. "Wendell has to comply with an order of discovery, but what if he doesn't? He could drag this out past the report date, and I'd have to go after him on a motion for contempt—"

"Gail, pass me the bread, will you?"

The baby fussed, and Digna held out her arms. Betty got up and carried him around to her. He opened his eyes and stared at his great-grandmother, then cooed in a toothless grin. When everyone broke into laughter, he started to wail. Digna shushed them and cradled the baby on her breast. Ernesto Pedrosa announced that this little *machito* already knew how to charm the ladies.

Then Pedrosa tilted his head to focus his glasses on the other end of the table. Anthony was talking about real estate with Xiomara's husband, Bernardo. Pedrosa broke in with a comment in Spanish, and Anthony disagreed. Pedrosa laughed and made a dismissive wave with one large, bony hand. Anthony returned a frosty smile down the length of the table and spun off some figures. The old man's glower turned into a shrug. He acknowledged that his grandson could be right for once. He allowed a smile before snapping his fingers for more *puerco asado*.

Gail had noticed the similarities—the physical resemblance, the dry humor, the pride—but they were not the same. Anthony had said so himself. He had a slight accent he couldn't shake, but his ideals, his political views, were not a holdover from fifties Latin America. She was grateful for every difference.

The conversation veered to houses, then to the one on Clematis Street, which Anthony said they would remodel— probably next year—and eventually, as Gail knew it would, the talk came around to the wedding.

Gail smiled, not really comfortable as the center of attention. No, she hadn't picked out her dress yet. Elena suggested a shop in Coral Gables. "Gail, you have to see it. You *must*. I'll go with you." And Betty wanted to come along too, because she had bought her wedding dress there. Gail shook her head, still smiling. "Please don't bother. I can find something easily enough."

But they carried on without her. Which couturier in the Gables was most suitable for a second marriage, and whether you could ever find the right dress at Dadeland—

"Dadeland?" Xiomara laughed. "*¡Que va!* Maybe at Saks, *pero* everything looks the same, *y la gente*—you have to walk sideways, it's so crowded."

The entire wedding had been like this—rolling along on its own, picking up speed. Gail's mother, Irene Connor, had volunteered to handle the details. An intimate wedding, Gail had instructed her. Family and our closest friends. Then Ernesto and Digna Pedrosa announced they would pay for the reception. They reserved the Alhambra Ballroom at the Biltmore Hotel. They would hire a fifteen-piece orchestra to play salsa, jazz, and pop. Flattered and thrilled, Irene caved in. She lined up a soprano with the Miami Opera to do "Ave Maria" at the wedding. The invitation list shot past three hundred names. *Darling, they want to invite the governor. How can you say no?* This was not a wedding anymore, it was an event, a political statement, a three-way detente among the exiles on the right, of whom Ernesto Pedrosa was a quintessential example, the more liberal new Cubans, such as Anthony Quintana, and the Anglo establishment. Gail felt as though she and Anthony were hanging onto a rocket by their fingernails. And somewhere during the last few weeks it had occurred to her that Pedrosa's stunning generosity was not because he liked her, or had a sentimental spot for weddings, but because he was luring Anthony home.

Leave him alone, old man.

The old man still had power. The article in the *Miami Herald* had touched only the surface, although bribery was too crude a word for what Pedrosa engaged in. Influence was better. To do favors for those in a position to return them. And when one had power, the favors were large. A judge on the circuit court, a Cuban American himself, had confided to Gail, *Where we came from, there was very little respect for government. We brought that attitude here, I'm afraid.*

Anthony had accused his grandfather of that very failing, and Gail admired him for having the guts to say so. Aside from loving Anthony Quintana, she respected him. He was a lawyer because he believed in the law, not for what he could get out of it. He loved his grandfather but didn't need his contacts or his wealth.

After the dishes were cleared, the cake was brought out, flaming with candles enough to make everyone laugh. They all sang "Happy Birthday," and presents were sent down the table to Aunt Adelita, who exclaimed over each one. *Que linda. Que preciosa.* A pretty blouse, some perfume, a framed photograph. Anthony had given her earrings and had signed Gail's name to the card as well.

By now Ernesto Pedrosa's head had sunk into his shoulders, and his eyes were closing. Soon his wife noticed, and she shook him gently. Standing up, she ordered everyone to stay, stay as long as they liked. The old man roused himself for the parade of good-night kisses and hugs. Then Digna wheeled him into the elevator and the door slid shut.

While the table was cleared, the guests wandered back into the living room. Gail wished she and Anthony could go home, but he had said that Hector Mesa wanted to talk to him. She wouldn't have cared, but she could never figure out what Mesa was after. He was a friend, not a relation. He had no particular occupation that she knew of, not in accounting or in the law. His card said "consultant." His suits were blue or gray, his hair was thinning, and in a group he would vanish. All one could see was a pair of black-framed glasses and a small gray mustache.

Drinks were made for those who wanted them. A tray of espresso was brought out. Gail went to look at the baby, and Betty let her hold him. His eyes were deep blue, and he had a fine blond fuzz on his head. "Well, aren't you a gorgeous guy? And heavy! Karen was only six pounds." Gail tickled his cheek till he grinned at her. "I'm in love," she said.

Aunt Adelita, even older than Digna, laid her papery hand on Gail's knee and patted it. *"Tú y Anthony, ¿quieren hembra o varon?"*

Did they want a girl or a boy? Embarrassed, Gail laughed and handed the baby back to its mother. "No, not for us. No babies." The meaning was too clear to need a translation. Adelita stared at Gail as if she were very strange indeed, then went on quickly to some other topic.

No children. She and Anthony had decided this months ago. He already had two children—and with Gail's career—Karen was enough. A sensible decision, one that did not have to be explained. Even so, Gail knew that she had been judged.

Elena pulled her closer, laughing. "Never mind Aunt Adelita. She's still in Havana, nineteen-forty."

Gail noticed Anthony and Hector Mesa in the hall, just past the carved wood that framed the entrance. Hector, touching Anthony's arm. Anthony with a smile that could mean anything. He had taken off his jacket. His dark green shirt was open at the collar and tucked smoothly into pleated linen slacks. He looked her way, and she pursed her lips in a little kiss. When Hector Mesa happened to glance in another direction, Anthony rolled his eyes up to the ceiling as if he were already dead of boredom.

Murmuring her excuses to the women, Gail went over to rescue him. She smiled at Hector as she took Anthony's arm. "They just brought the coffee in. Would you gentlemen like some?"

Anthony said, "Go ahead, Hector, I'll talk to you later."

The man made a slight nod in Gail's direction, his eyes obscured by the glasses and a wink of yellowish light on the lenses. *"Señora."* Then soundlessly he walked across the tiled floor and vanished into the living room.

"What did he want?"

"A legal matter. He was pulled over for speeding, and they arrested him for carrying a concealed weapon—a .22 caliber Beretta. He wants it back. I'll see what I can do."

"Good old Hector, playing with his toys."

"Hector's all right."

"If you say so. I've never heard him say more than three words in sequence. Do you want coffee? I don't."

"I don't either." Coming closer, Anthony brushed his lips across her ear. "I've got another idea."

"Really. What?"

"Come upstairs, I'll show you." The hall was tiled in terra cotta and paneled in dark wood. Sconces lit the way to the rest of the house. The stairs were behind him, curving out of sight. He pulled her toward them.

She said, "You're taking me to see your boyhood collection of Spider-Man comics."

"Oh, I wanted to surprise you." He walked backward, tugging her hand.

She laughed. "They'll look for us."

"No, they won't. Come on. Nena won't be back for half an hour."

"We can't!" she whispered. "It would be like doing it in church."

"So much the better." When she shot a glance toward the living room, he added, "Or we could listen to Uncle Humberto tell us again how President Kennedy sold out the exiles at Playa Girón."

He had been kicked out of here at twenty, but the small room upstairs at the far end of the hall was still his. He used it when he stayed over—not often, but sometimes. There were clothes in the closet, and some of his things in the bathroom.

Moonlight silvered the banyan tree outside the windows and came through faintly to illuminate the desk, a lamp, a bookcase, an armchair, a twin bed. Their clothes were across the bed, not to get wrinkled. She faced him on the armchair, knees on the seat cushion, her arms around his head. He had held her hips so tightly to his, she knew she would have ten little bruises on her behind.

The silhouette of leaves shifted in the window-shaped patch of pale light that angled across the wall.

She kissed his forehead. He kept his hair combed off it in thick waves. His eyes opened slowly. In this dim light they were black. She smiled at him. "Well. Better than Playa Girón."

The answer was a low growl in his throat. His eyes drifted shut. Cool air from the vent was blowing across her back. She awkwardly unfolded her legs and stood up. "Don't go away." In the bathroom she saw herself in the mirror. Not too bad. Nothing a brush and some lipstick couldn't fix—if only she had her purse.

While he took his turn in the bathroom she put on her underwear. There was a brush on the dresser, and she used it to fix her hair, checking herself in the mirror.

"Gail, I want to ask you something." His voice echoed on the tiles. "Why were you with Dave?"

"What?"

The water went off. "You said you were late because you were with Dave. Why?"

Gail walked to the door. Anthony was in his briefs, hanging a towel on a rod. He looked at her as he went to put on his shirt.

"I—we were talking about the psychologist the judge appointed. I had to arrange with Dave which of us should take Karen to see him. That's all." She shrugged. "We managed to get through an entire conversation without screaming at each other, so you could say progress was made."

Anthony finished the buttons and reached for his slacks. "You shouldn't be talking to him. That's what your lawyer is for."

Gail tried to decide if she was picking up any strange signals in his tone. "Well, it was my lawyer who suggested it."

"Why?"

She put on one shoe, then steadied herself on the chair and wiggled her foot into the other, bending to pull the narrow strap over her heel. She was conscious of Anthony watching her.

"Charlene believes that Dave wants Karen for some reason other than sacred fatherhood. If we knew where he's coming from, we'd be in a better bargaining position. So I went to see what I could find out."

"What did he say?"

She stepped into her dress and put her arms through the sleeves. "I asked, but if he has an ulterior motive, I couldn't find it. He says he wants a good life for Karen. He says he can spend more time with her than I can." Gail turned around and lifted her hair. "Do my zipper."

She felt the long rasp of plastic up her spine. Anthony said, "I don't want you to talk to him again."

"That's ridiculous. We had to discuss Karen."

"When you came in, I smelled beer on your breath."

Gail turned around to face him fully. "It was ninety degrees outside. I had a beer while we talked. And? And what, Anthony?" They had shared a beer. *Old times' sake.*

He held out his hand. "And nothing. I'm sorry." She didn't move. "Gail. Please?"

She put her arms around his waist. "You shouldn't be jealous of Dave."

Anthony gave a short laugh. "I'm not jealous of Dave. He's weak, a failure. Men like that can cause trouble."

Gail bit back her first response—to defend Dave against the word *failure*. She said, "It's better for Karen if her father and I get along, and her feelings are just as important to me as yours." To end the conversation, she went to turn off the bathroom light.

Anthony sat on the edge of the bed to put on his shoes. The desk lamp was still on, casting a small pool of light that left most of the room in darkness. He tied one shoe, then the other, then sat with his forearms on his knees, fingers loosely knit. "Did you ever consider going back to him?"

"No. How could you ask me that?"

"I think it's hard to forget someone you were in love with."

"*Was.* Not anymore."

His eyes were lifted to her, brow in horizontal lines. "You have my ring on your finger. Don't try to take it off."

She put a hand on her hip. "And what would you do about it, *machito*, shoot me?"

He slowly smiled. "No. I would find a way to keep you. He didn't. Too bad for him."

"My, my, my. You are just so irresistible."

He reached out and snagged the hem of her dress and pulled her next to him, arms circling her thighs. "Ah, Gail. We should have been married months ago."

"God, yes. I am so ready for this to be over."

"A simple ceremony at the courthouse. A glass of champagne, and *adiós*."

"That sounds lovely. I think they're planning a fountain with Dom Perignon."

"We could do it next week. Elope. Send a postcard from Las Vegas."

"All those invitations? The money? They'd kill us."

He laughed. "Yes, I think they probably would."

Gail stroked her fingers through his hair. "Anthony. Tell me why we came tonight."

"What do you mean?"

"This was all business. Maybe you didn't want to be left out."

"We are here because Nena asked us to come."

"She wants you at the head of that table someday."

"Probably. That doesn't mean I want to sit there."

"Every time I see Señor Mesa with his spidery little fingers on your sleeve, I want to push him away. He isn't related to your grandfather. Why are they so close?"

"Hector's a smart guy."

"So are Juan and Bernardo and Pepe. And Elena, if the women count."

Anthony slid his encircling arm down her thighs. "I think it's because of Hector's loyalty. As a kid, Hector used to shine shoes outside my grandfather's bank in Havana. When the revolution came, he begged to be taken to Miami. My grandfather liked his spirit and said yes. In return Hector swore his allegiance to our family."

"Hector wants you to take over, doesn't he? He and your grandfather are pulling you into the family business. You said you never wanted to get involved with it."

"Gail, who the hell cares what they want? I've never let anyone dictate what I do, and I'm not going to start. All right?"

"Very." She lightly kissed his lips. "That's one reason I love you."

"Oh? Give me another one."

She kissed him again. "You dress so well. I think I know how to lure you to Clematis Street. Kidnap your wardrobe."

"I'm devastated. This woman is in love with my clothes."

"And let's see . . . You dance! You're the only man who could ever teach me how to do the cha-cha, and hundreds have tried."

She involuntarily jumped at a sudden knock on the door, and

Anthony's hand tightened on her arm. He got up and went to open it as another knock came, louder.

A man in a dark suit stood just outside. For a split second his black-framed glasses swung in a small arc toward Gail.

Anthony said, *"¿Qué pasó?"*

Mesa's voice was soft but urgent. *"Tu abuelo se cayó en el baño."*

Now Gail could hear the commotion, growing louder. Someone running. Shouts. A woman's cry.

"¡Ay, mi Diós!"

She hurried to the door. "Anthony! What happened?"

But already he was sprinting toward the other end of the long hallway, outdistancing the man behind him. He pushed his way past people standing at the door of his grandparents' bedroom. Gail followed. She had never been inside, and images registered quickly—a four-poster bed, a TV, an armoire. Heavy velvet curtains. Framed snapshots and portraits everywhere. People were standing aside to let Anthony enter the bathroom. Gail could see white tile, the glare of lights, a broken ring from a shower curtain rod.

A thin voice cried out, "Anthony, *mi'jo, por favor, ayúdame."* Ernesto Pedrosa was calling him. Please, my son. Help me.

"Estoy aquí contigo, no te preocupes." I'm here with you. Don't worry.

Everyone backed away, and Digna came out trembling. Anthony followed with his grandfather in his arms, maneuvering his bare feet past the door. An old man, so thin and pale, a collection of long bones and loose skin. A towel was draped over his groin, and he struggled to keep it in place. As weak as he was, he still had his dignity. Anthony told someone to bring a robe.

Gail looked away, allowing them privacy, then went into the hall. She heard sirens. Xiomara ran past her in one direction, Alex in another. There were voices downstairs. Then the thud of heavy shoes. Men came up the stairs with their equipment. Gail sat on a cushioned bench out of the way, biting her lower lip.

A few minutes later Pedrosa was wheeled out on a gurney, an oxygen mask strapped over his face. His skin was gray. They carried him down the stairs. Hector Mesa followed.

The family surrounded Anthony, conferring loudly in Spanish. Aunt Graciela was weeping. Betty and Alex had to leave because of the baby. Elena and Pepe would bring Humberto. Xiomara and Bernardo's kids were already with his mother, who could keep them all night. Others organized a caravan.

Finally Anthony came over to Gail.

"I have to go," he said.

"Should I come with you?"

He shook his head. "Go home. There's nothing you can do. I might be there soon, maybe not. He'll be all right, I think. He's pretty tough. I'll call you."

Gail stood up when Anthony did. She said, "Call me and let me know. I don't care what time."

He said that he would. Then he kissed her and helped his grandmother and Aunt Graciela into the elevator. Digna Pedrosa carried a small bag, and her sweater was over her shoulders. She had been through this before and would again—unless this time her husband didn't come home.

The house on Clematis Street seemed hollow and empty as Gail unlocked the front door. She realized that she had never spent a night in it alone. Either Karen or Anthony—or both—had been with her.

She clicked on a lamp, then went to the kitchen to make some cocoa. The gas stove hissed at her, and she finally had to light it with a match. She put the water on, then went upstairs to change into her pajamas.

Please don't die, she prayed silently. And yet another part of her knew that if he did die, Anthony would be safe. It would be too late for Pedrosa to change his will. As far as she knew, he had cut Anthony out years ago and was still dangling the promise of power over his head.

She hurried back to the kitchen on the shrill scream of the kettle. She cranked the gas valve, and the flame sputtered and went out. "Dear God, I swear I don't want him to die. I am wicked even to think of it."

The old man cared for her. Who was she? Nothing to him. He could have turned his back. Instead he had welcomed her like his own blood. He and Digna wanted this wedding to be special, and she had seen only the machinations of a dying king. And when he fell, she had come home rather than stand vigil with the others.

Gail grabbed a napkin and blew her nose. She turned out the light and took her cocoa upstairs. For a while she sat cross-legged and watched the news, then hit the remote and the screen went dark.

These were the people whom Dave mistrusted. He didn't want Karen around them. This was the lifestyle he had said was wrong for his daughter. These people to whom family meant everything.

Gail turned off the lamp on her nightstand. She lay on her back in the dark, wanting Anthony to be there. Wanting to hear his footsteps on the stairs. The slight creak of the bed frame, the shifting of weight. His arms going around her. The heat of his body. Sometimes she would dream he was touching her, and the sensations would wake her up.

Dangerous, to want him so much.

You have my ring on your finger. Don't try to take it off.

How could I? When you look at me like that . . . When you touch me . . . I could never leave. I have no strength, none. This never happened before. Never. Not with any other man. You fill me completely. I am floating on the tide at full moon. Pulled under and swept away. Swept away. Crazy for you. Crazy.

In the distance she heard ringing. A telephone somewhere. Gradually she came awake and glanced at the clock: 12:37 A.M. There was a moment of knowing. The old man was dead. Anthony was calling to tell her.

She fumbled for the receiver, dropped it, then brought it to her ear. Her eyes were still closed. "How is he?"

A silence.

She cleared her throat. "Anthony?"

Then a voice like metal scraped across piano strings. *HelloGailConnor.*

Still groggy, she struggled to sit up.

Hellobitch. The hideous clanging resembled a laugh. *Timetodie.*

"Who are you?" Suddenly awake, heart pounding, she automatically clutched a handful of sheet at her heart. "Why are you doing this?"

"Goingtogetyou. Timetodie. Howdoyouwantit?"

"Go to hell." Gail saw the pale green light of the disconnect and jabbed it.

Within moments the ringing resumed. Gail turned on the light and squinted at the display. PAY PHONE. The same as last night? She couldn't remember. This time she left the number in memory.

She turned off the ringer. For a few seconds there was silence. Then a muffled jangle came up the stairs from the extension in the living room. She threw back the blanket and stood up, staring at the open door to her bedroom, the dark hallway beyond. She thought of calling the hospital, asking for Ernesto Pedrosa's room, then dismissed that idea. She couldn't disturb Anthony when he was waiting for word from the doctors. *Come home, I'm scared.*

The phone rang again downstairs, then went silent. In her room the display showed the same number as before, but the message light remained dark.

She thought of the argument with Peggy Cunningham. Peggy might have confronted her son with Gail's accusations. Might have punished him. Might have sent him to his room, where he sat fuming. He would look out the second-floor window and see her car in the driveway.

"Oh, stop it," she said aloud. "He's only fourteen years old."

She hastily put on jeans and a T-shirt and went downstairs to check all the windows and doors, and turn off the ringer on the extension. She sat in the dark in the living room, listening for noises. Her mind spun with visions of a face at the window. If Anthony was here, he would go outside with his pistol. Gail did not own a gun.

She dialed 911, heard it ring once, then hung up. The police had better things to do. *Yeah, some woman got a phone call and wants us to drive by and see if Freddy Krueger is hiding in the bushes.*

The ringer was off. What if Anthony called?

This is stupid, she told herself. Someone playing a joke, nothing more. She turned it back on, then went upstairs and turned on the phone in the bedroom as well.

I was past two o'clock in the morning when the call came through. Gail was wide awake. She saw MERCY HOSPITAL on the display and picked it up.

Anthony told her the old man's heart rate was irregular. They had him on medication, and the doctors were deciding what to do.

"Tell him I love him," she said. "And Digna. Be sure to tell her."

"I will," he said.

"I love you too, Anthony."

"I'll call you in the morning. Go back to sleep. *Te quiero.*"

FIVE

"**I** wouldn't say I'm *worried.*"

"Well, I'd be worried. You should notify the police. Promise me you will."

"I promise, Mother. If it happens again, I'll call them."

Gail had come to her mother's house to sit on the terrace, read the Sunday paper, and be fussed over.

A gust of wind off the water teased Irene Connor's sun hat, and she caught it and pressed it firmly on her head. Bright auburn curls framed her face, and her sunglasses were a conscious joke—hot pink frames with little flamingos at the corners. Karen had bought them for her in Key West. Extending her arm, Irene aimed the brass nozzle of a hose toward the periwinkle around the base of a palm tree.

"It's so *hot,*" she said. "Look at that poor plant, how droopy. I was just out here yesterday." Flat four-petaled flowers bobbed and swayed in the stream of water.

"My grass is dying," Gail said. "We just laid it, and it's turning brown. The roofers broke some sprinkler heads. They're still not finished with the job, and there are broken tiles all over the place. And they flattened that alamanda bush you gave me."

"They did? Well, I'll just bring you another one. Good

heavens, it's hot today. What's the rest of the summer going to be?" Irene gave the hose a jerk to free it and turned the sprayer on an arrangement of bromeliads, filling the pinkish centers with water. A small gray lizard scrambled out on Z-shaped legs and darted into the philodendron. "What I think," Irene said, "is that the person is someone you know. Why else would he disguise his voice? Did you hear any kind of accent?"

"Not that I could tell, just that horrible metallic scraping noise. And last time it was a robot. What next?"

"I hope there is no *next*." Irene said.

At this time of year the days were long, and the sun could bite till late in the afternoon. Outdoors, if one moved slowly, and wore shorts and a light, sleeveless top, it was possible not to get too sweaty, but Gail could feel the dampness on the back of her neck. The sea breeze gave some relief.

Half to herself, she said, "Someone whose voice I would recognize."

Irene bent down to inspect a leaf. Something had been chewing on it. "I think you ought to tell Anthony."

"I started to yesterday, but he was so tired. He'd been up all night. Then I forgot, and when I did think of it, he was on his way to the hospital again."

"Poor Mr. Pedrosa. I feel so sorry for Digna. I'd like to go by and see how she is. Do you think that would be all right?"

"Absolutely."

Gail had gone to see Anthony's grandfather yesterday afternoon, and would probably go again today. She had done little more than look in on him and sit with Digna for a while. Ernesto Pedrosa needed a pacemaker, his doctors had said. It would fit under the skin, a relatively simple procedure. The operation was scheduled for Tuesday. He had the best care available, but at eighty-four years of age . . .

"Anthony spent last night at his grandparents' house so he could take his grandmother to early mass. I haven't seen him to talk to since Friday night. He said he'd come by tonight for a while."

"Why don't you have dinner here?" Irene suggested. "Does Anthony like fresh asparagus? We could have a cold platter. I've got some lovely smoked turkey, if you don't mind leftovers."

"Oh, Mom, thanks, but we don't have time. He can't even stay the night with me. This is so hard, living apart. I hardly ever see him. If Dave wasn't putting everything I do under a microscope in court, I would ask Anthony to move in. Karen would just have to accept it."

Irene made a sly smile. Her lipstick matched her glasses— bright pink. "Separation isn't all that bad. Think how exciting your first night will be. Remember that scene in *Gone with the Wind*? Rhett Butler carrying Scarlett O'Hara up the stairs—"

"He had to. She wouldn't let him touch her. So all the way up the stairs, she's beating her fists on his chest. Rhett, Rhett put me *down*! That's not our problem."

The laughter bubbling across the yard seemed too big for such a small woman. In her bright yellow gardening clogs Irene stood barely five-two. Gail had heard people call Irene Strick-land Connor "cute," and they tended to dismiss her opinions. Gail thought that her mother liked it that way: She could sneak up on them. She had the organizational acumen of a CEO. Since the death of her husband, Gail's father Edwin, Irene had devoted herself to fund-raising for local cultural organizations.

When Irene gave a sharp tug on the hose, the reel on the back wall spun out more of it. A fine, cooling mist made silvery beads on the elephant ears and dripped from the red ginger plants, the cycads, and crotons. The grass pulled in moisture with a soft ticking sound. A gray striped cat watched them from a concrete bench under the cassia tree, which had come into bloom with pink flowers.

Gail's parents had moved into this one-story house just north of downtown Miami thirty years ago, and it looked the same now, with its brick facade and row of white columns across the front. The aluminum awning windows from the sixties had never been changed, and the Florida room still had its polished terrazzo floor. On Sunday mornings after church, Irene would sit on the porch by the pool, work the crossword puzzle, sneak a cigarette, and have her juice with champagne. She could look out past the seawall, past the little islands in the bay and see the skyline of Miami Beach in the distance. Pelicans and seagulls glided by. Boats hummed up and down the intracoastal waterway like heavy bees. The air was perfumed with orange jasmine and gardenia.

Gail had not lived here since going away to college at eighteen, but the word *home* always brought her these images. For Karen the house in South Miami was still home, and for Anthony it was his grandparents' mansion on Malagueña Avenue. Gail wondered how long it would take before the three of them felt a similar affection for the house on Clematis Street.

Irene took off her hat and fanned her face. "You know, I think the phone company has a service for tracing calls. But if it goes back to a pay phone, you still wouldn't know who did it, would you?"

"What's so weird is that there's just this disembodied voice that isn't even human, and he doesn't seem to *want* anything. I hung up quickly each time, so he didn't have a chance to say much. I wonder what he'd say if I stayed on the line."

"Don't give him the satisfaction."

"I almost want to listen so I could know *why*. It makes me feel so powerless. This person invaded my home, scared the hell out of me, and there is nothing I can do about it."

"Hang up, that's what you can do."

Gail followed her mother on the mildewy keystone that made a path to the side yard, where she grew her orchids. Hazy shafts of light came through the trees. Irene twisted the adjustment on the nozzle to mist an immense dendrobium with a cluster of stems four feet long. It had grown in that particular live oak tree as long as Gail could remember, and every spring it produced a half dozen spikes of white blossoms touched with pale yellow.

She had come to her mother's house to review plans for the wedding, but the files were still waiting in a box in the living room. Gail sat down on the concrete bench and petted the cat, who flopped over and exposed his belly for more.

"Mother, come with me to pick out a wedding dress. Anthony's cousins recommended a shop in Coral Gables." At the hospital today she had talked to Elena about it. Gail had felt bad for rebuffing the suggestion before, and worse for not having accompanied the rest of the family to the hospital the night Pedrosa collapsed. She added, "I need someone on my side, or else I'll spend too much."

"Well, don't expect me to put on the brakes. You should buy something that will knock his socks off."

The cat pushed its nose against Gail's hand, and she gave it a good scratching, feeling its throat rumble with purrs.

The spray went slowly across the row of miniature orchids hanging on the wood fence in little clay pots. "Darling, would you like to have my mother's earrings? You know—something old, something new. And this is the old part, not the borrowed. I want you to keep them."

The earrings were curves of diamonds set in platinum. Gail's grandfather, John Strickland, had gone all the way to New York by train in the thirties to buy them at Tiffany's for the woman he loved. Her father had refused to let her marry this young man with no prospects.

Gail said, "I have lusted for those earrings for years! But no, I can't keep them. They're yours."

"I never wear them. They're more classical, and they never suited me." Pointing the hose at an immense staghorn fern, she asked Gail when she planned to go shopping. "Not Tuesday, I hope. I have a meeting with the florist. But I could rearrange it. So just tell me when."

Gail had forgotten about the florist. "How much money do you have left out of what I gave you?"

"Well . . . I'm not sure."

"Mother. Please don't tell me you're using your own."

"What if I am? The flowers are from me, and that's that." She aimed the sprayer at giant maidenhair fern cascading from a tree, and a rainbow shimmered in the mist. "Aside from the neighborhood boy, who can you think of that has a grudge? Who's angry at you?"

Gail had explained what had happened in the gazebo, how she had yelled at Payton Cunningham. She shrugged. "Dave might be angry, but this isn't his style."

"I like Dave Metzger. Maybe he'll come to his senses. How is that going, by the way?"

"On hold till we see the psychologist and he makes a report. What do you mean, you like Dave?"

Irene's pink-flamingo sunglasses turned toward her. "Well, I do. Dave isn't a bad person. He's just making a mistake. I can't turn my feelings on and off."

"Sorry," Gail said.

An arc of water reached across the grass to the Boston fern along the fence. "You're worried. I can tell. You're pale and you hardly touched your breakfast." Irene looked at her. "You aren't pregnant, are you?"

Gail laughed. "No."

"It's too bad you and Dave only had one."

"Mother—"

She kicked at a weed with one yellow plastic clog. "I am eternally grateful, Gail, that I had two children. You know. Things can happen in this world."

Gail's sister, Renee, had died last year—viciously murdered. Irene did not mention her often, but Gail knew that the pain would never go away.

Gail followed her mother along the fence. "Charlene Marks thinks that Dave has a hidden agenda for wanting Karen. Is that plausible?"

"Hidden agenda? It's obvious to me that he's jealous of Anthony. Here's a man who's successful. He's rich and attractive. He has you, and Dave doesn't want him to have Karen as well. Male competitiveness, is what I think." Irene picked a rock out of the mulch and tossed it into the bushes. "Dave never was much of a businessman, was he?"

"Not in the past, but his luck might have changed."

"It will be nice for you, not to have to worry about money."

"I'm not marrying Anthony for his money."

"I didn't say you were." Irene turned the nozzle till the spray disappeared. "He has quite a few attributes. Still, it's better to have money than not, if a woman has a choice."

They started walking back toward the house. The hose dragged behind them, and occasionally Irene would flip it to get it over a stepping stone. "About those phone calls. I was thinking, what if one of your clients made them? Have you argued with any clients lately?"

"No, nothing that would justify such a weird response. Usually if a client is mad at you, they complain to the Florida Bar."

"What if it's someone you beat in court? What was that oil man you were telling me about? What's-his-name Sweet. Maybe he did it."

"Wendell." Gail walked for a while, then said. "No, the first call came before the hearing."

"And he wasn't angry with you before the hearing?"

Gail considered. "He's been angry with me for months, but I think the timing is off."

"You give people far too much credit for being logical. They aren't," Irene said. "They act on emotions, not brains. People don't like lawyers, and you're a tough cookie."

"Am I that awful? Whoever it was called me a bitch. 'Time to die, bitch.' "

"You're not awful!" Irene took her arm. "You're generous and kind. However, you can be prickly too."

"Prickly."

"You have to be, for your client, but the person on the other side might say you're cold and aggressive. It's all a matter of perspective, darling. If someone hates lawyers to begin with, and if a lawyer takes away what he has—particularly if the lawyer is a woman . . . Well, you've cut off his balls." Irene looked up at Gail over the top of her sunglasses and smiled. "So to speak."

"Did you know," Gail said, "that the legal profession now has the highest rate of suicide? We're more depressed than psychiatrists and police officers."

"Well, there's a bit of news we can do without." At the reel on the wall, she turned the crank, and the hose slid across the grass like a shiny green snake. "Why don't you come over for dinner one night this week? All three of you."

"I don't know. I'd have to check with Anthony."

"If I have one regret about your getting married, there it is. You're going to be so occupied with your new husband that I won't see you anymore."

"Mother—"

"How often do I see Karen as it is? One day she won't even recognize me."

"For heaven's sake. I'll ask him and if we're free, we'll come over."

"Terrific. Don't forget, darling—nothing is more important than family. I'm going to barbecue some chicken, that's what I'll do. Will Anthony eat lemon meringue pie?"

Laughing, Gail put an arm over her mother's shoulders. "He loves to try foreign food."

SIX

"Settle it, Sam. If we go to trial, you're taking a big risk. . . . Because we have a forty-one-year-old flight attendant, mother of three, with a medial meniscus. She can't squat, can't even stand for more than an hour. The jury will feel sorry for her. . . . Fifty? No way. We need at least a hundred. At least."

As Gail talked, she scanned the stack of mail on her desk she hadn't had time to get to on Friday. She would not have been surprised to find that the lawyer on the other end of the phone was signing pleadings while he explained why his client, an auto insurance company, shouldn't have to pay more than fifty thousand dollars for a torn knee, not that he believed what he was saying.

Gail noticed the receptionist at the door and motioned her in. "She's going to need arthroscopic surgery and rehab. The career she's had for twenty years is over."

Lynn had some checks to be signed. She stood by the desk, waiting for Gail to finish.

"Let me know soon, because I'm prepared to file the complaint. . . . Great. Talk to you then." Gail swiveled her chair to hang up the phone. "Thank God. I think we're going to get a settlement in Zimmerman."

"Congratulations."

"Let's see. If they give us a hundred . . ." Gail studied a printout of costs she had advanced in the case. "One third, plus I get all this back . . . That's about thirty-eight thousand dollars. You know what, Lynn? I used to turn up my nose at personal injury cases. That was before I had my own office." Gail uncapped her pen. "Now I just ask if there's insurance." When Lynn looked at her sideways, Gail said, "That was a joke. Honest."

"Oh."

Lynn Dobbert did not have the sparkle of Gail's full-time secretary, Miriam Ruiz, but she worked hard and rarely complained. Business had picked up enough to require another person to help out, but for every settled case, and every paid bill for services rendered, just as much seemed to go out.

The checks were drawn on the office account of Gail A. Connor, Attorney at Law, P.A. A check for malpractice insurance, another for dues to the Florida Bar. Then a payment on the leased computer equipment. Medical insurance. Rent and parking. Lynn drew each aside and placed it precisely on top of the one preceding. Gail did not usually interrupt her work to sign checks, but Miriam had sternly told her that they had to go out *today*, because most were overdue. A settlement payment had been three weeks late in arriving, and the funds wouldn't be available until Wednesday. Gail did not like kiting checks, but June so far had been a lousy month. The judge's ruling in the Sweet case had not helped. If Zimmerman came in, she would be all right—for a while.

The intercom buzzed, and Gail reached to pick it up. Miriam told her that Charlie Jenkins was on the line.

"Who? Oh, yes!" Gail swung around and pressed the right button. "Mr. Jenkins, I'm glad you called back. Do you remember me? I live on Clematis Street in the Grove, and you fixed my sink last week, and a toilet before that. . . . Well, I've got another emergency. There's no power in the kitchen. Did you say you do electric repairs?"

He assured her that he did everything.

Charlie Jenkins, a heavyset man with a short black beard, had been driving by in his van about a month ago and noticed the condition of Gail's house. He'd told her he was working up the street for the Cabreras. *I do it all—carpentry, electric, plumbing.* Gail had fibbed, telling him that she was dealing with a contractor, but Jenkins had taken a card out of his shirt pocket, assuring her he could do it for less, whatever it was. He had smiled, showing his dimples. *Besides, I speak English.* Gail had tossed the card into a drawer and forgotten about it until one Sunday morning when she couldn't find a licensed plumber to unclog a toilet for a reasonable amount of money. Just this morning she had left messages with two electricians about the kitchen problem, but neither had called her back. So she called Jenkins.

"Breaker box? . . . No, it has fuses, and they all looked fine to me. . . . Yes, I know we should redo everything, but right now I just need a refrigerator and lights in the kitchen. . . . Five o'clock, that's the earliest I could be home. . . . All right, see you then. Thanks."

She hung up and reached for the next check. "Poor Karen went downstairs for some milk last night, and *zzzzt!*"

"You should be careful with electricity," Lynn said. "Tom tried to put an extra outlet in the boys' room and shocked the heck out of himself."

Gail smiled. "I'll be careful." The intercom buzzed. "Yes, Miriam?"

Jamie Sweet was returning her call. Line two.

"Thanks, I'll take it." Gail told Lynn to have a seat for a minute. "Jamie, this is Gail."

She explained that she had talked to Anthony Quintana over the weekend. "Anthony said not to talk to Harry yet. First he wants to work out a plea with the prosecutors. I think he's being a little too cautious, but Harry is his client, and it's his call. Don't worry. There's still time."

Gail heard a child's muffled squeal of laughter, then Jamie yelling. "Ricky, you put that down! Excuse me, Gail." Ricky was three, the youngest. Gail heard a talk show in the background, and Jamie's voice over it. "You stay right there till I get off the phone." Then footsteps. Slightly winded, Jamie said, "I'm sorry, you were saying about Harry . . ."

"Yes. That I'm going to have to wait a week or so to talk to him."

"That's okay." A sigh came over the line. "I don't know if we ought to bother Harry. I don't know."

Gail heard the audience on the television laugh, then applaud. "Jamie?"

"I'm here. Wendell came by yesterday with the child support."

"The restraining order says he's supposed to mail it, not bring it in person." Gail added. "I hope he didn't cause any trouble."

"No, he didn't give me any trouble at all, just played with the kids. He fixed the tree house. They got all hot and sweaty, and Becky sprayed him with the hose, and they were laughin' and carryin' on. Then Bobby comes in and says, Mommy, can Daddy stay for lunch?"

Gail laughed in disbelief. "Jamie, you do not allow an estranged husband to hang out at your house."

"But he was being good, and the kids wanted him to stay. Gail, I swear, he was like the old Wendell again."

"The old Wendell used to beat you up."

"Well . . . we talked about that. He cried. I couldn't believe it. I cried too, Gail. He said he missed me and the kids so much—"

"Jamie, stop. Don't you see what he's doing? We busted his chops in court on Friday, and now he's trying to save himself. He has not, I guarantee you, miraculously repented."

"But he's not all bad. If he was, I wouldn't have stayed with him."

"You stayed with him because you have three children and no education. Wendell Sweet is a manipulative S.O.B." She heard only the catchy jingle of an ad for canned tuna. "Don't fall for it. We've already proved he lied to the IRS. He's afraid of what else we'll find—the cash that he didn't report. He's afraid he'll have to pay you and the kids a fair share of it."

Jamie Sweet started to cry.

"Oh, Jamie. I'm sorry. Let's see what Harry tells us, okay? And we'll go through Wendell's documents. When he comes for the kids, don't let him spend more than a minute. Just hi, Wendell, here are the kids, be sure to bring them back on time. The best thing is to have a friend there when he comes by. If he has any comments, he can call his lawyer, and his lawyer will call me. It has to be that way. Jamie?"

Her voice was so tight it came out as a squeak. "I'm so tired of this I could die."

"I know. I've been through a divorce myself, and it's hard. You've got to be brave. If you let him come back, it's going to be even worse. Come on, Jamie. Don't give up now. You're going to be just fine."

Gail murmured more assurances, and finally Jamie promised to tell Wendell that her lawyer had ordered her not to talk to him. Gail hung up. "Some clients," she said. "You just feel like screaming at them. Wake up!"

"She wants to take him back?" Lynn stood up from one of the chairs opposite Gail's desk.

Gail turned around to her computer. "No. What Jamie Sweet wants is for this to be over, and in the past that's how she made problems go away. She did what he told her." The Sweet file came up on the monitor. Gail typed a short memo, then hit the code for *phone conf w/client*. Two-tenths of an hour. It would show up on the next bill. "Fat chance I collect any of this," she muttered.

"If they do get back together," Lynn said, "I bet he won't pay the attorney's fees. You'll have to sue him."

"Afraid so. I've got over twenty thousand dollars in this. Wendell thinks a hundred bucks is too much to pay. People have no *idea* how hard they make us work, then they complain about the fees." She made a pistol of her thumb and forefinger.

"Stay away from my client, you varmint, my rent is overdue." Gail looked at Lynn. "That was another joke."

"I figured that." Lynn passed her the last check, waited till she signed it, then stacked them all neatly together. Her nails were short and unpolished, her hands adorned only by a wedding band and an inexpensive watch. She wore plain slacks and pullovers to work, and blond hair hung straight around her face. Her only makeup was a touch of color on high, almost Slavic cheekbones. Two months ago, when Miriam had met her in the cafeteria, Lynn had been working for a temp agency, and Gail had needed some extra help. The extra wages were starting to bite.

Lynn asked, "Gail? If it's no trouble, could I come in Thursday instead of Friday? Tommy's camp counselor said they need some parents to go along on a field trip to MetroZoo."

"Check the schedule," Gail said. "It should be all right." Lynn worked three days, but occasionally traded them around if something came up. That would not have been permitted at Hartwell Black and Robineau, where schedules were maintained and rules were enforced, lest the staff become spoiled.

"You'll have to bring the boys by sometime. I'd love to meet them."

"I should do that. They're a handful, though."

"Lynn, wait." She turned around at the door. "Have there been any strange phone calls lately, any hang-ups? People who call the office and don't leave a name?"

Her eyes widened. "No. Did you get a call like that?"

Gail shrugged. "Not here. I got a couple of crank calls at home." Last night she had seen it again: PAY PHONE on the caller-ID. She had not picked it up. She had ordered Karen not to answer the phone under any circumstances. Anthony had called once from his grandparents' house, and her mother had phoned. Otherwise the night had been quiet.

"What did they say?"

"Well . . . nothing worth repeating. I think it must have been kids. I suppose I should ignore it."

"Oh, don't do that. People are crazy, especially in Miami. Someone might be stalking you. Tom doesn't like me to go out after dark, and he's always checking to make sure the doors are locked. We had a woman in our neighborhood stabbed in her own house by a man who had followed her home. You should call the police."

Gail nodded. Whatever one might say, Lynn Dobbert had a disaster to top it. She went out with the checks she had brought in.

Tapping her pen on the desk, Gail looked again at the telephone, then dialed Jamie Sweet's number. An answering machine picked up, causing her a moment of distress before she said, "Hi, Jamie. This is Gail again. Just wanted to make sure you're all right. If you need to talk to me—anytime—please don't hesitate to call." After a second or two of searching her mind uselessly for a piece of memorable wisdom, Gail hung up. She laughed to herself, remembering Charlene Marks's advice about maintaining a safe emotional distance. *Don't be their mother or their pal.* Commercial litigation in the posh law firm downtown had not been nearly as messy.

She heard a click and looked around. Miriam had come in, closing the door behind her. She crossed the room, bouncy stride in high heels, curly hair swinging from a clip on top of her head. Bracelets jangled, and gold earrings spun. But something had ticked her off.

"*¿Qué pasa?*" Gail asked.

She was holding some papers, which fluttered as she extended her arm to show Gail. "Look at this. Look what she did. She put the South Miami Motors caption on an order for South Miami Hardware. And I just called the courier! This has to be filed at the courthouse this afternoon."

"Well, tell her to redo it."

"Why did you give it to Lynn?"

"You were out to lunch, Miriam, and it seemed simple enough."

"She hasn't learned the system yet," Miriam said. "She is so *slow.*"

"Inexperienced, not slow."

The red-lipsticked mouth, which had opened to vent another complaint, released a long sigh instead. "You're right." Miriam was only twenty-two, but had been Gail's secretary for three years at Hartwell Black. Gail had wooed her away with equal benefits and a raise. Miriam was worth every dime, but she took her seniority seriously.

"Oh, somebody left a message." The pink slip of paper that Miriam quickly handed her said that Elena Godoy could meet her at Lola Benitez Couture on Saturday morning at ten o'clock. Please call.

Gail set the message beside her telephone. "Elena Pedrosa Godoy is Anthony's cousin. She wants to help me pick out a wedding dress."

Miriam grinned, buoyant as a teenager. "I can't wait to see it! What will it look like?"

"I don't qualify for white. Something pastel and ankle-length, I suppose. Karen's outfit will be harder. Will she even agree to wear a dress?"

"She's going to look so cute."

"My flower girl," Gail said. "One of Anthony's nephews will be the ring bearer."

"Who's going to carry the *hadas*?"

Gail repeated it slowly. "Addas?"

"*Hadas*. With a silent H. It's like . . . money. Little coins."

"I've never heard of that."

"Oh, yes! After the rings the groom gives the bride the *hadas*. She holds out her hands like this, and he opens the little box and takes out the coins, and he gives them to her. It's to signify, like, I'm going to take care of you forever. All my worldly goods are yours. It's a custom in Cuban weddings. Or any Spanish wedding, I guess."

Gail smiled. "That's very nice. I don't know if it's appropriate for Anthony and me, but it's nice. Good Lord. We should have chosen the words for the ceremony already, but we've been so busy! Maybe we'll just do the usual thing. What was yours like, Miriam?"

"I wish I'd known you then. I'd have invited you!" Miriam leaned her little fanny on the edge of the desk. "We got married at Iglesia San Lazaro in Hialeah, and I had a long satin dress with a train, and Danny wore a white tuxedo. We had the *hadas*, and the *lazo*, and our mothers pinned the *mantilla* on our shoulders. Then we rode in a white limousine to the banquet hall. I should show you the video! All our friends and family were there, and we had a deejay and a mirrored ball in the ceiling!" She laughed. "The first dance was with my father. *Papi* couldn't stop smiling. Then he gave me to Danny, and we danced together. It was so perfect. We partied till one o'clock in the morning; then we drove to a hotel on Miami Beach."

With a giggle Miriam covered her mouth. "Oh, my God, Danny was so tired he fell asleep! We didn't . . . you know, make love till morning, but the sun was coming up over the ocean, and we heard the waves and the seagulls."

"It sounds perfect," Gail said.

"It was. You know we conceived Berto on our honeymoon? It was a total surprise. Danny says he wants to take me to Hawaii, we might have twins!" Miriam picked up the order that she had complained about earlier. "Well, I'd better redo this before the courier gets here." Hair bouncing on her back, Miriam vanished into the hall, her high heels clicking on the tiles, then diminishing.

Smiling, Gail watched her go. Miriam and Danny were blessed—unlike Wendell and Jamie Sweet, whose marriage had been cursed from the beginning. Since the failure of her own marriage, Gail had decided that there was nothing she could have done to save it, because the *passion* hadn't been there. They had not been lovers but two people occupying the same house. With Anthony . . . Gail closed her eyes and rested her chin on her fist. With Anthony no escape was possible. To leave him . . . She could not imagine it. Or that he would leave her.

Never. She remembered his words, spoken with such infuriating assurance as he sat on the edge of the bed in the room at his grandfather's house. *I would find some way to make you stay.* Looking up at her with those dark eyes. She had laughed, but if he had reached for her, she would have made love to him all over again.

With a start, Gail noticed the clock. Three-thirty already, the afternoon almost gone.

Next. Letters from attorneys who had read the ad in the *Business Review* about the spare office. One was from a recent graduate studying for the bar, who wanted to work as a law clerk. Another from a man in his sixties who wanted to practice part-time. Most were articulate, with substantial résumés attached. And all—every one—were from lawyers who wanted to be hired. Paid. Put on salary. The ad had clearly said, *Office space to share.* Desperation in the ranks, too many lawyers. Gail was grateful for her contacts. If her office went under, she could get a job. But it would be a job, not a business. It wouldn't be hers.

On the computer she quickly typed a form letter thanking the lawyers for their interest, etc., etc., with instructions for Miriam to customize it for each. The intercom signaled a call, and Gail picked it up without moving her eyes from the screen.

"Yes?"

Lynn told her that Mrs. Sweet was calling again.

If Gail had imagined that Jamie would listen to her advice when their last conversation ended, that mistake became quickly evident. Between sobs, Jamie told her that Wendell had just left. They'd gone upstairs to talk, hoping to settle things between them. Instead they had argued. He had said they wouldn't be going through this if Jamie hadn't been brainwashed by her lawyer. He had screamed at her for taking his children away, trying to ruin his life, stealing his money like the common slut she had been when he met her. She had screamed back at him to get out, and he had hit her.

"Oh, God. Jamie, are you all right?"

"My lip's busted, but it was my fault. I was yellin' at him, callin' him names."

"This isn't your fault! I want you to call the police. We're taking this to the judge."

"No, Gail! Please don't."

"Jamie—"

"I can't—I can't do this anymore. If it wasn't for the kids, I'd kill myself, I swear I would."

"Jamie, please—"

"Could you—Gail, I don't mean to be a bother—could you please come talk to me? Please." She sobbed. "I don't know what to do."

"Of course. Of course I will."

Gail scanned her desk, calculating what she could leave, what had to be taken with her. She flipped through her appointment book. A client was coming in. He could be rescheduled. As she stuffed files into her briefcase, followed by her laptop computer, she tucked the phone under her chin, speaking as calmly as she could. "Jamie, I don't want you to worry. I'll be right over. Do you have some tea? Good. Make us some tea, and we'll talk. I'll be there in fifteen minutes. If Wendell comes back, don't let him in."

"He won't be back. I told him if he came back, I'd shoot his sorry ass."

"I'm leaving right now," Gail said. She stuffed some files into her briefcase and grabbed her purse. Hurrying down the hall she glanced at her watch: 4:15. She would make a call to the day camp for Karen to take the bus. The bus would drop her off around five-thirty. Gail doubted she could make it home by then, but Karen had a key and knew to stay inside. At six-thirty Anthony would arrive to take them for a short visit with his grandfather; then they would go to dinner. That meant that Gail could not afford much time at Jamie's house. She would get her calmed down, maybe have a neighbor come over, then leave.

Miriam was at the copy machine. Lynn was working at the

desk behind the frosted window that opened onto the waiting room. When they looked around, Gail told them what had happened.

She was almost out the door when she remembered the repairman. "Damn." She came back to ask for a volunteer. "He'll be there at five, and I can't cancel it."

There was a quick discussion, a comparison of schedules, a shuffling of afternoon activities, kids, husbands. Lynn agreed to go, using Miriam's key to Gail's house.

Gail said, "I'll pay him when I get there, between five-thirty and six. And if you'd keep an eye on Karen too?"

Lynn stood up, nervously clasping her hands. "Be careful, Gail. What if Wendell comes back? What if he's carrying a gun?"

"I'll shoot him with Jamie's."

SEVEN

Wendell Sweet had struck his wife across the face, and her upper lip was swollen. She had bruises on her arms and a bump on her head where he had pushed her against the wall of their bedroom. They had gone in there for privacy, leaving the children in the playroom downstairs.

Gently probing her fingers through Jamie Sweet's thick red hair, Gail found the bump. Jamie had insisted she was fine, but Gail had to be sure. Jamie had also insisted that she didn't want to make a police report. Gail was mystified by this, wanting Jamie to be as angry as she was. It was as though Wendell had come in there and sucked all the air out of the room, leaving Jamie dizzy and weak.

Head bowed, she sat on a satin-covered ottoman in a bedroom overdone to the point of kitsch with gilded furniture, swagged drapes, and tasseled pillows. A gold-framed print of Monet's *Water Lilies*, in purple, occupied the space over a puffy white sofa. A pair of small chandeliers hung on either side of the canopied king-size bed. The gold silk comforter had fallen to the floor, and the air was heavy with the conflicting aromas of unlaundered sheets and perfumed candles burned to puddles of wax. The carpet was littered with toys and children's picture books. Jamie had fired the housekeeper, trying to save money.

"I'm *fine*," Jamie said again. She moved away from Gail's hand and smoothed her hair. Her blue eyes were puffy from crying and blotchy with mascara. She took another sip of tea. Gail left hers where it was on the dresser, too watery and already cold.

Frustrated, Gail said, "You are not fine. The man just beat you up! I should file a motion for contempt of court."

"This is my decision!"

"Don't be afraid of Wendell. He needs to be put in jail."

"No. I don't want my kids knowing—" Her voice caught. "Knowing the police came to get their daddy."

"But Jamie, isn't it better to show them that the law won't let him get away with—"

"Don't tell me what's better! My own father was in jail. I know how it feels." Jamie lifted her hands. "I'm sorry. Gail, I'm sorry. I'm not thinkin' straight right now."

Gail paced slowly across carpet so thick it nearly snagged her heels. She kept her eyes on Jamie, wondering how to make her listen. It would do no good to say, *I told you not to let him in.* "The judge has to approve a settlement. He won't let Wendell dictate the terms."

"What if I keep pushin', Gail? He could say screw you and leave the country. Then what would I do? The mortgage on this house is almost five thousand dollars a month. I'm so far behind now they're gonna put me out in the street."

"I won't let that happen, I promise. Wendell isn't going to get away with this. Without you he'd still be an oil rigger. You worked double shifts as a waitress to put him through college, and now it's his turn to take care of you. He is legally obligated, and you shouldn't feel the least bit guilty."

"Wendell says he doesn't have enough to keep me and the kids in the house, livin' so high, like we been doing."

"He is lying to you."

"This is such a big place. It wears me out. I got clothes in that closet there I never put on."

Gail could see their reflections in the wall of mirrored closet doors, one woman pacing, one slumped with her head in her hands. She went over and knelt beside Jamie and said quietly, "Okay. You feel overwhelmed right now. Maybe you should look for another place. No pool to take care of, a little less yard. But you'll want a good neighborhood for the kids."

With a wobbly smile Jamie lifted her head. Her eyes glistened with tears. "You want to hear something funny? When me and Wendell were talking—before we started fighting—he said he still loves me."

Gail took her hand. "It's not love to hurt someone. A man who hits you in the face does not *love* you."

"He used to. I used to love him too." Her voice was husky with emotion. "How do people stop loving each other? Was it real to begin with?"

Shaking her head, Gail said, "I don't know. People change."

Jamie focused on something across the room and quickly wiped her eyes. Gail turned to see a small face at the door. She rose to her feet.

"Hey, honey. Come here, baby." A little girl came shyly in, turning sideways as if that would keep her out of Gail's line of vision. "This is my friend Gail. She won't bite."

The girl climbed onto Jamie's lap and rested her head on her bosom. The tip of her forefinger was in her mouth, and her mouth had a rim of red liquid, as if she had been drinking Kool-Aid. Her hands and knees were dirty. Gail knew that she was five years old, the middle child. She had black hair, like her father.

Gail smiled at her. "Hi. You must be Becky."

"Aren't you going to say hi, precious?"

"No."

Jamie gently untangled the curls in Becky's hair. "Sometimes I think of going back home. A small town would be better for the kids. I never liked Miami much. It's too hot. I get so tired of hearing Spanish. I'm sorry to say that, because I know you're engaged to a Cuban man. I got to know him when he came into Harry's office. Did I tell you? He's a good-looking guy, always so polite to me." Jamie continued to stroke her daughter's hair. "You're lucky, to get divorced and have a man like that waiting for you. And you have your career. Look at me. I dropped out of high school. You know, I used to be pretty. Men would fight over me." She laughed. "I'm not so pretty now."

Gail said, "You are. You have to believe in yourself, Jamie."

The look that Jamie gave her was quick and sharp. *What do you know about pain?*

The grandfather clock in the hall announced the hour with five melodious notes. So little time left, Gail thought. She had come in here with her sword drawn, ready to defend her client, but had wound up slogging through a swamp of lethargy and despair, dragging Jamie behind her like dead weight. Gail was frustrated by Jamie's ambivalence, and by her own inability to break through it.

Gail smiled at the girl, then said, "I wonder if Becky would like to go play for a while longer?"

"Sure. Becky, honey? Would you see if Ricky's still taking his nap? Then you and Bobby can watch a video. Go on." The girl burrowed her face between Jamie's breasts. "Mommy's got to talk to the lady right now. Please? I'll come see you in a little bit."

"I don't want to!"

"Don't you make me count to three."

With a glare toward the intruder, Becky slid off her mother's lap and ran into the hall. Gail got up to make sure the girl had gone, but she left the door open in case of a noise from below signaling disaster. She looked back across the room. Jamie was standing by her dresser, arranging bottles of perfume. The surface of the dresser was almost completely hidden by a silk robe, a stack of CDs, toy trucks, empty glasses and cups.

"You know what Wendell said? He said . . . if I let him come back, we might could work it out."

"Oh, Jamie."

"My daddy was an alcoholic. My mama threw him out when I was twelve years old. We didn't see him much after that. Seven of us kids. He wanted to come back, but she never would let him. I had one brother go to prison and the other two don't amount to nothing, and only the youngest girl made anything of herself."

"All this because your father wasn't there?" Gail came closer and gestured toward Jamie's image in the mirror. "Look at that cut on your mouth. What does that tell Becky about what a father should be? What's she going to learn about the relationship of a husband and wife?"

When Jamie dropped her gaze and began to straighten the disarrayed clothes on the dresser, Gail knew that she had lost her.

Then the doorbell rang, distant chimes from the foyer. Jamie crossed the bedroom and pulled back the curtain. In the circular driveway Gail saw her own car and behind it a shiny red Lincoln. "Who is that?"

"Harry." With her forefingers Jamie wiped the mascara from under her eyes. "Oh Lord, I look like shit."

"Harry Lasko? Why is he here?"

"I left him a message about what Wendell did." As the doorbell sounded again, Jamie rushed out, and Gail followed her down the stairs. Bare feet pattering over the marble squares in the foyer, Jamie straightened the hem of her pink T-shirt over her jeans.

When she opened the door, the afternoon light flooded in, turning her hair to flame. A man's voice murmured, "Hey, baby doll."

"Harry, you didn't have to come."

"Of course I did. Let me look at you. Oohhh, that goddamn bastard." The words were barely audible. "Have you got company?"

"My lawyer. Come on in, you're lettin' the cold air out."

He came into the foyer, a tall, skinny, slightly stoop-shouldered man in a faded blue golf shirt and plaid shorts. The lenses in his sunglasses lightened to amber, revealing shaggy brows that sloped downward over inquisitive hazel eyes. His scalp gleamed through thinning white hair, and more white hair curled at the collar of his shirt. A gold chain sparkled on his neck.

"Gail Connor, Harry Lasko."

"How do you do?" Gail said, extending her hand.

His grin made deep creases in his cheeks. "Anthony Quintana said you were pretty. He lied. You're gorgeous."

"Harry's a big ole flirt." Jamie smiled up at him, then turned him by an elbow toward the living room. "Y'all come sit down."

Somewhat uncertainly Gail accompanied them, caught between the pressure of time and her raging curiosity about what Lasko might say. Gail still did not see anything wrong in talking to Lasko in advance of his sentencing agreement, but Anthony could be insufferably strict about his clients. She preferred to avoid the hassle of arguing about it.

Harry Lasko noticed the sofa cushions, which had been made into a fort. The carpet was littered with Legos, blocks, Barbie doll clothes, cookies. "Holy smokes. The Indians have raided the place. Did they tie up the maid in the closet?"

"I let her go." Jamie laughed. "Did you come to see me or my housekeeping?"

He studied her for a moment. Then he laughed and held his arms wide. "What the hell?"

"Right. What the hell." Jamie's face disappeared for a second against his blue shirt. "I'm glad you're here."

"I'm a louse for not coming more often." Harry Lasko took Jamie's hand in both of his. "You're okay, sweetheart? I expected to see the cops in here."

Jamie said, "I didn't call them. Y'all want something to drink?"

"Why didn't you call the police?"

She raised a shoulder in a shrug. "I just didn't feel like it, and that's all the talkin' I'm gonna do about Wendell, or me, or my damned marriage."

Lasko looked at Gail, his angled brows sloping down even farther. "You didn't advise this, did you?"

Gail shook her head. "It's Jamie's decision." She left it at that. If Jamie didn't want to explain, her lawyer could not speak either. She glanced at her watch: 5:25. Karen would be home soon. Lynn was supervising the electrician. Anthony would be there at six-thirty. Gail decided not to cut it any closer.

With a smile she held out her hand. "Mr. Lasko, I hate to leave so soon, but I need to get home—"

"You don't have five minutes?" Harry Lasko gave her shoulder a pat. "I'm going to ask the bartender to fix me a drink. What about you?"

She wavered. He wanted to talk to her, she could feel it. "A few minutes. Nothing to drink for me, though."

"Vodka and tonic, sweetheart, easy on the ice." When Jamie had disappeared down the hall, Lasko said, "Let's take a walk. I need a smoke."

He led Gail to the family room, where sliding doors opened onto a terrace. Pulling back a panel, he let Gail go first. Ceiling fans whirled slowly in the shade of the roof overhang. The air was like a heated towel. Lasko scanned the backyard with its half acre of parched, weedy grass. Algae had invaded the pool. Apparently Jamie had let the pool man and the gardener go too.

Lasko took a gold lighter and a pack of cigarettes from the pocket of his baggy plaid shorts. "I didn't know it was this bad. What's going on with her case?"

"I'll let Jamie discuss it with you, if she wants."

"Discretion. A virtue in a lawyer." He lit his cigarette. A Rolex circled his wrist. The sunglasses had gone dark again, but he was watching her through them. He exhaled smoke. "I suppose you know about my situation?"

She hesitated, choosing her words carefully. "I don't know the particulars. If discretion is a virtue, then Anthony Quintana is a saint."

"St. Anthony." Harry Lasko had a quick laugh that lingered in a smile. "I'm going to the federal slammer. The only question is, for how long? That's for Quintana to work out. Meanwhile, I'm closing out my business. I spend time with my family—my wife, my son and daughter. The grandkids. Terrific kids. They promise to write. How many people you know live in Florida, the grandkids are somewhere else? I have to look at it that way. I also have some friends. Jamie is one of them. I want to help if I can."

"I'm glad, because she needs your help right now," Gail said.

The sky to the west looked bruised. The tops of the palm trees moved, though the plants at ground level were still. It would rain soon. The air was hot and heavy with humidity. Gail took off the butter yellow jacket that matched her dress and laid it over the arm of a porch chair.

Harry Lasko drew on his cigarette. "What a dumb kid. She never asks me for anything, never says she's in trouble. Listen, Gail. Do what you can for her. Jamie doesn't need to go through a divorce trial. A settlement's the only way to go. Quick, so it doesn't bleed too much."

"You should tell Wendell that," Gail said.

"Well, Wendell and I aren't talking. Jamie owes you twenty grand in fees. Is that right? No, I'm not complaining. Lawyers are expensive, I should know. You want me to take care of it? I'm serious."

"No. When I said she could use your help, I didn't mean money. I'm fairly certain the judge will assess fees against Wendell."

This was odd, Gail thought. An arrest for money laundering usually resulted in the government's seizing everything the defendant owned, yet Harry Lasko had just offered her twenty thousand dollars. Obviously the government had missed something.

Cigarette smoke swirled away on the gathering breeze.

"Jamie said she met you on Bonaire."

"That's right," Lasko said. "One of my hotels was on Bonaire. Wendell and I had been friends for a while. We'd go deep-sea fishing, maybe do a little gambling in the casinos. So I invited him to bring the wife and kids down. Jamie and I, we really hit it off. Hell, we got up there on stage in the nightclub and did karaoke together. We had a blast. When Jamie and Wendell started having problems, she asked me if I needed anybody in my office here in Miami, and I said sure. She's a great gal. That accent! People—Latins—would come in and say, Where's she from? What'd she say?"

A bamboo wind chime suspended from a nearby shade tree swung around, clattering. Gail felt the pressure of time. "I should be going."

Lasko said, "Jamie called me over the weekend. You have some questions about Wendell's assets."

"And your lawyer doesn't want me to talk to you until he works out a deal with the prosecutors."

"Why?"

Gail hesitated, not wanting to sound critical of Anthony. "He's being careful."

"Careful? Jesus. He thinks he's my mother. Jamie says it would help her case if you could tell the judge that Wendell has money offshore."

"Mr. Lasko—"

"You're not talking to me, you're listening. And by the way, call me Harry. Wendell and I did some investing together. Some vacant land, some emeralds, nothing too complicated. About two years ago we acquired the Eagle Beach Casino on Aruba; then last summer we sold it to some investors from Venezuela. Wendell made about a million dollars on the deal. So don't let that snake say he can't support Jamie and the kids."

"Where's the money now?"

"My guess is Aruba, since it was handy, but you won't get any help from that end. Those bankers don't talk."

"Jamie doesn't know about this, does she?"

"Not from me. I never talked business with Jamie, even when she was working for the resort company. The feds questioned her, but she didn't know anything." He studied the end of his cigarette, rolling it between his fingers. "And it's a good thing. Damn government would have screwed her over too."

Recalling something Anthony had told her, Gail said, "What else was Wendell involved in? Does he have friends in the cartel?"

The amber lenses of Harry's sunglasses did not completely hide his eyes, which studied Gail as if to judge her motive for asking. "If you move among people with money, in that part of the world, some of them will be in the business. You want to know if he made any money that way. I don't think so. It's a very high-risk profession for an American."

There was more to this, Gail could sense it, but she knew that

Harry Lasko would not tell her. She said, "There's a hearing next month to reconsider the amount of temporary alimony and child support. Jamie could use your testimony. You don't have to go into detail, just say that Wendell made money on Eagle Beach, and how much—"

"That's not a good idea. You just tell the judge what I told you. Take him aside and tell him."

Gail shook her head. "It's not allowed."

"Not allowed." A deep chuckle vibrated in this chest. "Gail, some things ought to be done. Fuck the rules. Excuse my language. You're a lawyer, you have a job to do. Follow every last nit-picking rule, you wind up with nothing. Remember that."

She did not point out the obvious: Harry Lasko had wound up with a federal indictment. "What does Wendell do," she asked, "besides advise oil companies?"

"Oh, Wendell's a deal maker. Example. When I met him, about four years ago, he was working as a consultant with a drilling company out of Houston. They stayed at my hotel on Curaçao and went fishing with the brother or uncle, I don't remember, of whoever is in charge of Venezuelan coastal oil rights. Wendell got a fee for negotiating what the drilling company had to pay the politician's brother."

"Negotiating a bribe?"

"They call it a cost of doing business. Step two was, Wendell put the Texas company in contact with a Venezuelan company, proposing a joint venture. It went through and he got another cut, and more when the oil came in. He made money, and he asked my advice where to put it. Privacy was a concern."

"He wanted a bank that wouldn't report his deposits to the IRS," Gail said.

"Right. Some of his income he took back to the U.S., some he didn't."

And Harry Lasko had done the same thing, Gail assumed. She had more questions, but he was unlikely to say anything substantive.

She noticed that the wind chimes were making a racket, and the sky had darkened.

"Am I putting you in a spot with Quintana, talking to me? We don't have to tell him." Harry spread his hands apart, palms up, willing to do her a favor.

"Thanks, but Anthony and I like to be open with each other. He won't be thrilled, but when something falls in your lap, what do you do?"

"You gotta go with it." He grinned and winked.

Gail picked up her jacket, wondering precisely what she would say to Anthony. *I couldn't help it. Harry Lasko started running his mouth . . .* She intended to go back inside the house, but instead turned around to ask, "Harry, have you ever heard of the Old Island Club? It's on St. Thomas, but I can't remember exactly where."

"Sapphire Beach. Sure, I know the Island Club. Have you been there?"

"No, I just heard someone talk about it. What's it like?"

"I believe it was made from timbers out of an old shipwreck. At high tide the waves come right under the windows. They've got a big wooden deck and a pit for roasting pigs."

"Is it popular?"

"Oh, yeah. If you like tourists. I used to go when it was a hangout for sailors. It's still fun." Lasko took a last drag on his cigarette and dropped it into a planter full of dead philodendron. They walked across the terrace. Jamie was visible inside, sipping a drink.

"How did you get into the resort business?" Gail asked.

He slid back the door. "My dad ran a hotel in Baltimore, but I thought Vegas sounded exciting. I went in the fifties, when it was starting to heat up. I dealt blackjack, poker, ran the craps table. I bought my first hotel in Nassau with my wife, Edie. I met her in Vegas. She was a showgirl then. Could she dance. What a set of legs. Up to her neck, those legs."

He took the drink that Jamie offered him. "Jamie, you've seen my wife. Does she not have the best set of legs? And when she

was younger, breasts like ripe cantaloupes. Gail, am I embarrassing you?"

She smiled. "No, Harry."

"Edie used to be a platinum blonde, a tall girl, like you. And
smart! When I got to Vegas I was so green. I had dreams of
being a comic, to show you how dumb I was. Edie felt sorry for
me. She showed me the ropes, who was who. She actually
thought I was funny. When Edie laughed, I was in heaven."

Harry reached out and tapped Jamie on the arm. "Hey, come
here. You need a laugh."

"Sure." She curled up on the end of the rattan sofa, and Harry
sat beside her.

He said, "You know, I never asked Edie out at first because
she was going with a guy sent down from Chicago to keep an
eye on things in the casino. Joe Angionelli. Touch his girl, you
kiss your ass good-bye. One day I'm walking home, and I hear
this horn tooting at me. It's Joe's car, a fifty-eight Caddy con-
vertible, white with red leather interior, and Edie's behind the
wheel. She says get in, let's go. Go where? We're having a
picnic. I see a basket in the back. Then she scoots over and tells
me to drive. What? Are you nuts? Me drive this car? She says go
ahead, Joe's in L.A. till tomorrow, and I won't tell. She puts on
her sunglasses and her scarf, and we go tearing across the desert
and the dust rolls up behind us like smoke. I mean, here I am in
a Mafia goon's brand-new Cadillac, with this beautiful, gorgeous dame. We have a nice little supper by a lake. We have
some booze, we swim. The sun goes down, the stars come up.
Oh, those stars. You can't see them like that here, but wow. Was
I in love. We turned on the radio and danced. A corny old song,
'It Had to Be You,' which of course became our song. Edie still
likes me to sing to her. I think she hears me, I really do."

Harry Lasko took a drink, then said, "Anyway, coming back, I
swerve to miss something in the road and run the car into a
gulley and just cream the front end. Edie says don't worry,
don't worry, we'll think of something. We hitch a ride from an
Indian in a pickup truck, and all I'm thinking is, I'm dead.

When Joe gets back to Vegas, I'm dead. But the crazy thing is, the same night we were out there, the FBI arrested him in L.A. The next day Joe calls Edie to tell her to bring the car over, he's getting out on bail, and she says, Joe, it's gone. Whaddaya mean, gone? Where's my fuckin' car? The feds took it! The sons-a-bitches seized it and towed it away!"

Gail laughed along with the others. Jamie threw back her head and whooped, and her shoulders shook.

Harry's laughter trailed off. "We left Vegas that night and didn't look back. We worked our way over to the Bahamas and bought a little hotel, then a bigger one, then two in Jamaica. We traveled all over the islands. Edie loved the water, how clear it is, how blue. What a ride we had."

He stared down into his glass. Jamie reached over and put a hand on his wrist. He patted it, then took another sip of his drink.

Gail looked from one of them to the other, a little confused.

Harry said, "I don't mean to talk about her in the past tense. Edie's alive, but she has Alzheimer's. She doesn't know me anymore. When I go to prison, Edie won't be aware. You could say that's a blessing."

"Oh. I see." Gail felt the hideous irony like a weight on her chest.

Jamie said, "I wish I'd known Edie . . . before."

"You would have been great pals."

"You're a good man, Harry."

He laughed. "Tell it to the feds."

Tears shone in her eyes. "What am I gonna do when you're gone?"

"Jesus. I'm not gonna die, I'll be away for a while." Harry Lasko put his glass on the end table and stood up. He began dancing to a slow, jazzy beat of a tune that Gail did not know. "Ba-da-bop-bop-a-daaa." He took a step, then a turn, one hand on his chest, the other extended. He motioned to Jamie. "Come here. Dance with me."

"No, Harry—"

"Yes, Harry. Yes, Harry." He pulled her out of her chair, singing, "Bop-ba-da-da-daaah."

Jamie spun around under his extended arm, then around again, stopping precisely to face him, then around again. Her heavy breasts wobbled under the pink T-shirt. He dipped her backward. She shrieked, but he didn't drop her. Jamie's bare foot pointed toward the ceiling.

"This girl can dance!"

She laughed. "I'm so out of shape."

"No, you never forget. You got the moves, baby doll."

At twenty Jamie Sue Johnson had danced in *N'Awlins* in little more than long red hair, freckles on white skin, and a rose tattoo on her thigh.

Harry clicked the beat with his fingers, and his shoulders moved. The light gleamed on the frames of his glasses. "When I kissed youuuu, for the first time, it was the best time—"

Jamie laughed with delight, and Gail found herself smiling. Harry swung Jamie around and hummed the melody with a voice made husky by years of booze and cigarettes.

"Why wasn't Wendell *nice* to me, Harry? That's all he had to be. I wouldn't have filed for divorce if he'd just been nice to me."

"Wendell is a putz. You'll have better someday."

"You think so?"

"Would I lie?"

"It's the scariest thing, Harry."

"No, baby doll. There's worse."

She smiled. "I reckon there is."

"I reckon so." He sang again, putting his arms around her waist. "When that old yellow mooooon was hangin' up above me . . ."

Jamie's forehead dropped to his shoulder. She wept while he rocked her.

"And you said you loved me. Baby, what a time, oh, what a time we had."

CHAPTER

EIGHT

It was quarter to six, and raining hard, when Gail left Jamie Sweet's house. She slammed the car door and tossed her umbrella to the floor of the passenger side. Pausing at the end of the gated driveway, wipers sweeping sheets of water off the windshield, Gail hit speed-dial for Anthony's office.

Mr. Quintana was with a client. "Please tell him I'm running late. We'll meet him at the hospital." Gail had learned that the stereotype about Cuban time didn't apply to Anthony. He was punctual to the minute, and would keep checking his watch if he had to wait around for someone else to get ready.

With her headlights on, she hurried as fast as she dared on the narrow residential streets, barreling through puddles and swerving around a palm frond. She turned onto U.S. 1, the main artery through the south part of the county. A half mile later, taillights blazed, and she hit the brakes. Trapped in the middle lane behind a panel truck, Gail couldn't see what the problem was.

She called home. "Lynn? It's me, stuck in a traffic jam. There must be an accident. I'm going to be late. I'm so sorry." Lynn told her not to worry about it. She would phone her husband and tell him to take the boys out for pizza. Karen was upstairs taking a bath, and the repairman was nearly finished with the wiring. Gail asked her to remind Karen that they had to pay a visit to Anthony's grandfather tonight; then the three of them would go to dinner. "Tell her to put on something nice."

Gail said that there was some money in a drawer in the kitchen, and Lynn could pay the electrician from that. Gail accelerated to keep up with the truck, which had moved several yards ahead. Just in time she saw a car quickly cutting in front of her from the right. She slammed on the brakes, catching her breath when the car behind her nearly slid into her bumper. The driver in front turned around and gave her the finger. She could see his mouth moving in inaudible curses. She blared her horn at him.

The clock announced 6:02 in calm blue digital letters.

Rain obscured the strip shopping center to the east. A man ran across the parking lot with a plastic bag flapping over his head. Lightning flickered, and a crack of thunder followed. Summer thunderstorms were fierce but short-lived.

Gail's mind turned to Jamie Sweet. She had no idea what Jamie might do or what she wanted. In the space of ten minutes Jamie had gone from hating Wendell to loving him, then to wanting any settlement just to have it over with. Gail could feel her slipping away, preferring to drown rather than keep up the struggle.

"Selfish bastard," Gail said aloud. If Harry Lasko was right, Wendell had a million dollars or more in an offshore bank. If Gail could prove it, the judge would be likely to give the house, the stocks and bonds, the cars, the collectibles, the condo in Key West—everything within his reach—to Jamie because Wendell, in his greed, had flat-out lied to the court. The tricky part was finding the proof. She couldn't simply tell the judge that Harry Lasko supposed that Wendell had money. The supplemental documents that she expected on Friday might help, but Gail wanted to talk to Harry again, as soon as she cleared it with Anthony.

Before meeting Harry Lasko, Gail had not cared one way or the other about his going to prison, but now she could not bear the thought of it. She wanted Anthony to save him. Do something. Don't let this man die behind bars.

She found herself softly singing the tune that Harry had sung to Jamie. "When I kissed you . . . for the first time . . . Baby, what a time we had."

In south Florida rain might fall on one block and leave the next untouched. As Gail turned onto Clematis Street, the sun was sending golden light under the retreating clouds.

She noticed a group of kids by the low rock wall on the Cunningham property across the street. Payton Cunningham straddled his bicycle in baggy shorts and an oversized T-shirt, and his sister was combing another girl's hair. Two boys were hitting each other in the arm. As Gail's car approached, the group shifted to let her pass. Then Gail saw Karen sitting on the wall, swinging her feet. She jumped down and came slowly across the street in her hip-hugging bell-bottoms and a top that showed her navel. Gail stared at her, then turned to park in the driveway.

She couldn't. The space was taken up with Lynn Dobbert's old Toyota and a faded green van that Gail recognized as belonging to the repairman, Charlie Jenkins. She parked beside a half-empty pallet of roof tiles. The roofers were supposed to have finished their repairs today, but apparently they'd had better things to do.

Briefcase in one hand, her purse over her shoulder, Gail waited for Karen, who was taking her time. Her hair hung loose, and her bangs were in her eyes. She was as tall as the other girls, but too young for this crowd.

Gail noticed her mouth. "Where did you get that lipstick?"

"It's Jennifer's."

"What are you doing out here, anyway? You're still grounded from Friday." The only response was a shrug of narrow shoulders. "Never mind. Go change your clothes. And hurry. We're already late."

"I'm going with Daddy," Karen said. "I called him to pick me up."

Gail laughed in disbelief. "Well, you can just un-call him." She started toward the house. "Come on."

Not budging, Karen crossed her arms. "I don't want to go with you."

"Excuse me?"

"You embarrassed me, Mom. You told Payton's mother that he called you on the phone and said something nasty."

Gail glanced at the kids, who were avidly watching this scene. Peggy Cunningham had twisted what Gail had told her. "We'll discuss it later. Come inside, please. Now." She took the two stone steps to the front porch and saw Lynn Dobbert standing just inside the screen door.

"Ms. Connor, I told Karen to put on something nice, just like you said, but she wouldn't." Lynn stood back to let them come in. "I didn't know she called her father."

Karen rolled her eyes and flipped her hair over her shoulder.

"Lynn, I am so sorry. I apologize for her behavior." Gail dropped her briefcase and purse on the sofa, then said to Karen, "Upstairs. Now."

"Daddy's coming!"

"We'll leave him a note."

Just then a bearded man came out of the kitchen, wearing jeans and paint-spattered work boots. Charlie Jenkins was heavy enough that his belly hung over a scuffed leather tool belt. "Well, your electrical problem is resolved."

Lynn unfolded some bills from the pocket of her slacks and handed them to Gail. "This is what I found—sixty-three dollars. He wants a hundred and twenty-five."

Astonished, Gail looked at him. "For what?"

He looked back as if his feelings were hurt. "It's what I always charge. Fifty minimum to show up, plus twenty-five every half hour. It took some time."

She held up her hands. "Okay. Is everything working?"

"Like new." Charlie Jenkins extended an arm toward the

kitchen, and she went to see. Lynn and Karen trailed behind. He opened the refrigerator. The light was on, and the motor was humming obediently. Then he flipped a switch, turning the light in the ceiling on and off. "All right?"

Gail nodded wearily. She noticed Karen getting the box of kitten chow out of a lower cabinet, holding Missy around the belly with her other hand. The cat could not possibly be hungry.

She said to Jenkins, "What was the problem?"

"A short in the wall. I had to replace the wire. You got those old cloth-covered wires. Looks like something bit it, probably a rat. You'll find out in a day or so. They rot pretty fast in this heat we're having."

"Oh, wonderful." Gail retrieved her purse, finding eighteen dollars and change. She put that and the rest of the cash on the kitchen table. "That's eighty-three. Come on, Charlie, let me write you a check this time."

He sucked in some air through his teeth. "Well, you know my policy, Ms. Connor. Cash only."

"I'll make the check out to cash," she offered.

"I really hate banks. Hate to walk into those places, standing in line."

"Why is this happening? I'm supposed to be visiting someone at Mercy Hospital right now."

Lynn said, "I have some money."

"Would you?"

Charlie Jenkins took out his receipt book. "Your lucky day." He bent over the table, belly hanging, and began to write.

The doorbell rang. Karen sprinted for the living room. A second later her high voice rang out. "Daddy's here. Bye, Mom."

"Wait just a minute! Lynn, get the receipt, okay? Karen!" Gail ran after her.

Dave stood in the doorway, dressed in his usual fashion of boat shorts and Island Club shirt and billed cap. Gail pulled him onto the porch and closed the door, leaving Karen inside.

"Dave, I'm sorry, but there's been some confusion. Karen shouldn't have called you. We made plans for dinner tonight."

"All I know is, she said you weren't here, she didn't know where you were, she was in the house with strangers, and please, Daddy, come get me."

"She knew very well where I was. I had an emergency with a client. And my receptionist is not a *stranger*."

"What are you telling me? You won't let her come with me? Or what?" Dave's nose was sunburned, as if he had been outdoors all weekend. Karen had returned with her legs toasty brown, then white below the level of her tennis socks.

Gail momentarily closed her eyes. "I can't deal with this right now. All right, fine. You take her." When she opened the door, Karen rushed past, leaping into his arms, putting on a show. "Daddy!"

He whirled her around, bell-bottom jeans and clogs flying. "Hey, princess." He kissed Karen's cheek, then turned her toward his pickup truck, parked along the street. "Go get in the truck, honey. Daddy wants to talk to your mom for a second."

With a last wary look at both of them, Karen walked through the grass, picking her way around the roof tiles. The kids were still out there. The boys had come closer to the truck, a shiny new white one with double rear wheels and a boat hitch. Payton Cunningham was doing circles on his bike, skidding on the gravel.

Dave said, "I called Dr. Fischman and set up an appointment for Karen. One o'clock Thursday. I can pick her up from day camp."

The suddenness of this surprised her. Gail said, "You were going to call me. I can't make it Thursday. We were supposed to do this by mutual agreement."

"There was a cancellation, and if I didn't take it, we couldn't get in for two weeks."

"Karen shouldn't be dragged out of summer camp—"

"I'm not dragging her anywhere—"

"—to a psychologist, to be interrogated on a choice she is incapable of making—"

"Interrogated? I talked to Fischman myself on the phone. He's a great guy, very concerned about kids." Dave's face was turning red, making his eyebrows appear even blonder. "I love Karen. If I thought this would be traumatic for her, I wouldn't go near his office."

"Just don't make her feel it's her *fault* that she has to be there."

"None of this is her fault," Dave said.

"I know that. It's ours."

"Fischman wants to see us too." He laughed softly. "I don't know what to tell the man. Lay my guts out for him or what. Jesus. If he asks me why, I don't know what to tell him."

"Tell him you want an all-American lifestyle for your daughter," Gail said.

Dave's thin mouth drew in, and he shifted his weight to the other hip. His thumbs were hooked over his belt. "I'm taking her Thursday. You make your own arrangements."

Gail felt a rush of heat up her throat. "She's almost eleven. She's about to go through puberty, and she needs a mother. What you've done is unforgivable. She isn't going to live with you, Dave. I won't allow it."

The blue eyes grew frosty. "You won't allow it. What Gail Connor wants, well, that's the way it's going to be. Guess what. Karen wants to live with dear old dad. If she wasn't afraid you'd blow up, she'd tell you."

"That is such a lie."

"Yeah? Let's see what Fischman has to say about it." With a phony smile Dave stepped off the porch. "I'll bring her back tonight by nine-thirty. Try to be downstairs instead of in bed with *el macho*, like last time."

"Oh, really. Up yours, Dave."

"Nice language. You talk like that around Karen?"

He turned around and crossed the yard, got into his truck. The engine started with a deep growl. Karen waved from the passenger side. Gail waved back, smiling. She wanted to fall into one of the wooden chairs on the porch and cry.

Mercy Hospital had been constructed in a Mediterranean style, with a long portico along the front and a red tile roof. A modern parking garage had been added to one side. This time of day it was jammed with cars, and it took Gail awhile to find a space. The sun was lower but still shining brightly. She walked quickly to the main building under a covered walkway, caught her breath riding the elevator to the fourth floor, then took a right and a left to the end of the hall.

She glanced at her watch: 7:32. Bad, but not terrible.

As she had expected, the corridors were full of people, although the rules said only two visitors per patient. Most of the patients were Cuban, which meant that entire families would show up, bringing food and making trips to the cafeteria for espresso to stay awake, because they also paid no attention to the rule about leaving by eight o'clock.

Ernesto Pedrosa had a private corner room. Gail saw Anthony's cousin Betty in the hall, and they exchanged a kiss on the cheek. Betty said Anthony was inside. Gail peered around an older woman standing in the way. A City of Miami police officer in a dark blue uniform was posted by the door, which Gail found odd. He glanced at Gail without interest as she went through.

She saw the end of the bed, but Pedrosa was blocked from view by Aunt Graciela, fixing the pillow. Digna Pedrosa sat with other relatives on the sofa. Across the room a group of men were conversing in low tones. Most stood; a few were sitting. She saw a neatly creased trouser leg, a dark sock, and an expensive laced shoe of Italian design. She recognized the shoe. One of the men moved, revealing Anthony in profile—the long nose and full lips, the brown hair that waved back from his forehead. The collar of his shirt was open, his tie loosened. One elbow rested on the arm of the chair, and he gestured slowly as he spoke. The light caught the emerald on his last finger.

He looked up when another man in a dark business suit came over to see him. Then the quick smile that showed his lovely teeth. The handshake. But he didn't bother to stand, even for the mayor of Miami. The men spoke in rapid, colloquial Spanish. Gail understood now the presence of the police officer. The mayor, a fellow Cuban, had come to say good luck to Ernesto Pedrosa and, as long as he was here, to pay his respects to the heir to the throne.

Gail suddenly felt queasy. The aspirin, she thought. Bad to take it on an empty stomach.

A pair of dark-framed glasses that she hadn't noticed before suddenly gleamed with reflected light, and Hector Mesa leaned over to whisper to Anthony.

It took only a second for Anthony to locate Gail by the door. No smile. No indication that he wanted her to join them. He looked at her for only an instant—not even long enough for anyone to notice that his attention had been momentarily drawn away—before he resumed his conversation with the mayor.

The shock of this dismissal stunned her, and she was suddenly aware that she had not moved for several seconds, and that the other people in the room were behaving quite normally.

Hector Mesa seemed to be watching her, though it was impossible to tell. Gail abruptly turned her back on him and maneuvered through the visitors to Pedrosa's bedside.

Sitting nearly upright, the old man saw her and lifted one pale, spotted hand. She took it and bent to kiss his cheek. He had been shaved, and his lined face was smooth and soft. His pajamas had a design of fleur-de-lis and blue piping—not hospital-issue.

"*Señor, ¿cómo está?* I'm so sorry to be late. A client of mine called, and I thought she might kill herself, she was so upset. Her husband had just left after beating her up, and I had to make sure she was all right. She has three children." As Gail babbled on, she realized that it wasn't really Pedrosa she was explaining this to.

"You were on a mission of mercy." Pedrosa spoke as if it was an effort to do so, and Gail noticed how carefully he formed the words. *"No te preocupes por—* Don't worry about being late."* He swallowed and took a breath. "I will be here tomorrow."

"Is that a promise?"

"Oh, yes."

"Don't you need some rest? There are so many people here."

Digna Pedrosa, who had rejoined her husband, smiled at Gail across his bed. "The nurses will come and chase them all out very soon."

A slender hand went around Gail's elbow, and Elena Godoy lightly pressed their cheeks together. "There you are, Gail. We were starting to worry about you. How does he look? Very strong, no?"

"A tiger," Gail said.

"Did you get my message today about Lola Benitez?"

"Yes. I didn't have a chance to call you back. Saturday morning would be fine, if you still want to go." Gail managed a smile, although she was in no mood to think of wedding dresses.

"Nena wants to come too. Is that all right?" Without waiting for an answer, Elena asked her grandmother, "Nena, *usted quiere ir con nosotras el sábado, ¿verdad?*"

"*Sí, sí,* I would love to go with you. Gail, why don't you ask Irene to come too? I like her so much, but we don't see each other."

"Yes, she said she wanted to come," Gail replied.

She felt the light pressure of an arm against hers an instant before Elena said, "Anthony, we're going with Gail to look at wedding dresses on Saturday. But you can't come, of course. It would be bad luck to see the dress before the wedding."

He made a slight shrug. "Then I'll have to wait."

Pedrosa's grin was sly. "Women always make us wait. *Para*

ponernos deseosos en la noche de boda." To make us eager on the wedding night.

"*¡Abuelo!*" Elena lightly slapped his wrist.

Anthony was looking at Gail. "Where is Karen?"

"With her father."

"Ah." He nodded toward the door. "Come with me for a moment?"

"Oh, dear." Gail said to the faces around the bed, "Will you excuse us? I think Anthony wants to scream at me. And I'm trying so hard to be *cubana."*

She heard him exhale through his teeth.

The others exchanged glances. Digna raised her silvery eyebrows and made a slight nod. Gail turned around and walked through the door, not waiting to see if Anthony was behind her.

He was. In the corridor he took hold of her arm and pulled her close so no one could hear them. "Why did you say that to my grandparents? It was inconsiderate. It was embarrassing— for everyone."

"Was it? As rude as the way you treated me when I came in?" She took a ragged breath to ease the tension. "I should probably leave."

"Not yet." He led her down the hall, smiling at a couple of people but not stopping. It went through Gail's mind to jerk her arm away and leave him staring at her back as she stalked toward the elevator. Around the corner was a vacant room with two neatly made beds, both empty. They went inside, leaving the door open.

She threw her purse onto a chair and pushed her hair back with both hands. "What do you want me to do? Apologize to them? I will if you—"

"Harry Lasko called me." Anthony let that sink in, then added, "Would you like to know what he said?"

Gail dropped her hands by her side. "So that's why you're so mad. I was going to tell you."

"Were you?"

"Of course I was! Did you expect me to bring it up in there? Why are you making such a big deal out of it?"

"Big deal?" Anthony's voice was still soft, but the words were clipped, and his Spanish accent became more evident. "I told you I am in the middle of plea negotiations with the U.S. attorney's office. I told you not to contact Harry Lasko."

"I didn't! You weren't there, Anthony. Don't tell me what happened."

"Why didn't you call me? You have a telephone."

She laughed. "Call you? He just started talking! I didn't ask him to!"

Anthony tensed his mouth, and shadows undercut his cheekbones. "You didn't arrange a meeting at Jamie Sweet's house for the purpose of speaking to Harry?"

"If he told you that, it's a lie. No, Jamie called both of us this afternoon, and we independently came to see if she was all right. Wendell had just attacked her."

"Did you know Harry would be there?"

"Stop it, Anthony." Her voice rose. "Stop it. I hate it when you get like this."

He looked past her, and she sensed a presence at the door, knowing who it was before she turned around.

Hector Mesa made his customary little bow. *"Señora."* Then to Anthony, *"El señor Gutierrez está aquí."*

"Momento," Anthony replied.

Mesa vanished.

Gail was shaking with rage.

Anthony said, "I can't go to dinner with you tonight. My grandfather's lawyer—Jose Gutierrez—is here to draw up a power of attorney in case Ernesto is . . . temporarily incapacitated by the operation. The doctors don't expect that, but we want to cover all eventualities."

Gail took a slow breath. "And you will be the one appointed to take over. In case."

"Yes."

"You aren't going to ask me what I think?"

He frowned. "What do you mean?"

"I'm sure it doesn't matter, but I'll tell you anyway." Gail held onto the railing of one of the beds. "I think you should tell Mr. Mesa—because as chief court conspirator, he's no doubt behind this—that Bernardo can do it, or Elena, or one of the others."

"Ernesto asked for *me* to handle it. How can I refuse, when he's facing an operation in the morning?"

She could only laugh. "My God. You want this so badly, don't you? You told me you didn't, but I saw you with the mayor. You were eating it up."

"Gail, what is the matter with you?"

"You don't even see it. You're becoming something you said you'd never be—a puppet of Ernesto Pedrosa."

They stared at each other, Anthony's gaze going through her like a shard of ice. He said softly, "Why don't you go home? We can discuss this later."

"Later. Sure. When would that be? Tonight? Tomorrow?"

"Expect me around nine o'clock."

"Fine." Gail picked up her purse and walked out.

Mesa was standing outside the door, waiting for Anthony. His hands were loosely clasped, and he inclined his head. *"Señora."*

Through her teeth she said, "Go to hell."

He was still smiling under his neat gray mustache.

On the way down in the elevator she was barely in control. The tears started to come when the automatic doors in the lobby hissed open. She wiped her cheeks and walked faster, retracing her steps under the covered walkway, then to the parking garage. The last rays of the sun had faded to gray. She pounded up three flights of concrete stairs, footsteps echoing in the stairwell.

The heat and humidity bore down. Sweating freely, she hurried past car after car, looking for her light blue Mercedes. On the point of screaming with frustration, she went up another flight of stairs. Nothing there. Cars passed her, tires squealing on the turns. Her nose filled with the stench of exhaust. She took the stairs back down a level, certain she had not driven as far as the fourth.

On the third level again she pivoted slowly, looking down the row of cars, one end to the other. Just as she became convinced that her car had been stolen, she saw it.

She could see now why she had walked past it before. The color was wrong.

Red. There were stripes of red on the trunk that dripped slowly onto the slick concrete floor of the parking garage. She walked closer, staring. Almost without knowing it, she reached out and touched the liquid, then studied the smear on her forefinger.

Stunned, she walked along the driver's side between her car and the one next to it. More red flowed over the hood and dripped down the sides and into the air vents. Not my car, she said to herself. Someone else's. No one would do this to my car. Then she recognized the bamboo handle of an umbrella on the floor inside. "Oh, no. Oh, my God."

She could see a word scrawled at an angle across the windshield.

DIE.

Written in vivid scarlet, the color and consistency of blood.

NINE

"The police won't come out for a vandalism complaint." The security guard shook his head. "They say to send people to the station to make a report."

He sat in his golf cart with one black sneaker propped on the dashboard, waiting to see what would happen. Several yards away, Anthony paced back and forth, shouting in Spanish into his portable telephone. Gail waited in the car, trying to be inconspicuous.

The garage was clearing out, cars slowly circling down the levels. Faces at the windows turned to look at the Mercedes C280 covered with paint, and at the woman in the yellow dress stained with red.

People had stared at Gail when she'd gone back inside the hospital. They had seen her wild hair, the mascara under her eyes, and the smears of red on her hands. Someone asked if she had been injured. Shaking her head, she had hurried into the elevator, wanting only to find Anthony. Their argument didn't matter anymore, or the cold manner of their parting. One of Pedrosa's nurses brought Anthony out. When he saw her, his eyes widened. He rushed to her, touching her face and arms as if she might break. He had gone back inside his grandfather's room for a moment and how he had explained his abrupt departure Gail did not know. Or care. Anthony had taken charge. When security said they were extremely sorry, but there was nothing they could do, he demanded that the Miami police send a detective to the scene.

"We don't get much vandalism," the guard said. "We had some cars keyed or antennas snapped off, stuff like that. It usually happens to nice cars. That's true. I drive a Camaro, but it needs body work. I never have no problems." The security guard was somewhere in his thirties, with a tan uniform and a matching billed cap. His only weapons were a flashlight and a two-way radio.

Anthony folded his telephone. "They're on their way."

The guard sat up straight. "Who, the Miami PD? No lie? You must know somebody down there."

Ignoring the guard, Anthony told Gail he had parked on the second level and wanted to bring his car up. She went with him. He carried his jacket and put his arm around her waist. A humid breeze drifted through the garage, bringing the smell of decaying seaweed. He located his car and opened the passenger door for her, then went around. When the engine started, cool air came through the vents, and Gail felt her body sinking into the soft leather of the seat.

His hand touched her cheek. "Are you all right, sweetheart?"

"I thought you might not come."

"What? No. Oh, no." He reached for her across the console, and his arms went around her tightly. He was solid and warm, and the scent of his cologne was still in his clothes. "Gail, please forgive me for what I said to you earlier. I had no right to be angry."

She held on. "Who is doing this to me, Anthony?"

He lifted her face. His eyes seemed black in the dim interior of the car. "I swear to you, I will find him. Gail, you should have told me about the telephone calls. It wouldn't have been a bother—that's a crazy reason not to tell me."

"I thought it was just a kid. Payton Cunningham. That's what I thought at first."

"We'll change the phone number. I'll hire a private investi-

gator." Anthony kissed her softly. "Don't worry anymore."
Weak with relief, she began to cry. "No. *Deja de llorar, cielito.*"
He reached for his handkerchief, leaving his arm around her
while she wiped her eyes. After she had assured him at least
three times that she was fine, Anthony put the car into gear and
backed it out of the parking space.

On the third level a Miami Police patrol car was coming
along the ramp from the other direction. Anthony quickly
parked and walked toward it. The window slid down, revealing
a female officer with her coppery hair in a clip.

"Is there a Quintana here?"

"I'm Anthony Quintana."

The car pulled in diagonally, and both doors opened. The
driver was a short woman whose gun belt rode high on her
hips. Her partner had massive arms that strained the sleeves of
his dark blue shirt.

Brakes squealed, and a blue sedan with tinted windows rolled
to a stop behind the patrol car. Two men in sports shirts and
ties got out, badges clipped to their gun belts.

The security guard laughed softly. "Man, this is unbelievable."

The older man had fading blond hair and a fleshy neck. Deep
creases ran from a blunt nose to the drooping corners of his
mouth. His eyes swept over the car without particular interest.
He was not, Gail thought, happy to be here. "I'm Sergeant
Dennis Ladue. This is Detective Novick."

There were introductions but no handshakes.

Ladue walked around the car. "Looks like somebody repainted the girlfriend's Mercedes."

Anthony said, "This isn't a random act of vandalism, Sergeant. We believe it's related to telephone calls that Ms. Connor
received at home last week. The calls were anonymous, threatening her life."

The detective tilted his head, reading the word on the windshield. " 'Die.' That's nice." He gestured toward the paint can
near the left front wheel. "Is this the culprit?"

"We found it near the car," Gail said. Her shoe had sent

something rolling into the wall—an empty quart-size can of high-gloss enamel. Holding it by the rim, Anthony had set it upright, instructing her not to touch it. The lid lay beside it.

He said, "That can should be dusted for fingerprints. I'd like some photos taken of the car as well. Unfortunately, they don't have a video camera to record cars going in and out, but someone might have seen a person loitering near the garage."

One side of Ladue's mouth lifted, exposing the yellowed teeth of a heavy smoker. "Look. I got pulled off a homicide investigation to come over here, so I'm guessing that certain weight has been thrown around. But don't tell me how to do my job."

"Then do it."

"I don't care who you are, buddy, watch your attitude."

"You want to see an attitude?"

Gail dug her fingers into Anthony's arm.

The younger detective said, "Dennis?" He was unwrapping a stick of gum, rolling it into a tight spiral. "There's a camera in the trunk."

"Jesus. Okay, go ahead." Ladue said to Gail, "Tell me about the phone calls." Feet spread, he crossed his arms over his belly and leaned back.

"They came on Thursday and Friday nights from a pay phone—I have caller-ID. The same thing showed up on the screen Saturday too, but I didn't pick up."

"Same number?"

"No, it varied. And the voice was disguised. It sounded metallic, like a robot."

"Leading us to think that it's someone she knows," Anthony said.

"Yes. He called me by name and kept saying . . . 'die, bitch,' things like that."

Detective Novick, who had returned with a camera and flash, murmured for everyone to move aside. Chewing his gum between his front teeth, he went slowly around the car, crouching or standing at different angles. The flashes of light illuminated the red paint and made it look sticky and wet.

"Did you record the calls?" Ladue said.

"No, but I kept the numbers in memory—except the first time. I erased that one."

"Pay phones. That could be anyone."

Anthony said, "But if we could find out *which* pay phones, we would know where this person was when he placed the calls."

"How long were you away from the car?"

"Around . . . fifteen minutes."

Anthony nodded to Sergeant Ladue. "No more than twenty."

"Ms. Connor, you have any idea who would do this? Got any enemies? Anybody threatening you?"

"She and her ex-husband are in a custody fight," Anthony said.

Ladue made his half smile again. "Mr. Quintana, how about letting her answer the questions? What about it, Ms. Connor? Is the ex a possibility?"

"No, he's with our daughter. I don't know who could have done it. I have no clue." She turned her right hand over, which she had scraped more or less clean in a rest room in the hospital after telling Anthony what had happened. "I tried to wipe that word off my windshield." She laughed. "Enamel paint, half-dried already. When I saw it, I just . . . flipped. All I could think was, my daughter can't see this." Anthony's arm went around her.

"Ms. Connor, I realize this is distressing for you, but really there's not much we can do. We'll make a report, that's about it."

"Thank you for coming."

Ladue nodded, then turned to look for his partner. The other detective had picked up the empty paint can with a paper towel. "Mike, I've got to get back. Why don't you finish up here and catch a ride to HQ with the officers?"

"Sure." He dropped the can into a plastic bag. The two uniformed officers waited by their patrol car.

Ladue took a card out of his shirt pocket and gave it to Gail. "If anything else occurs, feel free to call." He got into his unmarked car, made a tight, squealing U-turn, and was gone.

While Anthony made arrangements to have the car towed, Gail took her own telephone out of her bag and dialed Dave's

apartment. His voice mail picked up. "Dammit." She disconnected. It was ten after nine. Dave had said he'd have Karen
home by nine-thirty.

Detective Novick was writing numbers on the evidence bags.
Gail said, "Excuse me. I wonder if we could finish this tomorrow.
My daughter will be home soon and no one is there."

"Where do you live, Ms. Connor?"

"Clematis Street in the Grove."

"That's not far. We can do the report at your house, and I can
get the phone numbers off caller-ID."

Gail hesitated.

"Is there a problem?"

"No. It's just—My ex-husband and I are having this . . . custody thing, and if the police are there, he'll wonder what happened, and I wouldn't want him to think that somebody is
threatening my life, if that's what it is. He might say that our
daughter was in danger. You understand."

Behind the glasses, his green-flecked brown eyes had not
wavered. "Okay. Tomorrow's fine."

Anthony was arguing with someone over the telephone
about towing the car out of here immediately. Gail shook her
head. "Never mind. There's no way he's going to let me put it
off till tomorrow."

From halfway up the block Gail could see it: a white pickup
truck parked along the street, leaving just enough room for
Anthony's Eldorado to swerve around it and park in the driveway. No one was in the truck. Lights shone through the windows in the living room and Karen's bedroom upstairs.

Anthony said, "What is he doing here?"

"They obviously got here early, and Karen let him in."

"He should wait outside."

"Anthony, for God's sake. Don't make a scene. Don't even
open your mouth."

The patrol car parked behind them. Doors slammed. A two-
way radio made its low, inarticulate chatter, and streetlights

shone on badges and patent leather gun belts. A neighbor out walking his dog stopped to see what was going on. Karen was at the front door before Gail got there. Her eyes grew round. "Mom! Why are the police here?"

"Hi, honey. It's all right, go back in."

"We'll wait out here," Novick said.

Dave appeared behind Karen, his hands on her shoulders. For a second he and Anthony looked at each other through the screen; then Dave stepped back when Anthony opened it.

Gail went in first, and Anthony remained where he was, holding the door open. Dave said, "Gail, no one was here, and I didn't want to leave Karen by herself—" His gaze fell to her dress. "Jesus. What's that?"

"My car was vandalized. Some idiot threw paint on it. The police are outside, and I need to make a report." She crossed the room to put her purse on the small table at the foot of the stairs.

Karen followed. "Who did it?"

"I don't know, sweetie."

"That's *awful*."

"Crazy people in this world." Gail hugged Karen around the neck and kissed her. Karen's hair was silky and warm. "I'm glad to see you."

Anthony was still by the door. "Thank you for bringing Karen home." His tone was polite—for Karen's benefit, Gail thought.

Dave looked at him. "You're welcome." He turned his back and said quietly to Gail, "What is this? You've got three cops outside. For a vandalism complaint?"

"Yes. Why is that strange? You'll have to excuse us, Dave. I need to talk to them." She inclined her head toward the door.

Dave was still trying to figure out what was going on. His eyes lingered on Gail as he pulled Karen close with an arm around her waist—a playful hold that had Karen laughing, her feet off the floor, long hair dangling. "Hey, princess, why don't you come home with Daddy tonight? Looks like Mom is busy, and you have to get up real early."

Gail pulled back the hand that automatically reached for her daughter. She would not start a tug-of-war. "Dave, this won't take long. Karen's already here."

"And I don't like what she's seeing."

"Daddy!" Karen squirmed till he let her down. She flipped her hair out of her face. "I want to stay here and help Mom."

"Looks like she has plenty of help."

"I want to stay *here*." Her square jaw was set, and her high voice was emphatic. Gail had to hold herself back from smothering Karen in a tight embrace.

"Okay. I'll see you on Thursday. Don't forget. Lunch with Dad." Dave kissed Karen, then said quietly to Gail, "Dr. Fischman. One o'clock."

As Dave left, the brief look between him and Anthony could have frozen molten steel. Anthony watched through the screen until the sound of a truck engine came across the yard.

The police came in. Karen stared at them. Detective Novick smiled at her. "Hi. I'm Michael Novick. These are officers Hernadez and Robinson. We're going to try to find out who damaged your mom's car."

Gail put an arm around her. "You know, sweetie, I missed dinner, and I'm so hungry I could faint. Could you bring me some juice?" Clearly seeing that she was being made to leave, Karen gave a theatrical sigh. She nevertheless went off to the kitchen without complaint, hair swinging on her back.

The female officer was carrying a clipboard. "I guess I can get your full names and addresses. Do you live here as well, Mr. Quintana?"

"Yes."

Gail was surprised by this but did not contradict him.

Novick said, "Mr. Quintana, if you'd give the officers the pertinent information, I'll get the phone numbers from Ms. Connor." The detective's manner was courteous and businesslike. Gail did not think he was faking it to please Anthony Quintana.

The caller-ID was in the master bedroom, Gail explained, leading the way. She flipped a switch, lighting the old brass sconces in the upper hall. "I'm sorry if you feel that Anthony twisted your arm. He's very worried."

"Well, I'd do the same," Novick said. "I heard his grandfather is Ernesto Pedrosa. I didn't know Pedrosa was in the hospital. What for?"

"He's getting a pacemaker in the morning." Gail had left a light on in the bedroom. The bed was unmade, file boxes and papers took up space on the dresser, and the shoes she had worn earlier were kicked off at the open door to the closet. "Sorry for the mess."

"No problem." He gave her a quick, boyish smile—the complicity of those who do not care about untidy bedrooms. He had brown hair so short he might have trimmed it himself with electric clippers in front of his bathroom mirror.

Gail bent over the nightstand. Her caller-ID was separate from the telephone, and she pushed the button to go back through the incoming calls. She looked more closely. "That's odd."

Novick tilted his head to see the screen. "It says 'no calls.' "

"Why isn't it—" Gail noticed that her clock radio was off by several hours. "Of course. The electrician. I had someone working on the kitchen wiring today. He must have cut the power."

"Those things are supposed to have battery backups," Novick said.

"Are they?" Gail turned it over. "Oh, I see. Well, no batteries, no memory. The first three digits were 4-4-3 on at least two of the calls."

"That's this area—Coconut Grove and Coral Gables."

"I should have written them down."

He was silent for a moment, then said, "You mentioned a 'custody thing' with your former husband. Have you had any trouble with him?"

"Not like that. I explained to Sergeant Ladue while you were taking pictures—Dave was with Karen tonight. Besides, he wouldn't do something so juvenile. If he wanted to get back at me, he would do just what he's doing—try to take my daughter."

"His also."

"Yes. His also."

"Get back at you for what? Leaving him?"

Gail shook her head. "The divorce was his idea."

"Because of Quintana?"

"Is that relevant?"

"If I knew in advance what was relevant or not," he said, "I wouldn't ask."

She could see neither idle curiosity nor judgment in the detective's face. His glasses made him look more like a teacher than a cop. "Dave left me before I was involved with Anthony. Then he changed his mind and wanted to come back. I refused."

"And by then you were involved."

"Yes. But Dave never threatened me. I mean, he'd be the last person to throw paint on my car."

Novick seemed to be studying his shoes—brown leather with heavy soles. He scuffed one along the carpet, which needed vacuuming. "What I've learned about people is that they don't always act in ways you can predict. It's good to keep an open mind. Is there anyone you can think of who might have less than friendly feelings toward you?"

She smiled at the euphemism. "I have a divorce case where my client's husband probably hates my guts. He's a violent man, but he had no way of knowing where I'd be tonight. I can't think of anyone. That's what makes this so infuriating. It comes out of nowhere."

"No, there's always a cause." Lifting an arm toward the hall, Novick let her precede him. "You should make a list of people who have shown any hostility, for whatever far-fetched reason. You're a lawyer, right?"

Following him down the stairs, she allowed a small laugh. "You mean I should list all my opponents? And my clients too?"

He smiled over his shoulder. "Only those you might have had a dispute with. I noticed that you're doing some work on the house. Maybe you've had disagreements with the contractor or one of the workers."

"All the time."

Pausing on the landing, he said, "It could be anyone. Neighbors, family, ex-lovers, business associates. A person from your past. If something suddenly reminds them of you, it could set them off. People get obsessed, and there's not much you can do, except find out who they are and what they want."

"I've been hanging up. Should I talk to him if he calls again?"

"I would. Don't show any emotion. Try to find out why he— or it could be a she—is doing this. That would help to know. Motive is everything."

When they reached the bottom, Anthony saw them and stood up. He told Karen to wait there, then crossed the room. "Did you get the numbers?"

Gail shook her head. "The electrician cut the power today, and the numbers were erased."

"What electrician?"

She let out a weary breath. "Later."

Novick spoke too softly for Karen to hear. "Mr. Quintana, I was about to tell Ms. Connor that since there has been no physical violence, she shouldn't become too agitated at this point. Usually the people who want to hurt you don't advertise it first—if that's of some comfort."

"It is," Gail said. "Thank you." She took the card he gave her. Michael C. Novick, Homicide Bureau.

"Let me know what happens. And get some batteries for that caller-ID."

Gail lay on her side, encircled by Anthony's arms, her spine curled into his belly. He wore nothing at all, and she could feel his skin radiating heat through her thin cotton nightgown. She knew by his breathing that he was awake. She had told him she didn't feel like making love tonight. That had surprised him— annoyed him—but he quickly let it go.

She watched the sky through the blinds, horizontal slices of dark blue.

Earlier she had fallen asleep in Karen's room while Anthony took a shower. In her nightgown and robe, she had sat on the bed to read Karen a story, but instead they watched the kitten go after Karen's toes, wiggling under the blanket. The kitten stared with its big green eyes, adjusted its rear legs, switched its tail, and pounced. Gail told Karen about the car. Probably some kids having fun. Nothing to worry about. Gail did not tell her about the word written in red across the windshield. Karen pulled the kitten onto her chest, scratching under its chin, where white fur made a bib. The kitten closed its eyes and purred. Gail said she wanted to explain about the phone calls. She had never actually accused Payton Cunningham of making them, and his mother was wrong to have said so. Karen asked who had called. Gail shrugged. Oh, who knows? But don't answer the phone till we change the number.

Gail pressed Karen's hand to her cheek. Her short nails were painted with pink glitter polish. There was a woven bracelet on her wrist, a scrape on one knuckle. Love you, sweetie. Karen wanted Gail to stay with her. Read me a story. Gail opened the book, and Karen cuddled closer. After a while Gail found it difficult for her lips to form the words. She heard Karen's steady breathing. Gail's eyes closed.

And then Anthony was whispering for her to wake up and come to bed.

He shifted his arm out from under her neck and rotated his fist, getting the numbness out, then propped himself on his elbow. He nudged aside a strand of hair and kissed the back of her neck. "Gail. You're not asleep."

"I was."

He slid his hand under the neckline of her gown, finding her breast, gently caressing. The nipple began to harden. He knew how to touch her.

She took his hand out and held it at her waist.

"*Bonboncita,* don't do this to me." He put his chin on her shoulder. "What's wrong? *¿Qué te pasa?* It's not about your car. You were all right earlier."

A long breath escaped her. "I keep going back to your grandfather's room at the hospital. Anthony, when I saw you with those men—Hector, the mayor, God knows who else—and you looked at me that way, so cold, and I said to myself, Oh, God, I don't even know this man."

"Gail, I said I was sorry."

"You're sorry? Well, it frightened me. I thought, What if this is who he really is?"

"What are you talking about?" Laughing softly, Anthony tugged on her shoulder till she lay flat. His face over hers was indistinct in the semidarkness of the bedroom. The ceiling fan revolved slowly. "Sweetheart, you know me. Don't say things like that."

"You asked me what was wrong."

"*Ay, Diós.*"

"Anthony, I didn't go to Jamie Sweet's house with the intention of talking to Harry Lasko."

"I believe you."

She sat up, swiveling to face him. "Now you do. Then you believed I had been deliberately, secretly talking to one of your clients after you told me not to. You didn't ask first, you just assumed." Gail's words came faster, and Anthony shoved his pillow against the headboard and leaned on it.

"And so what if I did talk to him?" she said. "My client is important too. If Jamie doesn't get some help soon, she might go back to Wendell. He hit her, and it's happened before, but she wouldn't let me call the police. She said she didn't want her children to think badly of their father. My God! She's barely holding on. Harry knew this, and he wanted to help. How can you not understand?"

"All right, Gail." Against this outburst Anthony could only lift his hands as if warding her off. "I understand." When she was silent, he said, "What did Harry tell you?"

"That Wendell Sweet has a million dollars, probably more, somewhere in the Caribbean. Wendell got it from a deal he and Harry put together."

"What deal?"

"He wasn't clear. A casino on Eagle Beach in Aruba. Harry knows more about Wendell, and I need to ask him."

Anthony raised one knee. The sheet barely covered his groin. Dark hair swept across his lean belly and the clearly defined muscles in his chest. Strips of light from the window curved over his body, but his face was in shadow. From overhead came the soft tick of the chain on the ceiling fan.

"Well?"

"I'm not sure I should allow it. In his desire to be helpful, Harry might say things he shouldn't. He could give you information that might be wrongfully used to incriminate him."

Gail let out a breath. "Fine. Then you tell me. Just give me something to go on. What about Wendell and Eagle Beach? I'm not going to the government with it. Don't you trust me?"

"Yes, I do. But Harry is my client, and . . . And I . . ." He sighed. "I am not accustomed to talking about my clients. All right. I'll ask Harry what's going on. He doesn't tell me everything. I never heard of this deal."

"Ask him about Wendell."

"I will."

"When?"

"I'll call him this week."

"Before Friday," she said. "I'm getting Wendell's documents Friday, and I need some clue what to look for."

"All right! *Que pena.* You are too much. Now, that's enough of this." He leaned forward and grabbed her hand and kissed it before she could pull it back. He had shaved, and his mouth was soft on her knuckles. He spread her fingers out on his upraised knee and shifted his thigh to place the engagement ring in a shaft of light that made the blue-white stone twinkle. "I think, *mi vida,* that I need to move in here right away, not wait till we're married. Being apart has created too many misunderstandings between us."

"You told Detective Novick that you live here already."

"This is my house," Anthony replied softly.

"Ours."

"Of course. Ours. You don't think that's a good idea?"

She shook her head. "Karen isn't ready."

"Gail, in less than two months I will be sleeping in this bed every night. She needs to get used to it. You treat her like a baby. You spoil her. I think you're afraid to make a mistake and then she'll want to live with her father."

"Not now, Anthony. Not with this custody case going on—"

He made a short laugh of dismissal. "I am tired of letting that case dictate what we do, when we do it—"

"*That case* is about my daughter!" Gail took her hand off his knee. "On Thursday Dave is taking Karen to see the psychologist. You and I will have to talk to him too, soon enough. Oh, sure, if Dr. Fischman goes against me, I can hire a rebuttal witness. A dozen of them. No problem. But it scares me, Anthony. The judge appointed this man, so he'll give greater weight to what he says. The judge knows that expert witnesses can be bought, and he knows you have money. What is Fischman going to see? A woman who spends sixty hours a week working on her law practice. And Daddy? He's teaching Karen how to play tennis. They go sailing. He reads her stories. Mom just doesn't have time. Mom loses her temper, but Daddy's always smiling."

"Ahhh." Anthony slid forward, and the sheets rustled. He leaned on one arm. "Is this why you're in such a mood?" He brushed her hair out of her eyes.

"This isn't a *mood*!" Gail found herself shaking, not from the cool air coming from the fan. "Maybe he's right. Maybe he's a better parent. He's there for her, and I'm not."

"That's bullshit. What does Charlene say?"

"She says there are no guarantees."

"What does that mean?"

"It means Dave could win."

"You didn't tell me this! Why?"

Gail smoothed the folds of her nightgown, which lay rumpled across her lap. "Maybe I was in denial. No. The fact is, sweetheart, you get crazy when I mention his name."

"Is that so? Well, perhaps—my love—that is because I see more clearly than you do." Anthony was angry but keeping his voice perfectly calm. "I wasn't going to mention this tonight, but I will. You told Detective Ladue that it wasn't possible that Dave vandalized your car, because he was with Karen. No, Gail. He wasn't."

Startled, Gail whispered, "How do you know?"

"She told me. While you were getting ready for bed, I talked to her. Well, Karen, what did you do tonight?" His voice lightened when he spoke Karen's words. "Oh, I watched *Titanic* on video. Did your dad watch it with you? No, he had to go to a meeting." Anthony waited for a reaction from Gail, who only stared back at him. "Don't worry, I was subtle. She won't feel that she has talked about her father behind his back."

"I can't believe he would do it."

"Where was he, then?"

"He had a meeting. She said—"

"Such a good father, leaving a young girl alone after dark."

"Dave never does that. She must have been with a sitter. Did you ask?"

"Why do you keep defending him?"

"Because I *know* him."

"You know him and not me."

"Anthony, please! This is why I didn't talk to you." She grabbed her pillow and swung her legs off the bed, but before she could stand up, Anthony's warm arms were around her from behind. He rose to his knees, leaning over her.

"Don't go." He kissed her cheek.

She turned her face away. "If you think, for one second, that I am still in love with Dave after what he has done . . . Leaving me. Deserting Karen for six months. Then trying to take her away because he's jealous of *you*. If you think"—her voice broke—"that I could want him after that—"

"No one will take her away from you."

Gail laughed and pulled in a shaky breath. "I saw her wearing *lipstick*, Anthony. Payton Cunningham was kissing her in the backyard the other night. And one of these days she's going to start her period. Dave doesn't know what that means, not really. She's his little princess, ten years old forever."

"Gail. Gail, it won't happen."

"She needs me. And . . . what would I do without her? What would I *be*?"

Anthony pulled her around. He made her look at him, and his black eyes seemed to pour into her. "Are you listening to me? Tell that psychologist to kiss my ass. If he throws mud at you, I will bury him in it. That is a promise." He embraced her, speaking softly into her ear. "No one—*no one*—is going to take Karen away from you. Not Dave. Not anyone."

A weakness settled in her chest, and she couldn't catch her breath.

"Do you believe me?"

She nodded.

"Then stop worrying about it."

He kissed her, tenderly at first, taking his time. Lips, cheeks, the point of her nose and chin, each eyebrow and the hollow under her jaw. Then her nightgown was going over her head. He held her bare upper arms and seemed to study the way the ribbons of light played on her body. "How beautiful you are."

She shivered and crossed her arms over her chest, shaking her head. "I won't be much good tonight."

He pulled her arms aside and kissed her breasts, one, then the other, drawing the tips into his mouth. His hand caressed her between her legs.

Gail didn't want this, but it was too late. It had been too late when she opened her mouth to tell him what was wrong, because he knew how to fix it. He always knew. She had wanted to remain wrapped in her comfortable blanket of fear and confusion, working out what she was feeling. And now she was feeling this. Not wanting to, but sliding beyond wanting to stop. She could hear the intake of her own ragged breath. Her head had fallen back, her hands clenched in his hair.

He pushed her onto the mattress, pinning her wrists. "No one is going to sleep on the sofa."

She laughed. "I knew you would stop me."

"Oh, is that so?" He moved slowly forward, then slid down again. Chest hair tickled her belly and breasts. His legs held hers tightly closed, but he was nudging between her thighs. "Is this what you wanted?"

"Maybe."

"I'm burning up. You feel it? You do that to me, *amor. Cuando me tocas se enciende mi cuerpo.*"

She moaned deep in her throat, wanting to touch him, but her hands were still pinned. Then he parted her legs with his knee and put his thighs between hers, opening her farther. He entered her slowly, then withdrew. She couldn't move.

He whispered against her mouth. "Why can't you give me everything?"

"I do, you know I do." She thought she might scream from wanting him.

"No. You hold too much back. *Yo quiero todo.*" He went in farther, only a little.

"Oh, God. Please. Anthony."

He pressed her into the mattress, holding her there, not moving. She could feel the heartbeat in his groin. He had aroused her, and now he waited, making her want him still more. His lips brushed across hers. *"¿Qué me das?"*

"I'll give you anything. Tell me what you want."

He told her, and her body caught fire.

CHAPTER

TEN

On Tuesday morning Gail rented a plain, mid-size Ford sedan for two weeks, the time it would take the Mercedes body shop to dig red Rust-Oleum enamel out of air vents, replace window seals, trim, and wipers, and do a complete paint job.

During the day, Gail parked next to the attendant's booth in the garage under her office building, in view of the security camera. At home, Anthony helped her clear out the boxes and miscellaneous junk taking up space in the garage so she wouldn't have to leave the car in the driveway. They stacked everything in the dining room, which had taken on the look of a secondhand shop. Her home phone number had been changed. Karen now knew not to pick up unless she saw a familiar name on the caller-ID screen. Gail spoke lightly of these precautions, even giving the caller a name—Bozo—that made him into more of a joke than a threat.

On Wednesday night Anthony drove Gail back to the hospital for a short visit with his grandfather, who was recovering from pacemaker surgery. Not wanting Karen to be anywhere near there, Gail took her to stay with her best friend, Molly, who lived in the old neighborhood. Circling up the ramps of the garage in the passenger seat of Anthony's car, Gail looked through the back window, but no one was following. Smudges of red paint on the concrete showed where she had parked the other night. She could see where her car had been pulled away by the tow truck. The tire tracks grew fainter and fainter until they were gone.

By Thursday morning Gail had begun to relax. She was starting to believe that the calls and the vandalism might have had no purpose other than the thrill of frightening someone. Hers could have been a name chosen by chance from the listings of attorneys in the phone book. She would be careful, of course. She would wait him out. Eventually Bozo would go away.

Coming back from an early motion hearing downtown, Gail rapped on the frosted glass and called out, "It's me." The door buzzed, and Gail pushed it open.

Lynn Dobbert swiveled her chair as Gail walked by. "I'll check for you. Could you hold on, please?" She pushed the button. "It's Theresa Zimmerman—the bad knee. She said you wanted to speak to her?"

"Finally. I left a message two days ago." Gail set her briefcase on Miriam's desk. "Where's Miriam?"

"In the storage room looking through old files. She said you asked her to."

"Oh, yes." Gail picked up the phone. "Hi, Theresa? This is Gail. Did you get my message about the settlement offer? Good news, huh? . . . What do you mean? . . . I can't ask for more, I already told him eighty . . . Why? Because it's what you wanted."

Lynn rolled her chair back so she could see past the edge of her cubicle. Gail pointed at the phone, then clenched her teeth and made a fist. When the voice on the other end had paused for breath, Gail smiled and spoke patiently. "Well, after the medicals and the costs are paid, you'll net around twenty-eight, which is more than you expected when we first talked. Remember? You said, 'Just get me twenty-five thousand dollars.'"

Gail made an exaggerated motion of choking someone, then smiled again as she said, "Do you recall that list of comparative jury verdicts that I sent you? With your particular injury, and the good prognosis for recovery, we are lucky to get eighty. . . ."

No. I would not advise it. A jury *might* give you more than that, but they probably wouldn't. Most verdicts in your kind of case come in around seventy. And consider this. Once the complaint is filed, my fees are forty percent of the recovery, not a third. If we go to trial, the fee is fifty percent."

She listened to her client complain about the high fees charged by lawyers, and for what?

"Theresa, I charge according to the standard fee schedule, which you agreed to—"

Lynn was listening intently while Gail paced, a hand on her hip, the phone cord stretching out, then back. "In my best judgment, you should take it. . . . They'll cut the check as soon as we give them a release. . . . Yes, I'll be here all day."

Gail hung up. "She said twenty-five, I got her twenty-eight, and she's complaining."

"I guess it's because you're getting more money than she is," Lynn said. When Gail looked at her, she added, "I mean, over thirty thousand dollars for some phone calls."

"I did more than make phone calls," Gail said. "Lynn, this case didn't require a lot of time, I'll admit that, but I have a few others that are driving me crazy. They all pay the same percentage. That's the system." Lynn was looking at her sideways, still unsure. "It's a business, Lynn. If I don't make money, I'd have to close my doors, and we'd all be out of a job."

"Okay," Lynn said. "Sorry."

Gail crossed the small secretarial area to stand by the monitor on Lynn's desk—a work station on the intra-office computer network that Gail had leased when she thought she had money. "Go ahead and prepare the release. The client is coming in right after lunch, and I'd like to have it ready before she changes her mind."

"A release? I don't know . . ."

"It's really not hard. Didn't Miriam show you? Here." Gail leaned over and started to do it herself, then said, "No, you should learn how. Call up the Zimmerman file . . . That's right . . . Now look at the documents list for a release . . ."

She watched Lynn's fingers tap hesitantly on the keyboard.

"No, no, that's a release for real estate. This is a personal injury case."

"It looks the same."

"Not at all. They're totally different." Gail pointed. "That one. Just bring it into the document you're working on. Merge it with the header on the Zimmerman case."

With a nervous little laugh Lynn dropped her hands into her lap. "I can't concentrate when people stand behind me looking over my shoulder."

"All right." Gail rolled Miriam's chair over and sat down, crossing her legs. She put an elbow on the back and brushed her fingers through her hair. Lynn started typing again. Gail resolved not to say anything unless Lynn hit a wall. She studied the photos, drawings, and clippings taped to the cabinet over the desk. The family vacation in DisneyWorld. A boy splashing in a backyard pool. Another with a cake with three candles. A clipping from Ann Landers, called "A Mother's Prayer." A child's drawing of a flower. And there was Daddy, a big man with thinning brown hair, holding a boy on each arm.

"Cute kids," Gail said.

"Uh-huh." Lynn's attention was fixed on the screen.

"How old are they?"

Lynn waited till she had finished a line. "Six and four."

"Really? They look younger."

"I haven't taken any pictures recently."

"Oh, you have to. Kids grow up so fast."

"Well, our camera broke, and I can't afford to buy another one."

Gail combed through her hair some more. Twelve bucks, she thought. Twelve bucks for a simple throw-away camera and five more to process the film. She wondered if Lynn had said it to make her feel bad.

She shifted to see the screen. "That's it. But don't double-space the caption."

"I know. I know. I hit the wrong key." Lynn shook her hands in the air as if the keyboard had scorched them.

Gail wondered what she'd been thinking of, hiring a woman

who knew nothing about working in a law office. Because she'll answer phones and run errands for eight dollars an hour, Gail said to herself.

A door down the hall slammed, and a moment later Miriam appeared barefoot, limping and laughing at the same time. "My leg is asleep! *Ay, que pena,* I've been sitting on the floor for two hours." She leaned an arm on the wall and held her right leg out, size-five foot dangling. Without shoes she was shorter than Karen.

The day after talking to Detective Novick, Gail had assigned Miriam the job of making a list. She told her to go through the files and pick out anyone who had caused trouble. Were there any letters of complaint? Anyone who could remotely be classified as a nut case?

"Did you find anything?"

"Like about . . . twenty names?"

"Oh, my God."

Miriam stepped gingerly onto her foot. "You remember that man who said you stole money from the closing on his house? He's on my list. I know he admitted he was wrong, but you said to write down anybody you ever had an argument with."

"Well, let's take a look." Gail started down the hall, then turned back to tell Lynn to print out the release. "Three copies," she said. "Proof it to make sure it's perfect. She might hang me for a misspelled word, the mood she's in." Gail laughed. "Twenty names? I'd better start being nicer to my clients."

In the small storage room, Miriam had pulled file boxes off the steel shelves that took up one wall. The rest of the room was crammed with books, old office furniture, and assorted junk brought from Hartwell Black. Miriam had cleared off a space on the floor, leaving several stacks of files.

"Gail, *te juro,* they aren't bad. I mean, I don't think any of them would want to *kill* you."

"That's a comfort." Gail crouched down to look through the files, handing them to Miriam to be returned to their proper storage boxes. "No maniacs here," she murmured. "No stalkers, no obsessives, nobody who claims to hear signals from outer space. Two complaints to the Florida Bar—resolved in my favor. Actually, these look fairly normal." She stood up.

Arms extended from the weight, Miriam slung the last box onto a shelf.

"Miriam, do you remember that case at Hartwell Black? I was in trial, I think, and the defendant kicked over a chair. He was coming after me, and the judge had to call the bailiff. Didn't I tell you about that?"

The brown eyes grew large. "Yes, you did. It was a foreclosure case, I'm pretty sure. He sent you a letter afterward—what you did was so bad, you put me out of my house, blah blah blah . . ."

Gail nodded. "What was the case?"

Miriam blew out a breath. "I forgot. It's been way over a year ago. Oh! What about that woman, the stockbroker, who was cheating her customers, and you told the FBI, and she was arrested? Do you think she's in jail?"

"I hope so." Gail turned off the light and shut the door. "You might as well look through the files at Hartwell Black too. Not tomorrow, because Lynn won't be here to watch the office. She has a field trip for her son, I think. Which reminds me. Tomorrow is Friday, and Wendell Sweet is supposed to drop off his documents. Do you think I would be risking my life to call his lawyer and remind him?"

An hour later Gail was sharing a table with three friends in the cafeteria downstairs, which at noontime buzzed with the voices of well-dressed men and women who joyously devoted most of their waking hours to the needs of clients and money. Impressive arrangements of tropical flowers decorated the ends of the serving lines, and halogen lights in the faraway ceiling shone down like small suns.

Gail sat opposite Charlene Marks, whom she had hoped to talk to privately, but two friends from the building had seen them in line and saved places at their table—Susan and Carol, both lawyers. Gail liked them very much. Carol, in fact, would be one of Gail's attendants at her wedding. But their chatter made her restless. Gail wanted to find out what trouble Dave's lawyer was making. Charlene had told her that Joe Erwin had called. Gail also wanted Charlene's opinion on Karen's appointment with the psychologist at one o'clock. Her father would be there, but Mom would be busy at her law office. What would this say to Dr. Fischman? Would Gail's absence hurt her chances of retaining custody? Or would her presence make her appear too controlling?

A deeper question was gnawing at Gail that Charlene Marks, as attorney, could not answer: Would Karen feel abandoned? A stranger would be asking her questions, and Karen might want both parents waiting for her outside. But it was already after noon, and Ms. Zimmerman with the bad knee would be in soon to sign the release. And Gail's afternoon calendar was heavy with appointments.

Charlene said, "Gail, tell them about your car."

Susan and Carol already knew about the phone calls. As she picked at her salad, Gail told them what had happened on Monday night.

Carol said, "Oh, my God. Aren't you petrified?"

"The police say not to be—unless he does something violent."

Susan was wolfing down her quiche. "The bastard. I hope you catch him at it and shoot him."

"I don't have a gun. They scare me. I'll let Anthony shoot him."

"Oh, pooh," Charlene said. "Come to my office, I'll show you mine. A darling little .38, never jams."

Carol's forehead was creased with worry. She swallowed her last bite of grilled portabello sandwich. "You don't have any idea who it could be?"

"Anthony thinks it could be my ex-husband," Gail said.

"*Dave?*"

Susan said, "Do you think so?"

"No." Gail laughed.

"*My* ex would do something like that," Susan said. "He was so jealous after we split up."

"Of course," Carol said. "He's a Latino."

Gail said, "Hey, watch it. I'm marrying a Latino."

Susan made a little face at Carol. "My ex isn't Latin, he's Italian."

"Same thing."

"No, it isn't. In Miami if you're Italian, you're Anglo. If you're Polish, you're Anglo. I'm Jewish and Anglo."

Charlene replied, "I married a Mexican when I was young and foolish. Javier. The man was hung like a *caballo*. It lasted a month. I walked out after he blacked my eye."

Carol protested. "Charlene! Don't say that in front of Gail."

"You're absolutely right. I apologize, Gail. I've known several other Latin men, and they were all pussycats."

Gail said, "The detective told me to start looking at my clients. Is that crazy?"

"Not at all." Susan gestured with her fork. "If you practice law, you get loonies. I was handling a probate case a few years ago for a man whose mother had died, right? And I thought he was a little strange when he said, 'Don't call me at home, my lines are tapped.' Then a week later he tells me the CIA murdered his mother because they thought she was a spy for the Cubans. He wanted me to sue the government. I said, whoa, buddy, I can't do that. So he sent a letter to everybody in the building accusing *me* of being in on this murder plot. People teased me about that for months."

"What finally happened?" Gail asked.

"I managed to withdraw from the case. Then"—she giggled— "then I sent him over to my ex-husband's law firm!"

Their laughter made people at neighboring tables look at them and smile, wondering what the joke was.

Carol whispered, "One of my clients sued me for fraud. Purely by coincidence, my boyfriend at the time bought the client's property at a foreclosure sale for a personal investment, but this woman was certain we were conspiring to steal her house. It was just awful. I had to explain and explain to the Florida Bar, even after the case was thrown out."

"*Not* a loony," Susan said. "That doesn't even qualify as funny, Carol."

"Well, I'm sorry. Nothing exciting ever happens to me."

Susan nudged Charlene. "Come on. You've had loonies. I know you have."

A low laugh came back. "Oh-ho, don't get me started." Charlene tapped slowly on the table with her long red nails. "I represented the owner of a nightclub in an uncontested divorce. The wife never put up a fight, and I couldn't figure out why. I mean, the guy had money. After it was over, he asked me out. I said no, I don't date clients. He kept asking. He sent flowers. He called. He said that he just *knew*, through some spiritual force, that we were meant for each other. I told him to get lost. Then one night I heard a noise outside my apartment and called the police. Guess who? He was carrying a pair of latex gloves, a roll of duct tape, and an eight-inch serrated hunting knife."

The other three at the table stared at her.

Charlene smiled. "He's in the state hospital. They said they'd let me know if he's ever released."

"Well." Carol let out her breath. "You win."

Susan patted Gail's arm. "Get a gun."

The two friends, having started their lunches first, were finished. They picked up their trays and told Gail to be careful. "Lock your doors," Carol said.

Charlene gave them a little good-bye wave, then turned around and looked across the table at Gail. A hammered gold necklace glittered at the neck of her black tank dress, and her gray hair sprang away from her face in thick curls. "Should I be worried about you?"

"Not really."

"Such a stoic." Charlene idly picked up a plastic straw and twirled it by the ends. "Any ideas who?"

"Wendell Sweet?" Gail accented her uncertainty with a shrug.

"So his wife hasn't taken him back yet."

"Bite your tongue, Charlene."

"I see it so often. The yo-yo syndrome." Realizing she was

playing with the straw, Charlene tossed it onto her tray. "I quit smoking twenty years ago, and I still want a cigarette. It's like sex. It doesn't go away."

Gail pushed aside her pasta salad, which she had barely touched. "Wendell is supposed to deliver his documents tomorrow, but I expect a call from his lawyer asking for a delay till Monday. Or next week. Or never. What would you do?"

"Tell his lawyer that unless Mr. Sweet has the documents on your desk by Monday at nine a.m., you will be in court at ten o'clock asking the court to throw his ass in jail."

"Jamie doesn't want him in jail."

Charlene lifted her eyes to the ceiling. "God, if there were only a way to keep the clients out of it. Let us fight and tell them afterward who won."

Gail said, "At the risk of interfering in my own case . . . What did Joe Erwin have to say?"

"Yes, I did call you for that, didn't I? Joe wants the judge to rehear the motion on visitation. Dave is allegedly concerned about the presence of the police at your house. Bad example for the child and so forth. As if in this town kids don't see cops all the time. He is further concerned that the vandalism to your car could have been carried out by one of Anthony Quintana's criminally minded clients, in which case we assume that Karen would be constantly exposed to such threats."

Gail rested her forehead on her palms. "This is making me crazy."

"Oh, come on. It's a ridiculous argument, and Joe Erwin knows it. The judge is not going to put this back on the calendar, I promise. What Dave wants is more access to Karen, obviously, and he hopes you'll capitulate. The good news is, Joe is probably charging him two hundred dollars in legal fees to make the phone call. Dave will see it differently when he gets the bill."

"So what's the strategy? Wear Dave down? And what about my bill?"

Charlene smiled. "This isn't on the meter. We're having lunch."

"We've had lunch a lot lately," Gail said.

"A person has to eat." Charlene asked. "Do you need to go? You keep looking at your watch."

"It's too late now, anyway."

"Too late for what?"

"Karen's appointment with Dr. Fischman at one o'clock. Dave's taking her."

Charlene sat up straight. "He is? What are you doing here?"

"I have a heavy schedule this afternoon. Should I go? Would it matter? It's not to talk to Dave and me, only to Karen."

"Of course you should go. Make motherly noises. Smile and pretend that Evan Fischman has a clue what he's doing."

"It's already twelve-thirty."

"So hurry."

Gail made it with ten minutes to spare, after running three red lights and using her portable phone to explain everything to Miriam. Apologize to the one o'clock client, Gail told her. Tell everyone it's a family emergency. And make sure Ms. Zimmerman signs the release.

The office was on a shady street just off Brickell Avenue downtown. It was one of those sleek, glassy buildings erected during the boom of the early eighties, when drug money poured into Miami by the billions. Since then the interior had been renovated, but the carpet in the corridor looked cheap. The metal plate on the door to 1225 announced EVAN R. FISCHMAN, PH.D., FAMILY COUNSELOR. Inside were the usual armchairs and department-store lamps. Gail announced herself to the receptionist. The smell of tuna sandwich came through the frosted window, which slid shut again.

Gail sat on the sofa, her purse beside her, and rested her hands on her knees. She had that peculiar lightness in her chest that accompanied nervous dread. She watched the entrance door, wondering what Dave would have to say about her being here.

A door opened from the other direction, and Gail turned her head to see a bald, bearded man around fifty, wearing a navy blazer over gray pants. He was indeed short, but made less so by the two-inch heels on a pair of brown-spotted snakeskin cowboy boots.

His inspection of her was just as thorough. He smiled. Thick glasses made his blue eyes seem small and far away. "Ms. Connor? I was told not to expect you."

Gail smiled as she stood up and extended her hand. "I had to rearrange a few things, but here I am."

"Come on in. Let's get acquainted." He held the door.

"Isn't this . . . for Karen? I should probably wait for her."

"Oh, I like to talk to Mom first. Sort of set the stage, as it were. We won't be long." Fischman's voice was so soft she had to watch his lips not to miss anything. "Can we get you something to drink? Coffee?" Gail, still smiling, said that she had just had lunch. He led her to his office, carrying a thin folder, tapping it lightly against his palm.

Fischman motioned her to the end of a blue upholstered sofa; he sat at right angles in a matching chair, the folder on his lap. He opened it. "Let's just see . . ."

An aquarium bubbled in the corner, bug-eyed goldfish swimming through a mass of green plastic seaweed. His desk was across the room, and diplomas and plaques decorated the wall behind it. The teak veneer was peeling off the bookcases. Shelves bowed downward from the weight of books. A box in the corner overflowed with stuffed animals, wooden puzzles, plastic blocks, and dolls. A man doll, a woman. A boy, a girl. Gail wondered if under their clothes they had the appropriate parts.

"So."

Gail looked around to see Fischman with his cheekbone propped on extended fingers. The lamp reflected on his gold-rimmed glasses."How do you feel about being here?"

"How do I *feel*? Fine. I have no problem with it."

"You're a lawyer. A solo practitioner."

She waited for him to go on. When he didn't, she said, "Yes."

"You were at a large firm downtown. Why did you leave?"

"I wanted my own business. I wanted more time with Karen. That was the most important factor. My daughter."

"And how has it worked out for you?"

Gail felt the flutter in her chest again. "Any new business is difficult in the beginning, but it's working out very well."

He smiled. "I meant with Karen."

"Oh." She searched for the right answer. "The freedom is helpful. Being able to rearrange my schedule. This afternoon, for example."

The smile remained. In his quiet voice he said. "You can relax with me, Ms. Connor. I won't bite. Tell me about your daughter. Do you and she have any areas you feel you need to work on?"

"Not really. I mean . . . nothing that any mother and daughter wouldn't have."

"Such as . . ."

"Our relationship is fine, Dr. Fischman. We love each other very much."

His pale eyes were distorted to little blue dots by the glasses. "All right. We'll leave it there for now. Let me ask about Karen's physical development. She's almost eleven, correct? Not menstruating yet, I assume." Gail shook her head.

"Does Karen have an understanding of sexual intercourse and reproduction?"

"Yes."

"And she feels free in discussing this with you?"

"I suppose so."

"But you're not sure?"

Gail resisted an urge to look away from this man, although her eyes had been pinned on the shiny curves of his glasses for some time. "Karen knows that if there is anything she is curious about, she can come to me. We talk quite openly."

"Usually initiated by . . . you? Karen?"

"It depends. I don't know."

He looked at her, then went back to his notes. Gail heard a jet outside the window, then muffled voices from the reception area. She didn't recognize Dave's voice, but he must have arrived by now, she thought.

Fischman was saying, "Going into fifth grade in the fall. Private school. It appears that her grades have fallen since the divorce." He glanced at Gail as if for some explanation.

Gail said, "Are you saying there's a connection?"

"Is there?"

"I don't know."

"Neither do I. I'm making an observation. All right?"

"Well, that's what you get paid for." She immediately regretted the sarcasm.

Fischman returned to the folder. "You are engaged to a lawyer. Anthony Quintana. Cuban descent. Forty-two. How long have you known him?"

"About a year and a half."

"Before your separation from Mr. Metzger."

"If that's a question, Anthony had nothing to do with our divorce."

"Mr. Metzger mentioned to me that you and Mr. Quintana were intimate before the divorce."

Gail took a slow breath. "Dave and I had already separated. He should have made that clear."

"And Karen was living with you at the time."

"At what time?"

"When you became intimate with Mr. Quintana."

After a few seconds' silence, Gail said, "Yes."

Fischman settled his chin back onto his fist. His beard covered deep acne scars. "What can you tell me about Karen's relationship with your fiancé?"

"They get along very well."

"Does he live with you?"

"No. He lives on Key Biscayne."

"Does he ever spend the night in your home when Karen is there?"

Gail's stomach tightened. "Occasionally, yes."

"Are you and he fairly open about sex in front of your daughter? Or not?"

"Meaning what?"

"Is there . . . fondling, that sort of thing, in Karen's presence?"

Gail laughed. "No. We are very discreet around Karen."

"You seem uncomfortable with this topic."

"Not at all—if it's relevant."

"It is most relevant." He laid the folder carefully on the corner table, pausing to shift aside a sculpture of a small frog clinging to a polished brass rock. "At Karen's age, her sexuality is beginning to assert itself. The presence of a man in the house—a man not her father, and with whom the mother is having an intimate relationship—often confuses the female child—"

"Karen is a normal, well-adjusted girl. She is not confused."

"If I may finish?"

Gail stared back at him. "Of course."

"Girls are sexually attracted to their fathers, but they know intuitively that it's wrong. It's the old incest taboo. When a man who is *not* the father moves into the home—or is sleeping with Mother—the child is still attracted. The girl will experience the same guilt, the same desire, but now she is confused because there is no natural barrier to that desire."

Gail's mouth opened. A small laugh came out. "You're implying that Karen is sexually attracted to my fiancé?"

Fischman scratched his cheek, then grasped some of his beard and tugged on it. His small lips were rosy and moist. "No. You asked me if the topic is relevant, and I am attempting to explain in a way that is easy to understand. The mother's sexual relationship with a man not the father can raise fears in the child's mind. Mommy threw away Daddy for someone else, will she throw me away too? Or, conversely, Mommy is my rival, but I feel guilty about hating her. Prepubescent girls are especially vulnerable. They are acquiring their sexual identity, taking clues from their parents, particularly the custodial parent. Many women entering second marriages, who have children, fail to consider these issues."

Gail dug her fingernails into her palms. "I was under the impression that you were asked by the court to find out if Karen preferred to live with her father or with me. And that was all."

"It isn't a simple matter," he replied. "A child doesn't often express her feelings well. And sometimes . . . what she thinks she wants isn't in her best interest."

Gail said, "Well, since you—and not Karen—are going to decide what she wants, then why bother to talk to her?"

"You seem upset."

"I seem upset? No, Dr. Fischman, I *am* upset. I am very upset." She grabbed her purse. "And that's about all we have to say to each other."

"Ms. Connor, I assure you, I was not making a personal attack on you or your choices." She stood over his chair. He smiled up at her. "This defensiveness is quite telling, you know."

Gail wanted to push his chair backward with him in it. "My daughter is not coming anywhere near you, I don't care what the judge ordered. Put that in your report."

She swung her purse over her shoulder and walked out. When she opened the door to the waiting room, and then swung it back, the doorknob accidentally slipped out of her grasp. The reverberation shook the frosted glass at the receptionist's window.

Dave and Karen sat on the sofa. Dave stood up. "Gail?"

"Find some other psychologist. I'm taking her out of here. Come on, sweetie." Gail held out her hand.

Karen's mouth hung open. She got up from the sofa.

"Karen, sit down." Dave grabbed Gail's arm. "What's the matter with you?"

"No. What's the matter with *you*? This is insane." Gail took his hand off her arm. "Come here, baby, we have to go."

"Karen, let me talk to your mom outside—"

She yelled at him, "Leave her alone! Go file another of your fucking motions. Call your lawyer."

Dave backed away. Fischman had opened the door and stood framed in the opening. "I'm sorry about this," Dave said.

Gail grabbed Karen's hand and pulled her out of Fischman's waiting room.

In the corridor someone was just getting into the elevator, and Gail ran toward it, dragging Karen along. She stuck her foot across the tracks. The door bucked, then came back open, and they went inside just as Gail heard Dave calling her name.

In the elevator she put on her sunglasses. The people already inside were trying not to stare.

Karen leaned against her and whispered, "Mom?"

"It's okay." Gail put her arm around Karen. "We'll go home, all right?"

Gail didn't let go of her hand as they hurried across the street and into the tree-shaded lot where she had parked the rental car. They had almost reached it when she saw a man in khaki pants and a denim shirt running from the building. Dave.

He looked up and down the street, then spotted them. "Gail! Wait!"

"Get in, Karen." Gail unlocked the passenger side.

Dave sprinted toward them. "What happened in there with Fischman? What's going on?" He followed Gail around the car and straight-armed the driver's-side door to keep her from opening it. "Talk to me, dammit."

She stared at him through the dark glasses, then went back around to speak to Karen. "Sweetie? Your daddy wants to talk to me for a minute. Can you wait here? It's shady, so you won't get hot. I'll be right over there, under that tree."

She walked a few yards away, gravel crunching under her shoes, then turned so that Karen couldn't see her face. Her voice was low. "David, I have let this go too far. I didn't want Karen to be hurt. I didn't want to warp her feelings about you. But this is too much, taking her to that man. Fischman implied that she hates me and desires you, and that if Anthony moves in, she'll want him too. Fischman hasn't even spoken to her, and he assumes this. What is he going to say to her? What is she going to think when he gets through with her?"

Dave only stared. He blinked, then looked up at the building they had just left.

Gail fumbled in her shoulder bag for a tissue. "That perverted little bastard. It's *his* decision. Not yours or mine, not Karen's. What are we doing? All right, fine. Just tell me what you want. You want her two afternoons a week? Three? Is that why you had your lawyer threaten to take me back to court because my car got trashed? As if I had something to do with it!"

"Gail, you're not making sense. Calm down, will you?"

"I don't want her going through this anymore," Gail said. "If she wants to live with you, I don't care. I do care, but if that's what she wants—I'd rather have her with you than miserable. To be torn apart."

Dave's hand was around her elbow. He was looking past Gail, his eyes fixed on her car and the girl sitting inside it. He said, "Karen didn't want to be here, but she came because I said to, and because she's a good kid. I don't want her to be miserable. I want—I want to be a good father. That's all. Just to be . . . in her life."

"Dave, I never tried to keep her away from you."

Fury rose in his face, shown in the tight set of his square jaw. "Yes, you did. You were so pissed off about me leaving and not calling her enough. Okay, I didn't. I know that. I couldn't sometimes. And then . . . things didn't go like I wanted. The cruise business slacked off. You said before I left that it would be a disaster. Remember that? 'Dave, you're dreaming. It's going to be a disaster.' So maybe . . . I was ashamed."

His eyes had reddened. "I wanted it to be good when I called her. But I thought about her, Gail. I did. Every day. She was in my heart all the time. I had to come back. I wanted to start over, to do it right. To be the kind of man—the kind of father—I should have been all along. You know what you said to me? 'So you're back. Well, you've lost your daughter.' "

Gail shook her head. "I don't remember."

"You said it."

"Did I? If I said that, I'm sorry. Yes, I was angry. I used to make up stories about where you were, and why you didn't call, so she wouldn't be disappointed."

"Oh, God, honey, I've been trying to make up for that. Trying like hell. All the mistakes. All the things I did wrong, going way back. Mistakes with you. We were so young when we married. I was twenty-three. I thought— Jesus. I thought I'd never lived. I was so wrong."

He put his hand on her shoulder, and when she didn't pull away, he left it there. He squeezed gently. "You're a great mother. We'll work this out, Gail."

Tears were running from under Gail's glasses. She wiped them away with trembling fingers.

Dave pulled her awkwardly against his chest. "I've missed you. When I left Miami, it was you I left. Because I was so screwed up and hurt."

She was so tense her body was aching. Her sunglasses pressed against his collarbone and tilted off her nose.

He held her clumsily at first, then more closely. "Oh, God, I'm so sorry. Sorry for throwing away what we had. You and me and Karen." His voice was tight and ragged. A sob tore out of his throat. "I threw it all away, Gail. How stupid . . . thinking I'd be happier. But I never stopped . . . loving you. Not one day."

When he kissed her, she let him do it, too shocked at first to move, then because it would have been cruel to shove him away, when his tears were on her lips. She let it continue because it was a chaste kiss, tentative and gentle, reminding her of the first time they had kissed, when she had been eighteen years old. It was familiar and comforting. His taste was familiar, and the way he held her, and she thought of the time when this had been natural between them, before their troubles had pushed them apart.

CHAPTER

ELEVEN

Irene made some peach-flavored iced tea, and she and Gail and Karen took the insulated glasses and pitcher outside to the gazebo. The old structure needed paint, and ferns grew from rotting floorboards, but lattice and vines created cooling shade, and a breeze from the bay softened the mid-afternoon heat. The two women sat side by side on the swing while Karen climbed onto the railing that circled the gazebo and steadied herself on a roof support.

"Don't fall, sweetie."

Gail had not gone back to her office. She had come home with Karen, changed into shorts and her swimsuit top, and called her mother. Bring over that new alamanda bush, she had said. The plant would replace the one that the roofing truck had mashed flat. Irene brought her wedding plans too, pleased about having a few unexpected hours to discuss them. But they talked about Dave. While Irene made the iced tea, Gail told her about the scene at Dr. Fischman's office—and what happened afterward. Irene had started to offer an opinion, but Gail told her she didn't want to talk about it anymore.

"Before we bought this place," Gail said, "I told Anthony we'd put a poinciana tree right over there, about halfway between the house and the seawall. They're in bloom now. The streets look so pretty, all those canopies of red flowers. When's a good time to plant them?"

"Fall is best. You'll have such a lovely home." The wind ruffled Irene's bright hair.

Gail pressed the half-empty glass of tea to her cheek. The temperature was only around ninety, but the humidity was vicious. She thought that if she tightened her fist around a handful of air, drops of water would fall to the ground. Swimming pools were as warm as bathtubs, and by dusk the mosquitoes would take over.

"My air conditioner is starting to wheeze," Gail said. "If it goes out entirely, we might camp at your house."

"Oh, this is not so bad," Irene said. "People get spoiled. My family didn't have air conditioning until I was Karen's age. We lived with fans, and on really steamy nights we'd sleep on the screened porch." She swung her feet. Her white sandals showed off her toenails, painted bright orange to match her shorts. Her oversized white T-shirt was knotted at the hip, and little green parrots swung from her earlobes.

Karen was circling the gazebo on the railing, skittering from one roof support to the next. Gail told her to get down. "You're going to slip and break your neck."

"Mom, I won't fall."

"Get down!"

Irene laughed. "Don't squelch the child's natural impulses, Gail. She's going to lead an expedition to Mt. Everest someday, won't you, precious?"

Karen flew off the railing and rolled to the grass, then sped up the slight incline to the old metal swing set, where she hung by her knees from a crossbar, looking at the world upside-down.

"What a little monkey," Irene said.

"A few days ago she was wearing lipstick." Gail closed her eyes and exhaled a long breath.

"Are you all right, honey?"

"Tired. I feel so dragged out."

The wooden porch swing in the gazebo went back and forth,

rattling the loose end of the chain on each pass. Irene said, "What are you going to tell Anthony?"

"What would *you* tell him?"

"Hmm." Irene's delicate auburn brows came together. "Well . . . not *everything.* Tell a man everything and you'll only start an argument. They hear what they want, and their feelings are hurt far too easily."

Gail curled her hand around the chain and leaned her head on it. "I don't even want to think about it right now."

"Well, then." Irene reached for the loose-leaf notebook she had laid next to the pitcher of tea on the small wooden table. The notebook was organized with multicolored index tabs. Irene turned to one marked FLOWERS. "I had a meeting with the florist yesterday, and he gave me some pictures of table arrangements with birds of paradise. Look how bright and pretty. You don't want the same old washed-out white orchids as everybody else, do you?"

"God no."

Irene looked at her for a moment, then said, "Well, do you like it or not?"

"They're wonderful. Gorgeous."

"All right. I'll tell him yes, then. Let's see. We have the photographer for the portraits, but for the video . . . Here's a list of videographers. Gail, we really should look at some examples of their work."

"I don't have time to look at videos. You decide, okay?" Gail pushed against the floor, and the swing creaked. The repetitive motion made her eyes drift shut.

"We ought to have valet parking at the reception, don't you think? Some of the guests will stay at the hotel, but that could be expensive, so I recommend reserving a block of rooms at the Holiday Inn as well. The Biltmore can do a lovely rehearsal dinner, which would be convenient because the church is right across the street." Irene's voice became mixed with the rustling leaves and the chirp of birds. "Gail, are you listening?"

"I'm sorry, Mother. What?"

Irene laid the book on the seat. "You know, I always find that when I'm feeling low, the best remedy is yard work. Why don't we go plant the alamanda?"

"In a while." Gail looked toward Karen, who was dragging a twig through the grass for her kitten to chase. "I wish Karen hadn't seen him kiss me."

"What did she say about it?"

"Nothing. I don't know what she thinks. Karen and I used to talk about anything. Now she hides her feelings. I don't know if she approves of me or what."

"She loves you! But girls have a secret life when they get to be Karen's age. You, for instance—a sphinx! You drove me batty." Irene laughed. "Payback time."

The phone in Gail's shorts pocket rang. She groaned, then stood up to reach it.

"Don't you ever turn that thing off?"

"I told Miriam to call with anything important." Gail's new portable had caller-ID, and she had recognized her office number. She sat on the railing, one foot on the floor. "Hi, what's up?"

Miriam told her that the bad-knee case had signed the release, and now the client wanted Gail to tell her when she could expect her money.

"I'm not going to call her now. It can wait till tomorrow morning." Gail leaned against one of the roof supports. "Anything else?"

Wendell Sweet's lawyer had called. He hadn't said what he wanted, only that it was urgent that Gail get in touch with him. Gail borrowed her mother's pen to scribble his number on a blank page in the notebook. "Thanks, Miriam. See you in the morning." She got a dial tone, then punched in numbers. "Drat, drat, drat."

"What is it?" Irene asked.

"A divorce I'm doing. I think I told you. The Sweet case. Bet you a dollar he wants an extension." She was correct. When Marvin Acker finally came on the line, he told her that Wendell wanted another week to turn over the documents that Gail had requested.

"No. Absolutely not. Marvin, your client is under a judicial order to produce the documents by Friday—that is tomorrow, not next week."

Marvin Acker said that Wendell was doing the best he could, that many documents had to come from Venezuela, and as a courtesy—

"Courtesy? Ask Wendell how courteous he was, beating up his wife the last time he was at the house. He should have been arrested. You tell him to get whatever documents he has to my office tomorrow, and the rest Monday morning by nine, I don't care if he has to fly down to Venezuela and pick them up, or I will be in front of the judge on Monday at ten o'clock asking that Wendell Sweet go directly to jail for contempt of court."

Acker said there was no reason for her to take that attitude.

"Don't blame me. Your client is creating the problems. Tell him what I said. Monday morning or his head is on the block." Gail disconnected and with an oath jammed the telephone back into her pocket.

Irene was staring at her. "Well."

"Well what?"

"I don't see this side of you very often. Thank goodness."

"Dr. Jekyll and Ms. Hyde? Mild-mannered mommy by night, fire-breathing bitch by day." Gail walked over to pick up her tea from the table. "You can't be nice to people like Wendell Sweet. Eight years of clawing and shoving at Hartwell Black taught me that if you don't go for blood, they'll walk all over you."

Irene made a little grimace. "I couldn't do it."

"Oh, yes, you could, if you had a client to protect. Wendell uses his fists if he can't have his way, and he'd be happy to see Jamie and their three kids living in a trailer and shopping at secondhand stores. He's got over a million dollars hidden somewhere, and I'm going to find it. If I give him more time, he'll use it to wear Jamie down, to force her into a lousy settlement.

Bastard. He's lying to save his own skin. You'd do the same thing I just did."

Irene said quietly, "I hope this doesn't carry over here at home."

"What do you mean?"

"Well . . . being so hard and uncompromising. Men are funny about that. You might ask yourself if this is one reason Dave left. Seems to me that Anthony would be even less willing to take it, given his culture and so forth."

"Anthony and I are not adversaries."

"Well, that's new in the history of the world."

"Mother!"

"All right." Irene lifted her hands. "A word to the wise, darling. You know I love you."

Gail continued to look at her. "You think I'm making a mistake to marry him."

"I never said such a thing."

"But you think it, don't you?"

"I do not. Anthony is attractive, intelligent, charming. I would never question your choice of whom you should marry."

"Yes, you would. What was the first thing out of your mouth when I told you what happened with Dave? You said it was a shame he and I got divorced."

"But you did, didn't you? Time has moved on, and a person just can't dwell on what-ifs." Irene took a sip of tea. "Never mind what I said. I guess I feel sorry for Dave Metzger."

"Why?"

"Because he always seemed to *need* you so much."

"Now, there's a good reason to stay married."

Irene stood up. "I think it's time to do some yard work."

"Oh, Mom, I didn't mean to snap at you."

"Well, you have a lot on your mind."

"That's no excuse." Gail meekly collected the glasses and pitcher and followed Irene down the steps to the yard. At the same moment she wondered where Karen had gone, she saw Irene walk toward the edge of the property, looking upward into the ficus tree. No grass grew in its heavy shade, and dark, tangled strands of air roots hung to the ground. The multiple trunks at the center made hiding places for lizards, cats, and children.

Irene called out, "Come down, jungle girl. Help your mother and me plant the alamanda."

A voice came back. "I'm busy."

"Of course you are." Irene smiled upward. "Busy being ten years old."

"*Eleven.* Almost."

"You want some company?" That brought a giggle. Irene put her little fists on her hips. "I bet I could climb that old tree."

"Okay. You can come up."

"Well, let me do some work first, then you can show me the secret passage." When Irene came back, Gail hugged her tightly. "My goodness, what's that for?"

Gail's eyes stung. "Because I love you. Because you're so good."

"Oh, hush."

The alamanda bush sat in its black plastic container in the driveway, where Irene had unloaded it from the trunk of the enormous burgundy red Chrysler she'd owned for ten years. She had to sit on a pillow to drive it. Opening the trunk, Irene took out her shovel, a spade, and a small plastic bag of fertilizer. Gail carried the plant to the bare spot in the yard where the roofers had ruined its predecessor. She wondered how in hell her mother had managed to heft the thing into her car.

The shovel was a short, slender one made to fit a woman's hands. Gail stepped hard on it, driving the point into the grass, then levered the dirt out and threw it to one side. She had worn her old sneakers. Already she could feel the sun burning her back, bare except for the thin strap of her swimsuit.

Irene reached into the front seat for her sun hat. "Do you need this, Gail?"

"No, I need a tan. I look like a mushroom."

Irene set the hat on her own head, then pulled on a pair of green gardening gloves. "What should I wear on Saturday?"

"Saturday?"

"To that Cuban dress shop."

"It isn't strictly Cuban, Mother. It's just—" Gail pounded the rocky ground with the shovel. "Just horrendously expensive. What should you wear? How about what you have on? The gloves go nicely with the parrot earrings."

"Are you making fun of me?"

"No, I just don't want you to feel intimidated by the Pedrosas."

"Me?"

Gail looked at her mother. "You're right. I'm the one they're after. They think I don't know how to dress. They want the bride to look as good as the groom, which is going to be a stretch."

"Gail, you're lovely."

"Compared to Elena, Xiomara, and the rest of his cousins, I have no butt, no boobs, and legs like sticks." She threw another shovelful of dirt to one side.

"Anthony thinks you're beautiful. He told me so."

"He makes me feel that way." Gail smiled.

A shiny black Land Rover approached, scattering leaves, and Gail lifted a hand. The woman inside didn't notice—or pretended not to. The vehicle turned between the coral rock columns on the property across the street.

"Who's she?"

"Peggy Cunningham, the queen of Clematis Street. Not the friendliest person in the world."

"Cunningham." The big daisy on Irene's hat still pointed toward the other side of the road. "Is her husband Bennett Cunningham? I believe I know his sister, Margie. She's in the Opera Guild."

"Peggy doesn't like me. I yelled at her son." Gail drove the shovel against the rocks, felt one give, and wedged in the point to lift it out. "I must be getting quite a reputation around the neighborhood. What should I do, go over there with a plate of cookies and apologize?"

"As long as they're homemade," Irene said.

"Sure. I have time for that." Breathing hard, Gail dropped the shovel and pointed at the hole. "Come on. That's deep enough, isn't it?"

Irene peered into it. "My father always told me, if you have a five-dollar plant, dig a ten-dollar hole. Take those rocks out."

On her knees, Gail chopped at the rocks with the spade, then started to pick them out of the hole.

"No, I'll do it," her mother said. "You don't have gloves on. You'll ruin your nails." She tossed the pitted white rocks into the grass. "Darling? This is just a thought. What if you wait awhile to get married? Six months, a year. If it was better for Karen—"

Gail sat back on her heels. "Anthony and I have talked about it, but we don't know for sure that Karen would be better off. We just don't know."

"Here." Irene kicked the pot a few times to loosen the dirt, then with an *umphh* of effort she lifted the plant by the trunk and set it into the hole, yellow flowers bobbing.

On her knees, Gail cleared away some dirt with the spade so the plant would sit level. "Karen told me last week—we were on our way to Dave's place—she said, 'I wish you and my dad and I could all be together again.' Then she said she knew it couldn't happen. You see? She doesn't want to make me unhappy."

A small hand patted her hair, then smoothed it down. Irene said, "Honey, I'd be glad to talk to her. You just say when."

"Would you? You'd get a lot further than Dr. Fischman."

Irene had brought a plastic bag with organic fertilizer, which she poured around the roots, a rich, loamy smell. Gail scraped the dirt back in with the spade, then stood up to tamp it down tight.

"Mom, what you said before . . . I'm not hard and uncompromising with Anthony. I wasn't like that with Dave. I don't think I was. I didn't drive him away."

"Oh, darling—"

"You know what Anthony said?" She laughed and wiped a knuckle under her nose. "He said he loves me because I'm such a challenge. But he's ten times stronger than Dave ever was. All right, maybe I should be more . . . what? I don't know what."

"Come on, let's go inside. You get cleaned up, and I'll fix us a real drink."

They put the shovel and spade back into the trunk, and Irene tossed in her gloves and straw hat. Gail took the plastic container out to the street and set it on the pile of trash that the city was supposed to have picked up last week but hadn't for some reason or other. "For you, Peggy," she said.

It was probably Irene closing the front door, going inside, that made Gail notice the mailbox beside it. White paper showed through the decorative hole in the black metal. The letter carrier had come while they were in the backyard. Gail lifted out what was inside, and the lid clanked back down.

She shoved the door shut with her foot and shuffled through the mail as she crossed the living room. An advertising circular on cheap newsprint, a catalog from Macy's, another from a cruise line. The electric bill. Visa. A letter from her cousin in Atlanta. And another letter with a Miami postmark but no return address. A plain white envelope with Gail's name and address written in block print, slightly crooked and off-center.

Her mother called out from the kitchen, asking if she had any vodka.

Gail felt a sickening rush of adrenaline surge through her. The envelope was light, not much inside. With the other mail clamped under her arm, she slid a finger under the flap. The paper tore. She noticed that her hands left smudges of dirt.

"Gail, did you hear me?"

"Yes. Just a second."

Though the opening she could see a sheet of white paper folded into thirds. She set down the other mail on the table by the stairs and withdrew the paper from the envelope. She unfolded it, a color copy of a photograph. Trees, a glimpse of blue sky. Gail recognized the playground at Biscayne Academy. There were a half dozen children, but the camera had centered on one of them.

Gail knew who she was before the details became clear. Light brown hair in a ponytail. Long, thin legs.

A pistol, crudely drawn in black marker, pointed at her, aiming right to left. The trajectory of a bullet was shown by thin lines. The bullet went through her head and came out the other side in a red explosion of bone and blood.

Gail's legs went weak, and she grabbed the finial post on the stairs for support. She heard the moan escaping her throat, and a few seconds later her mother's quick footsteps.

"Gail! What happened? What is that?" Irene pulled the paper out of her hands. "Oh. Oh, my God."

"Where is Karen?"

"I—I don't know. In the backyard—"

Gail rushed past Irene, through the hall, then the kitchen, finally throwing open the back door. The swing set was empty. There were no feet dangling from the branches of the ficus tree.

"Karen!"

She was by the seawall with another girl. Lindsay Cunningham. They turned around, and Karen called back, "What?"

Irene held onto Gail's arm. "Don't frighten her. She's all right."

Gail swallowed and moistened her lips. With a hand cupped at her mouth, she shouted, "Just checking! Stay in the yard, okay?"

They went back inside. Irene's eyes were enormous. "Let's call the police. Call Anthony."

"Yes, but first I want to call Dave. He has to know about this." Gail pulled her telephone from her pocket. She misdialed twice before getting the Island Club.

A man's voice on the other end told her that Mr. Metzger was expected back soon. Gail said to beep him, find him, tell him to call his ex-wife. It was important, regarding his daughter.

Irene had dropped the photograph and envelope on the

kitchen table. Gail stared at the picture, still not believing what she saw. She turned the envelope over. Nothing on the back. Then she read the address again as if this time it would offer an explanation. There was none. She slammed her hands down on the table until her palms stung.

Anthony arrived within fifteen minutes, leaving a client in mid-conference. Gail told him that the police refused to come. The detectives who had taken the complaint about the car were not available, and no one would do anything.

With a hand firmly around Gail's wrist, Anthony asked Irene if she would keep an eye on Karen. Keep her busy for a while, and tell her nothing at this point. Then he took Gail upstairs and told her to get changed while he made some phone calls. Gail took a fast shower and listened to him talk to the police while she grabbed a denim dress off a hanger and stepped into her shoes.

Anthony held the receiver an inch over the telephone before letting it drop. "They say to come in and make a report." He looked at Gail. "I expected that."

She nodded.

"We can go now if you like."

"Yes. How's my hair? I should brush it." She hurried into the bathroom.

Anthony leaned on the door frame, arms crossed. "We are not going to get into a panic. That's probably what he wants, to frighten you. If he wanted to harm you or Karen, he would have done it already." When the phone rang again, Anthony went to answer it. Gail lowered her brush. He said, "No, nothing is wrong with Karen. She's all right. . . . I'll let you speak to Gail."

She came out of the bathroom, and Anthony extended the receiver in her direction, nodding when she mouthed the name *Dave*. She sat on the edge of the bed while Anthony paced slowly, hands resting lightly on his hips, suit jacket pushed back.

Gail told Dave what had happened. Assured him again that Karen wasn't hurt. Explained that the phone calls and the damage to her car could be—had to be—related to this. Yes, she had called the police. She and Anthony were leaving right away.

She wished suddenly that Anthony was not in the room. She asked Dave, "Do you want to meet us there?" Not if Quintana is going, he replied, then said he wanted to come pick up Karen. "You don't have to. Mother is here. She's safe. I wouldn't leave her for a minute if I didn't think so."

When could he see the photograph?

"Anytime you like. I could bring it with me when I drop Karen off on Saturday. Dave, don't tell her anything. Not yet. Not till we decide what to do."

When Gail finally hung up, Anthony stopped pacing. "Is he coming with us?"

"No."

Standing directly over her, Anthony said, "Did he want to take her to his apartment?"

"I told him Mother is watching her."

"I'm going to move in. I don't believe that you or Karen are in any great danger, but even so, I need to be here."

"Maybe she should stay at Dave's. If . . . whoever is doing this is directing it at me, then maybe she should stay with him. What do you think?"

He made a soft laugh, barely audible. "That the timing is awfully convenient."

Gail stared up at him. "You think *Dave* sent that photograph?"

"I wouldn't rule it out."

"Oh, for God's sake! He would never do something so hideous. To his own daughter?"

"No. To you. To make you afraid—"

"That's insane."

He shook his head as if refusing to follow the argument further. "Fifteen years of criminal law—it makes you think the worst of anyone. Hidden motives. Lies." Anthony sat down and put his arm around her. "Gail, I don't know who sent that picture to you. What I do think is that it was meant to frighten you. A person who wants to kill doesn't usually spend his time telling you about it first."

"That's what one of the detectives told me. The younger one, Novick."

"You see?" He lifted her fingers to his lips. "It's going to be all right."

"What if it isn't? What if somebody wants to hurt Karen? Maybe that's what he wants. To hurt her to get to me."

"That won't happen. I won't allow it."

"Don't let him do anything to her. Please. I would die if anything happened to Karen!"

"*Niña,* don't." Anthony held her face. "Look at me. When I say something, you know that I mean it. Don't you? I love you, Gail. Nothing will happen to Karen. Or to you. I promise you this on my life."

TWELVE

Lola Benitez Couture. The gold script flowed across the red canvas awning that jutted over the sidewalk of Miracle Mile, between Mayor's Jewelers and Armani. With the heavy, polished brass door whispering shut on the traffic and heat outside, the shop seemed as secure as a bank vault.

Gail led Karen into a fantasy of crystal and gilt. Everything sparkled. Ultra-luxe career attire, evening wear along the opposite wall. Toward the back, traditional wedding gowns. In the center, beveled glass cases displayed jewel-like scarves and wispy lingerie.

There were a dozen women in the store, but Gail didn't see her mother, or Digna Pedrosa, or Elena—

"Mom, you're going to look stupid in a bride's dress."

"Who said I was going to wear one?"

Karen hadn't wanted to come along, but Gail had insisted. She was cautious but not fearful. Nothing had arrived in the mail yesterday, and there had been no odd numbers on caller-ID. At police headquarters Thursday evening, Detective Ladue had given the impression that the city had worse crimes to attend to. Yesterday Anthony had brought over three suitcases, a garment bag, and several boxes of personal papers. When Gail told Karen he was moving in, Karen had gone to her room and slammed the door. Gail decided against sending her to Dave's, reasoning that her own house was more secure, on a cul-de-sac where a strange person or car would be noticed. The counselors at Karen's day camp had been alerted to watch out for anyone taking photographs of the children. Short of hiring a body-guard, there was nothing more she could do.

Gail waded across some thick carpet to look at a raw silk jacket with feathers around the collar and cuffs. "Look, sweetie, isn't this gorgeous?"

"No." Karen crossed her arms over her striped polyester top, which hung loose outside baggy jeans. To complete this display of rotten temper, she had worn her oldest, rattiest sneakers. It had taken threats of being grounded again to make Karen brush her hair.

Gail was on the point of dragging her back outside for a lecture when someone called their names. "There you are!" Anthony's cousin Elena, arms out, came toward them in a stunning white linen dress and high-heeled sandals that showed off her red-painted toenails. "We just got here," Elena said. "Your mother is this way. Come on." She took them to the back, where a hall led to the fitting rooms.

"I found them!" she gaily announced.

This room was not a cramped little closet, but a space big enough to hold two cushy armchairs and a sofa. Digna Pedrosa sat with Xiomara and Betty, and Irene waved from one of the chairs. There was a table with a doilied tray of pastries and gold-rimmed cups for tea and espresso. Gail made her way around the room with kisses for everyone. No one here—except for Irene—knew about the photograph. Anthony had suggested it stay this way for now. If his relatives knew—especially the women—they were likely to throw themselves into a frenzy of worry.

Karen suffered through being asked if she liked the store, and wasn't it lovely, and wasn't she going to have fun helping her mother pick out a dress. Finally she slunk to a corner, where she sat on the carpet and put her forehead on crossed arms. Irene lifted her brows in that direction, and Gail answered with a tight smile.

A wheeled rack was waiting with a dozen dresses. The fitter was called, an ancient woman with a pincushion attached to her bosom. She took Gail behind a curtain, and Gail hung up her dress. The fitter deftly took her measurements and, in answer to Gail's inquiry, said in fractured English that she had been working for the Benitez family since she was a girl. The original store had been on Paseo del Prado.

Digna Pedrosa must have heard, because she said, *"Sí, sí, yo lo recuerdo bien."* She remembered it very well. The fashions had been always up-to-date, the latest from Paris and New York. But her wedding dress had not been purchased there. The family seamstress had sewn it for her, and she had worn it with a white lace mantilla that her grandmother had brought from Spain.

"Ernesto and I were married in nineteen thirty-eight in *la Catedral de la Habana*; then we walked to my family's house. We had champagne and hors d'oeuvres—but no dancing, no music. That's the way it was for us. The poor people had more fun!"

Through a crack in the curtain Gail could see Karen pretending not to listen to the women talk. The fitter dropped a dress over Gail's head.

Gail heard Irene's voice: "My mother and I bought my dress at Burdine's downtown, and then we went upstairs for lunch afterward to celebrate. I remember she was wearing a hat and white gloves. And she talked to me about marital love. That's what she called it." Irene giggled. "She said I might be shocked on my wedding night. Well, I wasn't *that* naive."

"I was." Digna's voice dropped to a murmur. Karen scooted closer. "Ernesto and I had kissed only a few times, when my aunt wasn't looking. I was never alone with him. On my wedding night . . . *Ay, mi Diós.* I cried and wanted to go right back to Havana, but I couldn't because we went for our honeymoon to Spain on a ship. First to New York, then to Europe. We were gone for three weeks, and when I came home . . . Well, I was very much in love with my dear Ernesto. And I was expecting our first child. A boy, Tomas." She was silent for a long moment, then crossed herself. "He was killed at Playa Girón by the communists."

The old woman finished pulling in the waist. Through a mouthful of pins she mumbled for Gail to show this one to the ladies. *"Vaya, enséñalas."* She held the curtain aside, allowing Gail, in borrowed pumps, to make a turn around the room.

The frothy pale ivory concoction made her feel she had been plunged feet first into a pile of meringue. There was appraisal. Comment. Dismissal. Karen rolled her eyes.

Behind the curtain again, Gail listened to a replay of her mother's wedding.

"Oh, it was just *huuuge*. Edwin and I were married at the Church of the Little Flower in the Gables, with a reception at the Riviera Country Club. The governor and his wife were there because my father was important in the state senate, and the whole thing was *so* political." Irene sat on the very edge of her chair with her legs crossed at the ankle, tucked away to one side, as if she were being interviewed for a vacancy in the garden club. Wooed, flattered, and seduced. Name-dropping like mad. And making sure that these women knew that her family had been pioneers in Miami and, before that, Carolina aristocrats, pre–Revolutionary War.

Just beyond the curtain, Karen had found some stray pins on the floor and was sticking them through the skin at the corners of her short fingernails. Gail whispered, "Karen, stop that!"

"It doesn't hurt." She waggled her fingers.

"Take those pins out this minute!"

"Mom, I'm bored. Can I go get something to drink?"

"No, stay here."

The fitter had just helped Gail off with a mint green taffeta thing that she'd known at first sight would not do when the curtain parted and Elena stuck her head in. "Hi. Can I show you this one?" Before Gail could reply, Elena murmured something in Spanish to the old woman, who nodded and went out. Elena held a champagne gold sheath under Gail's chin.

"This might look good with your hair." She put the hanger on a hook and opened the zipper. "Are you coming to the house afterward? Nena invited everyone for lunch. Did Anthony tell you?"

"Yes, we'll be there." Gail lifted her arms as Elena slid the dress over her head.

Elena's skin was pale as milk, a contrast to black hair cut bluntly at her shoulders. In a quiet voice she said, "I just wanted to tell you how happy I am that you're going to be part of our family. I've sensed sometimes that you don't feel comfortable with us. I hope I'm wrong."

Gail turned her back to be zipped up. "I don't know why you should think that. I'm very fond of all of you."

"I'm so glad." The zipper rose, and Gail sucked in her breath. The dress was a column of pale gold. Elena looked over Gail's shoulder, studying the fit. A pair of dark eyes met hers in the mirror. "Anthony's first wife was very sweet, but honestly, she didn't bring much to the marriage. The fact that you're *not* Latin is actually an asset for the family as well as for Anthony. So please don't feel like a stranger."

Gail smiled. "We won't be strangers. I know how important his family is to him." She turned sideways. Her hip bones protruded and her breasts had been flattened.

Elena squeezed Gail's arm. "I grew up with Anthony, so I know him very well. If you ever need advice, or somebody to talk to, I'm here for you. Okay? Remember."

"Yes. Thank you." Gail turned around. "Could you unzip this, please?"

A babble of voices drew their attention, and Elena pulled back the curtain. A woman had come in, purple caftan rippling as she crossed the room. A first impression said this was a woman in middle age—platinum blond hair was cropped at her ears, and her rouged cheeks were tight—but the veined hands and curved shoulders betrayed her. Seventy? Eighty?

Lola Benitez, without a doubt. She bent down to Digna

Pedrosa, and the women held each other lightly by the shoulders and pressed their cheeks together.

"*¿Cómo estás, mi amor?*"

"*Luces maravillosa, como siempre.*" You are looking as marvelous as ever, Digna told her.

Introductions were made, kisses given.

With a swirl of fabric Lola Benitez turned to Gail. "Ahhhh, *la novia*. The bride. How pretty you are. An elegant young woman. He will be happy, happy, happy." Señora Benitez's eyelashes were long, thick, and expertly attached. "Let me see the dress. I don't know. Maybe . . . more here." She lifted her own bosom, heavy as melons.

Karen put her hands over her mouth.

The lady imperiously turned to find the source of laughter. "And who is this?"

"Señora Benitez, my daughter, Karen."

Scrambling to her feet, Karen quickly held out her hand. "*Encantada, señora.*"

Lola Benitez took it in hers and pressed the other to her heart. "Oh! *Hablas español, que linda.*" Pursing her carefully outlined lips, she pressed her cheek to Karen's, then stepped back, holding her by the shoulders. "What a beautiful child! Skin like honey. And those eyes! So blue. I die. How old are you? No, no, don't tell me. Thirteen."

"Eleven," said Karen. "I mean, in about two weeks—"

"Oh, but you are so mature. Turn around, let me look at you. She has the shape of a model, so tall and slim, like her mother. I used to be pretty like you, Karen. It's true." She came closer, whispering, and her long lashes touched Karen's cheek. The fragile skin of her eyelids revealed the delicate veins beneath. "I broke the heart of many, many men. You will too, I see that clearly. What will you wear for the wedding, my lovely?" Señora Benitez made an arc with her open hand. "What kind of look do you want? Every woman must have a look."

"Well . . . I don't like lace. And I hate bows."

"Bows are for little girls, you are right. A sense of style

already, and so young." Señora Benitez snapped her fingers, and one of her assistants stepped forward. She told her to take *la jovencita* to look at the dresses. "Find a pair of shoes for her too. And stockings. And I think maybe a brassiere."

Karen gave Gail a wide-eyed look over her shoulder as she followed the clerk into the corridor.

With firm hands Señora Benitez swept Gail into the dressing area and pulled the curtain. Wooden rings clacked across the rod. She handed the gold silk sheath to the fitter, then made Gail stand on the pedestal. A finger to her cheek, she rested her elbow in her palm. Gail stared at the ceiling. Then Señora Benitez leaned through the curtain and ordered her assistant to bring the blue Louis Feraud gown from her office.

The dress was wheeled in on a rack, and the bag was unzipped as the ladies gathered around to watch. Señora Benitez lifted a padded hanger that held a silvery blue cascade of silk and organza. She took it into the dressing room, and she and the fitter helped Gail put it on.

Gail turned, staring at herself in the mirror. The color brightened her eyes and made her hair shimmer. The diagonal cut floated over hips and breasts, accenting what had seemed insignificant before. The neckline revealed her shoulders, which Señora Benitez judged particularly fine.

"Oh, my God."

"You were made for this dress."

"How much?" Gail turned her back to the mirror.

Señora Benitez tilted her head as if she hadn't quite heard.

"How much does it cost? It must be horrendous. I can't."

"But Mr. Quintana is paying for it. Yes! You did not know this? He called this morning. He said to let you have whatever you want and send the bill to him."

"I can't let him do that."

"You must!" Señora Benitez gave Gail a little squeeze around the waist. "If not, he will think you don't love him!"

"But how much—"

With a clacking of wood the curtain was flung back. "*Miren, todas.* Everyone!" She led Gail to the center of the room.

The women came nearer. "Not one ounce of fat," Xiomara said. "Not an ounce. I am so jealous."

"You look like a movie star," Betty said.

Digna Pedrosa blew a kiss from the sofa. Elena held out the skirt and let it slide from her fingers. "Beautiful."

Gail turned slowly in front of the triple mirror, and a laugh bubbled from her throat. "It is, isn't it? I mean, it really *is*."

Lola Benitez murmured, "He will love it. You will make him so proud."

Irene appeared with something in her hand. "Look, darling. Your grandmother's earrings. Put them on."

Gail did, but the diamonds were not as dramatic as she had recalled. They were smaller, almost pathetic in comparison to the elegance of the dress. The blue-white stone in her engagement ring sparkled more brightly. With a thrill that sent a tremor into her fingertips, Gail decided to go next to the jeweler's to find earrings that would do. She would mention it to Anthony. He would say yes. Yes, of course, *mi cielo,* whatever you want.

She heard a rustle and glanced toward the door. It took a moment for her mind to catch up to the reality that the girl who had come in was indeed Karen. Lilac silk skimmed her waist and flared into a froth of deep ruffles at her knee. Her feet looked tiny in sandals with delicate straps, and her legs glistened in hose the same shade as the dress. Someone had put her hair up in a knot, and strands of it framed her face. Her lips were glossy pink.

They stared at each other.

As the ladies rushed to see this new creature, Karen could not hold back a grin. She endured their caresses for a while, then went to stand beside Gail at the mirror. Lifting her chin, she studied herself through lowered lashes.

"This one's okay," she said. "Can I have it?"

* * *

After lunch Gail sat at the kitchen table, listening to Xiomara and Betty describe to Aunt Graciela in Spanish every detail of the dresses that Gail and Karen had chosen. Their husbands were watching a Marlins game, and Karen had gone somewhere upstairs with Elena's daughter. Digna was napping. Gail had lost track of everyone else, except Anthony, who an hour ago had kissed her cheek and said he and his grandfather's lawyer would be in the study for a while. But Ernesto Pedrosa had stayed in the kitchen. He parked Betty's stroller next to his wheelchair to make faces at the baby, who would respond with a toothless grin or wide-eyed stare, provoking chuckles from the old man.

Chin in her palms, Gail stole a quick glance at the clock on the stove: 2:10. She would give Anthony five more minutes, then see if he was ready to go. Fermina, the housekeeper, put away the last of the dishes in the glass-fronted cabinets. Gail remembered that two days' worth of dishes were waiting for her at home, and felt vaguely guilty about it.

Pedrosa held his eyes wide open with his fingers, and the baby's lower lip quivered. The old man laughed and gently patted his head with one huge, liver-spotted hand. *"No llores, machito."* Telling the little man not to cry.

Bernardo came in and took some beers from the extra refrigerator. Xiomara pretended to be shocked. "What is this? *¿Qué haces?"*

"Lighten up, woman. They're not all for me." Bernardo was forty and more than a few pounds overweight.

Gail wagged a finger. "No fighting."

"This isn't a fight!" Xiomara laughed. "The first time we had a fight—you remember our first fight, Nardo? Before we were married, we went to a friend's house for dinner, and you wanted me to serve your plate, and I wouldn't do it. I said, no, do I look like a servant to you? And you walked out! So I said okay, fine. Leave."

He grinned at Gail. "She married me anyway."

Ernesto Pedrosa turned to tap Gail's arm. "We were very useless men in Cuba. I remember my father and my uncle and I got up early to go fishing, before the women were awake. We boiled some eggs for breakfast, and my uncle had to ask my father how to open the egg to get it out of the . . . *cáscara*. What is that?"

"The shell," Betty said.

Laughing, cheeks going pink, Pedrosa mimed peering closely at an egg, shaking it, turning it around. "My uncle didn't know what to do with it."

Gail smiled. They would tell her these stories, explaining their culture as if she had just arrived from Nebraska. She didn't mind. It was good to be included. When the conversation moved on, switching to a discussion about what everyone was doing for the Fourth of July, Gail excused herself and went to find Anthony.

As she followed the long, tiled hallway, the voices and laughter faded. Her heels tapped on the floor, and she slowed as she walked past the paintings, a collection of contemporary Hispanic artists. She wondered what it would be like to live here, to throw parties. Gail held out her arms, seeing herself greeting guests. *Evelyn! Wally! I'm so glad you could come.* The paintings were lit, but even at midday there was something about this house that reminded her of the inner corridors of a castle. It ate light. It needed fewer curtains, a wall or two torn out, perhaps a skylight at the top of the stairs.

In the formal dining room the chandelier shone on polished wood. She wandered through the open double doors to the living room, pausing as if heads were turning upon her entrance. *Hello, everyone. Bienvenidos.* She smiled, presenting her cheek for an imaginary kiss.

A gold clock ticked on the mantel among the dozens of framed snapshots of grandchildren, nieces, and nephews. To the left of the fireplace, a wood-paneled door led to a small parlor. She turned the brass knob and went in, then pulled aside the fringed curtain to see out. The sun fell across a leather-topped side table, sparkling on a tiny crystal bird. Gail picked it up. Every corner of this house was filled with such treasures. No dust on any of them, no fingerprints around the light switches, no dead bugs under the furniture. A house like this required a maid, a cook, a gardener . . .

An odd sense that she was being observed made her glance toward the door. She involuntarily jumped, and the crystal bird slipped from her hand and dropped to the oriental rug. A split second later she recognized the gray suit and heavy glasses. Hector Mesa. It occurred to her that he had been waiting to see if she would slide the crystal into the pocket of her skirt. He watched Gail pick it up and set it back on the table, unbroken.

"I was looking for Anthony," she said, wishing too late that she had not made such an idiotic statement.

"He's in the study." Mesa's hands were loosely clasped in front. "He said that Karen has to be at her father's house soon, so he asked me to drive her there. You can go along if you want. I'll bring you back."

"I wouldn't dream of inconveniencing you. I'll borrow Anthony's car and take her myself."

Mesa hesitated, then said, "He's concerned for your safety."

Gail realized that Anthony had told Mesa everything. She automatically scanned his suit coat, finding no bulges but certain just the same that his .22-caliber Beretta was hidden on him somewhere. Karen had shown no distrust of this man. Indeed, she had found him geekily funny, but Gail did not like him. That he now stood at the door of this out-of-the-way room meant that he had followed her here, watching her slow progress through the house, making no sign of his presence.

She said, "That's very considerate of Anthony, but I'm sure we'll be all right. I'll speak to him. Has the lawyer left?"

"Yes, but Anthony is busy with some paperwork," Mesa said.

"Then I'll knock first."

With a slight nod, Hector Mesa stood aside to let her pass. His thinning white hair swept straight back over his skull and made frizzy little ringlets at his collar. He firmly closed the door.

Gail glanced back at him. "Tell me, Hector. What do you think about Anthony marrying an Anglo?"

"I have no opinion, *señora.*" She could not discern a reaction. His glasses hid his eyes, and he followed several paces behind her across the living room.

Over her shoulder Gail said, "You probably do, but you're right not to tell me."

"Nationality isn't so important," he said quietly. "His former wife was Cuban. Very beautiful, but greedy and ambitious. She married him for what he could give her, and when he found out the truth, he divorced her."

Barely holding on to her temper, Gail stopped and turned around. Mesa came no closer. "I'll make you a deal. You don't like me, and I don't like you. So let's keep out of each other's way. All right?"

She thought she saw his shoulders stiffen. Then he smiled, a slight lifting of the corners of his mouth. *"Con su permiso . . ."* He pivoted and vanished into the hall. She watched to make sure he was heading away from the study.

Ernesto Pedrosa's office was not a large room but completely masculine, with its old leather furniture, brass lamps, and dark wood wainscoting. A glass case held rare editions of poetry by José Martí. The desk was turned to the southwest, facing Havana, and a faded and torn Cuban flag hung from the wall behind it. Anthony sat with his forehead in his palm, writing. The lamplight gleamed on the waves in his brown hair and the heavy gold in his emerald ring. Cigar smoke curled from an ashtray.

Gail slid silently into the room, and his concentration was so complete that he did not notice her until she was almost on him. He leaned back to see who was there, and Gail fell into his lap. The big chair lurched on its wheels, then thudded back down.

"Ay, cuidado." Anthony laughed and held onto her.

"Smoking. Shame on you. Is that a Cuban cigar?"

"Don't tell the old man." He swiveled the chair to reach the ashtray, then took a last pull on the cigar and tapped the embers till it went out. He exhaled to the side, then smiled at the woman sitting in his lap. "Well. Look who dropped out of the sky."

Her legs hung over the broad arm of the chair. "Are you about finished?"

"It's going to take at least another hour. Did Hector find you?"

"Yes, he did, and no, I don't want him taking Karen to her father's. Let me borrow your car."

"If you can wait, I'll take you."

"Nothing's going to happen to us. Your car has tinted, shatterproof windows, for God's sake."

"You don't feel safer with Hector?"

"Frankly, no."

Anthony grinned. "Think of him as the family rottweiler. He won't bite you."

"I'm not family—not yet." Gail said, "Hector believes I'm after your money."

That brought a laugh. "No, he doesn't. I have to fight you to take it."

She played with the collar of his knit shirt, a deep burgundy one that brought out the warmth of his skin. "What is it with Hector? You said he used to shine shoes as a kid, and your grandfather brought him to Miami with the family. That isn't enough to turn anybody into a rottweiler."

"It was enough for Hector. In Cuba, both his parents were dead, and the aunt who took care of him was a whore. We were all he had. He promised my grandfather he would be of service someday." Anthony spoke softly. "There's a story, which you shouldn't repeat. My Uncle Tomás died at Playa Girón, as you know. He was among those captured. Because of his rank, they interrogated him, but all he would say was, *Viva Cuba libre, abajo Fidel.* One of the soldiers cut out his tongue and beat him to death in front of the others. The rest were eventually released, and when my grandfather found out what had happened, he wished the same fate on whoever had killed his only son. Twenty years later that same guard came over in the Mariel boatlift. And a few weeks after that . . . Hector brought my grandfather a small box."

A chill went down Gail's spine. "Was it a surprise package? Or did your grandfather ask him to do it?"

Anthony shook his head. "I don't know. And maybe it doesn't matter. That was a long time ago."

"Would you have done it for him?"

"No. Come on, what do you think I am?"

She swung her legs off the arm of the chair and sat on his thigh. The desk was covered with papers, stacks of documents, lists of figures. "What are you working on?"

"We're making an offer on a building in Fort Lauderdale. I'm going over the leases."

"We? Meaning you and . . . who?"

"Not me. Grandfather. His management company." From behind, Anthony put his chin on her shoulder. "Yes, Gail. I'm going to be helping him out for a little longer. His health is better. He's going to be around for a while, but . . . I don't know, he's not the same. He seems to have lost interest."

"Now that he has you, why not? Are you going to put a cot in the corner or sleep in your old room?"

"Gail." Anthony made a noise with his tongue. "How can I say no to him?"

"Be careful, will you? Too much of this, and there goes your law practice." She looked at him. "Anthony, does the rest of the family want you here? I get conflicting signals, especially from Elena."

"They do, they don't." He laughed softly. "They know that at the moment, at least, I'm in Ernesto's good graces. They want to know whose side I'm on, and I don't necessarily enlighten them. Xiomara and Bernardo want to divide up the businesses into separate companies. Elena and Jose want a family director-ship. Humberto, Alex, Graciela, the others all have their opinions. Nobody talks about it openly."

"Whose side are you on?" Gail asked. "Be honest, Anthony. What do you want?"

He looked at her for a long time, perhaps not trusting how she would respond to his answer.

She said, "Tell me. I want you to be happy. Not to be another Ernesto Pedrosa, or to do things in the way he has done them, but if you honestly feel this is where you need to be—"

"And you'd be with me?"

Her heart picked up speed, pushed by a rush of emotion. "Here?"

"Not now, but . . . I don't know. Someday. Perhaps."

She nodded slowly. "As long as you don't change who you are."

Releasing a held breath, Anthony rocked back far enough to look at the ceiling. "Of course it goes through my mind. Of course. But if I took over, it would be on my terms, not theirs. My grandfather has stayed too much with tradition. Too Cuban, if I can put it that way. Not part of the larger community. But why should they listen to me? I'm the outsider. They've been working for my grandfather for years, and here I am, coming at the last moment to take it away from them. I don't care if they love me or hate me, but I will have their respect, and I will not be anybody's puppet. You called me that, at the hospital."

"I shouldn't have."

"No one's puppet. Not for my grandfather, or a family directorate, or a committee, or the banks." He brought his gaze down to sweep across the room, over the old books, the yellowed photographs on the wall, the map of Havana, the memorabilia of decades of exile. He said, "There is too much of my father in me. They forget that."

"Luis, the revolutionary hero."

He smiled, then just as quickly narrowed his eyes. The normally slight Spanish accent became comically thick. "Luis Quintana Rodriguez, the son of a Santeria priestess who offered blood sacrifices to Chango and Eleggua." Anthony beat a slow, complicated rhythm on Gail's back. "I used to wake in the night and hear drums and chanting." His voice at her ear dropped to a whisper. "My grandmother Fulgencia, she used to twist the head off a chicken with her bare hands and drink the blood."

Gail made a face.

"I used to scare my cousins with stories like that."

"You must have been a terror."

"Let's just say we didn't get along."

"Elena said you and she were close."

"She said that?" Anthony laughed. "No, when my grandfather brought me out of Cuba, the oldest male grandchild—and maybe a substitute for my dead uncle Tomas, who can say?—my cousins hated me. Even Nena had her doubts."

"Digna didn't hate you. I would never believe that."

"No? I was the stain on the family honor. The physical reminder of what her youngest daughter did—not only to get pregnant at age sixteen, but worse, by the illegitimate son of a cane cutter. They could count six generations back to Spain, never a drop of black blood till my father. He was only one quarter, but Nena beat my mother when she found out she was pregnant. I never told you. You think Nena is so refined, such a lady. When I came to Miami, I wouldn't behave, I wanted to go home, let me go back to Cuba, I hate it here. She used to scream at me, your father is a communist, and you are just as bad. My cousins would call me names. Hey, *negrito*. Who is your father? My skin was as white as theirs, but if I hit them, they would tell our grandfather, and he would come after me with his belt. The funny thing is, my sister Alicia has the same blood as me, but she was never treated that way. You know why? Because she has the Pedrosa eyes—blue."

Gail looked at him wonderingly. "You still resent it, don't you? Almost thirty years, you're still angry."

"Not at all."

"Oh, you want to rub their noses in it. Yes. To take over from

Ernesto Pedrosa, *you,* the son of Luis Quintana Rodriguez, married to a blond American lawyer, coming in here to sit at this desk, maybe fire half of them for incompetence and make the others work as hard as you do. Scary."

Smiling, he stared down at the papers, ruffling the edges between thumb and forefinger. "Maybe it's not worth it. I don't know."

Gail shifted on his lap to put her arms around him. "I love you."

He focused on her face. "*Y yo te quiero más.* I would do anything for you, Gail. Sometimes I don't know where I belong. But there you are."

"Here I am." She smiled and kissed him, each corner of his mouth, then in the center, where his lips were warm and moist. She murmured, "I want to be good for you. So good."

"We're going to be good together," he said. "Wait and see."

"Anthony, I feel funny about letting you buy me those earrings." When he started to protest, she said, "All right, the dress. But the earrings. I shouldn't—"

"No, no." He nibbled her earlobe. "I like aquamarines. They would be beautiful with your eyes. I'll buy them. But you have to be good."

"Oh, is that how it is?" She struggled to get up, but he held her more tightly. She elbowed him.

"Ow, my head!"

"You deserve it." Laughing, she put her forehead against his. "I'm sorry for being such a pain about our house. My office has been on my mind. If you want to remodel, fine with me, but *after* the wedding. Maybe even a pool, but of course this means the yard will be a mud pit for months."

"Oh, my God! At last she is being reasonable."

She put her arms around his neck. "Spoil me. Go ahead."

"Should I?" He whispered against her lips, "Show me how good you are." She opened her mouth to him, and his kiss was long and slow and deep, tasting of smoky tobacco and below that, a complicated mix of rich coffee, bourbon, and Anthony himself. He moved under her, and she felt the hardness against her thighs. His hands slid down her back, over her hips. His tongue went deeper. She heard her own low moan. Then gradually realized where they were.

"Anthony." She pushed on his chest. "The door is open."

With a heavy exhalation that turned to a laugh, he said, "You should get up. I need to finish here."

"Do you have to do it now?"

"Unfortunately, yes. Tomorrow I have some cases to prepare, and a hearing on Monday. I'm so far behind. This thing with Karen—"

"Tell me about it. I hardly got anything done yesterday." Gail turned to look at him. "Did you speak to Harry Lasko?"

"What?"

"Anthony, you said you would do it on Friday. Wendell Sweet didn't deliver his documents, I doubt they'll come Monday either, and I really need to talk to Harry. I've only got three more weeks to track down Wendell's money."

"Oh, yes. Okay. I'll call him next week."

"Monday," she said. "And don't forget."

Anthony said patiently, "Look, Gail. Even if you find Wendell's money, your client is out of luck. The Bank of So-and-so might have an account in his name, but they won't let you have it, not even with a court order. Our courts have no jurisdiction—"

"Anthony. Darling. I *know* how it works. All I want to show is proof. I don't need to *take* it. Harry said Wendell made a million dollars from the Eagle Beach casino. Does Harry have any proof? Where's the closing statement? If I could show the judge that Wendell made that money, lied about it, and hid it offshore, he's going to award everything else to Jamie. She needs it, Anthony. She's right on the edge."

"All right, I'll talk to Harry and find out what's going on. But I am going to remind you, *bonboncita,* not to take this into your own hands." When Gail frowned at him, he lifted his brows. "What? What did I say?"

"Don't call me *bonboncita* when we're discussing legal matters."

"*Por Diós.* Yes, Ms. Connor, I am so sorry."

"I'm serious."

"You don't look very serious in this position, Ms. Connor." With one arm tightly locking her against her body, he pulled up her skirt.

"Stop it! Anthony!"

"Ms. Connor, where is your dignity?"

"I said, stop it!" She knocked his arm away and twisted out of his grasp to stand up.

For several seconds he looked up at her, both surprised and quizzical. He glanced to one side as if for an answer, then made a slight smile. "What did you do that for?"

She raked her fingers through her hair, smoothing the tangles. "I don't like it. Not in that context."

"*Ay, mi madre, me vuelves loco.* Let me finish this, then we can go."

Gail smoothed the creases out of her skirt and straightened a sleeve. "I have to take Karen to her father's place. I might as well go now."

"Let Hector take her."

"I don't *want* him to take Karen. Anyway, Dave wants to talk to me."

"Talk to you about what?"

"The photograph. What we can do. What to tell Karen."

Anthony leaned back in the chair. Color was rising up the planes of his face, and his eyes darkened. "If the photograph was that important to him, he could have come by our house."

"Not with you there. He said it would be awkward."

The chair rocked slowly. "Awkward. An interesting word. Was it his? Or yours?"

"Don't start."

"He doesn't want to see me face to face?"

"No more than you want to see him. I need to borrow your car. Please?"

Anthony sat without moving for a few more seconds, then

stood up and reached into his pants pocket. "I don't like you going over there."

"I know you don't."

"Why do you do it when you know I don't like it?"

She held out her hand. "The keys."

He tossed his key ring onto the desk.

She said, "You couldn't have given them to me? You have to throw them at me."

"I didn't throw them at you."

Her hand was still extended. "Give me the damned keys or I will call a taxi."

He hooked the key ring with one finger. The gold-trimmed Cadillac ignition key turned slowly. She reached out. He pulled the keys away before dropping them into her palm.

"I would like you back here within an hour."

Gail slammed the door on her way out of the study.

THIRTEEN

Dave's town house was one of a dozen in a U-shaped building, parking lot in the center, patios in back. A metal picket fence and electronic gate gave residents some protection against the urban crime that lurked at the fringes of Coconut Grove.

Karen would be spending the night and going with her father to a tennis tournament in the morning. She had brought her bag and her racquet, and on the short trip from the Pedrosas' house she had taken her hair out of the intricate knot acquired at Lola Benitez, and had brushed it into its usual style, a ponytail.

Gail pressed the buzzer. She had never been past the front door of Dave's apartment. She had seen it only from the walkway, dropping Karen off or picking her up, a glimpse of a tiled entrance and two bicycles.

The front door opened, and Dave held out his arms. "Heyyyy, it's my princess." He kissed Karen, then stood aside to let her pass. To Gail he said quietly, "One of the girls from the restaurant is going to watch her for a while."

The girl was the dark-haired waitress named Vicki, whom Gail had last seen behind the bar at the Old Island Club—there in tropical print shirt, here in a tank top and jogging shorts, glancing at Gail with brown eyes under upward-tilting brows.

She picked up her car keys and a fanny pack from the kitchen counter and spun herself off the stool.

Dave told Karen that he and her mom had to talk. They'd go to the marina later, but right now, what about a video at Vicki's apartment? Karen's lack of curiosity told Gail that she had been there before.

"Bye, Mom." She reached up for a hug.

"See you tomorrow, sweetie. Have a good time." Gail watched them go, her daughter and the woman with the tanned, muscular legs. The door clicked shut.

Dave came back in. He said, "Vicki and I aren't sleeping together."

"I didn't ask."

"You were wondering."

Gail lifted a shoulder. "Okay, I was wondering."

"And now you know. You want something to drink? A soda? Beer?"

"Just water. And a couple of pain relievers if you have any."

"Sure." He told her to have a seat. "Sorry for the mess. Things have been crazy at the Club. Welcome to my humble home."

"It's nice."

"I try."

Leaving her purse on the counter, Gail wandered farther into the living room. Past the dining area, which was tiled, the carpet was that neutral berber ubiquitous to rental apartments. Sports magazines and newspapers littered the coffee table. The brown leather sofa faced the entertainment center, with its enormous television and on either side black glass doors behind which winked the amber lights of a stereo system.

Stairs led to the second floor.

What did he do here? What was his life like, a single man of thirty-six? Gail realized that she knew exactly. She walked over to the patio door and saw the gas grill that she had expected would be there. He would have his friends over to watch sports on TV. He would barbecue some ribs, boiling them first in beer to make them tender. She knew the contents of the refrigerator,

and that in the trash she might find a folded pizza box—pep-
peroni and mushroom.

Two bedrooms upstairs. Gail did not know what Karen's
looked like, but about Dave's she had little doubt. If the bed was
made at all, the comforter would be pulled up over rumpled
sheets. He would probably have some condoms in the nightstand but no sex toys or dirty videos. His two good suits would
hang in garment bags in his closet, and slacks and some dress
shirts would be in plastic from the dry cleaners. He had dozens
of T-shirts, souvenirs of places he'd been or teams he liked. She
knew the shape of his shoes, the way his long first toes made a
bump in the leather. His closet would have the musty, male
smell of clothes tossed back on the shelf, not quite dirty enough
to require washing. Gail had complained, then given up. She'd
had her own closet, her own dresser, and her own side of the
bathroom vanity.

He liked to floss his strong, square teeth in bed while
watching the news, then turn it off with the remote and drop
the floss in a little pile on the nightstand to be picked up in the
morning, if he remembered. Then he'd turn off his lamp. When
they'd been married, her lamp would be on longer, and he'd
usually be asleep when she put her files away. She learned to
ignore the dental floss, and he learned to sleep with the light on.
If he was not asleep, he might roll toward her and put a hand on
her hip. *Are you tired?* Toward the end of their marriage the
answer had been yes so often he had stopped asking. But before
that, when things had been more or less okay, their lovemaking
had fallen into a pattern both comforting and predictable. Her
attempts at variation had been met with mild embarrassment.

Had he cheated on her in the twelve years of their marriage?
Gail did not think so, but the affairs would have been brief and
inconsequential. Dave had been more in love with the house.
He had kept a big red metal tool chest in the garage. Shelves
sagged with home-improvement manuals, garden sprays, and
fertilizer. Their lawn had been free of nematodes, chinch bugs,
mildew, and weeds. He had installed the sprinkler system him-

self, then stood in the center of the yard and told Gail to flip the switch. He had waited, hands on hips, feet spread, sunburn on his big shoulders, hard muscles in his legs, sneakers soggy with dirt. The pump had come on with a hum, pushing water through the pipes, the fittings, the sprinkler heads. Then the water hissed out in neat circles or semicircles to fit the shape of the yard, sunlight making rainbows over the thick grass and neat flower beds. Dave had strode around the yard with his screwdriver and wrench, adjusting heads, getting soaked, just for the pleasure of watching it go.

That he had wanted out of their marriage had surprised her. That he had sailed away to the Caribbean had not, because Dave was by nature a dreamer. Gail had stood on firmer ground. She knew how much things cost, how much debt his business was in, and what was needed to turn it around. Five businesses in twelve years, then the marina, the last fiasco. His dreams had done them in. So off to the Caribbean, away from everything. But he had come back. He said he had changed, but Gail doubted it. And if he said that he wasn't sleeping with Vicki-the-waitress, it meant he wasn't sleeping with her *at present*, though he probably had. Why else would a woman in jogging shorts agree to baby-sit indoors on a perfect Saturday afternoon?

Dave came out of the kitchen with a glass of water, ice tinkling against the sides. He put a coaster on the coffee table and gave her two pills. "That's ibuprofen. You shouldn't take aspirin on an empty stomach. I wasn't sure if you'd eaten. Is it bad?"

"Is what bad?"

"Your headache."

She swallowed the pills with some water. "It's been worse."

"You look like shit," he said.

"Oh, thanks."

"Want me to rub your neck?" He used to do that for her when the pain had been bad enough to make her cheekbones ache. His blunt-fingered hands were strong and sure. But she didn't want him touching her.

"I'm okay," she said, then laughed. "It's been . . . an interesting week."

His sun-blond eyebrows were drawn together. He was waiting for her to expand on that. She thought of telling him about Anthony. A long time ago she and Dave had talked to each other about anything, and he had always listened. He hadn't always come up with the answer she needed, but he had listened.

Gail said, "I brought the photograph."

"Okay. Well, let's have a look."

He followed her to the dining table, where she opened her purse and withdrew a small brown mailing envelope. She unfolded the clasps. Dave put his hands on his hips, blowing out a breath, preparing himself to see what Gail had already described over the telephone. The envelope slid out, color copy inside. Dave lifted the flap. His jaw shot forward, and his lips twisted as if he had tasted something vile. He swallowed.

Finally he set it down, and Gail could see the colors against the light wood of the tabletop. Blue sky and trees. The children's clothing. Karen's red shorts. And the immense black pistol aiming at her head. The three straight lines that marked the trajectory, the curves that indicated smoke, and the bullet crashing through her skull.

Dave spun around and walked stiffly to the sliding door, his back to the room. He sucked in a breath through his nose, and she heard the snuffle of liquid. He was close to tears. *"Fuck!"*

She folded the copy into its white envelope. Calmer now, Dave looked around and cleared his throat. "What did the police say?"

"There's nothing to go on. It's a common envelope, and anyone can make a color copy at a print shop. Mother and I handled the paper, so it would be hard to find fingerprints. He probably didn't leave any. There weren't any prints on the paint can. We assume it's related. The phone calls as well." Gail squared up the envelope with the grain in the table. "We might get more photographs. Letters, calls. Whatever. They've had cases of harassment that go on for months. Years."

"Jesus."

"They said it's good if he does send more. We might find out who." Gail picked up the envelope. "Do you want a copy?"

"No. Take it with you. I don't want it around." Dave blew out another breath. "Is she safe, Gail? What are we going to do to keep her safe?"

"I don't let her go out as much. She's never by herself. Anthony is living with us now. He has a gun, and there's an alarm system. We don't think anyone's going to break in. And the police say that a killer usually doesn't advertise his plans in advance."

Dave paced around the living room, thinking. "We could send Karen to my folks' house for the rest of the summer. What about that?"

"She wouldn't like it."

"I don't *care* if she likes it."

"I want her here, Dave. I don't want her out of my sight. It even makes me nervous to see her go with Vicki."

"She's fine. Vicki's place is a block from here."

For a while they talked about who might have done it. An angry client. A neighbor. Even the possibility that it was some-one Dave knew. Or someone Anthony Quintana knows, Dave suggested. Or Anthony himself.

Gail gave him a look.

"Why not? You get this photograph, the next thing you know, he's moving in."

"You're saying he sent it? That's funny. He said the same thing about you."

"If that's what he thinks, the man is sick. Truly sick."

They discussed what to tell Karen, if this happened again, and came to no conclusions. Maybe it wouldn't happen again. They would wait.

Gail asked if she could see Karen's room. "I'd like to know what it looks like."

"Sure." He led her up the stairs.

It was a small, sunny room across from his, with its own bath. In the old house on Clematis Street, with its wood floors and heavy stucco walls, Karen's tastes had gone modern. Here was a canopy bed with ruffles. A poster from the movie *Titanic* hung beside the dresser, stuffed animals covered the bed, and crystals on fishing line brightened the windows, sending rainbows dancing around the room when Gail set them swinging.

"This is pretty." She smoothed the lacy coverlet, then picked up a stuffed Paddington bear. "A neighborhood boy kissed her. Did she tell you about that? He's fourteen. Sort of cute, but she didn't want him to, and she got mad at him."

"Fourteen! I ought to talk to the kid's father."

Gail shook her head, smiling. "I've seen her watching him, and naturally he pays her no attention. She says he has a girlfriend who's thirteen."

"She's growing up too fast," Dave said.

As if her limbs were weighted, Gail sat on the small chair by the bed and closed her eyes.

"Are you okay?"

"I haven't slept much lately." He stood beside her, resting a palm on her hair. She said, "I don't know what to do, Dave. I try to tell myself I'm not scared, but that's a lie."

He squeezed her shoulder. "I know. It scares me too. They've got to find this son of a bitch."

"I think it's me he's after, not Karen. Someone wants me to suffer. I don't know who or why. I don't have a clue. If I knew what I had done, I'd fix it. I'd pay him, and if he doesn't want money, I could write elaborate letters of apology. On the phone, that first time, he said, 'Hello, bitch. Time to die.' I keep thinking, What have I done?" She laughed. "Oh, this is prompting all sorts of insights into the darkest corners of my mind. What sins have I committed that someone wants me to suffer like this?"

"Sins? What are you talking about? You ticked somebody off. Hell, maybe it's somebody you cut off in traffic, and he's doing this for the thrill. People are crazy."

"No. It's too personal."

He was stroking the back of her neck, and she didn't tell him to stop. Birds chirped outside the window, and a patch of sunlight fell on the carpet. Rainbows were still twirling across it.

"I haven't done this in a long time," he said.

She shifted to get up.

"No, don't. Aren't we friends, at least? Gail, I'm not going to attack you. Give me some credit."

"I shouldn't be here," she said.

"Yes, you should. That's the damn shame of this whole situation." He leaned over to press his lips to the top of her head. He stayed there a moment, his fingers moving gently over her temple. She felt his warm breath in her hair when he said, "You know, I've been seeing a counselor since I got back. Me. I never believed in that. Anyway, it's helping." He patted her shoulder and stood up.

"Jesus, you're so tense," he said. "Come on, just let me fix this. You remember that time you came home from a week in trial and it was so bad you couldn't turn your head?"

"Drugs," she said, laughing. "I need heavy drugs."

"You need to meditate and do some yoga."

"Dave, tell me you are not doing yoga."

"I have a video. Does that count?" He moved his thumbs down either side of her spine. "I've been working on letting go of a lot of issues. Like our marriage. I know why we had problems. You were—and are—a strong woman, and I didn't know how to deal with that. You always made more money, and on some level it bothered me. I had a lot of unprocessed anger. I wasn't really angry at you but at myself. Do you understand what I mean? When I filed the lawsuit to get custody of Karen, it was like: Look, I am capable of being a good father. A good man. A success in my business."

Dave stopped what he was doing and came around to sit on the edge of Karen's bed, facing Gail. "You want to hear some good news?"

"Sure."

"The franchise deal is going through next week. I didn't tell you before who I'm dealing with. It's Marriott. As in hotel."

"No."

"Did I tell you? Golden." He laughed, delighted. "They wanted the name and I have it. Now they're going to put an Old Island Club in every Marriott resort in Florida and the Caribbean. I didn't want to say anything till I was sure."

"Dave, that's wonderful. Congratulations. It's fantastic."

"There's going to be money coming in like you never saw. I can get a house with a yard, a pool. And a dock, because I want to buy another boat. Not a sailboat, a cabin cruiser. What do you think?"

"Me?" In a rush of comprehension she saw that he wanted her approval. "Well, I think a boat would be a great idea. But don't spend it till you have it."

"Oh, no, of course not. It's an investment. I could take the customers out. And Karen and I could take trips, wherever we wanted." But in the space of seconds the joy in his eyes faded, as if someone had yanked shut the curtains over the window. He reached for her hand and brushed his thumb over her engagement ring. "I could do this too."

She pulled her hand away. "I'd better go."

When she stood up, Dave put his arms around her. His mouth searched for hers, but she turned her head.

His forehead rested on her shoulder. "Two days ago I kissed you, and you kissed me back. Why did you want me to bring you upstairs? You know why." He held on more tightly. "You know what's right, but you're afraid to admit it. We need to be a family again. You. Me. Karen. She needs both of us."

"Stop it." With an effort she pushed him away.

His face was flushed, and his eyes glistened. "I almost called my lawyer today. I almost told him to drop the custody case, but something told me to hold back."

Gail stared at him. "But outside Fischman's office you said we could work this out."

"Well, I just changed my mind. Somebody has to care about

our daughter." Dave caught Gail's arm. "Your marriage won't last. I'm sorry to say that, because I don't want to see you unhappy, but it's bound to happen. I wish I had some magic words to make you wake up. I can't fight him for you. Jesus. He'd probably have me shot. But he is going to lose you. One way or the other, whether it's because you leave him or he finds some other woman, and when that happens, I hope—I pray—that you remember one thing. I loved you."

Gail drove the Cadillac to a shady park near the water and stopped with the engine running and the air conditioner on. At irregular intervals, feathery needles and hard brown seedlings dropped from the pine trees, tapped on the roof, and slid down the windshield. She watched a man throwing a Frisbee to his dog. Bicyclists. No joggers in this heat. She cried for a while, then rummaged in the glove compartment for a napkin and found nothing but neatly folded maps, a small flashlight, and the car manual. She reused her soggy Kleenex, then tilted the leather seat back. Her head spun, and she seriously wondered if she was going crazy.

She thought about what she would tell Anthony.

Nothing.

Or how she would explain the fact that she was late.

Sorry. Deal with it.

If he became angry, she would remind him of his own behavior, throwing the keys in a jealous pique.

But she would certainly not disclose what Dave had said to her. It would be impossible, in any event, to follow his abrupt turns in logic and make sense of the contradictions. Not that Gail couldn't see the point: Dave wanted his life put back. He wanted her. And Gail had been profoundly astonished to feel, when his hands had been gently massaging her neck, a sinister uncurling of desire.

This would not be the first time she had withheld the truth from Anthony. He had asked her if she had ever thought of going back to Dave. This question had come after he had made love to her upstairs in his grandfather's house. Put his mark on her, then assured himself that there was no reason to suspect her loyalty. And she had lied. Who would not have lied at that moment?

A lie to avoid misunderstanding. To keep his feelings from being hurt. Not even a lie but an avoidance of an issue that had become irrelevant. Or so she had told herself at the time.

A few months after she and Anthony had become involved, and just after her divorce had become final, Dave showed up at the house late one night. He had been drinking. He wanted to come back, to try again, and when she said no, he had wept.

Go home, Dave.

I don't have a home anymore.

For God's sake, you'll wake Karen.

Gail, don't turn me away. I need you. I can't live without you.

She could reconstruct the events of that night and see herself walking to the front door, opening it. Telling him to leave. Gently, and without hesitation: *Dave, please go.* Then the sound of his pickup truck fading from the quiet street.

But it hadn't happened that way. They had gone to bed. She had wanted to be sure. Or hadn't wanted to hurt him. Or had done it simply out of habit. Easy to be with Dave. And easy to let him go. She had told him before dawn that he couldn't stay, and he'd left without protest. The next day she had called him. *It's over, Dave.*

Of course she had lied to Anthony. In matters of sex, truth was a matter of interpretation, and by then she had been aware of his jealousy and pride. The truth—or what he thought was the truth—would have eaten away at them like acid.

After repairing her makeup, Gail put the car into gear and drove back to Coral Gables, turning onto Malagueña Street and parking behind the high iron gates of the Pedrosa house. She had been gone over two hours.

Anthony was watching the last inning of the Marlins game. She said she was sorry for being late, and he gave her his usual shrug—the slight lift of shoulders and brows, a downturn of his mouth. They waited until the game was over, then said their good-byes to his family, most of whom were leaving too.

As the car turned out of the driveway, she unfolded her sunglasses and put them on. "We were thinking of sending Karen to stay with Dave's parents in Delray Beach."

"I told you, nothing is going to happen to her. If you want a bodyguard, I'll get you one."

"Nothing scares you, does it?"

He glanced at her but said nothing.

Sunlight flickered through the branches of a poinciana, a brilliant canopy of red and bright green. Around a curve they entered a dark tunnel of ficus trees. He waited until the stop sign at the end of the street to ask, "Did you make love to him?"

Her exhalation of breath was so sharp it could have been a laugh. "Are you crazy? No. We didn't make love. He didn't kiss me. I showed him the color copy, and that's what we talked about. That and Karen and what the hell we're supposed to do about it."

Anthony said, "I'm sorry. It was a terrible question, but it was going through my mind because I know what he wants."

"In your imagination."

"No. It's in his eyes when he looks at you." Gail was glad for her sunglasses, but he seemed to look through them. "If I were Dave," he said, "and I had lost you, I would want you back. I would hate the man who has you, and I would do nothing but think of ways to take you away from him."

"Well, Dave isn't you, is he?"

"It hasn't occurred to you—not at all—that he did this? That he is the one person who could have come that close with a camera and nobody would have thought it strange? The photograph brought you to his house."

"Oh, please."

"Didn't it?" The dark eyes searched her face. "What did he say, I wonder? What would get to you? Our daughter is better off with mommy and daddy in the same house. Did he say that? I would have. Yes. We make an appeal to your mother-hood. You might even forget that he never contacted Karen for weeks at a time."

"Anthony, leave it alone," she said through clenched jaws.

He glanced in the rearview mirror, then accelerated through the stop sign. There was not much traffic on Saturday afternoon in this part of the Gables. His long fingers tapped on the curve of the steering wheel, and his ring glittered.

"What else would I say if I were Dave? That I need you? Need. Yes, that's a word he would use."

Gail glared at him. "Not a word that Anthony Quintana would use, is it?"

"You're right. It's not my word. I want you. I love you. But I don't need you. There's a difference. He needs you because he's a loser. He needs your money and your brains. He needs to lean on you, like he leaned on you for twelve years in your marriage."

"How reassuring it must be to think that," she said. "Dave is doing quite well. Next week he will sign a contract to franchise his restaurant with Marriott hotels, with more to follow. It's apparently a lucrative deal, and I'm very happy for him."

"How nice. If it succeeds."

"It will, but I'm sure you hope otherwise."

Anthony glanced out the side, then took a right. They were on Granada Boulevard, passing one luxurious home after another. "Why did he tell you about this deal? Did you ask yourself that? This deal that will make him so much money? Because he wants you to think he can support you. He wants to be petted on the head like a dog. And we like dogs because they never challenge us, never question what we do. Go fetch, Dave. Be a good boy."

"Shut up, Anthony."

"What else did he say? That I'm Cuban, and don't all *latinos* cheat on their wives?"

With her fists she came down hard on his shoulder, and the car jerked, then straightened. "I said shut up! Dave was never as irrational, so jealous, so emotionally violent, as you are. Jealousy is not attractive. I am not flattered by it. If you want to make me unhappy, if you *want* me to leave, then just keep it up!"

They drove the rest of the way in silence. Gail turned her face to the window, so tense that the muscles in her neck sent white flashes of pain down her spine.

When they arrived at the house on Clematis Street, Anthony took the mail out of the box and found another plain white envelope with Gail's name on it.

He held it out of her reach and opened it, and his expression turned icy.

Gail demanded to see it, and he showed her.

As if at a long distance, she saw herself sinking to the floor, Anthony catching her. In the bathroom in the downstairs hall, she threw up until her throat was raw. He helped her to the bedroom. When she wanted to call Dave to tell him about it, Anthony brought her the telephone. She made Dave promise to keep Karen inside and to tell her nothing, not until they had decided what to say.

Around two o'clock in the morning, she woke up, trembling violently. A small lamp was on. Anthony had dressed her in her nightgown.

"Come here." He pulled her into his arms.

She had dreamed of the knife in the photograph. Someone cutting Karen into pieces, flesh from bone, such honey soft flesh. The knife enters, severing muscles and arteries, slashing open the breasts still unbudded. A gush of blood soaking her long hair, filling her mouth, bubbling in the severed throat. It's too quick for pain, but there is terror more hideous than pain, seeing the body sundered, the inner parts spilling out, the knife flashing upward, then down, again and again.

He held her tightly. "Gail, you're all right. Karen is all right. I sent someone to make sure. Nothing will happen to her. I swear it." He kissed her forehead and told her again that Karen was safe.

Finally she slept.

FOURTEEN

Flowers were delivered to Gail's office on Wednesday morning, an arrangement of six red roses with green fern and sprigs of baby's breath. Miriam, thinking that perhaps Anthony had sent them, carried the flowers back to Gail's office and waited, smiling expectantly, for Gail to open the card. Lynn peered in from the hall.

Gail, who was eating lunch at her desk, put aside her sandwich. Anthony had not sent them, she knew that immediately. His would have been deep pink roses, not red ones. This was a cheap arrangement in a plain glass vase.

"Those are nice," Lynn said, coming in a little farther. "Tom bought me red roses for our anniversary last week."

A small envelope was held aloft by a plastic holder stuck through the foliage. Her name had been printed by a computer. GAIL CONNOR. Underneath that, the office address.

Another envelope—the third one—had appeared in her mailbox on Monday. The police had told her not to open any more of them, so she had taken it still sealed to the detectives working the case. They had hoped for fingerprints but found nothing. It had been another photograph of Karen at play, but Gail had not wanted to see it. Her dreams had been bad enough.

"Tell us who. We're dying to know." Miriam crossed her arms and rotated her foot on the heel of her pump.

Gail took the envelope out of the holder and slipped out the small, flat florist's card. When her vision came back into focus, she cleared her throat and said, "Miriam, who brought these?"

"Someone from Exotic Gardens." Picking up something in Gail's tone, Miriam looked at Lynn.

"Right." Lynn's blond hair fell to one side as she tilted her head. She frowned at the roses as if they might be a toxic species someone had slipped past her. "What's the matter?"

Gail's hands trembled as she lifted the vase, took it to the bathroom in the hall, poured out the water, then dropped the flowers into the trash and tied up the bag. The women stared at her.

"I need to talk to both of you. Come back to my office, please."

They mutely followed, sitting side by side on the sofa under the window, Miriam in her red miniskirt, Lynn as plain as a potato. Gail showed them the message.

With sympathy on the loss of your daughter. From Renee.

"Oh, my God," Miriam whispered. Her brown eyes widened. "Oh, Gail."

"But Karen's not—" Lynn looked again at the card. "Who is Renee?"

Gail took the card from her. "My sister. She died over a year ago."

Lynn's mouth fell open. "Why is her name here?"

"Because someone is using her death as a sick joke." Gail pulled a chair closer and sat down, crossing her legs. She refused to allow emotion into her voice. "You know that someone has been harassing me. The phone calls, the paint on my car? That isn't all. There have been three photographs. Now these flowers. They were sent here, to the office, so I think you need to know the rest of it. This person—whoever he is—has decided that I wouldn't scare easily. So now he's using Karen."

She described the pictures—not in detail, but it was enough

to make Miriam press her fingertips to her mouth and stifle a cry. Lynn sat silently staring.

"We're working with the police, naturally. I spoke to them last on Monday. Looks like I'll be going again this afternoon."

On Monday she and Anthony had taken the second photograph to the Miami Police Department headquarters downtown, a modern red-brick building a few blocks from the courthouse. Dave had met them there. The men had minded their manners, knowing what was important—this vile thing that depicted the butchery of a young girl. Toward the police Anthony had maintained icy control; Dave had demanded that they do something, find the bastard, call in the FBI.

Gail said, "They told me not to open any mail that looks suspicious, but take it directly to them so they can examine it for fingerprints. If we get anything like that here, don't open it, just bring it to me. All right?"

Lynn and Miriam nodded.

"I don't expect you to have any problems, but you should be aware, in case you see something unusual. I'm being very cautious, especially with Karen."

Miriam scooted forward to grab Gail's hand. "Why would anybody *do* this?"

"Because they're crazy. Who knows why?"

Lynn's voice shook. "I wouldn't have signed for them if I'd known."

"No, it's better you took them. The police told me that every time he makes contact he leaves a clue. Maybe the florist will remember who placed the order, or trace the charge." Gail stood up. "Okay, back to work. God only knows how many potential clients were clamoring at the door while we talked."

She called out to Lynn to wait a moment.

"Yes?"

"I wonder if you could call Charlie Jenkins for me. You remember him. He worked on my wiring. Now the air conditioner is about to die." She flipped through her Rolodex. "I shouldn't have let it go for so long. We woke up last night sweating."

She was copying Charlie's number when the phone rang. She punched the intercom. Miriam told her that Theresa Zimmerman was on the line. Could Gail take it?

"Oh, God." The client with the bad knee, whom Gail had meant to call back on Friday. "All right, I'll take it." Gail doodled dollar signs on her legal pad, then 28,000. "Hello, Theresa. I'm sorry I didn't get right back to you. It's been so hectic." Ms. Zimmerman wanted to know when she could collect her money from the insurance settlement. "Probably on Friday," Gail told her. "It was an out-of-state check, and they always take longer. . . . Yes, call me Friday, and I'll make sure the funds are available."

She hung up, then stared at the telephone. "Believe me, I'll be as happy as you to see that check clear."

Lynn said, "The check is good, isn't it? Couldn't you just give her the money?"

"No, because if, by some remote chance, the check bounced, I wouldn't have money for the next client, and he'd tell the Florida Bar. Lawyers get in trouble screwing around with their trust accounts."

"Oh."

"Here's Charlie Jenkins's number. See if he can come around five o'clock."

When Lynn was gone, Gail stood by the window, noticing how normal the world seemed on the other side of the glass. Traffic flowed on the expressway, and the mall had its usual crowds of South American shoppers. He could be driving through the parking lot. Or standing outside one of the stores, staring back at the window that marked her office. Thinking of what else he could do. What cleverness next? How long could he play with her before he closed in? And meanwhile people were walking around him left or right, unaware.

When Gail turned away from the window, she noticed the box on her credenza. Miriam had spent Monday and half of

Tuesday going through old cases at the law firm downtown. She had come back and flopped into Gail's chair, curls bouncing, bringing gossip about all the people they knew. Gossip and a banker's box full of photocopies organized into labeled folders. Overkill, Gail had told her, but the efficient Ms. Ruiz had not missed a case in which anyone—client, opponent, witness, or lawyer—had squabbled about tactics or outcome. She had gone back no more than two years, since they decided that nobody was likely to hold a grudge without acting on it longer than that.

Gail walked her fingers through the files, certain that there had been a couple of cases having to do with trust accounts. Real estate deals that had fallen through. Or someone laying claim to an escrow account. Gail recognized the names of her clients, surprising given the staggering number of cases she had worked on at any one time. Hartwell Black had offered her a partnership, but she'd been sick of the bureaucracy, the tyranny of time sheets, the monotony of commercial litigation. Six months later, working just as hard for less money, she was beginning to wonder what she'd been thinking.

Too wound up to eat, Gail dropped the rest of her sandwich back into the deli bag and tossed it into her trash basket. She pulled one folder from the box, then another. Miriam had not copied the entire file, only the client information sheet, the complaint, the answer, the final judgment, and any pertinent letters or records of phone calls. Most were of no interest. Petty complaints. Misunderstandings. She skipped over cases in which the dispute had been with a corporation. Corporations did not send flowers from a dead woman or draw bloody knives on a picture of a ten-year-old girl.

She went more slowly through cases where she had filed suit against an individual, not a company. There were three residential-foreclosure cases, and Gail sat down in her chair with the folders on her lap. She sipped her iced tea and set it back on the napkin. *Atlantic Financial Savings* v. *Yancey*. The homeowners, Simon Yancey and his wife, Rita Yancey, had not filed an answer, so Gail had asked for a judgment in her client's favor. Yancey had appeared at the hearing. When Gail won her motion, he had cursed and kicked the furniture, then turned on Gail like a maddened bull. The judge had screamed for the bailiff. Yancey had crashed through the swinging gate, then pushed the exit door so hard it slammed into the wall. Nervous laughter rose among the lawyers waiting for their own cases to be called. Gail had been shaken, but with so many other things on her mind, Yancey became only an anecdote to relate in the coffee room. A week or so later a typed letter arrived in the mail:

Dear Ms. Gail Connor:

I hope you can live with yourself. You have succeeded in taking away the house which my wife and I made faithful payments on for five years. We had some bad luck, but you would not give us a chance to bring the loan current. Does it make you happy to see a decent, hardworking American family out on the street? My wife is on medication from the stress. You are a sorry excuse for a human being who wants to do high-fives with the mortgage company over the house you stole from us.

Sincerely,

Simon T. Yancey

That was the last she had heard from Yancey. He'd been angry—the letter pulsed with anger—but there was also a curious politeness and adherence to form. *Dear Ms. Gail Connor. Sincerely, Simon T. Yancey.*

Gail tossed the file onto her desk, remembering that at the time she had felt bad about the Yancey foreclosure—but not bad enough to tell the company to give the man an extension. She recalled billing about a thousand dollars in fees on the case. Her client hadn't cared about the fees, which were tacked onto the judgment and collected on resale. Atlantic Financial had wanted the loan called. Maybe the interest rate had been too low. Or they wanted to get out of that area of town. Gail had not questioned their motives, and could not have done so without risking her chances for a partnership. Hartwell Black had not become one of Miami's most powerful law firms by being squeamish about pulling the trigger.

She opened the second folder—another homeowner angry about losing his property, blaming the court this time, and blaming Gail for being a pawn of the system.

When the intercom buzzed, Gail picked it up.

Charlene Marks told her that she had just received a copy of a report filed by Dr. Fischman in the custody case.

Gail closed the folder. "What does he say?"

"Come on up," Charlene said. "We'll chat."

When a drink was offered, Gail did not turn it down. Charlene came back with two vodka martinis over crushed ice in heavy glasses, adorned with twists of lime.

The report was on Charlene's desk where Gail had tossed it, upside down. *The mother's controlling personality . . . signs of instability bordering on pathological . . . unsuitable living arrangement with the mother's lover . . . risk of emotional damage to the child . . . leaving her frequently in the care of others . . . A recommendation that sole custody of said minor child be granted to the father.*

Gail took one of the glasses. "I wonder. Even if I'd known he would write something like that, could I have restrained myself from screaming at him?"

"You should have, of course."

"Maybe I'd have drowned him in his aquarium. He'd be hanging over the edge with his goldfish swimming around his head." Gail closed her eyes. "What am I going to do?"

Charlene sat down in the adjacent chair and crossed her legs. "You are not going to panic. We'll hire another psychologist. Fischman's report is so far off, he looks rabid."

"I'm running out of money."

"Then ask Anthony to help you. He will, you know. Gladly."

"I don't like asking him for money. He just paid for my wedding dress. I could become used to it, and then what?"

"This is not a wedding dress. This is your daughter's future."

Gail held up a hand. "Okay. You're right." She laughed. "This morning I got a call from the couturier asking me to come in for a fitting. And of course it should be soon, because the portrait photographer wants to take pictures well in advance of the ceremony. My mother thinks I should put off the wedding till all this is over."

Charlene's brows arched. "No. Don't give in to your fear." She swung her foot. "But I can't say I'm not nervous for you. You and Karen. Are you eating? You've lost weight."

"I have no appetite anymore." Gail sipped her martini. "God, Charlene, is there *any* vermouth in this?"

"Sissy. Drink up."

"I have a hearing at one-thirty," Gail said, "so I need to maintain an appearance of sobriety. It's the Sweet case, and I'm going to ask the judge to throw Wendell's miserable ass in jail. He didn't give me the documents." She took another sip. "I don't know why I'm working so hard. Jamie could slide right back to him. I want to help her, but how can I when she won't let me? She still thinks this guy who slammed her in the teeth is worth loving! What am I supposed to do?"

"Do? Make sure your bill is paid up. What do you mean, *do*?"

"I hate divorce cases. Nobody wins." Gail leaned back in the chair. "When I worked for Hartwell Black, I was so tough grown men would shake. I had that huge legal machine behind me, you see. Now I've got myself and one and a half secretaries, and the only recourse is to be a bigger s.o.b. than the next guy—the only way to survive on your own."

"Do you see me that way?"

"No. I didn't mean you." Gail exhaled. "I meant . . . me."

Charlene smiled. Her salt-and-pepper hair was like fine strands of pewter, wiry and strong. "Well, you could go back to the machine. Or you could give it up entirely and live on Anthony's money. Or move to a women's commune in Arizona or some damn place and make pottery." She pointed at Gail. "You're a lawyer. You like it, bloody knuckles and all. You will continue to go into court because you believe that whether or not your client is dumb enough to love the guy who slammed her in the teeth, she still deserves to be fought for."

Gail smiled. "Why, Charlene, all this time I thought you were such a cynic."

"I should feed you martinis more often."

On Monday Gail had expected hundreds of pages of documents from Wendell Sweet relating to his offshore investments. When he sent fewer than fifty, Gail telephoned Judge Ramirez's office to schedule an emergency hearing, and lucked into a cancellation at one-thirty on Wednesday.

Jamie Sweet didn't have to be there, but Gail asked her to show up, hoping that Jamie's innocent, motherly expression would catch the judge's attention. They sat on a bench in the hall to wait. The court reporter arrived with her machine, and she and Gail made some chitchat. At 1:29 Sweet and his lawyer got off the elevator. Marvin Acker smiled, double chin showing. "Well, well. Ms. Connor." Wendell Sweet sullenly lagged behind, hands in his pockets, shoulders slumped like James Dean.

"I hope," Gail said, nodding at Acker's fat briefcase, "that you've brought the documents I asked for."

"Wendell says they don't exist, and he gave you what he has."

Without moving her lips Gail murmured, "Do you really believe that, Marvin?"

"Sure. I never doubt a client's word—unless he stops paying my bills."

Wendell Sweet was staring at his wife. His black hair glimmered in the dim light of the hall, and his little red lips were pursed like he'd been sucking a lime. Jamie stared back at him. Her freckles stood out on her bloodless face. Gail grabbed her by the elbow and escorted her inside.

The hearing was held in chambers, a narrow room with windows looking west, the Everglades a hazy green line in the distance. The style was bureaucratic *moderne*—bookcases and plaques, long table with chairs along either side, judge's desk at one end. The court reporter set up her machine, and Gail put Wendell's documents in the center of the table, a stack less than a half inch thick. With only ten minutes allotted, she quickly stated her case: The court had ordered Wendell to produce, he hadn't, and now he should get slapped for his contemptuous disregard.

The judge, who was about to go on the bench in another case, took his robe off a hanger behind the door. "How do you know, Ms. Connor, that he didn't give you everything? Maybe this is it."

Out of the corner of her eye she saw Wendell Sweet smirk behind the fist supporting his chin. "Mr. Sweet has done business as a consultant to oil companies in the southern Caribbean for fifteen years. To give me fifty pages is ludicrous. It's insulting to the intelligence of the court."

The judge chuckled. "Sometimes I wonder."

Marvin Acker laughed, showing he could appreciate a joke. Then he grew serious. "Judge, most of Mr. Sweet's business is done on a handshake basis. He gave Ms. Connor what he has. Anything else would be in the custody of the companies he worked for."

Astonished and appalled, Gail could feel the case lurch out of her grasp. "Does Mr. Sweet expect us to believe that he has no records?"

The judge looked at his watch. "I don't know how you expect to prove what Mr. Sweet did or did not turn over, and frankly, Ms. Connor, there's not much I can do about it."

"Judge, it was clearly stated in our last hearing—by you—that Mr. Sweet was to produce all records. Everything. Look. Here's a copy of your order. And now he's telling us that he doesn't have copies because they're in the custody of persons whose names we don't even know."

"Well, file a motion to compel Mr. Sweet to divulge the names." The judge zipped up the front of his robe. "When you have the names, have them served with a subpoena."

"Most of them are out of the country!" Gail lowered her voice. "I hope that the court is not going to allow Mr. Sweet to play these games."

"Don't get mad at me, Ms. Connor. I don't make the rules. Excuse me, folks. Gotta run."

Marvin Acker stood up. "Is there an order, Judge?"

"I'm ruling that the respondent, Mr. Sweet, is in substantial compliance."

"And you'll reconsider the alimony and child support at the next hearing. You said you would, Your Honor, if Mr. Sweet doesn't have the means to pay."

"If I said it, then sure, we'll reconsider." With a swirl of black robe he was gone.

Gail's hands were clammy with perspiration. She wanted to scream at the judge, *You should be thrown off the bench. This is outrageous!*

Wendell smiled, not bothering to hide it. He leaned across the table and patted Jamie's arm. "Hey, honey. Tough luck."

"Get your slimy hand offa me." Her fluffy red hair was like fire around her face.

Acker pushed his heavy frame out of the armchair. "Come on, Wendell, let's leave before the ladies throw a hissy fit."

Gail smiled through clenched teeth. "Marvin, you are very close to the line."

"Well, ya win some, ya lose some."

"We're not going to lose this one. Count on it."

The court reporter snapped her machine back into its case. "Ms. Connor? Would you like a transcript?"

"I'll let you know." She turned to Jamie Sweet. "I swear to you, Jamie, it isn't supposed to go this way. I want to file an appeal. Honestly, this is so wrong."

"Wendell don't make it easy. Never has." Jamie slung her heavy purse over her shoulder and straightened the hem of her jacket. "Don't appeal it. I want to get this over with."

Gail gritted her teeth as she and Jamie Sweet rode down in a packed elevator. Anthony had promised her he would talk to

Harry Lasko. Had *promised*. By Friday. On Monday. Next week. Sorry, Gail, he's out of town. I'm in trial. I'll call him in the morning. *Bonboncita*.

The polished chrome doors of the elevator opened, disgorging passengers into the echoing lobby of the family courts building. Outside, the sun glared brightly. Squinting, Gail reached for her sunglasses. Wind snapped the flags on the plaza.

"Jamie, listen. When you go home, search the remotest corner of your mind about Wendell's activities. Who he talked to, who his associates were. Try to remember who you met in the islands. If we can find just one or two people willing to testify at trial, we could nail him."

When she got no response from the woman beside her, Gail stopped walking. "Jamie? Come on, you can't give up. Did you see the way he was gloating?"

Jamie bit down on her lips to keep them from trembling, and Gail realized she was at the point of tears. "If you want to keep on fighting him, go ahead, but I can't pay you. I'm done."

Standing close, Gail tucked her arm through Jamie's. "What do you want? Just tell me. Never mind the fees. What would you like to do?"

"Oh, Lord. If it was just me, I'd say, Wendell, you horse's ass, give me what you want, and if you give me nothing, that's all right. But he shouldn't do the children that way. He's thinking of his own self more than what they need, and that's wrong. So I guess I'd like to keep going."

"Yes. Good." Gail nodded. "We'll start preparing for your trial. You don't need to worry about it. Okay?" She squeezed Jamie's hand and felt the fingers close tightly around hers.

"I feel so tired. And I can't stand seein' Wendell look at me like I was dirt on his shoe."

"Do you *care* what he thinks?"

"You know, it's funny, but I do. I still do. Just weak-minded, I guess." She laughed. "I keep thinking how he used to be."

"But the bad side was there too. And it's not going to go away."

"I'm just a prisoner of love." She laughed. "I had a lot of men, I guess you know that, but Wendell . . . Oh, my. You are the queen of Egypt and I am your slave. He'd say shit like that. I'll get over him, like I got over drinkin'. Give up a bad habit, you sure miss it, though. I might find me a nice guy one of these days, somebody who won't do me like Wendell. But I don't know if anybody's gonna touch me in my heart like he did either."

At the bottom of the escalator to the Metrorail station, Gail put her arm around her. "You'll be fine, Jamie. You'll be great."

"I keep hoping. Thank you, Gail."

Sunlight glinted on the escalator, and Jamie rose slowly, a beautiful woman with freckles and milk white skin, her red hair blowing around her face like a flag. Gail waved, but Jamie didn't notice.

The parking garage was a block away, and by the time Gail reached it, she had taken off her jacket, letting the air get to her sleeveless linen shirt, although the breeze was nearly useless in this heat. She took the elevator up to the fourth level and automatically glanced around before getting off. Nearing her rental car, she shifted her briefcase to reach the keys in her shoulder bag.

Because she had been careful she did not expect to hear footsteps behind her. She looked over her shoulder and saw Wendell Sweet. Her heart seemed to squeeze the blood through her chest in one massive surge.

She pulled in a breath. "What do you want?"

"Well, hi." A lopsided smirk lifted one side of his little red mouth. His collar was open, and his tie was loose. He had stowed the coat to his thousand-dollar business suit somewhere. In his car, Gail realized. They had parked in the same garage, and he had spotted her, probably by chance. His face glowed with rage, and his eyes danced with it. "I would like to ask you a question, Miz Lawyer. What kind of satisfaction do you get out of destroying a marriage? Does it make you feel powerful? Are you a man hater? Is that it?"

Gail was calculating the amount of time it would take to run to her car, turn the key in the lock, open her door, get inside . . .

Her voice was level and calm. "Your marriage was over before Jamie hired me. If you want someone to blame, start with yourself." Keeping an eye on Wendell Sweet, Gail walked toward her car.

He followed, closing the gap. "You ought to be ashamed, brainwashing my wife. Jamie and I love each other. That must be hard for a dried-up dyke like you to comprehend."

"Stay away from me." She backed toward the door. "I'll scream."

"Oh, my goodness. Would I hurt you, even though—yes, let's admit it—you probably need your jaw fractured?" He stood by the rear door, trapping her between her car and the one in the next space.

The key rattled against the lock, then slid in. "Touch me, you're dead. My fiancé would come after you without a second thought."

His mouth made an O of feigned alarm. "Quintana? I don't think so. He knows better."

Gail gripped the door handle but did not turn it. "What do you mean?"

"There's information I possess. Are we curious? I'll make you a little bargain. You advise my wife to drop this, I won't take Quintana down. Deal?"

"What are you talking about?" Gail demanded.

"Why don't you ask him?" Wendell Sweet blew her a kiss, a moist smack off the tips of his fingers, then turned and walked away.

FIFTEEN

Greeting Gail by name, the receptionist at Ferrer & Quintana told her that Anthony had just called. He wanted to let Ms. Connor know that he was running late but would arrive shortly. Would she care to wait in the conference room? No, the lobby will do, Gail told her. Would Ms. Connor like something to drink while she waited? Tea would be lovely, thanks.

She found a seat on a long sofa that curved to follow a wall of glass blocks. The outside light made a wavery grid on the silver-flecked granite floor. The monotones of the lobby were relieved by a series of abstract paintings that looked like bright tropical plants.

Gail sipped her tea while thumbing through a news magazine, and only by chance looked up and saw a gray suit and a pair of black glasses. Hector Mesa. He was noiselessly crossing the polished floor, and his image moved with him, upside down. Spots of light from the ceiling fell on his shoulders as he passed under them. The man and his double glanced at Gail but did not stop. He punched a code on a panel of the interior door. It opened, then swung shut behind him. She had not known he could come and go as he pleased.

How would it be, Gail wondered, to have a guard dog like

Mesa? One who did not question. Who might say, if he were ever asked, that it would be impertinent to demand explanations.

Her teacup was empty when Anthony came in. There was an immediate smile, and he held out his arm, waiting. His jacket was a light wool and silk tweed, brown flecked with cream. Gold flashed at his cuffs. She had still not become accustomed to the sight of him when he smiled at her across a room. Her breath would stop.

He kissed her cheek. *"¿Cómo andas, amor?"*

He took her to his office, where Gail told him that she had just lost her motion for contempt in the Sweet case.

"Lost? What happened? Sit down and tell me." He gestured toward the sofa, a leather sectional. Deep, boxy chairs faced an atrium, where sunlight danced on water burbling down ferny rocks. His desk was in a corner, curving into the room, lit by pinpoint halogen lights on thin wires.

Gail was too restless to sit. "The judge said that fifty pages of documents was substantial compliance. An insane ruling, but we'd lose the appeal. At the next hearing, Wendell Sweet will ask for a reduction in alimony and child support because he can't pay. On what he gave me, I can't prove otherwise. I was hoping that you might come through for me and talk to Harry Lasko, which you promised to do last week."

"Sweetheart, sit down. Please." When she remained standing, he said, "I spoke to Harry this morning."

"Finally."

"You're right to be upset, but this was the first opportunity Harry and I had to talk."

Gail leaned on the arm of a chair. "What did he say? Can he give me any information about Wendell's offshore assets?"

"I asked him. Harry and Wendell made some profits from the sale of the Eagle Beach casino, as you know, but Harry has no idea what Wendell did with his share. It was over a year ago, so he could have spent it or lost it in a bad investment. Harry suspects he still has a considerable amount, but he doesn't know where."

"Can we assume they didn't report their profits to the IRS?"

After a moment Anthony nodded. "They bought the casino using a complicated trust agreement and a corporation registered in Grand Cayman. There is an argument to be made that the income wasn't subject to U.S. tax laws, but it's questionable whether a jury would buy it. I've been talking to the prosecutors. They might agree to a sentence of seven years on the current indictment, but if they find out about Eagle Beach, Harry could die in prison. You see why I've been so careful."

She looked at him awhile, then walked over to the glass door, which led to the atrium. Dappled light fell across philodendron and ferns, and she could hear the muffled splash of water on rocks. "After the hearing I accidentally ran across Wendell Sweet in the parking garage. He offered me a deal. If I stop brainwashing his wife, he won't divulge certain information about you." She turned to look at Anthony. "What does he mean?"

A slight frown of confusion passed over his face. "Information? About me? I have no idea."

"He said he could take you down." Gail leaned a shoulder on the door frame and watched the fountain. "On the way over here I realized how little I know about what you do—aside from practicing criminal defense law, and the investments you rarely mention. I saw Hector Mesa come in. What does he do here?"

"He's a courier, Gail. He goes to the bank for us. Sometimes he acts as a bodyguard for our high-profile clients. There is nothing sinister about it." Anthony spread his arms wide. "What do you want to know? Ask."

"All right. What was Wendell talking about?"

"He was handing you a plate of bullshit."

"Were you doing business with Harry and Wendell?"

His brows lifted. "Is that what you think?"

"I don't know, Anthony. Were you?"

He seemed amazed that she would ask such a thing. "Absolutely not."

"I have a right to know," she said. "I would rather hear it

now than find out after we're married." Anxiety stirred in her chest, and she took a breath. "I would never tell anyone else. Not ever. We have to trust each other."

His eyes stayed on her for a long moment. "Yes, we do. When I say I don't know what Wendell Sweet was talking about, that is exactly what I mean. Why do you question it?"

"Please don't be angry."

"Sweetheart, I'm not. Not at you, certainly. Listen to me. How can I disprove what he said? He said nothing. A vague allegation to . . . what? Was he specific?"

"No."

"Come on, you see what Sweet is after. He wants his divorce case settled on his terms, and he's trying to scare you. I have never spoken to Wendell Sweet, never met him. If he would care to elucidate on what 'taking me down' refers to, then I could answer. Until then I do not know. I can't even guess." Anthony took her hands and squeezed them for emphasis. "Gail?"

She shook her head. "I'm sorry. This case is getting to me."

"Yes, I would agree with that." He pulled her closer and softly kissed her lips. She let herself lean against him, inhaling a scent of cologne, light but distinctly male. He said, "Why don't you to go to bed early tonight?"

"Do I look awful?"

"A little tired, that's all. Come with me." He led her away from the glass doors and across his office. "I want you to try something." He swiveled his black leather desk chair and held out his arm. "Sit here."

She laughed. "Why?"

When she was seated, he tilted the chair back. She clutched the arms. "Not a bad fit," he said. "Gail, I have a proposal for you." He sat on the edge of the desk with both feet on the floor. "I've already discussed it with Raul. We want you to join Ferrer and Quintana."

Her mouth opened. She said, "You mean . . . a partnership?"

He hesitated. "No, not . . . right away. You'd be an associate, and then we'd see. What you have, Gail, are the old Miami

Anglo contacts that we lack here. Raul does real estate and business. I'm in criminal defense. You're an expert in commercial litigation, eight years with one of Miami's oldest and best law firms. We have associates in a number of other fields, but none with what you would bring to it. It would be perfect." He smiled, creases deepening along either side of his mouth. "Well?"

"Anthony, I . . . What about my office? Miriam and Lynn?"

"Bring them with you. I know you wanted your own business, but this is crazy. You're barely getting by. You think I don't see what's going on?" He reached out and lifted her face. "You're working so hard. Look at you. The shadows under your eyes. I hate to see you like this, *cielo.*"

Gail kissed his palm. "Since when is fatigue a qualification?"

"No, that's my ulterior motive," he said. "What qualifies you is that you're a damned good lawyer. This isn't charity. We could use you here. We need what you know and *who* you know. Put in as many hours as you want. Take more time to be with Karen. You see? There's another reason to do it."

Gail thought of the report that Charlene Marks had shown her. Time with Karen. Dr. Fischman had noted how little she had of it. Rocking back in the chair, Gail swung it around, her gaze passing over the ultramodern lights in the ceiling, the glass-fronted bookcases, the atrium, the leather chairs around a granite-topped table. There were two partners, seven associates, three paralegals, a dozen support staff, a library, two conference rooms. . . . "This is all very seductive," she said. "One could become accustomed to this, I suppose. But"—she spun the chair faster, lifting her feet—"would we get on each other's nerves, working in the same office? You and I are independent creatures, more so than most."

Anthony leaned forward, stopping the chair's motion with a hand planted firmly on each leather-upholstered arm. His silk tie swung into her lap. "No, Gail, our biggest problem at work"—his lips brushed across hers—"would be how to get anything done."

She tugged on his tie and smiled. "I'll think about it."

"How can you say no?"

"I'll say maybe. I have a lot on my mind."

"Of course. You don't have to decide now." He kissed her forehead.

"What should I do about Wendell?" she asked. "Ignore him?"

"*Claro que sí.* Yes, forget about Wendell. But if he bothers you again, tell me."

"Don't beat him up on my account, Anthony."

He put a hand on his heart. "Oh, Gail. Where do you get these ideas, that I would do such a thing? I promise, I am the most gentle of men. *Te juro.*" He shrugged. "Unless he touched you, then I would have to kill him."

"Funny." Gail got up and stood between Anthony's thighs. Under the warm brown fabric of his trousers, his legs were trim and hard.

He slid his hands down her hips, pulling her tightly against his groin. "Would we get any work done? Hmm. *Un problema muy grande.*"

"Anthony, I forgot to tell you. Bozo sent roses to my office."

Leaving Ferrer & Quintana, Gail went by Miami Police head-quarters with the envelope that had come with the flowers. At the information desk she was given a pass to clip to the lapel of her jacket and told to take the elevator to the third floor. She knew the way, having been here two days ago. Anthony wanted to come along, but had already made an appointment with a client. Gail assured him she would park in a safe place and, yes, look around before getting out of the car. *Anthony, for God's sake, I'll be surrounded by cops.*

The older of the detectives assigned to the case, Sergeant Ladue, met her in the hall and took her to the room used by homicide and personal crimes. Windows looked east, but an apartment house with faded turquoise paint obscured a view of the water. Detective Novick looked up from a phone call and acknowledged Gail with a nod. Ladue held a chair at the end of his desk, and she gave him the card.

He remained standing, belly thrust out for balance. A pistol in a scuffed brown holster rode on his belt, along with a badge. Sergeant, Miami Police Department, the city's palm tree logo in the center. He took a pair of glasses out of his pocket, shook them open, and set them on his short nose.

Gail held her purse on her lap. "Renee is my sister. She died last year. A homicide."

"Uh-huh." Ladue flipped the card over, found nothing, then dropped it onto his desk. "You want a copy?" Gail said she didn't. Ladue said, "I heard about your sister. Apparently our guy did too. Okay, we'll call the florist, see if they have a record."

Opening her purse, Gail withdrew some folded pages. "Detective Novick asked me to make a list of people I've had disagreements with in the recent past. There are about a dozen people whom I'd consider remotely possible as suspects." She had listed names and addresses and a brief description of the dispute, most of which had been amicably resolved.

She tapped the top of the list. "This one, Simon Yancey, was the defendant in a foreclosure case I handled April a year ago. Here. I made you some copies from the case file. He wrote me a letter."

Novick, who had finished his phone call, came to look over Ladue's shoulder. While they read, Gail idly looked at the stuff pinned to the wall. Cartoons and drawings. A cap from the 1998 Pig Bowl on a pushpin. Lists of names and telephone numbers. A three-month calendar with court appearances marked in red. Ladue had a stapler with an old derringer welded to it and a miniature electric chair with a lightbulb in the seat. Behind Novick's desk, which was considerably less cluttered, several snapshots of snow-topped mountains were tacked to a cork board. In one Novick and a dark-haired woman stood in the foreground, arms around each other. Elsewhere in the room, conversations went on. A phone rang.

Novick finished reading the letter and pulled a chair closer. "Do you get a lot of letters like this?"

"No, they're very rare. Whoever that lawyer is he's complaining about, I don't recognize her. She isn't *me*."

He had a pleasant smile. "We who deal with the public are often misunderstood."

Ladue dropped his bulk into his swivel chair. "Our resident egghead. He actually graduated high school."

Gail turned the letter around to see the signature. *Sincerely, Simon T. Yancey.* Small, cramped letters. The turns were sharp angles, not curves. "Can the document examiners compare this to the writing on the envelopes?"

"Not likely," Novick said. "The envelopes were addressed in block print. When a person makes a deliberate attempt to disguise his handwriting, it's almost impossible to make a match."

He leaned in his chair to reach a pen and notepad on his desk. "Can you give us a description of Simon Yancey?"

"He was big—not fat, but strong. He kicked a chair over. I can't remember his face. He was in his early thirties. Brown hair, sort of long." She touched her collar. "In court he said, 'You'd better watch out, bitch.' Something like that, but definitely the word 'bitch.' "

Novick held the pad on his lap, and words flowed quickly into neat lines. "Did he have a distinct accent? The electronic device on the telephone could have been used to disguise an accent."

Gail thought. "Accent. Not really."

Swiveling his chair, Ladue picked up the telephone and dialed the information operator. He asked for the number of Simon Yancey. He waited, then hung up. "No listing in this area, not even a unpublished number."

"After I stole his house, he had to live on the street."

"Yeah, no wonder he's pissed—if it's him." Ladue glanced down at his beeper. "We'll run a computer check, see if we can track him down. The license bureau will have a picture. I gotta go, Mike. They want me in court." Ladue stood up and took a blue jacket off the back of the chair. "Ms. Connor, keep in touch, anything else arises."

She thanked him, then looked back at Detective Novick. "Would it be possible to ask you something unrelated?"

"Sure."

"Have you ever heard of a man named Wendell Sweet? Black hair, late thirties. He's a consultant in offshore oil. Spends a lot of time out of the country."

Behind his glasses Novick's brown eyes went out of focus for a moment, then returned to Gail. "In what connection might I have heard of him?"

"Narcotics?"

He shook his head. "I don't generally handle narcotics cases, unless they turn into homicides, which they often do."

Gail asked, "Do you know the name Hector Mesa? Mid fifties, Cuban?"

That brought a slight nod. "He's an associate of your fiancé's grandfather, Ernesto Pedrosa. What do you want to know?"

"I was just curious. Nobody talks much about Mesa."

"He came to our attention in connection with some anti-Castro activities. Of course, in Miami that's half the population."

"Has he ever come to your *particular* attention?"

Novick smiled. "You mean, questioned in a homicide? No. Are Sweet and Mesa acquainted?"

"Not that I know of. Wendell Sweet is married to a client of mine. They're going through a divorce. There was some abuse in the marriage, and today, after a hearing in court, he said I should have my jaw fractured."

"I can't arrest him for that."

"I know. I'm just telling you."

"Is he on your list?"

"It isn't likely," Gail said. "He has three kids, and he's never been violent with them."

Novick tapped the pen on the notepad like a small drumstick. "Well. We should probably put his name and information in the file. People can surprise you."

"All right. I'll call you." Gail put the strap of her purse over her shoulder.

He stood up. "Ladue says you didn't want to see the last photograph."

"Two were enough, don't you think?"

"If you don't mind, Ms. Connor, there could be something you recognize. The more you know, the more help you'll be to us."

Anxiety, which had played with her all day, began to rise up her throat. She took a long, slow breath. "Show me." She put her purse on the desk while Novick went to his four-drawer file cabinet, returning with a manila envelope marked PROPERTY MPD. He pulled out the three color copies, putting the latest one on top, then holding it for her to see. Gail stood stiffly, not touching it, gripping the back of the chair.

The first two pictures had been taken on different days, obvious from the fact that Karen had been wearing different clothes. Blue shorts the first time, red the second. In the third Karen's clothes had been blackened. Black with ashes, burned to dust. Her body was on fire. Her mouth was a gaping black cave of agony. Red and orange streamed out behind her as she ran. Her hair burned. Flames shot up from the school, visible at the edge of the picture. Fire consumed the trees and blotted out the sky.

Novick's quiet voice pierced the silence. "Ms. Connor, do you recognize anything in the way it was drawn? The color, the lines?"

"Nothing." She took a breath through her teeth. "Who would do that to a child? Who would *think* of it?" She glanced at the detective. His steady brown eyes must have seen worse things, not in altered photographs but in reality. Real blood, real children bludgeoned, stabbed, burned.

He slid the color copy back into the envelope with the others and returned them to the file cabinet. Her fingers trembled on her cheeks as she swept away some tears.

"Please. Sit down." His hand was firm on her elbow. "This is difficult, and I appreciate your willingness to help."

"Of course I'll help. I'll do anything. Oh, God." She took in a long, shaky breath. "I wish I knew *why*, then I could deal with it. This is like punishment without a trial. Without even an accusation. You said there's always a cause. I wish I knew what it was."

"This may sound strange," he said, "but did you pick up on any sexual references in the way the photographs were altered?"

Gail looked at him. "No."

"I didn't either. There's usually a sexual basis to that kind of violence against children." Novick leaned forward, elbows on his knees. "Ladue and I worked a case a couple of months ago, a man who was parked outside a school. One of the children noticed that his pants were down and called the police. They took him in, and we searched his apartment. He had hundreds of nude drawings of children—boys in this case. If he drew a gun or knife, it was used in a violent and very sexual way. Do you understand?"

"Yes." Detective Novick's understated words conveyed content so chilling that Gail shivered. "But the photos of Karen weren't sexual. What does that tell us?"

"I don't know." The light reflected on his glasses. "We'll keep it in mind."

When she stood up, she noticed again the photographs of mountains, misty blue in the distance, folds of white at the craggy peaks. "Where were those pictures taken?"

He turned toward the wall behind his desk. "Oh, those. Near Whistler in British Columbia. It was a hiking trip last spring. Give me a steep incline, I'm happy."

"What are you doing in Miami?"

A smile accompanied his shrug. "If you live in the mountains, you stop seeing them."

Gail leaned closer, picking out a small blue lake, its surface reflecting the peaks behind it. "I suppose that makes sense. Detective Novick, how many cases like mine have you had?"

"Like this? Not many. Usually we know who it is going in."

"And if not, do you find out?"

"Eventually."

"Sooner rather than later, I hope." She extended her hand. "Thank you, Detective."

He walked with her to the elevators and pressed the button for the first floor. Gail turned in her badge at the desk.

Biscayne Academy, out for the summer, offered a day camp that Karen attended. The children would get lessons in dance, music, and art, visit galleries, and take field trips to study local history. The staff called it an "enriched" program—which meant it cost two hundred dollars a week. The camp ended at four o'clock, with aftercare until six at an additional charge for parents who worked. Past six o'clock the charge zoomed to fifty dollars every fifteen minutes. Gail had often pushed the limit, and if she couldn't break free she would send Miriam or Lynn to pick Karen up and bring her to the office.

It felt strange to be here so early, among other parents—mothers mostly—who had found shady spots along the sidewalk to wait for the doors to open. The women were in shorts and light tops and sneakers, greeting each other, clustered in groups. Gail knew some of them from parent-teacher meetings during the year. She smiled and returned a few hellos, but continued to walk along the chain-link fence that bordered the play yard, picking her way over the root-buckled sidewalk in high heels better suited to carpeted corridors.

One could become accustomed to this, she thought. Accustomed to arriving at this hour every day. To being here when the children returned from their trips or came running out of the building. It would not be so hard to get used to. Picking Karen up, taking her for ice cream. During the school year they would be home before dark and fix dinner together—fresh, grilled fish instead of microwaved meat loaf. There would be time to decorate the house for Christmas, to have holiday parties, to shop ahead rather than dashing frantically through the mall the weekend before. Karen would get stories every night. Her grades and her behavior would be exemplary.

Dr. Fischman could go screw himself. Gail would be a model mother. Another Peggy Cunningham, she thought, imagining a pool in the backyard of the house on Clematis Street. Peggy might even become a friend. On Saturdays they might lie on lounge chairs, do their nails, and discuss neighborhood events while Karen and Lindsay splashed in the pool. Gail would have a tan. She would join a health club.

Working as an associate would mean being an employee again, but a partner's wife would be treated well. And there would be no kiting checks at the end of the month, or having to put off her own salary to pay Lynn's and Miriam's.

When Karen was older—sixteen or so—Gail could go back into the law full-time. If she felt like it. Or stay with her part-time schedule, devoting herself to charitable causes. Only during the day, because her nights would be taken up with Anthony.

Could this happen? She wanted to believe it, but at no time in her adult life had she been taken care of. When she was married to Dave, the burden had been on her shoulders, but she had carried it, there being no alternative. It was the way it was. The prospect of someone else taking care of her was disconcerting, like floating in midair.

Anthony Quintana wanted to make her happy, and he had the means to do it. Dear God. His eyes lit up when he talked about the things he would do for her. And for Karen. He would keep her happy too, if he could. And safe. Karen would be in no danger as long as Anthony was there to protect her.

The academy's play yard adjoined the building. Trees shaded the sidewalk, but blue sky showed through over the field. The blue sky of the photographs.

With a sudden shortness of breath, Gail recognized this scene. Karen had been no more than fifty yards distant when the camera had been aimed at her. Someone could stand unobserved in this group of moms and a few dads who waited, chatting, for the doors to open. What had he seen? The children whose parents would arrive later had run to claim spots on the swings or the big wooden play set. The older ones, the tens and elevens, had brought out balls for four square or toss. The girls sat in the shade, combing each other's hair and talking about girls they didn't like and the boys they did. In the second photograph Karen had been leaning against the tree. A bloody knife had been drawn as if pinning her to it, and the others flashed around her.

The first photo, and the third, showed Karen in motion. She had been playing kick ball in one, running in the other, hair streaming out behind her. The pistol had been the easiest to draw. The flames had been the most elaborate, the entire play yard and school burning, black smoke billowing. The camera had caught Karen leaping, nothing blurred. It had not been a cheap camera, Gail realized, but one with adjustable shutter speeds to catch a girl in mid-stride. And compact, not to be noticed.

Gail walked along the sidewalk, shifting her perspective. At this distance, too much background would have showed. The camera must have had a telephoto lens. Or he had cut around the part he wanted and enlarged it to the proper size on a copy machine. Simple.

The play yard was still empty. The swings moved slightly in the breeze. A squirrel ran across the top beam of the jungle gym.

Near the school entrance a woman pushed a stroller. A man walked a dog on a leash. More parents had arrived, filling the space between the sidewalk and street. Car engines stayed on, and windows were rolled up to keep the cool air inside.

Easy to park here unnoticed behind tinted glass, wait till the children came out, then walk to the fence like any parent . . .

A white pickup truck turned the corner. It moved slowly up the narrow street, then found a place on the other side, in front of the Presbyterian church. Dave got out, wearing his khaki shorts and tropical shirt, coming from work. The sun flickered on his hair as he jogged across the street.

Gail wondered what he was doing here. Coming early to be with his daughter before the wicked mother arrived? *The mother's controlling personality . . . signs of instability bordering on pathological . . .*

Dave saw her and nodded, then made his way around the bumper of a minivan too far over the sidewalk. He stopped beside her. No smile. The muscles in his face seemed too tight for that. "Your office said you'd be here."

She picked out a leaf caught between metal pipe and mesh. "Do we have anything to say to each other? I read the report from Fischman."

"Yeah, he didn't waste any time. I called my lawyer today and told him to drop it. The case is over."

She turned around to look at him. "Do you mean that?"

"It's over, Gail. I'm sorry it took me this long."

Almost afraid to believe him, she put her hand on his shoulder. "We can work this out. We'll decide what Karen needs and go from there. We can do this."

He took her hand and held it in both of his. "I need to talk to you. Could we go somewhere? It's important."

"Now? No, I can't. Karen expects me at four o'clock. Talk about what?"

"I need a favor. You're the only person I know who could help me out."

Already she sensed herself drawing away. "A favor. As long as it doesn't involve time or money, I'll be glad to."

"This is serious, Gail. I need a loan till Monday. No risk to you. None."

She stared at him. "I can't give you money, Dave."

He was squeezing her hand, holding it to his chest. "Please listen. My deal with Marriott is going down the tubes if I can't borrow some money fast."

"Go to the bank." She pulled her hand away.

"I can't. Would you listen? Five minutes. Please."

Gail unhooked her arm from his grasp and walked farther

along the sidewalk. A banyan tree grew on the corner, and she moved into its deep shade. Dave followed closely. Twigs and dried leaves crunched underfoot.

"I'm not lending you any money," she said. "Let's get that straight before you say one more word."

He tapped his clenched fists together, then took a breath as if he were going to dive off the ten-meter platform. "I told you about the Old Island Club—the one on St. Thomas. How I bought the name—the right to use the name. The owner is Armand Dubois, a Frenchman from Guadeloupe. He bought the Club about ten years ago, and when I was in St. Thomas, he needed money, but he didn't want to sell. I offered him a deal. He'd let me use the corporate name in the States and copy his menu, his decor, everything, for two hundred grand."

"Good Lord."

"Gail, that's nothing. It was a steal. I sold the boat for seventy thousand, scraped up another five, and said I'd pay him the rest in six months. I gave him my interest in the Old Island Club in Miami as security. The last payment is due Friday."

She held up both hands, palms out. "Let me guess. You can't pay him, he knows about your deal with Marriott, and he's going to step in."

Dave nodded. "Armand was here over the weekend. He said if I don't get the money to him by Friday, he's going to take the Club away. He can do it. We signed an agreement."

"Didn't you have a lawyer in St. Thomas?"

"No, we used his."

She closed her eyes. "Idiot."

"Gail, I have to pay him." Dave walked around her when she turned away. "The deal with Marriott was supposed to go through today, but somebody at the resort in Key West didn't fax them the restaurant lease, and they need a couple of days to review it. The closing is reset for Monday, but by then it will be too late, if I don't get the money to Armand."

"Stop. Just stop for a minute." Gail stared at the twisted air roots of the banyan tree, then at Dave. "Your bank will understand. Do you want me to call them? I will. You can show them the contract with Marriott."

"I'm at my limit already."

"It doesn't matter. Just show them the contract. You said *no risk*, didn't you? They would be happy to lend you the money."

"They'll want to see my books." Dave shook his head.

"I see. You've been playing around with the accounts."

"Gail, I had to. The liquor distributors made me pay cash. And the salaries, the insurance—"

"One set of books for the IRS, showing you don't make anything, and one for your creditors, to show them that you're making so much money, they can lend up to the maximum—which now you have exceeded."

"Gail, please—"

"Do you owe employment taxes too?" The anger pounding in her head felt sickeningly familiar. Gail said calmly, "And you bought yourself a new truck. A big-screen TV."

"The deal with Marriott is going to pay for all that."

"Oh, my God. Déjà-vu."

"This wasn't supposed to happen! Jesus Christ. If the closing had been today, like it was supposed to be, I wouldn't be here begging you on my knees. I could pay off everything and have money in the bank. People do it all the time! It's how business works." His face was red. "I saw the opportunity, I went with it, and it's going to pay off—if I can just get past Friday."

Years in commercial litigation had showed Gail that people would operate on air, on hope, on good expectations, *knowing* that it would all work out. They could trust the other guy, trust the market, trust fate. They would sell an empty box, intending to fill it before the other guy flipped up the lid.

Sweat shone on Dave's upper lip. "If this deal doesn't go through, I could go to jail. Do you realize that? Prison. For tax evasion. How would that be for Karen?"

"They wouldn't send you to prison. You would have a tax lien for as long as it took you to pay it off."

"They'd take everything I have, Gail. Everything." He moistened his lips. "I told Karen we'd take a trip over Christmas. That's off. She's going to see her father with nothing. No money, no house, *nothing*, if you don't help me."

"Don't you lay this on me!"

"Okay. I screwed up. I should've put the money aside, but I didn't. I spent it on upgrading the restaurant. Now what? For lack of a hundred and twenty-five grand, which is fucking peanuts in this business, I'm going to miss the biggest chance of my life because *somebody* at Marriott forgot to fax one *lousy piece of paper*." Dave sucked in a breath. He was shaking. "I'm not asking you to *give* me the money. It's a loan till Monday."

"No."

"I need the cash by Friday at noon. You'd get it back Monday. The closing is at two o'clock. Look." He grabbed his wallet out of his back pocket and pulled out a business card. "This is the lawyer for Marriott. His name is Jeffrey Barlow."

Gail read the card. Barlow worked for Davis & Seitz, one of Miami's biggest law firms. "I know Jeff Barlow," Gail reluctantly admitted. "We co-counseled a case last winter."

"Then call him. Tell him to give *you* the money, not me. I'm supposed to get a hundred-fifty up front, more as the franchises come on line. They already gave me twenty, so I've got one-thirty coming, less some expenses. You want all of it? I don't care, I'll give it to you. Make five thousand. I'll sign an agreement, whatever you want."

Gail laughed, finally biting her lip to stop.

"What's so funny?"

"I don't have the money. This is true, Dave. I have a personal-injury case settling this week, and I'll make money from that, but not *a hundred and twenty-five*! It *is* funny. I thought you were doing well. You thought I was doing well." She extended the card. "Take it back."

"What about your mother? Could you borrow it from her for a few days? Irene and I always liked each other. I bet she would help."

"I'm not going to involve my mother in this."

"Don't you have stocks? Retirement?" He gripped her arm. "Gail, you've got to help me out. Call him."

Gail studied the card.

"Please. It's for Karen too. It's for Karen."

"Leave her out of it." She looked back along the sidewalk, hearing engines starting, the happy shrieks of children in the play yard.

"Honey. Don't let me down. Don't kill me like this." He put his forehead on the point of her shoulder. "One banking day. One day. Please."

"All right. I'll call him."

Dave embraced her. "Thank God. I knew you'd come through." His lips pressed against her cheek. "You've always been there for me. I love you so much, Gail. Thank you."

"Stop it." She extricated herself. "Do you want to take Karen today?"

He wiped under his eyes. "I've got to get back to work. I'll say hello to her, though. She's a super kid." Dave put his arm around Gail's waist. "We're going to take good care of her, Gail. We're going to do all right."

They started walking back toward the school.

Gail slowed her steps. "Dave, there's something I have to tell you about. I got a nasty bouquet at my office today."

CHAPTER

SIXTEEN

Gail stood under the shower massage, and the cool water came out with a low, pulsating buzz. She dug her fingers into tense muscles and rotated her head.

Karen was in her room, allegedly cleaning it, and chicken *cordon bleu* was marinating in the refrigerator. Seven-fifty a pound at the gourmet market. Coming home, Gail had checked the mailbox. No envelopes from Bozo. Perhaps he thought that flowers would be enough for one day.

With sympathy on the loss of your daughter.

"You son of a bitch. If I knew who you were . . ."

With a moan Gail leaned her forehead against the tiles and told herself to shut up. They would have a nice dinner. She might watch some TV with Karen. *Dawson's Creek* or that angel show. A couple of hours on her files, then to bed with Anthony. Or to bed with Anthony, then the files.

With sympathy—

"Shut *up*." Gail spun the knobs, and the water went off. Pipes clanked in the wall. Wrapped in a towel, she went into her bedroom. She put on her bra, then opened another drawer and pawed through the panties, looking for red satin bordered in lace. Anthony had given them to her in his office. He'd pulled them slowly out of his briefcase and told her to try them on. And she had.

Tonight they would have a nice dinner, some wine, watch a little TV like normal people, then go to bed. Read Karen a story first, *then* go to bed. Get up early, do the files in the morning.

She went back to the bathroom to blow-dry her hair.

A minute later she thought she heard a noise. Hair dryers do that, she had noticed. Turn one on, you hear a phone ringing. A doorbell. Music.

Gail clicked it off. The whine went silent. She listened for a moment, then set the hair dryer quietly on the vanity. She unhooked her short cotton robe from the back of the door.

No mistake—there had been a series of metallic taps. An odd noise, nothing she had ever heard before. She crossed the hall and looked into Karen's room. Karen was not there.

The noise was coming from downstairs. Her bare feet made no sound on the carpet in the hall or down the steps to the landing. She heard a scraping noise, then a man's voice, humming a tune.

She looked over the railing. Someone was half inside the air-conditioning closet. The wood creaked, and the man below slowly backed out of the closet. A face with a close-trimmed black beard looked up at her. Charlie Jenkins. Gail let out an audible breath.

"Hi. Didn't mean to scare you. Your daughter let me in. She recognized me from last time."

Gail said, "I forgot you'd be coming. Is Karen down there?"

"She went out." Jenkins pointed with a thumb toward the rear of the house. His eyes moved over Gail's legs, then back up. He smiled. "The air handler is clogged, nothing major."

"That's good to know." Holding her robe closed, Gail went upstairs to get dressed. Karen had not asked to go out, she had just gone. Her room was passably clean, and she would argue, when confronted, that her mother was being unreasonable. Gail thought Karen was probably right. A sunny afternoon, a quiet neighborhood. But she could not quell her unease. She threw on shorts and a T-shirt, stepped into her sandals, and hurried back downstairs.

"If you see her, tell her to stay indoors."

"Is everything okay?"

"Yes, I'm sure it is."

She opened the back door. "Karen!" The swing set was empty, and there was no movement in the gazebo. "Damn." She circled the house, stopping to peer up into the ficus tree.

At the street she looked both ways. A car passed, then Gail ran across, going through the twin columns of coral rock, then up the gentle, curving slope of the Cunninghams' property, a colonial-style house with a weather vane on top. An American flag waved from its holder on one of the four columns across the slate porch. Miniature boxwoods bordered the old brick walkway. Gail lifted the brass knocker, and after a minute, Peggy Cunningham appeared.

"Have you seen Karen?"

"Yes, she's up in Lindsay's room." Peggy's blue eyes widened. "My goodness, what's the matter?"

Gail was shaking with relief. "I guess I should tell you."

"Come in."

The house was spotless, everything in its place, glowing with furniture polish. White-painted woodwork accented polished oak floors and oriental rugs. Cranberry glass sparkled in a window. There were Limoges porcelain boxes on the mantel, silk shades on the lamps, fresh flowers on the mahogany sideboard, and needlepoint seat covers on the dining room chairs. Everything had that slightly worn look achieved by inheritance.

Peggy Cunningham, in a flowered lilac jumper and Keds with little white socks, led Gail through the kitchen, where the smell of roast beef curled from the oven. A pie sat cooling on the tiled countertop. Gail's mouth watered. A golden retriever followed them, tail swishing, nails tapping on the floor.

They reached the back porch, which was glassed in and cool, furnished with old white wicker and flowered cushions.

Another woman sat at a card table strewn with papers and index cards.

"You know Ana, don't you?"

Gail said she did. Ana Cabrera was Jennifer's mother. Jennifer was upstairs with the other girls. Quickly moving aside some file boxes, Peggy explained that they had been working on the Fourth of July benefit for Gulliver Academy, which her children attended, but that Gail's visit was no bother at all. Peggy told Gail to sit down, then brought her some iced tea with a sprig of mint. Gail could see the herb garden from where she sat, a sunny spot with a bird bath and trellis of ivy.

Peggy Cunningham told Ana Cabrera that Gail had come over white as a sheet, and that something had happened.

The women were staring at her. She said, "It started about two weeks ago with a phone call. Peggy, I am so sorry. I know now that Payton could never have made such a call." She told them about the paint thrown on her car, then the photographs of Karen, which she described only briefly. The women's mouths fell open. Ana Cabrera whispered, "Why is he doing this?"

"I don't know."

"You have no idea *who*?" Peggy asked.

"The police said to make a list of clients who might have it in for me. Not that I don't get along with my clients," she added quickly.

"What about the gardener?" Ana asked. "Or one of the work-men? You've had lots of men over there working at your house."

"We don't have a gardener," Gail said, "only somebody who comes by and cuts the grass when he feels like it. Nobody else is working for us right now. Except Charlie Jenkins." She said to Ana, "You know him. He's done work for you."

She frowned. "I don't think so."

"He's about thirty, black hair, a beard, sort of chubby? He drives an old green van. He gave you as a reference."

"Oh, yes. About a month ago he came by, but I didn't hire him. I don't hire people who just drop by. He didn't tell you the truth. You should have called me."

If she had not been so distant from her neighbors, Gail thought. If she had not been embarrassed that her roofers had thrown trash in the street and she had yelled at a kid for smoking in her backyard. She had imagined that they saw her as a negligent mother, a pushy bitch lawyer, a woman whose behavior with her lover was shocking to adolescent sensibilities. Maybe they did think this after all, and here she was, laying out her life to these women who appeared so sympathetic. Sympathy or curiosity? Gail saw the greedy fascination on their shocked faces and knew that this would be all over the neighborhood before dark. People would ask each other, Who is Gail Connor that she has brought this to our safe, respectable block?

She smiled and said, "Well. I need to go start dinner."

At the bottom of the stairs Peggy called up for Lindsay, whose face peeked over the railing. "Tell Karen her mother is here, and it's time to go home." A minute later three girls came clattering down the stairs, three pairs of eyes looking at Gail. Karen said to the others, "Bye! See you tomorrow." The girls waved.

At the door, Peggy came out too. When Karen was out of earshot, Peggy said quietly to Gail, "You're going to be careful, aren't you?" Gail assured her that she was. Peggy nodded, then said, "Gail, I don't want you to take this the wrong way, but I think it would be better if Lindsay and Karen didn't play together for a while—till this is over, I mean."

Gail hesitated, then asked, "At my house? Or . . . what?"

"Not here either," Peggy said. "I'm sorry, but I just don't feel right exposing Lindsay to a risk like that."

"Well, she doesn't have a contagious disease."

A bluejay hopped across the porch, then fluttered away. Peggy was staring at the ground. She shook her head. "I'm sorry, Gail. I just can't." The door closed, and the brass knocker made a soft clunk.

Gail looked over at Karen. She was not in the mood to chastise her for disappearing. "Come on. Let's go home." She could have added, Your mom has just screwed up every friendship you had in this neighborhood.

Halfway down the driveway, Karen said, "You lied. I asked Jennifer and Lindsay if they ever heard of that stalker, and they said they didn't. You made it up. You don't want me to go out because you're afraid I'll do something with Payton. That's what Lindsay says." Her eyes were narrowed, and her mouth was a thin line—like her father's when he was angry.

"We'll talk about it later."

"Your red bra is showing right through your T-shirt! That is so embarrassing." She walked past Gail.

Gail touched her hair and found it still damp. "I—I ran out of the house so fast."

"You always embarrass me."

"I didn't know where you were." Gail's throat ached. "I couldn't find you." She leaned against the rock column.

Karen stared at her. "What's the matter? Mom? Don't cry!" She put thin arms around Gail's waist and held on. "Mommy, I didn't mean it. Please stop!"

"It's okay." Gail held Karen's face tightly and kissed her on both cheeks, then once on the lips. "I love you more than anything. Never, ever forget that."

Karen's chin wobbled. "I love you too, Mommy. I swear."

Arms around each other, they crossed the street. Gail decided that tonight, between dinner and story, she would tell Karen about the photographs. It would be even harder to explain why she couldn't go to Lindsay Cunningham's house anymore.

The green van was still in their driveway. Passing it, Gail made a mental note of the license plate, aware of how ridiculous it was to do so. She peered inside through the dirt-grimed side window. Tool chests. A broken chair. An old tire. Paint cans. Putting Karen behind her, she opened the front door. The house was cold as a wine cellar. Charlie Jenkins sat on a wooden chair by the arched entryway to the hall, hands on his thighs, feet spread.

"I was just about to go look for you." He stood up. "I'm all done."

"So. It was the air handler," Gail said.

"Sure was. When was the last time those coils were cleaned? I bet you don't know how." He walked toward the hall. "Come here, I'll show you."

"No. I'll see it later."

He was still pointing in that direction. "It only takes a minute."

"I'd rather not. How much do I owe you?"

"Seventy-five dollars. Cash."

"Do you mind waiting outside? I'll be right back." She held the door.

His brows rose. "O-kay."

She locked the door, ran upstairs to take the money from her purse, then back down. She opened the door far enough to give him the money. "Thank you so much."

He looked at her strangely. "You have any trouble, give me a call."

"Yes. Thank you. I will." After she heard the engine crank up, she pulled the curtain aside and watched the van back out of the driveway.

She found Karen in the kitchen, holding a piece of sliced ham just over Missy's head. The little cat meowed and batted at it. "Oh, Karen, don't tease her." Gail took the rolled chicken breasts out of the refrigerator and put the pan into the oven. She cranked the temperature gauge to 325 degrees, lit a kitchen match, and stuck it into the hole where the pilot light would be, if it worked. The gas hissed. "Come on, come on." With a pop, blue flames spread out under the black metal plate at the bottom. Gail slammed the door.

"Mom, can I take Missy outside?" Karen nuzzled her nose in the white fur under the kitten's chin. "She has to pee."

"Put her in her litter box."

"She likes to go in the grass."

"Fine. Stay in the backyard." Gail went out on the terrace to make sure. "I mean it." Karen sat on a swing and spun around, twisting the chains. Missy was stalking a lizard. Gail called out, "Don't go anywhere."

"I *won't*."

As Gail went back inside, the telephone started to ring. They had put caller-ID on every phone in the house, including the one on the wall in the kitchen. The screen said W. SWEET, but she recognized the number at Jamie's house.

Jamie was drunk. Not roaring drunk or falling-down drunk, or even giddy. It was a dark, lonely drunk, one that wants to sleep and never wake up, and had even thought of ways to do it, but Bobby knew how to call 911, and what if they got here too soon? And anyway, Jamie told Gail, the kids haven't had dinner yet.

Then she laughed.

They sat in the chaos of the living room, talking over the whir of the fan in the window. Jamie had turned off the air conditioner to save on the electric bill.

Gail said, "I'll be right back." She went out to the back porch, where Karen was keeping an eye on the three Sweet children. Gail had explained the situation in general terms: One of my clients is sick, and she needs to talk to me. Could you help with the kids? While Gail was changing clothes, Karen packed her backpack full of Beanie Babies, coloring books, and markers. They had been here fifteen minutes, and already Karen was organizing the construction of a house out of old cardboard boxes and duct tape. The older boy was taping, the girl was drawing a window, and the toddler went in and out the door.

"Karen, you want to see what there is in the kitchen to eat? It's after six o'clock. I'll bet they're hungry."

"Okay." She stood up and said to Becky, "While I'm gone, color some flowers on the side. Not yellow, it doesn't show up."

Gail had explained it more fully in her note to Anthony, which she had left on the kitchen table at home. Wendell had paid his wife another visit. She was threatening to kill herself. Gail had added a postscript. *Take the chicken out at six-thirty. I love you.*

Arriving at the Sweet house determined to call the police regardless of what Jamie might say to the contrary, Gail had been surprised to find no bruises or blood. She had found the half-empty bottle of Southern Comfort that Jamie had been sipping all afternoon.

When Gail came back to the living room, she sat on the edge of the coffee table. "Jamie, I have to leave soon. Could you call the lady next door to come over?"

"Yeah. I'll call her. She said to, anytime. I'm sorry for draggin' you out here. I'm glad you came, though. Real glad." She pushed her fingers slowly through her hair, lifting it back from her face. Her hair was bright on the ivory-colored sofa.

"Are you sure you're all right now?"

Jamie smiled. Her lips were pale. "You want to know what Wendell did?"

Gail looked at her. "Tell me."

"He . . . made me do it with him. He said it would show me what I been missing." She laughed. "It wasn't near as good as I remember."

Barely able to speak, Gail whispered, "Oh, Jamie." She reached for her hand. "Let me call the police."

She shook her head. "I'm not hurt."

"Yes, you are."

Jamie suddenly put her hands over her face.

Gail said, "Where were the children?"

"In the playroom." The hands fell away. "They didn't see anything."

"Call the police. Please."

"No. He would say I wanted him to."

"But you didn't."

One side of Jamie's mouth rose. "I don't know. I don't know if I did or not. Isn't that weird? At first, I mean. And then . . . I just wanted it to be over." She closed her eyes. "I want it all to be over, Gail. Please."

Harry Lasko owned—and after sentencing would lose to the U.S. government—a penthouse at the Seacoast Towers on Miami Beach. By the time the elevator opened in his foyer, the building was casting a long shadow across the sand.

Harry had just been for a swim, and he was still wearing a striped terry-cloth robe. His rubber sandals slapped on the marble floor as he led Gail and Karen into his apartment. Low sofas faced each other across a glass table. Windows were reflected in a mirrored wall, and the room seemed endless.

Gail had called Harry Lasko from the lobby downstairs, having obtained his address from Jamie. She had not, however, called Anthony to say she planned a detour before coming home.

Walking over to the hall, Harry called out, "Dorothy?"

A woman appeared in the tunic and heavy shoes of a nurse's assistant. Gail assumed she took care of Harry's wife, Edie.

"I think this young lady needs some cookies, maybe a little juice, whatever she wants. She can watch TV in the kitchen. How's that, Karen?" He patted her cheek. His inverted eyebrows canted at even more of an angle when he smiled. Karen thanked him and said she would rather draw, since she had brought her colored markers and some paper.

Declining a drink, Gail followed Harry across the living room. He slid open a door, and they went out on the terrace.

"That's a very bright girl," Harry said. His robe was loosely belted, revealing a brown, leathery chest, curly white hair, and a chain with a gold starfish.

"I hope you don't mind her coming along."

"Naah. I love kids. My grandkids are great. My son is an idiot, but what can you do?" He set his drink on a small plastic table between two chairs.

Gail leaned on the railing. Her hair blew back from her face. The sea was dark blue at a distance, paler at the shore, breaking into lace on the beach. The heat had let go, and dozens of people were out, tiny from this height.

"I'm gonna miss the view," Harry Lasko said.

She turned around. He had sat down and lit a cigarette. Age had thinned his calves, and a sandal dangled from his toe. The wind teased the thinning white hair on his sun-browned scalp. The lenses of his glasses had darkened only slightly here in the shade, and she could see through them.

"What do you need, Gail?"

"It's what Jamie needs. You said you wanted to help."

"Name it."

"Your records on the sale of the casino at Eagle Beach."

Still looking at her, Harry exhaled smoke, and the wind swept it away.

Gail said, "You and Wendell both participated in the sale. He won't give me any of his documents, but if you have Eagle Beach, at least I'll have something to go on."

"Have you talked to my lawyer?" Harry Lasko chuckled and reached for his drink. "Dumb question. If Quintana knew, you wouldn't be here."

"The records won't be filed in court," Gail said. "I won't tell Wendell I have them. I just want to *see* them."

"This divorce was supposed to be settled already. Jesus. I thought you could negotiate with Wendell's lawyer and get Jamie a decent settlement."

"I thought so too, but Wendell's trying to wear her down." Gail sat in the other chair. "We lost in court today. The judge is going to reduce Jamie's support if I can't prove Wendell can afford it. Jamie won't last, Harry. She's been drinking. She's so depressed I'm afraid of what she might do to herself. The children are what's keeping her going. She might go back to Wendell because she thinks she has no other way to take care of them, or because she's too tired to fight anymore."

"Tell her to forget Wendell. How much does she need for the kids? I can help her."

"Why should you? They're Wendell's kids. If he has the money, he should damn well support them."

Harry made a noncommittal noise and picked up his drink. He wasn't avoiding her, he was thinking, so Gail sat back in her chair and waited. Finally he said, "Gail, I can't do it. If this got to the feds . . . Do you understand?"

It was on her lips to assure him again, to remind him that he was the only one who could help, that he had to . . . Gail nodded. "I understand." She watched the ocean for a while through the railing. "Maybe it's personal. I hate to lose. I was so angry at Wendell. I lost today, and I wanted so badly to win."

Harry pointed his cigarette at her. "In my business, you win if you can walk out with what you came in with." He picked up his drink, then put it down again. He shifted in his chair. "I don't have documents. Not like you see in a usual closing. It wasn't like that. It was memos, a handshake, and some wire transfers. Besides, our names don't appear anywhere, so even if I gave you everything I've got, it wouldn't help." He took a deep drag on his cigarette.

He was changing his mind. Afraid to push him too hard, Gail spoke quietly. "You could tell me what the memos mean, though. Couldn't you? And . . . explain how the money came in and where it went?" Gail remembered what Anthony had told her: Wendell Sweet and Harry Lasko had bought and sold the casino using a corporation registered in the Caymans, which in turn had hidden their names under layers of trusts. "And if there are any documents or trust agreements showing ownership . . ."

"What are you doing to me, sweetheart?" His laugh trailed off into a long sigh. "You could make sure Jamie gets everything here in the States?"

"I think so, yes, if I can follow the trail and find out where his money is."

"What the hell." Harry looked over at her, brows in a quizzical slant. "Should we tell my lawyer? It's up to you."

"He should know," Gail said. "Let me handle it."

Harry got up and leaned his elbows on the railing, smoothing his hair, looking out at the ocean. "That fucking Wendell."

Gail stood beside him.

"Guy like that ought to be taken care of. It would be no problem. I'm tempted."

"Don't do that, Harry."

He flipped his cigarette over the edge. "In life you don't get a lot of people you really click with. Four or five if you're lucky. People who, if you didn't see them for twenty years, and then bam, there they are, you could pick up the same conversation where you left off. My Edie was one of them. There was a guy I knew in Vegas, but he's gone now. Couple of friends still in the business. And Jamie. She's another one. She told me, Harry, when you get out, I'm gonna throw you a party like you never saw. And she will. She'll be there."

Gail smiled at him. "I think you're a little in love with her."

"Come on. She's a kid." Harry leaned his back against the railing, arms spread. "I still say it would be easier if you let me give her some money. Not all at once—that draws attention—but whenever she needs it."

"Keep it for yourself and Edie."

"I have enough, and there's somebody to take care of things while I'm away, so don't worry about whether she'd get it or she wouldn't."

Gail ventured to ask, "Who?"

He shrugged. "Someone I trust."

Meaning someone he trusted to manage a great deal of what was probably illegal cash maintained somewhere beyond the reach of U.S. authorities, and whose name he preferred not to reveal.

Gail stepped on the bottom rail and leaned out as far as she dared, and the wind whipped the hem of her shirt and tossed her hair. The clouds that towered over the eastern horizon reflected orange and pink from the west.

She felt Harry's hand on the back of her shirt, holding on. "I'm sure gonna miss this view," he said.

At the house on Clematis Street, Anthony was in the study downstairs working. Gail had used it as a storeroom, but when Anthony moved in, he had turned it into a small office, pushing the boxes against one wall, adding shelves and a desk.

The sky past the window was gray, and he had turned on the lamp. The papers on the desk were not pleadings in a criminal case but financial statements, most likely another project for his grandfather.

She bent down to kiss him. "Did you eat already?"

"No, I was waiting for you and Karen." He turned toward her. "Your mission of mercy went well? How is your client?"

"Not good. We'll talk about it later. I'm starving, aren't you?"

At the door Karen said, "Mom, I forgot to bring Missy inside, and I called her, and she won't come."

"She will. Call her again."

From the desk Anthony smiled at her. "Hi, Karen. How was your day?"

"Fine." She looked back at Gail. "What if she's lost?"

"She's not lost. Cats like to explore. Put some food out, she'll come home." Gail turned Karen toward the door. "Why don't you set the table? We'll be right there." When Karen's running footsteps had faded—she rarely walked—Gail held out her hand toward Anthony. "Dinner is served."

"In a minute. Close the door."

Smiling, she clicked it shut and went over to him. Anthony put a hand on her waist and tugged twice at the belt loop of her slacks. "And how was your day—aside from the Sweet case?"

Gail could sense something but didn't know what it was. "I didn't really learn anything new from the police. I took them the list. And they showed me the other photograph of Karen." His tie was loose, and Gail untied it. "I'm going to talk to her tonight. She needs to know—not everything, but enough."

"Yes. She should know. Nobody likes to be in the dark." Anthony pulled his tie out of his collar and folded it. "So what else happened? Anything of interest?" He raised his eyes.

"Not really. Why?"

He put his tie on the desk. "I asked Hector Mesa to go by Karen's school to see if he noticed anyone with a camera. Today he saw you with Dave. Could you tell me about that?"

Stunned into silence for a moment, Gail finally said, "So Hector was looking for someone with a camera. I don't believe that. Did you ask him to follow me?"

"I asked him to go by Karen's school." Anthony's words were like sharp pebbles, tossed one after the other. "I suggested that it would be a good idea to watch for anyone suspicious, and to make sure Karen was all right, and for the past three days Hector has been there. Today he saw Dave and you, together, and I would like to know, if you don't mind, what you were doing."

"Why didn't you ask me that when I came in?" Her cheeks burned. "Oh, let's see if Gail tells me on her own. I mean, if she doesn't tell me herself, then she is obviously guilty. Guilty of *something.*"

His head turned to follow her across the room. With his back to the light, his face was in shadow.

"And what did Hector say? I can imagine how he embellished it. What did he say, Anthony? I would like to know."

Anthony's palm lifted from the desk. "That he had his arms around you. That he kissed you."

"Too bad Hector didn't have a directional microphone. He could have heard Dave telling me that he dropped the custody case. It was emotional, and I'm not going to apologize." Gail looked steadily at Anthony. She would not tell him the rest of it. The loan. How Dave had begged for her help.

Anthony reached for her. "Forgive me." He put his head on her stomach. "*Discúlpame, cielo.* I was going crazy sitting here, waiting."

"You have to stop this." Gail wound Anthony's hair around her finger, then stroked his temple. A few silvery strands glistened in the rich brown. "I love you. Nobody else."

They both heard the scream, then the footsteps coming nearer. They looked toward the door, which flew open. Karen hurtled across the room, her mouth open in a high-pitched wail of terror.

Gail caught her and stumbled backward.

"No! Mommy, no! Mommy mommy mommy—" Karen was hanging off Gail's arms, jumping up and down at the same time. "Maaaaaaaaaaa—" Her legs went out from under her, and she fell to the floor, still clinging.

"Karen! Karen! Oh, my God!"

Kneeling, Anthony pulled her around, touching her quickly. "Is she hurt? I don't see anything."

"Karen! What happened? Sweetie, please!"

"M-M-Missy is killed! She's dead!"

"Dead?" Gail looked at Anthony.

"Where? *Díme, mamita.* Where is she?"

Still the awful keening went on, punctuated by ragged gasps for breath.

Gail wiped her sweaty bangs off her face. "Karen, tell us. Maybe she's all right."

"She's not, she's not."

"Where is she?" Gail rocked her. "Where, baby?"

"The—the swings."

Anthony held her shoulders. "Karen, listen to me. Is anyone out there? Did you see anyone?"

"No." She gulped in a breath. Her eyes opened, reddened and swollen.

He looked at Gail, then stood up.

With her arm around Karen, Gail followed Anthony through the house. The kitchen door was open, and a flashlight lay on the floor, where Karen must have dropped it. She had been out looking for her kitten.

He picked up the flashlight and flipped a switch on the wall. Light flooded the terrace, illuminating the metal railing down the steps, then gradually fading to darkness. The tubular frame of the swing set was barely visible.

Holding Karen tightly, Gail stood inside the screen door, watching Anthony's white shirt as he walked quickly toward the dim outline of the swings. Gail pushed open the door a few inches. "Shhh, Karen. We're not going out." Karen had stopped crying, but stood with her arms wrapped around Gail's waist, her face pressed against her shoulder.

Anthony was following the pool of light along the stepping stones, and where they ended came a quick flare of green. The light moved over the grass for a few yards before reaching the swing set. It swept over the ground under the three seats, found nothing, then climbed the frame, moving across the top bar, then quickly backing up.

There was a rope thrown over the bar between two of the swings. The circle of light slid down the rope and stopped. Anthony's hand appeared in the light, turning the rope, and a shape at the bottom moved with it. His hand jerked back, and the thing spun slowly. There was a dim flash of white, then black, then white . . . The beam suddenly flew out into the yard, swerving wildly before once again appearing on the grass to light Anthony's way back to the house.

In those few seconds Gail had seen what Karen must have seen—the limp body of a small cat suspended by its rear legs, and the hideous pink of severed flesh. Its head was gone. She pulled Karen away from the door.

As Anthony came in, she could see the revulsion on his face. He blew out a breath, composing himself, then came over to speak to Karen. He crouched beside her.

"Karen. Listen to me. Missy is dead. I don't know who did that to her or why. Someone very sick. A coward, maybe someone doing this for fun. There are people like that in the world, but he won't hurt you. He won't hurt you or your mother, and I promise you, he won't come here again. Don't worry. Okay? Karen?"

Her eyes came open. "Yes."

"Good. The police will come here and talk to you, so you help them as much as you can. All right?"

"Okay."

He kissed her as tears continued to stream down her face.

When he stood up, he said quietly to Gail, "Take her upstairs. I'll call the police. And I want to call my family's doctor to see about her, if that's all right with you."

Gail nodded. "Thank you."

Upstairs, she laid Karen in the big bed in the master bedroom and curled up beside her, murmuring softly and stroking her face. She told her that everything was going to be all right, even though she knew it could get even worse.

CHAPTER

SEVENTEEN

The doctor who came that night gave Karen something to help her sleep. He took a look at Gail and prescribed the same for her. The next morning, Anthony suggested that they move to his grandparents' house for a few days. It was nearby, it was familiar, and he had already spoken with Ernesto and Digna, who would welcome them. The swing set would be removed and new sod laid so that when they moved back, no trace would remain.

Seeing the wisdom of this, Gail asked Irene to take Karen for the rest of the day, and she and Anthony moved what clothes and personal items they needed to the house on Malagueña Avenue. Gail felt unsettled, uprooted, but believed this would pass as soon as they were home again and Karen had recovered.

She returned to work on Friday, and just after ten o'clock Dave came to pick up his money.

Gail had found time yesterday to call the attorney hired by Marriott to handle the deal. Jeff Barlow remembered her, but hadn't known she was Metzger's former wife. Small world, he had said. Coming into work early, Gail drew up an agreement for Dave to sign and faxed the draft to Barlow for his approval. He made a joke about wishing his ex-wife was so generous, then told Gail that after the final papers were signed at two o'clock on Monday, he would disburse a check to Gail A. Connor, P.A., in the amount of $125,000.

Lynn and Miriam came in to witness Dave's signature and went out again. Gail had told them nothing of this transaction.

She took her desk-size checkbook out of her credenza and wrote out a check to David Metzger, the top check in a row of three, and added the notation OLD ISLAND CLUB. She signed it, tore it neatly out of the book, and slid it across the desk.

Dave looked at it for a while before picking it up. "I've had Karen so much on my mind, this doesn't seem that important anymore." He folded it and put it into his wallet. "Have the police come up with anything since we talked?"

She had called him that same night, not wanting him to hear about it on the news. TV reporters, alerted by God-only-knew-what telepathy, had descended on the house with their video cameras. The details were compelling: a quiet neighborhood in the Grove, a devastated child, a decapitated kitten, the missing head. Cameras panned over the street, the house, then focused on the door. There were shots of the empty swing set until Anthony ordered them out of the yard. He requested the Miami Police not to mention the other incidents, and so far they had complied.

Miriam and Lynn had filtered calls to the office, many from friends. Others had been pranks. One elderly voice offered to pray for Karen, and another accused her of Satan worship. Still another suggested a *santero* to cleanse the property of evil spirits.

Gail told Dave, "The police are going to follow up with a couple of people. The kid across the street, which should endear me to his parents, and a handyman who was fixing the air conditioner. His name is Charlie Jenkins. His background is a little spotty, but I don't think he would have killed a pet at the same house where he'd just been working. That wouldn't be smart."

"Sickos don't have to be smart," Dave pointed out. "Listen,

I've been thinking. What about taking Karen to my folks' place for the rest of the summer?"

His folks' place was a condominium in Delray Beach, fifty miles up the coast. Gail said she thought that this was an over-reaction. "Karen is perfectly safe with the Pedrosas."

"For how long? You plan to go back to your house, don't you? She's not safe here, Gail, not in Miami. Mom and Dad would love to have her. You know she loves them, and they don't see her as much since we got divorced. There's a summer camp down the street and kids in the neighborhood. The building has a pool and a rec room."

"Anthony's going to hire a security guard. There is no way Bozo can get close."

"Bozo. How about . . . Dark Angel of Death?" Dave got up, too nervous to sit. "You don't want to let her go. You want to decide what happens. It's the same damn crap all over again."

"That's not true!" Gail followed him across the office. "Bozo—whoever—he could get to her easier in a small town."

"Not if he didn't know where she was!"

Gail opened her mouth, then said, "I'd be sick with worry."

Dave looked at her, then reached out and hooked an arm around her neck. "I know. I don't want to send her away, either, but it's not like she's going to Alaska. You can get there in an hour. We could drive together."

She laughed a little. "I don't think so." She let herself lean against Dave for a moment, then said, "Let's wait. We'll see what happens."

"Wait? Wait till he does the same thing to her that he—"

"Don't!" Gail turned away. She took a breath. "I try not to think about that. The only reason I don't dream about it is that Ernesto Pedrosa's doctor has very kindly given me some sweet-dreams potion. Otherwise, I would probably go out of my mind."

Dave put a hand on her shoulder and squeezed gently. "We'll wait, then. Not too long, okay?"

She nodded.

He went over to her desk for his copy of the agreement, which Gail had put into an envelope. "Thank you for this," he said. "I told Karen that we'd go to every one of the Old Island Clubs as they open. She asked me if I was going to be rich." Dave smiled. "I said, Princess, your daddy is already rich if he has you. But you and me, we're going to have ourselves a whole lot of fun."

Gail smiled back at him. "I'm happy I could help. Honestly."

"You should have believed in me a long time ago." He kissed her quickly on the lips before she could pull away. "See you on Monday, okay? I'll call you right after the closing and bring you the check myself." He saluted with the envelope and opened the door to her office.

Gail walked him out. In a good mood, he paused to say hello to Miriam, whom he had not seen in a year, and to smile at Lynn, warning her not to let Gail work her too hard.

When he was finally gone, Miriam said, "Wow, he looks just the same."

"A good tan does wonders." Gail took the mail from Miriam, who had sorted it. Back in her office the checkbook for her trust account was still on the desk. She flipped it open and computed the remaining balance in her head—just under $8,000. The client in the Zimmerman case expected her money today— $28,650 and change. The doctors would want to be paid also, but they didn't even know the case had been settled. Gail would have to explain the slight delay to Ms. Zimmerman.

The risk, Gail had decided, was negligible. Dave had been right: Business *was* done this way. Never by her until now. Some lawyers did it frequently, flagrantly. Gail would see their names listed in the *Florida Bar News* under "Disciplinary Actions." This lawyer suspended, that one disbarred for using their clients' money. Knowing she wouldn't profit from this made her feel slightly better. She reminded herself that it wasn't even for Dave but for Karen.

Gail put the checkbook into her bottom drawer.

Theresa Zimmerman's number was in the computer. Gail hit the button for automatic dial, then turned on her speaker phone, listening to the ringing on the other end. She shuffled through the mail and saw what she was looking for—an envelope from Harry Lasko. Miriam had slit it open and left the contents inside.

"Oh, *yes!* Harry, I love you." There were letters, most of them in Spanish. Fax numbers showed at the top. There were pages of figures that appeared to be income and expenses from the casino. What appeared to be a disbursement statement was typed in Spanish. She noticed $3,200,000 to Pan-Caribbean Holding Company. Harry had penciled in the initials HL. There was another figure, $1,050,000 to Yellow Rose, Ltd.—who else but a Texan would have named it that? As if confirming Gail's guess, Harry had written Wendell Sweet's initials. The buyer was a company called Inversiones Venezolanos, owned or managed by one Ricardo Molina of Caracas. Gail shuffled back through the faxes. One had been addressed to an R. Molina at the Commodore Club, Miami. Gail knew the building—tall, glitzy, and overpriced, just off Brickell Avenue downtown. Many wealthy South Americans had condos in Miami. Gail wondered if Molina knew Wendell Sweet. She wondered if Molina would be willing to talk. Why not? The deal was over.

With a start, she became aware that Theresa Zimmerman had answered the phone. She took it off the speaker. "Theresa, hello. It's Gail Connor. I wanted to let you know about your settlement. There's been a slight delay." Gail explained that the settlement check had not actually gone into her trust account until two days after she had received it, due to some mixup in her office, for which she took full responsibility.

The mail had slid off a heavy brown bubble envelope on the bottom of the stack. Gail noticed the return address: Ferrer & Quintana, P.A. Miriam had not opened it because someone— Anthony or his secretary—had typed PERSONAL next to her name and underlined it. There was a boxy shape inside.

With the phone tucked under her chin, she turned the envelope over and picked at the zip-release tab. "But I'll mail you a check Monday, if that's acceptable."

Anthony rarely sent gifts to the office, but Gail pulled from the envelope a pound-size box of Godiva chocolates in a gold paper box with a red ribbon. She looked back into the envelope for a note but found none.

Ms. Zimmerman's voice cut into her thoughts. No, mailing the check on Monday would not be acceptable. She would come pick it up. She needed the money immediately.

Gail felt a flutter of anxiety. The check from the Marriott deal would be issued on Monday afternoon. "The money won't actually be available till Tuesday," she said. "If you care to come in then, I'll have the check for you."

Tuesday? Ms. Zimmerman protested that last week Gail had promised her the money *today*.

"No, I said it would probably be available, but I'd have to confirm it." Gail slid the ribbon off the box. She interrupted the irate voice on the telephone to say, "I'm so sorry about the mixup. There's no problem, I assure you." She lifted the lid, then frowned, seeing a snapshot of Karen's room. A three-by-five color photo showed the unmade bed and too many clothes strewn on the floor. Gail took it out and found two more pictures taken from different angles, then the white and gold tissue that covered the chocolates.

She heard Theresa asking if Gail was keeping her money to earn a few extra days' interest, and if so, she didn't appreciate it one bit. Gail said, "No, it's just—"

The paper rustled softly between her fingers when she turned it back.

"It's . . . " She felt dizzy and grabbed the edge of the desk for support. "I'm sorry. Tuesday. Call then." She dropped the phone twice before she managed to put it back.

Gail stood up, backing away from the box. Her stomach heaved, and she stumbled for the bathroom.

*   *   *

When the detectives arrived a half hour later, Gail led them to her office. She had not been inside since the gruesome discovery. She stood at the door, Miriam and Lynn behind her, as Ladue and Novick went to take a look.

The older man lifted the tissue with the end of his pen. "Holy shit."

"We might as well take it in," Novick said.

Ladue leaned closer, sniffing through his short nose. "He's got a pretty good seal on that bag."

"Clear duct tape," Novick said. He asked Gail if she had a storage box. Miriam brought one, and he put the gold-trimmed box inside and interwove the flaps. "We'll dust for prints, but I don't expect to find any." He set the box by the door, then looked at the three women standing there. "Ms. Connor?" She came in, and he smiled at the others. "If you could hold her calls for a few minutes?"

Gail picked up the envelope. "This isn't from Anthony's office. I should have noticed. The address label is plain white. Theirs is preprinted with the firm name, Ferrer and Quintana. This means something, doesn't it? Whoever sent it knows who Anthony is and where he works."

"Not that hard to figure out, is it?" Sergeant Ladue laid the photographs in a row on the desk. His hands were ruddy and thick. "Take a close look. Can you tell when these were taken?"

Gail picked up one photograph, then the next. "No. I hate to say it, but her room frequently looks like this. Charlie Jenkins could have taken these two days ago. I went to look for Karen and left him in the house for about a half hour."

Novick said, "But you said that your daughter saw the cat after Jenkins left."

"He could have come back. Did you speak to him yet? I was sure he couldn't have done it, but now—"

"I went by his apartment," Ladue said. "The landlord says he lives alone. He wasn't there at the time, but we'll try again."

Gail remembered something and picked up one of the

photos. "No. These weren't taken Wednesday afternoon. Her room was clean that day. I'd told her to straighten it, and she did, then she went out."

The detectives exchanged a look.

"Someone else was in my house taking pictures. My God. I don't know when. How did he get inside? I can't believe this."

Novick asked, "Aside from you and your fiancé, who has a key?"

"A key? My mother." Gail tried to think. "My secretary, Miriam. Karen has one in her book bag. No one else. Wait. Charlie Jenkins has been to my house before. He did a few things for me last month, then he came again last week. Monday. Yes. Lynn Dobbert—my receptionist—used Miriam's key and let him in because I couldn't be home. I was there the other times, but not last week."

"Could we speak to Ms. Dobbert?" Novick asked.

"Yes, of course." Gail buzzed her on the intercom.

When she came in, Gail reminded her of last Monday, the day that Jamie Sweet had called and Gail needed someone to meet the handyman, Charlie Jenkins, at the house and let him in.

Gray eyes rolling from the detectives to Gail, then back again, Lynn picked at a fingernail and said yes, she remembered.

Sergeant Ladue put himself directly in front of her. "Ms. Dobbert, when you were at Ms. Connor's house, was Charlie Jenkins ever out of your sight?"

She shook her head, and her straight hair swung. "I kept my eye on him, like Ms. Connor asked me to."

Gail said, "Lynn, it's okay. We're not accusing him of anything. Was there a time when he could have gone upstairs without your seeing him? If you were in the bathroom, perhaps?"

"I would've heard him," she said. "The house has wood floors."

Ladue asked, "You were with him the entire time?"

"Well, I . . . I remember now that I went to the gazebo, but when I came back he was still in the kitchen."

"Why did you go the gazebo?"

"Because . . . I wanted to see it. I've only seen them in pictures."

"How long were you down there?"

"I don't know. Five minutes. Maybe longer, I don't know."

Ladue nodded. "Okay."

Lynn whispered to Gail, "What did Charlie do?"

"We're not sure." Gail opened the door. "Thank you."

Ladue took his hands out of his pockets and wandered back to the desk, where he stacked the photographs. "We need to get going, but to bring you up to date . . . " He gestured toward the sofa. Gail sat on one end, and the detectives took the chairs.

"Exotic Gardens. We called about the flowers you got on Monday. They show a cash payment on Monday in the name of Renee Connor—your sister."

"A woman placed the order?"

"Maybe, maybe not." He held up a hand. "You could go in there and say you're placing an order for Joe Blow. We don't know who the clerk is that took the order, and they said they were too busy to look it up. We could get a photo of Charlie Jenkins from the DMV and take it in, but frankly, due to the homicides we're working, other things tend to get stacked up."

"I understand." Gail wondered if the FBI could be called in to help with the investigation. "They have jurisdiction, don't they? The U.S. Postal Service was used."

"Technically, yes. But let me tell you. They don't come in on something like this unless (a) your daughter was kidnapped, or (b) the case has a high publicity value for the Bureau." He spread his hands, then dropped them on the arms of the chair. "Novick, what was that thing you had to show her?"

"Simon Yancey." He reached into the breast pocket of his sports shirt and withdrew a single sheet of paper, which he unfolded. "Last year Yancey moved to Winter Springs, just outside Orlando. I called up there, and the department is small, so they remembered the case." Novick gave Gail a copy of a newspaper clipping from the Orlando *Gazette*. He sat forward, as seemed his habit, with his forearms on his thighs. "This is from last December. Yancey was intoxicated and got into an argument with his wife. He shot her and their two boys, then himself. The children died, but the mother survived, although the clipping doesn't indicate that. Apparently he had lost his job just before Christmas."

Horrified, Gail scanned the body of the article, which ran two and a half columns.

FAMILY TRAGEDY: MAN SHOOTS WIFE, KIDS, SELF. *Winter Springs . . . late Tuesday night neighbors heard gunshots . . . Yancey had been employed as a drywall worker . . . Rita D. Yancey, 28 . . . sons Timothy and Jason, 3 and 5 . . . each shot twice in the chest . . . Yancey's mother said her son had been depressed since the couple lost their home in Miami to a foreclosure action—*

"Oh, my God." Gail let the clipping fall to her lap.

Novick said, "It isn't your fault."

"You said everything has a cause."

His eyes were gentle behind his glasses. "This was a chain of events. You didn't cause it."

"Well." She slowly folded the sheet of paper. "At least we can scratch one person off our list."

Ladue looked at his watch, then pushed himself out of the chair. "We need to get going."

Gail stood up. "Thank you for coming."

Novick held up the photos. "Do you want these?" Gail said she didn't. He dropped them into the empty bubble envelope, then said to Ladue. "Dennis, I'll carry this, and you take the box. You're bigger than I am."

"Guy's a comedian." Ladue went over and picked it up.

Gail walked out with them. In the corridor she said to Detective Novick, "Karen's father wants to send her out of town for a while—to his parents' place in Delray. Do you think I should be that worried? Anthony is going to hire a guard when we go back to Clematis Street."

Ladue turned around. "Someone chopped the head off your daughter's cat and mailed it to you in a Zip-Loc bag. The photographs are his way of saying he could get to her too."

"Hey," Novick said.

"I'm sorry, Ms. Connor," Ladue said. "You didn't ask me, but if I were in your shoes, and my girl had a place to go, I'd send her there—for my own peace of mind, if nothing else. When we have an arrest, you can bring her back, safe and sound."

Novick looked at Gail. "It's a thought."

"Considered and decided," she said.

"And you will change your locks, won't you?"

"Absolutely." She opened the entrance door for them, then went out into the hall. "I have another question."

They turned to look at her. Ladue had the box under one arm.

"Ricardo Molina. He's a Venezuelan with a condo on Brickell. I believe he also owns a casino on Aruba. Does that name mean anything to you?"

EIGHTEEN

The Pedrosa house was as still as a museum when the relatives were gone and the old people were there. Ernesto and Digna. The aunts. Uncle Humberto.

The maid was mopping the floor when Gail came into the kitchen. She explained what she wanted. *Leche en un . . . una copa. No frio.* Warm milk in a cup. *Por favor.* The woman found a mug in the high, glass-fronted cabinets and rattled on in Spanish about Karen's state of mind.

"Karen's feeling better—" Gail started over in Spanish. *"Ella está mejor."*

"Gracias a Diós. Pobrecita."

The milk was warmed in the microwave and put on a tray with a napkin and a slice of chocolate cake. *"Para la niña."* The wrinkled face smiled.

"Muchas gracias."

Anthony had stayed late at his office, preparing for a trial that would begin Monday morning. He was likely to spend tomorrow and Sunday there as well. Now that the old man was a little better, Anthony needed to catch up. Gail had brought some files, which she'd been going through in Karen's room, but her mind wandered. She worried about ever catching up.

Not to jostle the tray, Gail walked carefully through the tiled hallway, passing the gallery of paintings. She had just reached the stairs when Hector Mesa came around the corner from the study. If he had not already seen her, she would have darted into the living room. His eyes floated over her, and invisible strings lifted the corners of his mouth and just as quickly let them drop. He turned toward the foyer and she toward the stairs. She waited, a foot on the bottom step, until she heard the click of a latch and the soft thud of the front door closing.

She set the tray on the floor between the stairs and the grandfather clock and walked silently toward the study, wondering if Anthony had arrived. Light from inside the room fell onto the tiles. She was aware of cigar smoke, then the low murmur of Spanish—at least two men, possibly three, but Anthony wasn't among them. Ernesto Pedrosa growled, and someone gave an answer that he didn't like. *"¡Coño! No, voy a'blar con mi nieto cuando regrese a casa."* I'll talk with my grandson when he comes home.

The old man was planning to take up the rest of Anthony's evening with business. When he comes *home*, as if it were Anthony's home, and nothing would happen until he got here. The voices grew louder, approaching the door.

Gail fled. Around the corner she picked up the tray. She turned at the landing and looked back down. Pedrosa— swinging his cane like a pendulum—was talking quietly with his lawyer and a man from the bank. Gail had learned one thing at least: Pedrosa was not as feeble as he pretended.

"You conniving old fraud," she whispered.

Upstairs at the end of the hall she pushed open the door to Anthony's old room. Digna had given it to Karen and brightened it with flowers and a pink comforter. Karen's eyes came open. She had already taken her pill and would not be awake much longer.

"Where were you, Mommy?" She groggily sat up.

"I had to chase the cow all over the backyard. There's some cake too, sweetie." Gail set the tray on the nightstand and gave Karen the mug, but kept her hand poised underneath. Karen gulped half the milk and said she was full. Gail set the mug on the tray. "Sweetie? Daddy and I talked today about letting you go to Nonna and Poppa's house for the rest of the summer. We thought it might be fun to be with them for a while. You could go fishing. Do you think that would be all right?"

Karen thought about it. "Is it so nobody can find me?"

Gail sat on the edge of the bed. "Nothing's going to happen to you, I promise. It would just make us feel better. We wouldn't worry. Okay?"

"Would you come see me?"

"Of course I would. I'd drive up every weekend. Daddy too." Gail held her hand. "It's only for a little while. Two or three weeks. A month. It depends."

"Can I come back for the wedding?"

"We wouldn't have it without you."

"I told everybody about my dress. Lindsay and Jennifer want to see it. They can come, can't they?"

"They're on the list. You'll be so pretty. People will say, Who is that stunning creature in the purple dress?"

Karen laughed. "A creature. Oh, great. Mom, are we living here now?"

"No, we're just visiting for a few days."

"This house is like . . . huge. There's a wall all around it with spikes on top. They have servants here and everything."

"Not *servants*, Karen. They have people who help with the house."

"The old lady with those really thick glasses—*Tia* Fermina? She made my bed this morning and hung up my clothes. She called me *Señorita* Karen. If we lived here, my room would be a lot cleaner."

Gail could only laugh.

"And they would bring me breakfast in bed every day."

"Oh, certainly. And draw you a perfumed bath every night."

Karen looked down her nose. "Bring me some more ice cream—in a crystal goblet this time."

"On a silver tray," Gail added. "One for *la señorita* Karen and another for *la dama* Connor de Quintana."

"What?"

"That's me, after I marry Anthony. I'll be Gail Ann Connor de Quintana—if we used the old Spanish system. Actually, I'd use my mother's name too. So my whole name would be Gail Ann Connor y Strickland de Quintana. But they really don't do that anymore, and I plan to keep my own name."

"Who am I?"

"Oh, let's see. Karen Marie Metzger y Connor. Your gramma is . . . Irene Louise Strickland y Quarterman, *viuda de* Connor. That means she's the *viuda*, the widow, of Edwin Connor, your grandfather."

"Weird." Karen yawned, and her eyes opened again, but slowly.

"Time for bed." Gail was standing up to rearrange the pillows as a soft knock came at the door. Anthony came in, still wearing his shirt and tie from the office. One hand was behind his back.

Karen watched him. "What have you got?"

It was a teddy bear with curly brown fur. Anthony dipped him forward in a bow. "I don't know the name of this fat little gentleman, but he said he wanted to meet you. He was very insistent, so I brought him with me. *Señor,* this is the young lady I told you about." Anthony held his ear to the bear's mouth. "Ah. He says you are very charming, and he would like . . . What? To spend the night? Well, I don't know about that."

Karen held out her arms. "Yes. He can stay. Thank you." She hugged Anthony around the neck, then placed the bear on her raised knees. "What's his name?"

"Oh, I think he will tell you when you get to know him a little better."

Gail and Anthony exchanged a smile.

"Can I take him to Nonna and Poppa's?" Karen waggled the bear's ears. "I have to go live there."

"You do?"

Gail put a hand on his arm. "For a little while. We'll talk about it."

His eyes lingered, pulling away as he said, "*Señor* Bear may go with you wherever you like." He bent to kiss Karen's cheek. *"Que te duermas bien."* Sleep well.

"*Buenas noches,* Anthony."

He said to Gail, "I'll be in our room."

The guest room across the hall had not been redecorated, Anthony had told her, since he had first seen it as a boy—still the big four-poster bed and green walls accented with gold-framed ink drawings of old Havana. An armchair and ottoman angled out from the corner, and curtains were held back on brass knobs. French doors led to a small balcony overlooking a golf course. Gail had stood there this morning with her coffee at dawn, and rain had obscured the city.

When she came in, Anthony turned around from the doors, which now were dark, except for a few lights twinkling behind him through the glass. He had showered and put on his robe. The deep red silk made his skin glow as if from an inner fire. He held out his hand.

Gail crossed the room. "That was sweet of you, getting a bear for Karen."

"How is she today?"

"Improving. The sedative helped her rest, and of course Nena ordered everyone to treat her like a little princess. She'll be spoiled rotten." Gail slid her hand up the lapel of his robe. "I expected you to be waylaid by your grandfather."

"He said he had something to discuss, but I told him"— Anthony locked his arms behind her waist—"that I had other business upstairs."

"He's laying a trap for you."

Anthony laughed. "I know that. I will fall into it when I am ready." He pulled her close. His kiss was deep and warm, and her bones seemed to soften. The scent of his skin made her dizzy with need. He gently bit her lower lip. "Do you know, *mi rubita,* that we haven't made love in a week? Incredible."

She tugged on his belt. It slid out of its knot and his robe fell open. She found what she wanted, like heated satin. He hardened in her hands. She inhaled the warmth of his chest, left a kiss over his heart, and stepped away. Laughing softly, he retied his robe. "You like to torture me."

"I'll be back in a few minutes. Don't you dare go anywhere."

He caught her wrist. "Ten minutes or I'll come look for you."

In the bathroom, gleaming with marble and gold-plated fixtures, she showered quickly, smoothed on body lotion, brushed the cake out of her teeth, then dabbed perfume on the places he loved most to kiss. She dropped a nightgown over her head, bias-cut white satin with thin straps. She frowned into the mirror and drew her fingers across her collarbones. She hadn't been eating enough, and there were dark circles under her eyes.

As if it had been shoved in front of her, she saw a gold paper box and a plastic bag darkened with dried blood and matted black fur. Small white teeth. The eyes . . . She felt chilled and clammy, and leaned on the sink with both hands.

Anthony's muffled voice came through the door. "Fifteen seconds. Fourteen—"

"Coming." She drank some water from a disposable cup and opened the door.

He lay on the bed in his robe, hands behind his head, feet crossed. The small lamp on the nightstand made a soft glow. "I like that thing you have on," he said.

"You should. You bought it for me."

"Turn around."

She pivoted slowly, looking at him over her shoulder.

Anthony's eyes, so dark in the shadow cast by his arm, moved slowly over her body. *"Ven aca."*

"Why should I?"

"Because I want to know what you have on underneath."

"Only myself."

"Come here, I said. Let me see."

She walked barefoot across the carpet and stopped a short distance from the bed. With a finger she pushed a strap off her shoulder, then let the fabric fall to expose the top of one breast.

"Take it off."

She grasped the nightgown at her knees and it rose up her calves, then stopped on her thighs. He told her to keep going. The satin gathered into her hands, pulled by her fingers, inching higher.

His arm shot out faster than she could react and went around the back of her thighs. Laughing, she fell forward, then gasped when he buried his face between her legs. She felt his teeth, then the wet heat of his tongue. Moving to kneel before her, he left kisses up her belly, pushed her nightgown over her breasts, and drew one, then the other, into his mouth till the tips hardened. Her fingers dug into his shoulders.

Putting her nightgown back into place, he raised his eyes to look at her.

She was breathless. "Anthony—"

"I need to ask you something," he said. "It's bothering me."

"What?"

"It's about Karen staying with Dave's parents. Whose idea was that?"

"Oh, God. Don't. Not now."

"Was it his?"

"It was mutual. Dave and I discussed it this morning. I wasn't sure, but after what I got in the mail, I decided he was right. It was more than that disgusting thing in the box. Anthony, someone got into our house. They took pictures of Karen's bedroom. She isn't safe in Miami."

"You don't believe she is safe in this house?"

"Perfectly. If she doesn't go out. If she doesn't see her friends—"

"Why didn't you discuss it with me first?"

"Please don't make this into something it's not." She started to move away, but he held her upper arms.

"Gail, listen to me. You can't take Karen out of here. It's too dangerous. The man is psychotic. He's ruthless and obsessive. He could find her."

"When do we get to the real reason you don't want her to leave?" She twisted out of his grip and straightened her nightgown.

Anthony sat on the side of the bed. "And what is that?"

"You think Dave suggested it to lure me away. Where Karen goes, I go. If she stays here, I do too."

"What I think, *querida,* is that he is taking advantage of your fears, and I don't like that."

"I don't need your permission or your advice regarding my daughter."

He stood up, smoothing his hair. "You talked to him this morning? Where?"

"At my office."

"He couldn't have called?"

"We had to talk about Karen."

"It's always about Karen." He circled her. "Why do I so frequently have the feeling that you aren't telling me everything? Why is that?"

She pivoted. "Because you're naturally suspicious and irrational?"

"Is it irrational to believe that he wants you back? And that he's using Karen to get to you?"

"And you're using her to keep me," Gail said.

Anthony held his hands in the shape of a tube and looked at her through them. "Why does she evade the question?"

She clenched her fists. "The answer is, it doesn't matter what he wants. I'm in love with you—if you don't make me completely crazy."

His hands fell to his sides.

She turned her back on him and walked to the French doors. His reflection appeared in the glass.

"Gail, let's go to bed. I'm sorry I brought it up."

She brushed away some dried paint on the inner frame. "In a minute. I need to tell you something, so you won't accuse me later of hiding it from you. I'd have told you already, but I've had other things on my mind." She flicked the paint off her thumb.

"I told you Wednesday about going to Jamie Sweet's house. What I didn't tell you was that after I left there, I went to see Harry Lasko. I told him what happened and asked for anything he had on the casino at Eagle Beach. His copies of documents came in the mail today."

Anthony stood so still he could have been carved from wax.

Gail turned around. "I had to, after what Wendell did to her. He might as well have punched her in the face again—it would have been more obvious. What he did was worse than rape."

"So . . . you went to see Harry."

"I did what I thought best for my client."

"And if Harry Lasko has to spend the rest of his life in prison, well, *que lástima*. So sorry."

"As if that would happen," Gail said. "I promised him—and you—that nothing of what he gave me will be used in court."

There was more astonishment than anger on Anthony's face. "And what will Wendell Sweet do, Ms. Connor, when he finds out what you have?"

"Who's going to tell him?"

Anthony laughed. "He has to know. He will wonder how you got so smart, and it won't take him five minutes to figure it out."

"He can't say a damn thing. He'd incriminate himself."

The belt on Anthony's robe swung out when he turned and paced in the other direction. "Wendell Sweet would sell out his mother to avoid prosecution. If he knew—if he even suspected that his interest in the casino could be established, he would run crying to the government for immunity from prosecution. He would spill his guts, and *adiós*, Harry."

"You lied to me. You said you never heard of Eagle Beach."

"Call it a lie if you want. I chose not to discuss a client's business."

"How self-righteous you are. What conceit." She laughed. "How dare you accuse *me* of holding back?"

He pinned her with a fierce look. "That is not the same thing. *Coño cara'o*, how did we get into this?"

"Who are you really protecting?" she asked. "Yourself? What did Wendell Sweet mean when he said he knew things to take you down?"

Anthony stared back at her.

She said, "The casino was purchased by a Venezuelan named Ricardo Molina. He made his money transshipping Colombian coke through his country, then to the U.S. The DEA knows about him, so do the Miami police. I believe that he bought the casino as a way to launder his profits from the cartel. My question is, did you know *before* Harry and Wendell sold it to him, or after?"

"Harry is not involved with the cartel," Anthony said, "and neither am I, if that's your question. And no. I didn't know about the sale in advance. Are you finished?"

They were circling each other. Gail said, "One more question. Harry has money in an account offshore—a lot of it. He has someone to manage it when he goes to prison, but he didn't say who. Would that be you, by any chance?"

"Is that strange to you? My helping a client? And his choosing to maintain his privacy—which you are so intent on invading?"

"Is the money dirty, Anthony?"

"No."

"It wasn't from Molina? Or it isn't what Harry Lasko has skimmed off his casinos for years? Did you help him do it?" She took a breath. "Is that what Wendell Sweet was talking about? Tell me that you won't be taken away in handcuffs. Tell me I won't have to worry about that."

His brows rose, and he said patiently, "My relationship with my clients is none of your business. Wendell Sweet is full of shit. You don't have to worry. Are we finished now?"

Rage was a tight ball in her chest, pressing outward. "Maybe we are. Tomorrow morning Karen and I are leaving. I'm taking her to her grandparents' house."

"Is that right? And where will you go, back to Clematis Street? Or home to your mother?"

"Where I go is none of your business." She held onto the back of the armchair. "And you can stay right here. You and your grandfather are a perfect pair."

"Maybe you can go live with Dave."

"I might do that. At least he respected me. He treated me decently. He never lied to me."

"And you never lied to him. Did you?"

"No. I didn't."

Anthony smiled, showing his teeth. "I'll tell you why. You didn't have to. He is too dumb to have known the difference."

"Really." She smiled back. "When you and I were dating, he came to my house, and I slept with him. But of course you must have known. You asked if I'd ever thought of going back to him. I said no, but that wasn't true either. He asked me again the other day. Maybe I should reconsider."

"And did you sleep with him the other day? Or this morning in your office?"

"That's none of your business."

His right hand lifted, then froze. Anthony's lips were so tight they were bloodless, and anger snapped in his eyes like electrical charges in a black sky. She expected him to strike her, but didn't care. He exhaled and the back of his fingers brushed across her breast, then cupped it gently. "Who do you want?"

She stepped back. "Don't touch me. Again. Ever." She flung open the closet door and grabbed her robe off a hook.

"Where are you going?"

"To Karen's room."

"Stay here." It was not a request.

She put her arms into the sleeves. "I am not in the mood, Anthony. I am so far out of the mood that if you touched me, I would probably hit you."

He was around the end of the bed before she could reach the door. He grabbed her by the waist, and she found herself spun around, her back against his chest, his hand over her mouth.

"Shhh! Do not scream in this house. Someone will think we are being murdered and call the police. Karen will wake up." When Gail kicked, his voice became a heated whisper in her ear. "You are going to frighten everyone. Stop acting crazy."

Gail reached for her engagement ring. It was halfway off when Anthony's hand clamped over hers.

"Don't take that off."

"Stop it! That hurts!"

"*¡Déjalo!*"

She swung at him blindly, connecting with solid flesh. He pinned her arms. She found herself facedown on the floor, able to see the shimmering silk of his robe, a bare leg, and a foot on the carpet.

When she stopped struggling he let her sit up, and she shook her hair off her face. He remained crouched beside her, poised. They were both breathing hard. She leaned over, her stomach queasy from rage. Her body shook from it. "I have never hated anyone in my life as much as I hate you."

He stared back at her.

She couldn't look at him anymore and turned away.

"Gail. *Perdóname.* I lost my temper. I swore I wouldn't." He put his hand on her shoulder, and she jerked away. "I can't let you do this. Take Karen to Delray Beach? That's insane. What this has done to you . . . You aren't thinking clearly. I knew that and still I lost my temper." Anthony's arms went around her, holding tightly. "Sweetheart, don't. *Deja de pelear conmigo.*" He scattered kisses across her face. "If you sent Karen away and he got to her, it would destroy you. If it's in my power to prevent it, I will. You aren't yourself these days, and I shouldn't have become angry. Maybe I don't know the right things to say, but I can't let you take this risk."

"Let her go." Gail wept. "I'll stay here."

"*Ay, Diós.* You aren't my prisoner. That's not what I want. Shhhh." He held her tightly. "All right. We'll talk about it tomorrow. Tomorrow. Not now." He pressed his cheek to hers.

Utterly exhausted, Gail fell against him. When she began to cry, he put an arm around her back and lifted her up. He carried her to bed and took off her robe, then pulled the sheet up. He came back with some tissues from the bathroom, then turned off the light.

"Go to sleep."

Gail heard the slide of silk, then the rustle of sheets. The mattress shifted. He let out a heavy breath and crossed his forearms over his eyes.

She put her back to him. Her body was like a piece of twisted steel. Her throat ached, and she sobbed into the pillow until she gradually stopped. Past the French doors, stars seemed to dance between the shifting fronds of a palm tree. Cool air came through the ceiling vent for a while, then went off.

Anthony rolled onto his back. She tensed.

He took a breath. Then another. "Gail?"

She didn't answer.

He said, "Harry Lasko became a client about eight years ago, some trouble with the IRS. I advised him how to avoid future problems, but a client doesn't always listen. Harry likes people. He trusts them. Like Wendell Sweet. Harry didn't know about Molina. He just wanted a buyer so he could retire, and Wendell found Molina. I only found out when Harry did. The deal was underway. I told him not to go through with it, but he said, No, you don't back out on a guy like Molina. Meanwhile the government was on to Harry about some other matters. He says he was creative with his accounting, they said he was doing it with criminal intent, and I was trying to save him from prison. The prosecutors offered a deal. No time if he'd give them Molina. They didn't know about Harry's interest in the casino, but knew that Harry and Molina were acquainted. They wanted him to wear a wire. Harry wouldn't do it, although I argued with him, at great length. My grandkids would be shark bait. That's what he told me. So I'm doing what I can with his sentence, and there isn't much anyone can do—except not to let it get any worse for him."

Anthony shifted on the mattress. His voice came from another place, as if he had turned toward her and propped himself on his elbow.

"After eight years of knowing Harry, I became more than his lawyer. This happens, you become friends with a client. He asked me for help. He was worried about his wife when he went to prison. Who would take care of her? How could he be sure she was treated properly? And the grandchildren—he is crazy on that subject. He wants them to go to college. If he gave the money directly to his son and daughter to handle these things, the government would seize it, and Harry doesn't think either can be trusted not to loot the account. So I said yes. And I could be disbarred for unethical, not to mention illegal, acts, even though I'm not receiving any payment beyond expenses. But I said yes, and I would do it again. I think Harry must have told Wendell I was helping him, and that's what Wendell meant when he talked to you. Wendell could make trouble for me, and part of my reluctance to talk was because of the risk to myself. And because . . . I didn't want to disappoint you.

"I wish you didn't know about this, but I don't apologize for what I do for my clients either, just as you don't. I ask you—I *hope* for your understanding."

He was silent for a moment, then said, "You are angry now, and you have a right to be angry, but I think that whatever happens, we will be together because we have . . . we have *passion* for each other. To say love or want or even need isn't enough. I don't know the right words to say. I want so much to touch you. Not to make love. It would be enough only to touch you."

There was a sigh. He turned over, plumped his pillow, and lay quietly. Gradually his breathing became slower and deeper, and occasionally there was a soft snore.

Gail knew that she could, if she wanted, creep out of bed, open the door, and go across the hall. He might wake up, but he wouldn't stop her.

She turned her head and saw the curve of his hips, a bare shoulder, his dark hair on the pillow. He was leaving her alone. Letting her decide. As if there was a choice.

The satin nightgown slid easily, and she nestled beside him, curled against his back. Her open mouth pressed against the smooth skin of his shoulder, and her leg went around him. He caught her knee and held it, then turned toward her.

She held his face and kissed him. "Anthony. I'll always want you. Always."

He was ready and entered her quickly in a single thrust. She clawed to get closer, finally moving on top of him, bracing her hands on his, entwining their fingers.

NINETEEN

Gail sent Karen to stay with her grandparents after all. Even with Anthony's assurances, she could not dismiss her fears, and he agreed, finally, to allow Karen to leave—*if*. If the Metzgers would allow a private security company to keep an eye on the building, at his expense. Dave complained to Gail that Anthony Quintana had no right to set conditions on Karen's going any damn where her parents wanted her to go, but Gail begged him not to make an issue of it. She delivered Karen to Dave's apartment on Sunday morning, and Karen was in Delray Beach by noon. Anthony was pleased that Karen had taken Señor Bear along.

Three days without Karen had sent Gail across the hall to gaze at the empty bed. She had curled up in the armchair, and Anthony had found her there one evening, asleep. Telephone calls were of some consolation, and Gail called at least twice a day. Karen sounded happy, but said she would be glad to come home again. Then she had asked, "Where do we live now, Mom?" Gail had not been able to answer.

Gail had called Dave a few times, but not to discuss Karen. She wanted to know about the Old Island Club. What in hell was going on?

The deal with Marriott had been canceled for Monday and

reset to Wednesday. Dave wasn't sure why—some mixup at the head office—but he wasn't worried. "Give their lawyer a call," he had told her. Jeffrey Barlow, apologizing for the confusion, said that the general counsel had wanted to review the documents, but by two o'clock on Wednesday afternoon—barring some event he could not imagine—a cashier's check for $125,000 would be hand-delivered to Ms. Connor's office.

Gail had spent all day Tuesday attempting to placate the increasingly shrill and suspicious Theresa Zimmerman. Her excuses had been so lame she herself had blushed to hear them come out of her mouth. *I need to go over the figures one last time. The check was inadvertently mailed to the wrong address.* She had stopped taking Ms. Zimmerman's calls. Ms. Zimmerman had left a message: *If I don't get my money, I'm calling the police.*

The Pedrosa family physician had prescribed Xanax the night Karen's kitten had been killed, and Gail was still taking it. Otherwise, she said to herself, the situation with Zimmerman would have finished off what little of her sanity remained.

In late June the weather was too oppressive to sit outdoors in the sun, even in the morning, but the terrace outside their bedroom was shady, and the French doors were open to let the cooler air drift out. Gail could hear the shower going. Still wearing a pink cotton nightie, she nibbled on toast. Fermina had just brought breakfast—toast, juice, and *café con leche*, along with this morning's *Miami Herald*. Gail had read the sports section. Fermina would come back later to collect the dishes and wipe off the little glass-topped table. Softly singing gospel songs in Spanish, she would change the sheets, scrub the bathroom, and straighten the towels.

Just as Gail lifted the little silver pot to pour espresso, a leaf fluttered into her cup. She frowned, shook it out, then poured an inch or so into her cup and Anthony's, then filled the cups with hot milk. Added sugar. Stirred. After breakfast, she decided, she would get dressed and try to make it to work by ten o'clock.

There was a situation to be taken care of with the bank. Last

Friday, computing her trust account balance in her head, she'd made a mistake. She didn't have $8,000 left in the account, but a $12,000 deficit. Other checks would have bounced, but the bank had cleared them for payment. The bank officer had called: *Ms. Connor, could you drop in and see me tomorrow morning?* Gail had been forced to confess everything to Miriam, who was covering for her.

Today—unless a disaster occurred—Gail would deposit a cashier's check for $125,000, which Jeff Barlow would send to her office by two o'clock. And then she would mail Ms. Zimmerman a check for $28,650.27, the amount due from the insurance company as payment for one bad knee.

Gail was filling glasses with orange juice when Anthony came out and kissed the back of her neck. She inhaled spicy cologne. He sat down, adjusting the knee of his trousers. The sunlight fell through the trees like bright coins in his lap. His hair was polished mahogany, and his hands would have made a sculptor weep.

Full lips turned upward in a little smile. "What are you thinking about, *chulita?*"

Gail hesitated. "My wedding gown. Lola Benitez left another message that I need to come in for a fitting."

"I can't wait to see you in it." He kissed her mouth, then turned his attention to the newspaper. "*¡No!* The Marlins lost to Cincinnati, six to four. I owe Raul twenty bucks."

"Poor baby."

Anthony picked up the section and scanned the story. "I talked to Harry Lasko last night. We have a proposal on the Sweet case we want you to consider—you and your client."

Gail stopped her cup on its way to her lips.

He flipped the paper to the bottom half. "Harry is worried about Jamie. Aside from that, the divorce proceedings could drag out for months, and we are concerned what Wendell might do—as you and I have already discussed. So it would be to everyone's benefit, your client's most of all, if Harry takes care of her expenses—hers and the children's—minus what

Wendell would probably pay without protest. I would make sure that money gets to her on a regular basis. Of course, we need to arrange a way to do this, not to draw attention, but if it's handled properly, Jamie will be free of Wendell, Wendell can do as he pleases, and Harry will have no reason to worry. So if you could prepare a list of her expenses"—Anthony tapped the refolded section on his thigh—"and your fees. What is it— twenty-something? Twenty-two?"

"Twenty-two thousand, five hundred," said Gail. "Less my retainer, which Harry already gave me."

"Harry will take care of your fees as well, since Wendell is making a big deal out of having to pay opposing counsel." Anthony smiled. "Well?"

Gail was astonished. "I don't know how Jamie could refuse. That's extremely generous."

"Harry is fond of her."

"Yes. And of the idea of not spending any more time in prison than he has to." The sun twinkled on the juice glasses. "I'll call Jamie today."

"Good. Harry's sentencing is in two weeks. I would like to have this settled before then, if possible." Anthony lifted the napkin that covered the basket of toast. He picked up a piece and bit a corner off with perfect white teeth. His tongue darted out to catch a crumb, and he brushed something off his tie. The pattern was intricate Moorish swirls, green on gold, and the color matched the subtle stripes in his socks. His attention went to the newspaper that Gail had dropped in disarrayed sections between their chairs.

She was aware suddenly that a dismal mood had settled over her, but she didn't know why. The Sweet case was finished, or would be within days. Anthony had tied the solution up in a package, and all she had to do was carry it to Jamie. What bothered her, she decided, was that she hadn't thought of it herself. She had been too insistent that Wendell pay, and maybe it was her own pride that had jammed up the case. She had been beating against an iron door with her fists, when all the time Anthony had been twirling the key around his finger.

What kind of a lawyer was she, anyway? Still in her night-clothes at eight-thirty in the morning. Fuzzy on Xanax. Avoiding her office, with a lease payment she couldn't afford. Avoiding the paperwork stacking up on her desk. And avoiding the client whose money Gail had borrowed for *one* day to save her ex-husband's sweet ass on a deal he had promised would be *no risk to you, Gail. None.* She felt herself sliding toward catastrophe, a sickening, swirling rush—

Anthony broke into her thoughts, and she realized he had been talking for a while. ". . . might as well call the same sales agent we used when we bought it. What was her name?"

"Silvia Sanchez." Gail sipped her coffee, but it was too sticky sweet. She put it back on the table.

They had decided to sell the house on Clematis Street. Karen didn't want to go back there, Gail did not care for the neighbors, and Anthony could only see years of remodeling. He had broached the idea; Gail had agreed. They would look for something else. And meanwhile they would live here.

"If you have her number, would you mind giving her a call?"

"All right."

"*¿Qué pasa, mamita?*" Anthony took her hand. "It's not an easy decision. I have mixed feelings too. Should we keep the house?" The look on his face answered the question.

She formed what she hoped would pass as a reassuring smile. "I'll call Mrs. Sanchez. Maybe I can show her the house on Saturday. I'd like to visit Karen on Sunday."

"I'd like to see Karen too. May I go with you?"

"Of course." Gail had wanted time alone with Karen, but she didn't want to disappoint Anthony.

He tipped his head back to take a big breath of morning air. "As a boy I wanted to get out of here. It was a prison to me. You know, at that age, coming from rural Cuba, where I could roam around the countryside barefoot . . ." He laid a hand on Gail's arm. "I want you to think about something. We could live here.

Last night Nena said to me, Why do you want to buy a house? We have so much room, and we wouldn't charge you anything. If you want, help with the groceries."

Gail propped her cheek on her fist. "A few cans of black beans now and then."

He laughed, then became serious. "She has a point."

"We wanted our own place."

"They're going to leave this house to me in their wills."

"They are?"

"Nena told me, but I'm not supposed to know." He squeezed Gail's hand. "Don't think about it now. There's time." He leaned over and kissed her cheek. "When this is over—when Karen comes home, then we'll talk about it."

She held onto his shoulder before he could pull away. "Where are you, Anthony?"

"What do you mean?" He frowned, smiling a little. "I'm right here, as always. *Siempre tuyo.*" He kissed her again, on the mouth, lingering. "Always yours."

A soft electronic ringing noise was coming from the bedroom. He turned his head. "Is that your phone or mine?"

"Yours. I turned mine off."

He got up to answer it.

Of course they would live here, Gail thought. It was inevitable. Not so bad, really. The house had appeared in *Architectural Digest*, and the grounds had been photographed for a book on South Florida gardens. Meals would be prepared. There would be no cleaning to do, which would make Karen happy. It was quiet—except for the parties and dinners—which occurred two or three times a week and which, living here, she would have no way to avoid—

"Gail."

She turned to see Anthony in the open doorway.

"That was Harry Lasko. He's at Jamie Sweet's house. The police are there too. Last night they pulled Wendell out of the Miami River."

"He's *dead?*"

"Very."

Wendell Sweet had been murdered by drug dealers. Or by someone who wanted it to look that way. His BMW had been found in a park upriver with an empty gym bag in the trunk—empty except for some white residue at the bottom and a few scraps of silver duct tape, the sort commonly used to seal kilos of cocaine. Wendell had been shot in the chest twice at close range with a small-caliber weapon, then once again in the back of the head. His body had been dumped in the river. Gunshots were not unusual in that neighborhood, and no witnesses had turned up. His wallet and car keys were still in his pocket.

On an ebbing tide Wendell Sweet had floated down the dark, narrow river past rusty Haitian freighters tied to docks, past yachts at the Bertram yard, past barnacled wood pilings and small houses with banana trees in the backyards. He had drifted on the brackish, oil-specked water with rotting coconuts, plastic jugs, and sodden wood, and finally had come into the lights of an outdoor seafood restaurant, where one of the patrons had stood up and pointed at the shape bobbing a few yards away.

Miami homicide detectives, using the address on the victim's ID, had arrived at eight-fifteen in the morning to break the news. Mrs. Sweet came to the door. The police discovered that Mr. Sweet had not lived there since a restraining order in his divorce proceedings had ordered him out. Mr. Sweet's demise would leave his wife in full ownership of their jointly held property. They also discovered an overnight guest at the house, a former business associate of the victim.

Five minutes after the phone call from Harry, Anthony's car was accelerating out of the driveway at the Pedrosa house. Five minutes because he had allowed Gail only that much time to get dressed.

Anthony had told Harry Lasko to keep his mouth shut and to tell Jamie Sweet not to say anything else until he got there. With morning rush-hour traffic, they made it by nine o'clock.

"Exactly who do you represent, Mr. Quintana?"

Detective Evaristo Garcia had been assigned to the case, and he asked the question at the door.

Anthony said, "By complete coincidence, I represent both of them. This is my associate, Ms. Connor. We'd like to come in. They're expecting us."

There was another detective inside. Harry Lasko and Jamie Sweet were sitting on the sofa. Anthony nodded to them and smiled. "Good morning, Mrs. Sweet. Mr. Lasko." Anthony held his hand out to Jamie Sweet. "Let's chat for a few minutes."

Jamie glanced at Gail, then led Anthony toward the kitchen. Gail heard a door close. The detectives looked at Gail. She said, "Harry?"

They stood out of earshot in the foyer.

"Where are the kids?" Gail asked.

"Upstairs, still asleep." Harry Lasko's beard had grizzled his face, and his rumpled hair stood on end. His eyes were wide. "How about Wendell? Holy smokes. The guy was dealing."

"You knew him pretty well. You never suspected?"

"It's a surprise to me."

"Who do you think shot him?"

"Come on. It was a drug rip-off. They took the coke, kept the money. Wendell shouldn't have gotten involved with those guys."

"You sold your casino to one of them."

"That's different."

Gail asked, "What were you doing here last night, Harry?"

"It's not how it looks. Jamie called me, feeling blue, and I came over. We talked. I played with the kids for a while—that Bobby kept me up till two in the morning! I fell asleep on the couch in the playroom. My back is killing me." Harry's slanted brows shot up. "Say, did Anthony tell you what I wanted to do for Jamie?"

"This morning he did."

"What a break." His eyes danced with amusement. "I'm trying not to smile around the cops, but it's hard."

Gail continued to look at him.

"Uh-oh. I know what you're thinking, doll." Harry pointed at her. "I remember what I said at my condo when you came over, but I swear, on the head of my grandchildren, I did not pull that trigger."

Hearing Anthony's voice, Gail took Harry back around the corner. He went with Anthony, and Gail went over to see about Jamie. She had apparently thrown on her clothes this morning in some haste—old jeans and a big T-shirt stained with grape juice or Kool-Aid.

"Hey, Gail." She hugged her, then asked the detectives if they'd like some coffee. "I should've fixed a pot already." They said that sounded like a great idea, and looked at their watches. "Y'all want some pecan Danish? It's leftover from yesterday, but it's still good." They declined.

The kitchen had such a shine on it Gail nearly blinked. The floor had been mopped, dishes put away, and the cabinets were clean.

Jamie smiled and pushed her unruly red hair behind one ear. "Harry did this last night. I was upstairs givin' the kids a bath. Isn't he precious?"

"Too bad he's not thirty years younger."

"Well. He's special to me, and he knows it." Jamie ran water in the coffee maker. "I'm gonna miss that old bird."

Gail pulled out a stool at the counter. "Harry thinks Wendell was dealing cocaine. Did the police ask you about that?"

"They asked, and I don't believe it. Wendell had some friends I knew were in that business, but Wendell swore to me he wouldn't touch it."

"Not even if he was desperate for money?"

Jamie concentrated on measuring coffee into the filter. She shook her head. "I could tell when Wendell was lyin' to me."

"What did Anthony say to you?"

"Mostly he wanted to know where Harry was last night. And if Harry had anything to do with Wendell." She pressed the button to turn on the coffee maker. "Anthony didn't put it that way, naturally, but that's what he was gettin' at. He's pretty cool. Like . . . I'm not gonna tell you what to say to the police, but they're gonna be looking at Harry for this." Jamie flipped a switch on the machine. "And I told him, Harry didn't do it. We were here all night, talking and playing with the kids. You ask my oldest."

She took mugs from the dishwasher, which was still loaded with clean dishes. "And he didn't hire nobody either." She put the mugs on the counter in a row, five firm thumps, then looked at Gail, daring her to say otherwise.

Gail rested her cheek on her hand. "He told you that?"

"Who, Harry? No, he didn't tell me. He didn't have to. I *know* what kind of a man Harry is. I know he wouldn't do the kids that way. Wendell was their *daddy*. Harry wouldn't have taken away their daddy. They loved Wendell. They only saw the good in him, and Harry knows that kids don't have much these days to believe in, and if they don't have their daddy . . ."

Jamie watched the coffee drizzling into the pot. "They're gonna wake up in a little while. I don't know what to tell them." She closed her eyes and quickly turned away. Her shoulders began to shake, and she grabbed a paper towel.

Gail moved close and put her arms around her.

Jamie wiped her eyes. "Wendell wasn't a bad man, not in his heart. I'm sorry he's gone. I wished him dead more'n once, but I'm not happy he's gone."

TWENTY

It was nearly eleven o'clock by the time Gail reached her office.

She threw down her purse and found Jeffrey Barlow's number in Dave's file. Barlow was not in, but his secretary said that as far as she knew, the papers would be signed and payment made at two o'clock. Mr. Metzger had called to say he would be there.

Gail thanked her and hung up. "Praise the Lord and all the little angels," she breathed. She pressed the intercom and asked Miriam to come see her. Whatever happened with Dave's deal with Marriott, Gail knew that expenses had to be cut. When Miriam sat down, they discussed options for the office. Turning in the elaborate computer equipment. Breaking the lease and taking a smaller space. Letting Lynn go.

Gail said, "Anthony wants me to come to work for his law firm. You too, of course. I'm considering it."

Distressed, Miriam cried, "But you wanted your own office."

"Don't put that in the past tense yet," Gail said.

With a sigh Miriam sank into her chair. "We've been together for more than three years! If you go with another firm, I'll go too." She added, "I want *you* to set my hours, though."

A knock came at the open door. Gail told Lynn to come in.

"Theresa Zimmerman just called again. She said she wanted

to come by and pick up her check this afternoon, so I said okay. I hope that was all right."

"You *what*?"

"Well . . . I heard you tell her that you'd mail it this afternoon, and so . . . it would be easier if she picked it up."

"You told her to come here?" Gail stood up from her chair. "You don't *ever* tell a client to pick up money unless you have my approval."

"But if you're going to mail it—"

"Call her back and tell her you were mistaken. Tell her you needed to ask me, and I was in court."

Lynn's brow furrowed. "I don't like to lie."

Gail erupted. "You *idiot*!" She clapped her hand on her forehead. "I'm sorry, I didn't mean—"

"Don't call me an idiot! I do the best I can, and you yell at me all the time."

"All the *time*? I am extraordinarily patient."

"You're a terrible person to work for!"

Petite Miriam, long hair bouncing, ran from one of them to the other like an agitated dog. "Calm down! I'll take care of it! Lynn, it's okay, Gail is really stressed because of Karen."

When the office was quiet again, Gail cut a Xanax in half with her letter opener and swallowed it dry. Her heart was doing somersaults, swinging from rib to rib. She noticed how the miniblinds made stripes of light on the carpet. She kept them closed these days against the possibility of a bullet crashing through the glass. They reminded her of bars in a jail cell.

She pulled her stack of files to the center of her desk and reached for a pen. The intercom buzzed. Gail exhaled tiredly. "Yes, Lynn?" It was a Mr. Ferrer from Ferrer & Quintana.

"Raul?"

"Yes, he said he had to speak to you."

Gail gritted her teeth. "I told you, I'm not here."

"Oh. Well, he said it was important, and I thought—"

"Never mind. I'll take it." She picked up the phone. "Raul, this is Gail."

It took a few seconds for her brain to catch up with what she was hearing—a voice, a stuttering, high pitched whisper, like the laughter of a demented child locked in an echo chamber.

Gai-ai-ail Connor-or-or. It's been-en-en a long ti-i-ime.

Slowly she stood up from her chair. "What do you want? Why are you doing this?"

Did you li-i-ike-ke the choco-o-o-lates-s-s?

"Do you want money? You're out of luck. I don't have any. My daughter? No way. She's gone. You'll never find her. You want me? Here I am. Come on, you coward, walk through my door."

The echoing whisper filled her ear. *What I wan-n-nt—bitch-ch-ch—is you-u-u . . . dea-e-e-ed. Like the ca-a-at-t-t. I wan-n-nt you to die-ie-ie. Cut off-f-f your lying-ing-ing hea-e-e-ed, you fu-u-ucking-ing-ing bitch-ch-ch.*

"Same to you buddy. Tell me. Do you have a name? Can I call you something besides Bozo the Clown?" There was a silence. "Maybe Donald Duck? Dopey? Grumpy? Wheezy? Don't stop now, I'm recording this. Please go on."

"My na-a-a-ame is Dea-e-eath-eth-eth."

"Oh, really. How original. Is that Mr. Death? Do you carry a scythe and wear a black robe?"

"Sa-ay-ay your prayer-er-ers. He-ell-ell-ell is waiting-ing-ing." There was a click on the other end.

Gail slammed down the telephone, then screamed at it. "Son of a bitch! I will find you and rip out your heart!"

She heard running footsteps. Miriam stopped herself on the door frame, swinging then hanging on. "Gail! What happened?" A second set of footsteps followed. Lynn stared, open-mouthed.

Gail shouted, "Lynn! Who was that on the phone?" She came around her desk.

"What—the one that—it was—it was Mr. Quintana's law partner—"

"No, it wasn't. It was our favorite psycho, Bozo the Clown, *aka* Mr. Death. He asked if I liked the chocolates."

Lynn's eyes widened to gray circles in her white face. "But he said—he said—"

Gail put her forehead in her hands. "Lynn, I didn't mean to yell at you. It isn't your fault. Listen to me. What did he sound like? When you answered the phone, what did he say?"

"He—he—"

"What did he *say*?"

"Uhhh . . . Hello. This is Raul Ferrer from Ferrer and Quintana, I'm Anthony Quintana's law partner. Could I speak to Ms. Connor, please? It's important. Something like that." Lynn took a breath. "I don't remember what he said exactly."

"Did he have a slight Spanish accent?"

"I—I don't think so."

"Well, the genuine Raul Ferrer does." Gail paced. "Okay, think, Lynn. You've heard Charlie Jenkins speak, haven't you?"

"Who? Oh, the man who worked on your house." Lynn shook her head. "No, it didn't sound like him. The voice on the phone was . . . sort of . . . deep? Oh, Ms. Connor, I don't *know*!"

"It's okay." She patted Lynn's shoulder. "From now on, I don't care if God is on the phone, get his number and I'll call back. I will not take any more phone calls."

"What about Karen or Anthony or your mother?"

"Of course I'll take their calls. I meant, I won't take any calls from people you don't personally know. All right?"

Lynn nodded.

"Miriam, go buy a recorder for this telephone, and order caller-ID immediately."

"It's a good thing you sent Karen away," Lynn said.

"Well, she's staying away till we catch this freak."

"What if you never catch him? What if he doesn't stop?" Lynn swallowed. "He could come after Miriam and me. Or our kids. We have a tabby cat that's been with us for ten years, and if she died, my boys would go crazy."

Gail looked at her, then nodded. "Yes, well, let's all get back to work. I'll report this to the police, for what it's worth."

Without interruption, Gail worked steadily on the computer, composing six letters, drafting two complaints for damages in commercial cases, and preparing interrogatories she had meant to get to for weeks. Around noon Miriam brought the tape recorder in and hooked it up to Gail's telephone. The economy model— forty dollars from the security shop at the mall across the street.

Just after one o'clock, Gail gave Lynn ten dollars and told her to go downstairs and get her a chicken sandwich from the deli. Lynn stuck the bill into the pocket of her slacks and rolled her chair under her desk.

On the desktop Gail noticed the message slip, a piece of pink paper, one in a neat row of them. *11:35 p.m. To: Ms. Connor. From: Mr. Jeff Barlow. Message: Transaction canceled for today. Please call.*

"Oh, my God."

"Ms. Connor?"

"Why didn't you give me this?"

"You said you didn't want any phone calls."

"The *message*. Why didn't you give me the damned *message*?" Gail leaned against the side of Lynn's cubicle. Lynn stared back at her blankly.

"Okay, that's it," Gail said. "You're leaving."

"What?"

"I'm sorry, but I've had more than I can take."

"Are you firing me?"

"Yes. I can't stand this anymore."

"*Why?* What did I do?"

"Look. For one thing, I can't afford your salary anymore."

"You pay me *peanuts*!"

"Which you agreed to take, for the experience. Remember?"

Lynn's eyes narrowed. "Well, I'm not surprised. All you care about is money. You and your rich la-de-dah boyfriend. I know what you did. You used Ms. Zimmerman's money for yourself, and now you can't pay her back."

Gail called out for Miriam, who stuck her head out of the extra office, where she had been working on the books. "I want you to write a check to Lynn for whatever her salary is for the week, and give her two extra weeks' severance pay."

Miriam's eyes widened.

"She's firing me," Lynn said with a tight smile. She continued to glare back at Gail as she followed Miriam into the office. She came out again a minute later, folding a check. Her feet thudded on the carpet in their flat, laced shoes, and her hair swung side to side. Passing Gail, she said, "My husband is going to have something to say about this. We might hire a lawyer and sue you."

Seated at the other desk, Gail watched her from under the hand arched over her forehead. She watched Lynn take down her children's crayon drawings, the snapshots, the clippings. Lynn cleaned out the drawers in her desk and put everything into a box. Her lips moved, but Gail could not hear what she was saying.

"Lynn, I'm sorry about this."

"No, you aren't. You're such a bitch. You really are. You don't care what you do to people. I've got two kids at home to feed and clothe, but you couldn't care less."

The door slammed behind her.

Miriam looked around. "Oh, my God."

Gail said, "Miriam, I need to make a phone call. Then I might be out the rest of the day. Can you handle it?"

"Of course. Gail?" She caught up to her in the hall. "I didn't know about the message from Mr. Barlow. It's not good news, is it?" Gail shook her head, then felt Miriam's small hand grip her wrist. Miriam said, "Should I call Ms. Zimmerman and say not to expect the check? Or . . . wait till she calls?"

Gail opened her mouth, then said, "I don't know. If she calls—and she will—tell her tomorrow. She'll get it tomorrow."

Rain was spitting on Gail's windshield when she reached Coconut Grove, and coming down in fat, intermittent drops when she pulled into the parking lot of the Old Island Club. At nearly two o'clock, the lunchtime crowd was gone, but locals still were lingering with their beer under the umbrellas on the deck, ignoring the rain.

Gail went inside and shivered in a blast of chilled air. Busboys were clearing the wooden tables, and reggae pounded from the speakers. Stuffed parrots in fake banana trees jerkily turned their heads and squawked at random intervals. An overhang made to look like a tin roof ran along the food-prep area, and Gail spotted someone she knew behind the cash register—Vicki, wearing her usual little shorts and flowered Island Club shirt. She was tapping at the multicolored squares on a computer screen.

"Hi. I need to speak to Dave. Could you tell me where I can find him?"

Vicki looked around, and her tilted, black-penciled eyes flicked over Gail in a quick, dismissive appraisal. "And you are— oh, hi. Is he expecting you?"

Gail wanted to slap her. "Just tell him I'm here." She smiled. "Thank you."

"I'll be right with you." Vicki finished what she was doing. "Would you mind waiting over there? I'll see if he's available." She turned and walked into the back, the muscles in her calves bunching under sleekly tanned skin.

The rain was falling harder, obscuring the mangrove islands around the marina. It seemed to move in a curtain across the parking lot, finally reaching the deck, where it coursed off the umbrellas and made people pick up their feet to keep dry. A few of them ran inside, laughing and brushing the rain out of their hair.

"Gail?" She turned around. Dave had called to her from a doorway behind the phony storefront of a Caribbean market. When she got there, he said, "I tried to call your office just now. Miriam said you'd left."

"We need to talk."

The grimness of her expression took the smile off his face. "Sure. Come on." He led her down a short hallway stacked with boxes of napkins, cups, and toilet paper, then into his office, a small room just as cluttered. He closed the door.

"I know what you're going to say, and I'm sorry, I don't know exactly what's going on, but Jeff Barlow says it's just a matter of a few days. The general counsel at the head office wants to look at it again." He extended his arm toward a chair. "Do you want something to drink?"

"No. I talked to Jeff. He is not nearly as optimistic as you are."

Dave held up his hands. "I talked to the man too. It's fine. Would you relax?"

"Where's the money I gave you?"

"Where? Gail, I wire-transferred it on Friday to Armand Dubois." He tugged on her arm. "Honey, come on, sit down. You look like you're about to snap into pieces."

"Do not call me honey."

"Okay. Sorry."

"What is going on, Dave? Jeff was in the middle of a meeting and he couldn't talk."

"It's just . . . some crap about the name. They want to make sure Armand had the right to sell it to me, something like that. And he did. We signed a contract." Dave's hand smacked his palm, accenting his words. "Armand's lawyer drew it up, Armand signed it, I paid the money, and I own the name, the logo, the look—everything. It's like . . . owning the name 'Hard Rock Cafe.' "

Gail's mouth was dry as sand. "But . . . nobody knows the Old Island Club."

"Oh, you're wrong. The place is a legend."

"To anyone with a boat maybe, who sails in the Caribbean. But I'd never heard of the Old Island Club. Marriott won't get involved in a dispute over the name. They will just . . . forget it."

"They paid me eighty thousand dollars already!"

"A cost of doing business."

Dave was pacing around his small office. "If they try to back out, we'll sue them."

Gail laughed. "You can be sure they put an escape clause in their contract with you. I didn't even think to ask Jeff Barlow for a copy before I wrote the check. There wasn't *time*. I was so worried about Karen. I wasn't thinking. I must have been out of my mind."

"You're making this into a big problem," Dave said. "I really don't think it will be."

"How long did Barlow say it would take them to decide?"

"A couple of weeks, maybe more. They have to get in touch with Armand, and he's usually sailing this time of year."

Gail sank into the chair. Dave crouched beside her. "Gail? Honey, are you all right? Your skin is so cold. Here, put your head between your knees. Take a couple of deep breaths. Come on."

She raised her head. "I took the money from my trust account."

"Your trust account." He looked at her blankly. "Well . . . can't you transfer some money over?"

"From *where*? I have nothing to cover the shortage with. My checks will start bouncing. I will be sued. I could be disbarred from the practice of law. *Do you understand?*"

"Gail, calm down."

"How could I have done this?"

"Please don't blame me."

"No. I blame myself. I let myself forget that every business venture you have ever touched has turned to *shit*!"

"I'll . . . give you whatever cash I have on hand."

"I need forty thousand dollars."

He stood up and spun to face the wall. "I don't have that much."

"How much do you have?"

"About five grand."

"I want it."

"Gail, it's for payroll and rent."

"I don't care."

"I can give you a thousand. Ask your mother to spot you the money for a couple of weeks. Ask Quintana."

She stared at him. "I deserved this. I must have deserved it for something wicked I have done. It's all coming back."

"Gail, stop talking crazy."

Someone knocked at the door, which slowly came open. A

woman with short, dark hair stuck her head through. Gail focused.

Vicki gave her a smile. "Hi." Then she turned to Dave. "Mr. Metzger? You're wanted out front."

"Who is it?"

"It's somebody about catering." A lie. Of course a lie. And Dave knew it. She was rescuing her boss from his ex-wife, this screaming bitch.

"Tell him I'll be right there." When Vicki was gone, he turned to Gail. She could see the panic starting to creep in at the corners, like slowly rising water in a leaking hull, too far from shore. "Barlow said to wait. He didn't say it was off. Something is going on. Armand is pulling some shit. I'll straighten it out. It's going to be all right." He reached for his wallet and thumbed through the bills. "Here's about five hundred dollars. Take it. *Take it.*"

He unlocked a drawer in his desk and took out a heavy metal box. "I've got two thousand in cash. You can have it."

Gail put the bills on the desk. "It's no use," she said. "Five hundred, five thousand."

"I swear to you, it isn't my fault. Please. It's going to be all right. It will. In a couple of weeks . . . Don't leave like this. Honey, please."

Dave followed her out of the office. At the door to the restaurant she glanced back and caught a glimpse of him standing under the tin roof of the Caribbean marketplace. She put her jacket over her head and dashed for her car.

TWENTY-ONE

Irene came out of her house with a bright yellow umbrella, a spot of color bobbing toward her Chrysler sedan in the driveway. As Gail's headlights swept over the yard, the umbrella paused, turned, and came toward the driver's side. Gail got out and huddled under it with her mother.

"Hello, darling. Was I expecting you?" Irene asked.

"I should have called."

"It's just a little meeting with Friends of the Opera, but I have to go, since I'm presenting . . ." Irene looked more closely into Gail's face and took a breath. "Oh, my. Something happened. What is it? You're scaring me."

"Mom, I'm in trouble. If you have some time, just a little—"

"Come on, let's go inside."

Irene propped her umbrella in the stand in the foyer, then told Gail to start some tea while she made a phone call. *Evelyn, I'm so sorry, but I've run into a little situation.* They took their cups into the living room, Irene curling up on the end of the sofa, Gail in a floral-print wing chair. Nothing in this room had changed since Gail could remember. Her mother reupholstered the furniture from time to time or repainted the walls, but the pieces were in the same positions they had always been. The leg of the coffee table was dented where Gail had run into it with her skates twenty-five years ago. Grandmother Strickland's mantel clock ticked from the sideboard in the dining room. Sliding glass doors gave a view of the screened porch and the pool, and as Gail spoke, she saw the rain gradually come to a stop. Occasionally water would drip from the screen into the pool, making circles that widened outward.

"I've never done anything like this before. I can't explain it."

"Your motives were unselfish."

"That's no justification."

"Haven't you ever made a mistake?"

"I feel so embarrassed, asking you for money."

"Gail! Don't hurt my feelings by saying that." Irene smiled at her. "It will be yours anyway, yours and Karen's. Let me think. Forty thousand. I only keep about ten in my savings account. If I gave you a check off my money-market account, it would take a few days for it to clear. I bet I could raise at least eighteen thousand for Ms. Zimmerman with some phone calls tonight. Yes. I'd give them checks on my account, and they'd give me the cash. Would that work?"

"I don't want anyone to know about this."

"Heavens, no. I'd say it's for an emergency. No one will demand explanations."

"Mother, I'm so sorry."

Irene took her hand. "May I suggest something to you? And this isn't because I don't want to help you. Tell Anthony."

"Oh, God."

"Don't you think you're underestimating him?"

"We had a horrible fight about sending Karen to Nonna and Poppa's house. He thinks Dave had ulterior motives in suggesting it. If he knew that I lent Dave a hundred and twenty-five thousand dollars—"

"Listen to me. Let's say that he does become angry and unpleasant. Say he punishes you by withholding his affections, or he even calls off your engagement. Well, I say good. That's right. *Good.* You should be happy to find out something in advance that many woman don't discover until it's too late."

"Mother, things just aren't that simple!"

"Excuse me, but yes, they are. If this is all it takes to lose a man who supposedly loves you, then was he worth having?" Irene drew herself up. "Do you want a relationship where you can't confess the mistakes you've made? Trust me, darling, he will make his share, and you must be just as forgiving. Your father had his faults, heaven knows, but on that point I had absolute confidence in him. I could tell him the worst thing I'd done, ask him to forgive me, and he would."

Gail laughed softly. "Mother, you are such a contradiction. You once said that women can't tell men everything."

"I was referring to trivial matters. Little annoyances. This is far different. This goes to the foundation. No, I won't refuse to help you. I will not force you into a corner with Anthony, because I see that you are in no state of mind to think clearly about it. I'm going to go out and speak to my friends, collect what I can, and unless you say not to, I'll be at your office tomorrow morning, bright and early. I'll bring some coffee cake for the girls."

"There's only Miriam. I fired Lynn today. I went crazy, I think. I'd gotten another call from Bozo, who is now calling himself Mr. Death."

"At your *office*?"

"He got through by pretending to be Anthony's law partner. He said, 'Hell is waiting.' Hell couldn't be much worse than this, could it?"

"Yes, darling. Much worse. Karen is safe."

Gail went to sit beside her mother, and for several minutes, she rested her head on Irene's shoulder, unable to speak.

In the morning Anthony would have opening arguments in an attempted murder case at the criminal courthouse. This meant staying late at his office with his associate and the client. Gail was more or less expected for dinner with the Pedrosas, but she called to say she had errands to run. Karen needed some things from their old house, and Gail had to pick up a few pieces of clothing for herself as well.

Gail was aware of her reasons for leaving most of her clothes where they were—a stubborn protest against the inevitable. Soon enough the house would be sold and everything she owned would be shipped to Malagueña Avenue, behind the gates of *la Casa Pedrosa*. Outside the domain of her law practice, modest and stumbling as it currently was, the house on Clematis Street retained the last vestiges of the person she had been.

The street was overgrown, foliage brushing the sides of her car, dripping rain, when she arrived just before sunset. The roofs and treetops were touched with gold.

Turning into her driveway, Gail noticed the new alamanda bush that she and her mother had planted two weeks ago. She got out and went to look at it. A branch was snapped off, and tire tracks had been left in the soggy grass.

She heard a young voice. "I didn't run over it." Payton Cunningham was circling on his bicycle.

"Hi, Payton. I know you didn't. It was a car."

"I think it was a van." He circled closer. "I saw a van in your driveway."

"Did you see who it was?"

"It was that man who works for you? I passed by here and saw his van."

"His name is Charlie Jenkins." Gail stared at the house. "When did you see him?"

"About . . . six o'clock? I rode over to the park, and when I came back he was gone." Payton rolled to a stop, big sneakers on the driveway. He flipped his curly blond bangs out of his eyes.

"How long have you been here?" Gail asked.

"I got back about fifteen minutes ago."

She looked at her watch, which said 7:35. Charlie Jenkins had been here around six o'clock, but why? "Did you speak to him?"

"I didn't see him. I only saw his van."

"Was he inside it?"

"I don't know." Payton spun the pedal with the toe of his sneaker. "Well, I have to go. Mom said to be home for supper."

Gail said, "I'm sorry I yelled at you in the backyard. Remember that?"

"Oh, yeah. I don't smoke at lot. I mean, I tried it, that's all. Too bad about Karen's cat. Did they find whoever did it?"

"Not yet."

"You don't live here anymore, right?"

"We've been staying with my fiancé's family."

"Are you going to move back?"

She smiled and shook her head. "I don't think so."

"Tell Karen I said hello. She's a nice girl."

"I'll tell her. Bye, Payton." He did a wheelie on the street, shirt flapping open behind him. The bicycle skidded, swerved into the driveway of the Cunningham house, and disappeared behind the hedges.

Gail took an empty suitcase and a garment bag out of the trunk and set them on the front porch. All normal explanations would have Charlie Jenkins knocking on her door, waiting a minute or two for someone to open it, and when no one did, getting back in his van, clipping the alamanda bush as he backed out of the driveway. That he had come here in broad daylight, at a time when the occupants were likely to be home, made her wonder if the police were right in suspecting him.

There were no notes stuck in the door. She opened the mailbox and found the usual junk mail and bills. The key turned smoothly in the lock. She pushed open the door and stood on the threshold, listening. She flipped the switch for the lamp at the end of the sofa.

"Scaredy cat," she said under her breath. She dropped the bags in the hall and checked the back door, which was secure as well. The sun had gone behind the trees, leaving the yard in shadow. The swing set was still there. No one had come yet to take it out. The police had taken the rope.

In the kitchen the old fluorescent tubes in the ceiling came on with their familiar annoying buzz. Dropping her keys in her shoulder bag, Gail walked back to the hall and turned that light on too. A yellowish glow from the old sconces lit her way up the stairs.

She paused at the top to shift the strap of the garment bag on her shoulder and saw as if for the first time how narrow and cramped this house really was. Anthony had been right—minor fix-ups would never have been enough.

The wheels on the suitcase rolled smoothly over the carpet past Karen's room. Karen had asked for her tennis racquets, more shorts and shirts, extra sneakers. Karen wanted all her Beanie Babies. She wanted her diary, and Gail had promised not to read it. But someone had gone into that room, aimed his camera, and captured a piece of her daughter's life. So easily. Click click click.

In her own room, the windows were the colorless gray of approaching night. She looked down at the front yard, able to see a slice of driveway. What had Charlie Jenkins wanted? Checking to see if she had a spare job for him to do perhaps. She remembered the baseball cap and work boots, the paunch, and the smile in a short black beard. Such an open, friendly face. What was it that people said when they found out that the man next door was a serial killer? He seemed like such a nice guy, never any trouble at all.

She dropped the suitcase and garment bag on the carpet, burdened by fatigue so bone deep it had taken her breath. She needed to rest. To go home. Calling Anthony earlier, she had said that word without effort. Home. *What time will you be home?* At the Pedrosa house the family would be making final plans for their annual Fourth of July party on Friday. They would be trooping en masse across the golf course to see the fireworks at the Biltmore Country Club, then home again to a salsa band.

Gail unzipped the garment bag on the bed, wanting to be out of there before dark. An unreasonable fear, but even so, her senses were alert to every sound—an engine in the driveway, the creak of a stair tread. From her closet she took a short black cocktail dress, two tailored dresses for the office, a beige linen jacket, and two pairs of shoes. She hung the bag on the door, went across the hall with the suitcase, and flipped the switch at the door to Karen's room.

The light was in the ceiling fan, whose wooden blades began to revolve, picking up speed.

Gail took a few steps before her movements became jerky. She froze, staring across the room. A man was lying on Karen's bed, looking back at her. His mouth was open, and his beard was red.

Her knees hit the carpet. "Ohhh . . ." A low groan caught in her constricted throat. The room revolved with the fan, and her vision dimmed. She braced her hands on the floor, and when she looked up, he had not moved.

She saw work boots and jeans, a big stomach. The man was leaning against the headboard, falling sideways on a pillow trimmed in yellow ruffles. Blood from his nose and mouth had reddened his beard and soaked the front of his white T-shirt. His pants were unzipped.

Crawling backward, she dragged herself up on the door frame, then fled downstairs.

The police had found a gun on the floor, a .38 Smith & Wesson revolver. They had found gunpowder residue on Charlie Jenkins's hand, along with blood spatter from the wound. Pending the medical examiner's report, it appeared that Jenkins had inserted the barrel of the .38 into his mouth and pulled the trigger.

Gail sat in the kitchen, as far away from the activity as she could get—feet thumping up and down the stairs, red and blue lights flashing through the living room windows, the squawk of radios. So far the reporters had been kept at bay. Neighbors stared from the other side of the crime-scene tape. None of the neighbors reported having heard a gunshot—not surprising since this time of year windows were closed and the air conditioners were humming. In any event, gunshots from the bad side of the Grove were so common no one paid much attention anymore.

She had decided not to disturb Anthony at his office in the middle of trial preparations. She had, however, called Digna Pedrosa to explain why she might be late getting home, and if Anthony finished early, to send him to Clematis Street.

Detective Michael Novick put a mug in front of her. Gail had told him where the instant coffee was, and he had made himself at home. She had told him everything she could remember. Another of the detectives had gone to find Payton Cunningham.

Wooden chair legs rattled across the floor. Novick sat down and leaned forward, resting his elbows on his thighs.

"We found three photos on the bed of Karen—one taken at the playground and the other two on the swings out there in your backyard. The angle is from the door to the terrace. He probably used a zoom lens to get close." Novick hesitated. "He had taken a pair of your daughter's panties out of a drawer and wrapped them around his genitals. His pants were open."

"Oh, God." Gail's hand lifted to cover her mouth. Her fingers were icy.

While she caught her breath Novick told her what else they had found—a loose house key in the back pocket of Jenkins's pants, which Novick had tried in the front door before bagging it as evidence. He asked Gail how Jenkins might have obtained a key to her house.

"I have no idea."

"Perhaps you keep a spare on a rack? Some people do."

She shook her head. "We don't. But . . . he could have taken it from Karen's backpack. She would routinely leave it downstairs. Last time I saw it, I put it in her closet."

Novick leaned back in the chair far enough to see out the

kitchen door. He told the uniformed officer standing there to go look in the girl's closet for a backpack and bring it down here.

"Weren't you going to change your locks?" he asked Gail.

"I intended to," she said, "but—" She lifted her hands off the table. "This has not been a good week."

Novick told Gail that they had found a note on a piece of paper torn out of the spiral notebook on Karen's desk. In block print were the words, *Hell is waiting for me.* Jenkins's signature was at the bottom. "We'll have the document examiners compare it with a signature from his apartment, on a check or a letter."

Gail said, "Why? Aren't you sure?"

"I don't like to start assuming I know the answer. If we assume that Charlie Jenkins was a pedophile, then what do we make of the threats to you? I can understand his stalking Karen and taking photographs of her. That fits. But you have to ask, Why did he write 'die' on your car in red paint? Why did he send you the cat's head?"

"I don't *care* why. Just tell me he did it so I can bring my daughter home."

His partner came into the kitchen with a red and yellow backpack dangling from one finger. "Mike, is this for you? One of the officers said you wanted it."

"It's for me," Gail said. "The key you found might have been in here." Holding the bag on her lap, she unzipped the various pockets. "It's not here!" She looked at Novick. "Well? He must have taken it."

Sergeant Ladue took another mug out of the dish drainer. "May I?" Gail said to go ahead.

Novick asked Gail if Karen had noticed the key missing.

"She didn't say anything. She wouldn't have noticed if I let her in with my key."

"Where else might she have carried the bag, other than camp?"

"To her father's place sometimes, or to my mother's, if either of them picked her up, but other than that, it was always here. He could have taken it easily the day he fixed my wiring."

Novick asked, "Did he ever show any unusual interest in Karen?"

"Well . . . not in front of me."

"Maybe a comment about her being a pretty girl, anything like that?"

"I don't remember."

"Give it up, Mikey. The guy ate a bullet." Ladue tapped instant coffee into his mug.

Novick looked at him. "I'm not saying he didn't. However, since you bring it up, where's his van?"

Ladue filled the mug with hot water. "Down the street."

"They found it?"

"Just now. My theory is, Jenkins moved it out of the driveway so Karen would find him first. If the van is there, and no one is in it, Ms. Connor might call the police. She won't let her daughter go in the house. But if they come in as usual, and Karen goes up to her room—"

"They aren't living here now," Novick said.

"Well, he didn't know that, did he?"

"He knew Karen was gone," Gail said. "I told him when he called today that she was out of town."

"He thought you were lying to him." Ladue sipped his coffee.

"Apparently so," she said.

Novick said, "Except for a few traffic offenses and one arrest for petty theft, which was never prosecuted, his record is clean. I'm surprised we didn't find a history of violence. Cruelty to animals, an assault and battery, stalking—"

"You know what we have here." Ladue gave Novick a tap on the shoulder with his fist. "Ten dollars says he's got kiddie porn all over his bedroom."

When Ladue had left the kitchen, Gail said, "Detective Novick? Tell me what the problem is. Charlie Jenkins killed himself on my daughter's bed looking at her photographs and masturbating into her panties. My house key was in his pocket."

Her voice shook. "If he isn't the one, then who is? Do we have someone else out there? Or can I bring my daughter home?"

Novick studied his laced fingers, tapping his thumbs together. Then he looked up at her and smiled. "Life is messy. Not much about it fits. Sure. Bring her home."

Anthony arrived just as Gail was about to turn the house over to the police. He asked if she was all right, chastised her a bit for not calling him, then had a talk with Novick and Ladue. By then Charlie Jenkins's van had been searched, and crime-scene technicians had found a camera with zoom lens in the console between the seats. Inside a wooden chest in the back they had found, wrapped in an old towel, a hunting knife with black fur caught in the serrations on the blade.

Anthony went upstairs to get the clothes Gail had left in the bedroom. She wrote him a list of things to put in the suitcase for Karen.

Coming back down five minutes later, Anthony told Gail that Charlie Jenkins's body had been moved from the bed to a gurney and zipped into a bag.

The clock showed 12:45 A.M.

"Anthony? Are you awake?"

"Mmhmm."

"Anthony, wake up."

"I am awake. What is it?"

"I have to tell you something. This is not easy. Please try to understand. I have done something stupid. I did it, I think, because . . . I didn't want Karen to be disappointed in her father. That's the main reason." She paused to assemble her words in the proper order.

Anthony said, "What are you trying to tell me?"

She took a breath. "I told you about Dave's contract with Marriott, remember? A week ago he came up to me outside Karen's school—that was when Hector Mesa saw us together—

and he was desperate. If he didn't make the final payment to purchase the name of the business, Old Island Club, then he would lose everything. The closing was set for Monday, and he could pay me back. So . . . I lent him the money."

"How much?"

"A hundred and twenty-five thousand dollars."

"*Ay, mi Diós.*"

"I gave it to him out of my trust account. Now Marriott is holding up the deal, and he can't pay me, and my checks are bouncing, and a client is threatening to turn me in to the Florida Bar if I don't have money from a personal-injury settlement for her tomorrow, which I promised to her last Friday." Gail could feel the tension in Anthony's body. "I know what you're thinking—How could she have done something so stupid? To have gone behind my back? I'm sorry for that most of all—not telling you. I was afraid to. I'm not anymore. After seeing Charlie Jenkins . . . Right now there isn't much I'd be afraid of. But . . . I am afraid of losing you. Afraid you'll forget that I love you."

She came to a stop, not sure what else to say. She listened for a reply, but there was none. Crickets were chirring outside the window.

"Anthony, please say something." She turned over to look at him. It was not too dark in the room to see that his eyes were wide open. "Anthony . . ."

With a rustling of sheets and comforter, he slowly sat up. The long curve of his back was visible in the dim light from the windows, and his arms lay unmoving in his lap. Gail sat up too, trembling. Waiting. Quietly he said, "How much do you need?"

She stared at him.

"Tomorrow. How much cash do you need?"

She found her voice. "Twenty-eight for my client, and another twelve to cover my account. It's twelve thousand in the red."

"Which brings your balance back to zero. That's not good. All right. Forty thousand in cash to your office, and another eighty-five thousand to your account. A check would be all right for that, no? Or a wire transfer. That would put the money in your account the same day." He nodded. "We'll do it that way."

"You're so . . . calm. I thought . . . you would . . ."

He waited, then asked what she had thought he would do.

"Scream. Threaten to kill Dave. Hit me. Throw me out. I don't know." She said, "I'll pay you back."

"No. I don't expect you to."

"If I get anything from Dave, you can have it. I'll sign over my interest in the house—"

"I said I don't *want* it." Anger ricocheted across the bedroom. He closed his eyes for a moment.

Gail's voice was tight. "Anthony, can you forgive me?"

"Forgive you. I think . . . the best thing to do . . . is to forget about it."

"How can we? Won't it keep going through your mind?"

"No. It's done. Over. The wedding is less than a month away, we'll be married, and there is no reason to discuss this again." He reached out and put his arm around her neck. She nestled against his chest, feeling the warmth of his skin. "Listen to me. I want you to close your office. It's too much for you." He kissed her gently on the lips. "Will you do that? For me?"

Limp with relief, she could only nod.

"Good. We'll talk about it later. Now go to sleep. I have to make some arrangements." He threw back the comforter and stood up.

She buried her face in her pillow.

Tying his robe, he came around the bed. "Gail? Sweetheart." He bent down to kiss her and stroke her hair, murmuring in Spanish, telling her it was all right, to stop crying, he loved her. *Olvídate de eso, cielito. Tú sabes que te amo.*

TWENTY-TWO

Theresa Zimmerman arrived at Gail's office at 9:05 the next morning. She signed a receipt for the $28,650.27 in cash that she had demanded, then announced she intended to write a letter to the Florida Bar regardless. When she was gone, Gail went upstairs and told Charlene Marks everything. Not to worry, Charlene replied. Gail would receive sympathy, not censure, after what she'd gone through the last month. Who would not forgive such a lapse, under the circumstances? Then Charlene had hugged her. "You and Karen are damned lucky to be alive."

Gail had called her mother the night she found Jenkins's body. She called her again in the morning about the money. She and Anthony had talked, and everything was fine. It was wonderful. He had been incredibly forgiving. Irene was happy to hear it, and even happier that Karen could come home.

By Friday other facts about Charlie Jenkins became known. The film in his camera produced more photographs of Karen at play. A search of his apartment turned up colored markers, copies of photographs, and the electronic device he had used to terrorize Gail in the telephone calls. His signature on the suicide note matched the handwriting on his canceled checks.

There was a woman he occasionally dated, but she hadn't seen him in a couple of weeks. The woman, his friends, and his family were all shocked that Charlie Jenkins had led a secret life. In the end, his shame must have been too much to carry. Jenkins had used a key stolen from Karen's backpack to enter the house. In her bedroom he had written his last words, *Hell is waiting for me.* With her underwear in his pants and her image in front of him, he put the gun in his mouth and pulled the trigger.

Gail read the latest details in the newspaper at breakfast on Friday, which had been sent up to their room. Anthony gulped his coffee, kissed her, and was out the door for a meeting with a bunch of Little Havana politicos at the mayor's residence. Ernesto had asked Anthony to fill in for him, a lousy thing to do to someone on a holiday.

Still exhausted, Gail went back to bed, hoping to sleep till noon or so, but she found herself watching the French doors, where a shaft of sunlight slowly moved across the carpet. She thought of Karen, who would be coming home tomorrow. Tonight Karen would see the fireworks with her father and grandparents in Delray Beach, and Dave would bring her back on Saturday. It was not Karen's return, precisely, that Gail was thinking of, but Charlie Jenkins. He had not seemed like the sort of man to have an interest in little girls. On the other hand, he would hardly have printed "pedophile" on his T-shirts.

Of course it had been Jenkins. And yet Detective Novick had asked *why.* Why had he written "die" on Gail's car? Why had he sent her the cat's head? Why did he hate her? Surely not because she had hassled him about giving him cash the day he fixed the wiring. He had come to the house a month or so before the first phone call. Had she done something then to offend him? And how had he known about her dead sister?

Gail was dropping a sundress over her head when she heard a querulous voice coming from outside the house. She quickly fastened the buttons, then went over to the French doors to look out. She heard it more clearly, a man yelling in Spanish. Stepping onto the narrow terrace, she held the wrought-iron railing and looked over the edge. From this angle she saw a straw hat and the shoulders of a tall, gaunt figure wearing a short-sleeved white guayabera. Ernesto Pedrosa. She saw the bushes move and heard a metallic snipping sound. The gardener came into view with a big pair of clippers. Pedrosa pointed with his cane, shouting, *"Mir'allí, ¿no tiene ojos?"*, asking if the man had eyes. The nurse stood nearby with the wheelchair, but clearly Pedrosa was in no mood to be coddled.

"What's going on?" Gail asked.

The hat swiveled around, then tipped up. Ernesto swept it off and held it over his heart. *"Buenos días, mi niña."*

"Buenos días, señor."

"The bushes have to be trimmed away from the house. People can hide there and look in." He glanced at the gardener, who had stopped working. *"Córtalo al suelo."* The gardener murmured something and gestured toward the bush, shaking his head. *"¡Al suelo, te digo!"* He raised his cane, and when the gardener rushed toward the bush, Pedrosa laughed. The clippers flashed through the foliage and the branches fell to the ground.

Pedrosa backed up to be able to see Gail more easily. "Manolo doesn't listen. I want the bushes removed, but he tells me no. What do you do with a man like that?"

Gail asked, "Why are you taking the bushes out?"

"So no one can hide there."

"But who would hide in the bushes?"

"The communists! Here in Miami the FBI arrested ten spies of the regime, but there are more, many more. Where is my grandson?"

"He's . . . having a breakfast meeting at the mayor's house." Gail glanced at the nurse, who lifted a shoulder in a shrug.

"Yes, I remember." Pedrosa smiled at her. *"Que linda eres. Mi nieta.* May I call you my granddaughter? You are very pretty there on the *balcón.*"

He took another step backward and stumbled. Gail gasped. He tottered and stretched out his arm for balance, catching himself on his cane. Leaning on it, he slowly bent over to retrieve his straw hat.

"You really should sit in your chair."

"To hell with the chair. The bricks are loose." He turned around. "Manolo!" He yelled at him to forget about the bush, come fix the walkway immediately. The gardener dropped the clippers and came to see about the bricks.

Pedrosa fanned his face with the hat. "*¿Dónde está Anthony?* Ah! He's in a meeting with the mayor." He smiled apologetically at Gail and dropped his hat back onto his head. "Forgive me for deserting you. I have much work to do." He went to stand over Manolo to supervise the adjustment of the offending brick.

Gail wondered if she should find Nena or Aunt Graciela and tell them that Ernesto was not himself today. But the nurse was on hand, and the old man occasionally took these mental detours. In any event, the women were busy decorating the house with red, white, and blue banners and balloons before the rest of the family arrived.

She heard her telephone ring and went back inside to pick it up from the dresser. The male voice on the other end said, "Ms. Connor? This is Michael Novick. I thought I'd find you in today. I hope I'm not disturbing you."

"No, please. It's all right. Is there a problem?"

"Could you drop by the station early Monday? There are a couple of things I wanted to discuss with you."

"About Charlie Jenkins? What is it?"

"A couple of things I noticed. I can't talk now. I was just on my way out."

"Don't tell me that, then make me wait till Monday," she said. "Karen is coming back tomorrow. Should I leave her with her grandparents?"

"Where are you calling from?" he asked.

"The Pedrosa house."

"Do you have time to meet me for coffee?"

* * *

On the western edge of Coral Gables, where green and shady streets became a sunburned collection of strip shopping centers and small stucco houses, there was a drugstore from the fifties that still had a counter with rotating stools covered in red vinyl. The radio was tuned to the oldies station, and the wall was decorated with an airbrushed painting of a gleaming '57 Chevy coupe. Elvis portraits were prominent.

Gail got there first and ordered iced tea. Detective Novick arrived ten minutes later in shorts, sneakers, and a T-shirt with a leaping swordfish on the front. She didn't recognize him until he unclipped his sunglasses from his regular frames and walked toward the booth where she was sitting. He wasn't wearing a gun, but his short haircut said cop. He sat across from her. The waitress came over with a coffeepot, and he ordered breakfast.

When she was gone, Gail said, "I'm grateful for your time."

"No problem. I live down the street."

Over his coffee Novick recounted the evidence so far, then said, "We didn't find anything at the scene to suggest that Charlie Jenkins did *not* commit suicide, let me say that right away. However, any unwitnessed, violent death is open to interpretation; otherwise defense lawyers would be out of a job. Like the Simpson case. You start poking at the small inconsistencies, you start wondering, even though common sense tells you what the answer is. With your case the answer is, Jenkins was behind the harassment and he shot himself. If you make a list of all the evidence that he did do it, and put it on this side"— Novick held his hands like a balance scale, letting his left hand sink to the table—"and you put issues you can't resolve on the other, then the evidence far outweighs the anomalies."

"I know the evidence," Gail said. "What are the anomalies?"

"First—and this isn't in any kind of order—there are the questions that you asked on the phone. Do his actions at the scene match his harassment of you? Second, the sexual connotations. Sex was obvious in the way he died, but absent in the calls, the vandalism, and particularly in what he did with the photos of Karen."

"You brought that up before," Gail said. "When I saw the photos, you asked if I saw anything sexual in them, and I didn't."

"The medical examiner found no semen on your daughter's underwear, but it could be that Jenkins was unable to climax, or that he wasn't even trying to. There are reasonable explanations, just as there could be a reason he mailed you the head of the cat. You could devise a theory how he found the name and address of your fiancé's law partner and how he knew the name of your deceased sister. But then there's the florist. My partner called last week, wanting to know who placed the order for the roses that were delivered to your office. The manager finally called back yesterday. They can't find any record of flowers being sent to you at that address, and no record of anyone named Renee placing an order."

Gail frowned. "Does that mean they can't find it or that there wasn't one?"

"Well, there could be several explanations." Novick sipped his coffee. "Their record keeping is bad. Someone stole one of their envelopes. Or Jenkins had the flowers sent to his address under another name."

Gail was shaking her head. "They were delivered to me."

"Did you see who brought them?"

"No, but my receptionist did."

"Maybe she can describe the man she saw."

"If it had been Charlie Jenkins," Gail said, "she would have recognized him."

"Here's a theory: It was a friend of Jenkins, doing him a favor."

"Well, it's a theory."

The waitress appeared. Novick took his arms off the table to make room for the plate. "Here you go, hon, two sunny side up with hash browns and bacon. Miss, are you sure you don't want anything?"

"No, I'm fine, thanks. Maybe some more tea."

Novick reached for the salt and pepper. "I have a question on another subject, if you don't mind." Gail asked him what it was. "It's about Wendell Sweet."

"Are you handling that now?"

"We stay up on each other's cases when possible, and this one interests me because his wife is your client." He tapped pepper onto the eggs. Gail averted her face from the glistening yolks staring back at her.

"What do you want to know?" she asked.

"Ricardo Molina's name came up at Mrs. Sweet's house. Garcia, who is the lead detective on the case, told me that Mr. Quintana mentioned that name as a possible suspect. Do you recall that?"

"No, I might have been in the kitchen with Jamie at the time."

With his fork Novick dragged a piece of toast through the eggs. Gail's stomach lurched, and she concentrated on the little boomerang shapes in the laminate on the tabletop. Novick said, "We don't think Molina's organization did it. This wasn't Molina's kind of transaction. He deals in multiple hundreds of kilos, not a few sold out the back of a car in a gym bag. We don't know who did it. In fact, we can't link Wendell Sweet to any dopers. He wasn't even on our radar screen."

"Someone made it look like a drug deal," Gail said.

"It's been suggested." Novick forked some hash browns. "The day you were at the station looking at the color copies, you asked me about Wendell Sweet. Then you asked about Hector Mesa. Last week you asked me about Ricardo Molina." Novick gazed across the table at her through his glasses.

Gail said, "And?"

"And you might want to tell me if there's a connection here we could have overlooked."

"If there is, I don't know about it."

He had an odd way of looking at a person, Gail thought. He didn't blink, but he didn't stare either. His brown eyes were neither accusatory nor suspicious. They were patient.

"Detective Garcia says that Mr. Quintana came over to Mrs.

Sweet's house after a phone call from Harry Lasko, who had spent the night at the house—"

"They aren't intimate," Gail said. "Jamie and Harry are close friends."

"Friends, then. And Mr. Quintana is, I believe, an associate of Hector Mesa—"

"No. Mesa is an associate, or employee, or friend, of Ernesto Pedrosa, Anthony's grandfather."

That brought a slight nod. "I think I heard that Mesa is employed by Mr. Quintana's law firm."

Gail reluctantly said, "This is true. He's a courier. What is the point?"

"There isn't one. I just have these names—Lasko, Quintana, Sweet, Mesa, Molina—and I stack them up and turn them around one way or the other, seeing what fits."

"The other night you said not much of anything fits."

"But sometimes they do. Garcia went to talk to Hector Mesa, but he's out of the country. His wife said he left Monday, but the neighbor says Hector was around on Tuesday. Wendell Sweet was killed Tuesday night."

"Why are you telling me this?"

"Why? Because I thought you were the kind of person who's intrigued by anomalies."

"Oh, I am." Gail looked back at him. "Did you invite me for coffee so I could ask you about Charlie Jenkins, or so you could ask me about Wendell Sweet?"

He smiled. "It could have been both."

"You don't really expect me to speculate on anything having to do with my fiancé, do you? Or his clients? Or people he knows?"

"I suppose not. That's all right. There's nothing wrong with loyalty."

She realized that Detective Novick assumed she was protecting someone. "I'm not sure I like the way you put that," she said.

He spread his hands, a mute apology.

Gail said, "So. Do I bring Karen back tomorrow or not?"

As before, he took his time answering. "If she were my daughter . . . I probably would. But this time I'd be careful with my keys."

The musicians from Jamaica, three men in bright pink shirts, were setting their steel drums on stands under the palm-frond hut. Gail had driven under a banner at the entrance to the parking lot announcing that they would play for the festivities at the Old Island Club. The restaurant was not open yet, but one of the cooks was loading charcoal into the split-barrel barbecue grill in the side yard.

Gail saw Dave carrying one end of a long wooden picnic table. He and the waiter on the other end maneuvered it into the shade of a coconut palm. Dave dusted his hands and nodded at Gail.

She said, "I'm here to collect the other half of my beer."

Dave sent the waiter for one Red Stripe and two mugs. He and Gail sat down at an umbrella table on the deck. A parade of sailboats and motor yachts moved out of the marina, and sunlight glittered like broken glass.

"This ought to be some party," she said.

"See that barbecue grill? And the beer kegs? Totally illegal. No city permit." Dave laughed. "What the hell. One final blow-out for the staff. They deserve it. They've worked hard for me. But . . . it's over. Next week I'm handing the keys to the bank." His smile faded as he looked at Gail, who sat on the bench beside him. "The deal with Marriott is dead."

"I didn't have much hope for it," she said.

"Their lawyer told me yesterday. I don't know how I'm going to pay you back."

"Don't worry about it for now. I'm all right." Gail folded her sunglasses and set them on the table. "Do you have any idea what happened?"

"Nope. They were hot for the idea a week ago, and all of a sudden they backed off. Barlow admitted he can't get a clear answer. I thought of suing them, but I have no money for a lawyer, and like you said, there's all that fine print in the contract."

"Do they want the eighty thousand back that they gave you?"

Laughing, Dave made a gesture of defiance—fist up, other palm on his bicep. "Good luck, guys. Stand in line."

The waiter brought the beer, and Dave poured half into Gail's mug, the rest into his. "Cheers." Behind them the Jamaicans started to play around on the steel drums—bell-like music chiming in scraps of melody, pattering like rain.

"I'll stick around till about four, then split for Delray Beach. My manager can handle the party tonight. I ought to be here, but to be honest with you, I don't have the heart."

Gail said, "Let me tell you about the conversation I just had with Michael Novick. I talked to him because I had to know if we should bring Karen home yet. Some of the things he had said on Wednesday night bothered me. Today I don't feel much better about it."

She told Dave what they had discussed—the evidence and the oddities. He listened without comment, but a skeptical frown appeared. He finished his beer.

"I don't know what to do, Dave. I'm nervous about this."

"Sure, anybody would be if they'd seen what you saw—walking into Karen's room, that pervert lying there with his brains blown out. Novick is making too much out of this. No, I say Karen's coming home. I wouldn't bring her back if I thought she was in danger, I swear to God. She wants to come home, and I want the time with her." He added, "I'm leaving Miami."

"You are? Where are you going?"

"I have a job on St. John, managing a restaurant at a resort in Cruz Bay. It pays pretty well. A friend of a friend called me about it. I don't know the guy, but he heard about me and they needed someone, and there it is."

"St. John. That's so far away."

"I have nothing here, Gail. My credit is shot to hell. Down there I get a place to stay. I don't need a car. It's a decent life, no stress, no traffic, no hassles. The drawback is, I won't see Karen as much. And that's hard. That is very hard. We had these big plans, Karen and me, going around to see all the Island Clubs. She was so excited. I heard her bragging about it to the kids in the building. I don't know what the hell to say to her."

"When are you leaving?"

"In a couple of weeks. When the rent on my apartment runs out. Say, you wouldn't like a good deal on a big-screen TV, would you?"

Sensing someone's presence, Gail looked around.

The dark-haired waitress with the short shorts—Vicki—was pretending Gail wasn't there. "Dave? The liquor distributor needs to talk to you about the order for the party."

"Tell Pete to handle it."

"He's not here yet."

"Then you do it." Dave held out his arm. "I grant you my authority and permission to sign my name to whatever order for however much he will give us. Go for it."

Vicki's eyes shifted to the restaurant, then back at Dave. "Okay."

"And bring us a couple more beers. Gail? You want one?"

"Why not?"

"Now all we need is the steel drum version of 'Nearer My God to Thee.' " He gave Vicki the empty bottle of Red Stripe. "Go see if they know that tune."

"Oh, come on." With a roll of her eyes, Vicki left.

"Does she know you're leaving?"

"No one does yet. I guess I don't want to believe it myself. I wish you and Karen were going with me. Why don't we do that? Let's all run away to St. John." He took her hand and held it to his cheek. "You know, Gail, we came close. We almost made it, didn't we?" His face emptied, and he looked out toward the bay. He seemed to struggle for words, then said, "I've got a lot of nerve to ask you this. I'd like to bring Karen down there for a week before school starts, but I don't have enough right now for the airline ticket. You think you could lend me the money? I could pay you back. I mean, three or four hundred bucks is not impossible." His eyes closed. "I'm so sorry, Gail. So damned sorry."

The party at the Pedrosa house started around three o'clock and would proceed at seven to the Biltmore Hotel, everyone bringing lawn chairs, blankets, and coolers, to sit on the grass and listen to the military band, after which they would enjoy the fireworks display put on by the city. Then home again for more food and a live salsa band. Elena told Gail, as they stood in line for hamburgers, that every year the decorations were more elaborate and the house more crowded. Rows of American and Cuban flags waved from stanchions in the driveway. Every politician in the county dropped in. Family and friends clogged the hallways and poured onto the grounds. There was a carousel for the little ones and a magic act at four in the living room. Folding chairs had been put in rows, and every one was filled.

Around five o'clock Gail went upstairs to find something for her headache. She lay down on the bed, but teenagers below her window had a boom box playing Spanish rap music. Ernesto had spent most of the afternoon napping, so by default Anthony had been playing host. Gail had not seen much of him, except for the times he had introduced her to this person or that. *Mi novia. Encantada.* Where are you going on your honeymoon? The lake district of Italy, a cottage on a mountain. How romantic.

The air conditioning drifted out onto the terrace, keeping it less torrid than the rest of the yard. People ate at picnic tables with checkered cloths, and the caterers cleaned up behind them. Somebody set off a firecracker, frightening the babies. A radio was tuned to old Spanish ballads, and another played hip-hop.

Wandering back downstairs, Gail spotted Ernesto Pedrosa in his wheelchair across the yard by the goldfish pond. He and some of the younger children were tossing bits of food into the water. He had changed his straw hat for an exquisite white Panama, and an American flag had been stuck at a jaunty angle in the ribbon around the crown.

Gail stood beside his chair. "Are you enjoying the party?"

"I always enjoy parties."

He held out a crust to a toddler, a little girl in a bright red dress. The girl grabbed for the bread, but Pedrosa pulled it away. She shrieked and stamped her feet up and down. He relented and let her have the bread, then chuckled when she ate it instead of throwing it to the fish.

Gail sat on the low, ferny wall of the pond. When the bread ran out, Pedrosa held his hands open to show the children there was nothing left. *"Más. Buscan más."* They ran off to find more. Gail stood up and grasped the handles of his chair.

"Where are we going?"

"For a little walk." She wheeled him along the brick walkway. People smiled and said hello, and he lifted his hand like a monarch in a carriage. She stopped around the corner of the guest house and sat down on a shady bench beside him.

"I heard a story about Hector Mesa—his devotion to this family. Your son, Tomás, was captured in the invasion at Playa Girón. When they questioned him, all he would say was *viva Cuba libre.* One of the Cuban soldiers cut out his tongue and beat him to death. Many years later Hector Mesa brought you that same soldier's tongue in a box. Is this true?"

The old man did not deny it. "Those were difficult times."

"Have you ever heard the name Wendell Sweet?"

He pursed his lips. Spittle had gathered in the corners. "No, I don't know this name."

"He was shot to death, and his body was found in the Miami River."

"Ah. I remember. It was on the news. He was dealing drugs. Those people deserve what they get."

"Hector Mesa left town the morning after Wendell was killed. Do you know why?"

The big, liver-spotted hands went outward in a shrug.

"But he must have told you. You're his *padrón*. He works for you."

Ernesto Pedrosa's eyes shifted slowly to fix on her. They were pale, watery blue, the color of ice. His pink-rimmed lower lids drooped, pulled by shadowy pouches and weighted by the things he had seen in his life. Black pupils fixed on Gail, and as through a chink in a wall, pure lucidity shone out.

"Olvídate de Hector. No me preguntes más." With a wave of his hand he directed her to take him back to the others, and she did.

Forget about it, Pedrosa had said. Forget about Hector. Don't ask about it again. Gail wondered why he had chosen to be under her balcony today with the gardener. Calling her granddaughter, his pretty *nieta*, making her feel sorry for an old man's infirmities.

She left him with the old people listening to *boleros*, and he rose shakily from his chair to dance a few steps with one of the ladies. Gail walked toward the house. She saw Anthony standing on the terrace, the center of a group of men. He held a cigar. How relaxed he looked, laughing with them. He wore pleated linen pants and a pale blue shirt. A child toddled by and he patted her on the head.

The heat, the noise were too much. Gail felt dizzy from it.

Anthony noticed her and smiled, motioning for her to come there, to join them. The men looked at her.

Gail backed up, turned, and hurried through the crowd, pushing her way, running past the guest house, going faster until she came to the back of the property and the gate in the wall. Anthony's voice came from behind her. She lifted the heavy iron latch and pushed open the gate. The golf course undulated left and right, curling around small lakes and white sand. She walked straight across, then around a dense stand of ficus trees. In the distance she could see the bell tower of the hotel and could hear the band. She went over a rise in the ground, then down, and there was a lake and she could go no farther.

"Gail!"

Annoyed, out of breath, Anthony stood at the top of the berm. "What are you doing? Why did you walk away when I called you? Everyone saw it." When she didn't answer, he let out an exhalation of forbearance and trotted down the slope toward her. The setting sun turned his hair deep copper.

Coming closer, he frowned. "Are you all right? Are you feeling sick? What's the matter?"

"What I saw— You and those men. It was like Ernesto. Exactly."

"Gail, come back to the house with me. I'm going to call the doctor."

"Don't touch me!" She swerved out of his grasp, and he stared at her, stunned. She said, "I'm going to ask you something, and I'd like the truth."

He exhaled, showing his patience. "Okay. Ask me. What do you want to know?"

"Did you talk to Hector Mesa about Wendell Sweet?"

"*Por Diós,* what kind of question is that?"

"Did Hector know about the offshore account you're managing for Harry Lasko? Did Hector know about the sale of the casino to Ricardo Molina? Did he know?"

"No. I don't discuss that kind of thing with Hector. Why are you—"

"What about your grandfather? Did you tell him?"

Anthony hesitated. "Yes. We talked about it."

"Did your grandfather ask Hector Mesa to kill Wendell Sweet?"

His mouth opened. "No. Why in the name of God would you think that? Wendell was killed in a drug deal."

"Was he? Wendell knew things that could get you disbarred, if not criminally prosecuted. You have the key to Harry Lasko's offshore account, money that Harry got from a drug trafficker. You're taking the risk because Harry is your friend, but Wendell could have ruined you. Couldn't Hector have solved the problem? Couldn't your grandfather have asked him to? Ernesto is an old man, and you're his life."

"You just accused my grandfather of murder! This is insane."

"Why don't you ask him?"

"I won't ask him that!"

"Of course you can't. What if he said yes? What would you do then? Turn him in? You can't even accuse Hector. He's going to get away with it."

"Let's go back to the house." He grabbed her wrist. "We're not going to discuss this now. We're going to the Biltmore with the family, and you will behave normally. If you can't, then you will stay in our room until I come back."

Laughing, she jerked away. "Oh, my God. Listen to yourself."

He put his hands on his hips. "What do you want me to do? Leave you here? Everyone is wondering what happened. What am I supposed to tell them?"

"I don't give a damn."

"*Ay, mi madre, que pena.*"

Voices came nearer, and Gail realized the Pedrosa family and their friends were on their way toward the hotel already. She saw them moving through the trees, and gradually they came into view with their chairs and coolers. But not Ernesto. He would watch from the upper floor of the house with his wife and the others who could not make the walk.

Anthony's cousin Bernardo saw the two standing over by the pond and made an exaggerated shrug, asking what was going on. Anthony gave him a dismissive wave.

"Look at that," he said. "They know we're having a fight. *Ay, Diós mio.* Gail, come on. I'm tired of being out here like this."

"I have one more question."

"Enough questions." He grabbed her elbow. "Do you want me to carry you back? I will do it. Don't think I won't."

Gail planted her feet in the grass. "What did you do to Dave?"

"What?"

"Did you kill his deal with the Old Island Club? Did you do that?"

He laughed. "No. What are you talking about?"

"You're lying. When I told you what I did for Dave, you didn't scream about it. You said we should forget it. Remember? No one has an answer why it fell through. Then miraculously someone offered him a job at a resort on St. John. Harry Lasko is in the business. He would have done you a favor."

Anthony stared at her, and the defiance in his expression told her the truth.

"Oh, God, the irony. I cleaned out my trust account to help Dave with a deal that you had already poisoned. And when I told you—Well, what could you do but pay me the money back?"

He dropped her arm. "Yes, and I would do it again. Dave wanted to take you away from me. He filed the custody case for that reason. He used Karen as a tool to drive us apart. You lied to me about what you felt for him. Every time I talked to you, I learned something more. You even slept with him after you and I were together. What guarantee did I have that it wouldn't happen again?"

"So you left him with nothing but a job on the other side of the Caribbean."

"You still love him. Go on, admit it." He shouted at her, "What you did—lending him one hundred and twenty-five thousand dollars! *Que barbaridad.* Admit it!"

"Yes. I admit it. He's been part of my life since I was eighteen years old. He's Karen's father. We had our differences, but he always treated me with respect. He isn't as smart as you are, not as clever or rich. He failed at business, and God knows, he might have failed with the Old Island Club too, but he was never cruel. What you did to him was cruel. Unbelievably heartless."

"Are you going back to him?"

She closed her eyes. "No."

"*Que sí.* You should. Go. Go to Dave Metzger. You would be

back here in a week." Anthony paced in front of her. "Why do we play these games with each other?"

Gail said quietly, "All I thought about was you. I wanted you so much that nothing else mattered. Neither of us wanted to live in that house, but there we are. You work for your grandfather now, and you didn't want to do that. And I won't have a law practice anymore, except what you give me. I've been erased."

"All right. If you want your own office, then keep it. All you had to say was no."

"The price of fighting you is too high."

"That is very weak, Gail. Weak and selfish. You fight for Jamie Sweet, and for Karen, but not for me. Not for us."

"Why should I?" She looked up at him. "I'm going to move my things out of here tonight."

"What? No. That's ridiculous. I won't let you do it."

"You can't stop me."

"I said no."

She started up the slope.

"Gail!" He turned her around. "We're going to be married in three weeks. You'll come back to your senses. You can't do this!" His breath came quickly. "You can't. I love you. You know this. No one else could love you as much as I do." He put his arms around her. "*Corazón*, we belong to each other. Don't frighten me like this."

She turned away from his kiss.

"All right. I understand what you're saying. I was wrong. I am sorry. What do you want me to do? Tell me. What does Dave want? I can arrange it. Does he want money? Another restaurant? Even here in Miami. Tell me."

"I don't want anything from you."

He held her face. "You don't mean that. Please don't. This is crazy! What do you mean, you want to call it off? I don't believe you."

She took his hands away and backed up a few steps. "Jamie Sweet explained to me how she knew that Harry Lasko hadn't murdered Wendell. Do you know what she said? Because Harry was a good man. He was kind, and he loved her children. Harry knew how much their father meant to them, and he wouldn't have taken him away. He wouldn't have *hurt* them like that. That's what you did, Anthony. You hurt Karen by destroying Dave, and no one—*no one*—does that to my child!"

"I didn't—No. You see it that way, but Gail, remember what her father did. He deserted her for six months! Karen has been safe here. She has anything she wants. Haven't I treated her well?" Gail started to walk up the slope, but he blocked her path. "We have both—you and I—been under some pressure. Gail, sweetheart, *por amor de Diós*. Do you want me to apologize? I will. I will every day of my life, on my knees, but I can't lose you. I don't even want to say that. I won't let it happen."

"It's too late. I've seen who you really are."

He put his hands out as if to steady himself. "We'll leave here. We can find another house. We'll get out of here and go wherever you want."

"You can't leave. You've wanted this ever since the old man dragged you out of Cuba, and your miserable cousins despised you for being his favorite. You'll never leave because you want it too much. Your grandfather knows that. He isn't as feeble as you think. He knows how to play you, and you go right along because at heart, you're just like Ernesto—controlling, manipulative, and ruthless."

Gail took the ring off her finger and shoved it into his hand. He stared at it.

"I don't want it. I don't want you."

When he looked back at her, his eyes had reddened, and his lips turned white with fury. He grabbed her upper arms, and she cried out from the pain. *"Puta mentirosa. Ingrata."* He shoved her away so hard she fell, catching herself on her outstretched arms. *"¡Que tonto fuí en haberte querido!"*

Her elbow was bleeding, but she barely felt it. She hated him so thoroughly that if he had come after her, she would have spat in his face.

Gail stood up, pushing her hair out of her eyes. "Ask your grandfather. Go on, ask him. Not now. Don't spoil the holiday, but someday, ask him if Hector Mesa committed murder to save you. What will you do when he says yes?"

Anthony extended his arm and pointed at her. "*¡Separate de mi!* Get out of my sight. I don't want to see your face. I don't want to hear from you. Don't call me. Don't come around here again." His voice cracked. He took a breath. "Do not write to me. Do not ask anyone else to contact me. I don't know your name."

"You're pathetic." Gail laughed. "If you can live with what he did, you deserve each other."

He tossed the diamond up and down in his palm, then strode quickly to the lake.

"Anthony!"

But his arm went back, and the ring was flying up, sparkling for a quick moment before it plummeted downward, splashed, and was gone.

He turned around, stumbling as if momentarily blinded. In that same moment Gail might have run to him, fallen to his feet and begged him to forgive her, because she had gone crazy, driven mad by what had happened to her daughter, and her fears had driven out all rational thought. He would have screamed at her, perhaps would have hit her, but he would have taken her back.

As she watched, his expression settled into stone. He turned and walked away. Gail went to the top of the rise and looked after him awhile. He didn't look back.

TWENTY-THREE

The decision came easily: The offices of Gail A. Connor, Attorney at Law, P.A., would move to smaller quarters. After some haggling, the building management allowed the lease to be transferred to a suite one floor down in the back. One office for the lawyer, a tiny secretarial area, and no view. The computer network and the extra copy machine would go. Miriam, with her usual optimism, said it would be cozy.

Gail had not heard from Anthony, nor did she care to. Her friends said it was better to make a clean break. Gail and Karen would stay with Irene for now. Karen didn't mind; she had a friend across the street. She had taken the news of her father's impending departure well enough. Gail thought it was because she had never really become used to having him around. Or because her mind was on her party. Tomorrow all her friends would gather at her grandmother's house to celebrate her eleventh birthday.

By late on Friday afternoon, Gail and Miriam had organized most of the files, papers, office supplies, and assorted junk into boxes, ready for the move the following weekend. Gail wanted to start over as soon as she could.

Thin arms extended, curls swaying, Miriam lugged a box full of computer software manuals down the hall, preceding Gail, who carried old magazines from the Florida Bar. Every day this week they had deposited two boxes into the Dumpster on their way home.

Gail dropped her box on the floor by the exit, and Miriam dropped hers on her desk.

Miriam held up a big brown envelope. "I found some things of Lynn's when I was cleaning out her desk. She took most of her stuff, but she missed this. It's like, lipstick, a mirror, some quarters and dimes, and pictures, new panty hose, breath mints—"

"I still feel bad about firing her," Gail said.

"Awww." Miriam gave Gail a little hug. "Don't worry. She'll find something else."

"Not easily. She doesn't have much going for her. Well, wrap it up and put it in the mail on Monday."

Miriam turned out the light over her desk. "I talked to Danny, and he can get some of his friends to help us move next weekend, if you'd like." Miriam's husband, who worked for fire-rescue in Hialeah, spent his spare time on the weight machines.

"I'd like that very much," Gail said. "Tell them lunch is on me." She turned off the light in the hall. "Miriam, do you mind awfully much that we have to move? Things haven't worked out as well as I'd hoped, and I won't be able to give you a raise for a while."

Brown eyes widened, and the red-lipsticked mouth went into a big smile. "Gail, no, it's okay. If you can't pay me right now, that's okay too, I can wait."

Gail laughed. "No, I promise, that isn't necessary, but thank you." She slid the frosted glass window shut, then stepped back to stare at it. "Miriam? Do you remember the day I got the flowers?"

"Oh, *those* flowers. I remember. Why?"

"Where were you when they were delivered?"

She shrugged. "I don't know. In the extra office working on the books, I think."

"You didn't see the delivery man at all? Not a glimpse?"

"No. But it wasn't a man. It was a woman."

"A woman? Nobody ever told me that."

"Well . . . nobody asked. I heard the door opening, and Lynn said, Can I help you? And then this woman's voice, but I don't remember what she said. I wasn't really listening." Miriam looked closely at Gail. "Are you still thinking about that?"

"It still bothers me why the florist had no record. Who was that woman, I wonder? A friend of Charlie Jenkins? Lynn would have recognized him if *he* had brought the flowers. And how did he know about Renee?"

"Maybe he went through all your stuff at home." Miriam gave a theatrical shudder. "Scary, scary. I am glad he's dead, even if you had to be the one to find him. Do you *dream* about him?" She stopped herself, quickly lifting her hands, palms out. "*Olvídalo.* I'm sorry for reminding you. No more talking about it."

Gail put her purse over her shoulder and found the right key to lock the office door. She said quietly, "Yes, I dream about him. I'd like to find a way to stop. I dream about a lot of things I shouldn't."

Lynn Dobbert's house was west of the city in a nondescript neighborhood off the expressway where narrow town houses with minuscule yards were jammed one next to the other, and too many cars had worn away the grass to weeds and white rock. Gail parked between a pickup truck whose rear axle was supported on two jacks, and a low-riding Honda Civic with a Nicaraguan flag on the antenna. Gail had retrieved her Mercedes this week from the body shop, and it seemed out of place here.

Identical poured concrete walkways led to the long row of tiny porches and doors. Gail glanced at the envelope on which she had written Lynn's address before leaving the office. A graying woman in the next yard swept the front steps and kept an eye on this tall, skinny blonde in sunglasses, coming toward her in a dress that showed too much of her legs.

"Excuse me. Do you speak English?" When the woman nodded, Gail asked if she had the right town house. Did that one belong to the Dobberts?

"She no home."

Unsure if the woman had understood, Gail said, *"¿Es la casa de Tom y Lynn Dobbert?"*

"I spik Englee," the woman said, insulted.

"Oh. Of course. Well, could you tell me—"

She narrowed her eyes suspiciously. "Wha' you name?" The woman was around sixty with a sleeveless plaid shirt that revealed bra straps and the pale skin of her loose upper arms.

"Gail Connor. Lynn used to work for me." Gail held up the envelope. "I want to talk to her."

"Leeng no home."

"She has to be home. I called her a half hour ago and said I was coming."

"She no here."

"Is Tom home?"

"I don' know abou' no Tom."

"Her husband."

"Leeng don' have no husban'."

"Yes, she does. *Tom.* She's married to Tom Dobbert."

"She don' have no man in there."

"She has a husband and two boys."

"Boys?"

"Yes. Joey and Tommy. Little boys." Gail held her palm about waist high. "Two of them. *Dos niños.*"

"She don' have no sheeldren."

Wondering if this woman had a few circuits unplugged, Gail studied the green street sign on the corner. One of these streets could look like the next. "Thank you anyway," she said.

The woman went back to vigorously scraping the sidewalk. Gail hesitated a moment, then walked toward the door she had first intended to knock on. The numbers matched. Still unsure, she shaded the window glass with her hand, but a curtain blocked the view. She noticed some mail in the box, glanced around, then lifted the lid. There was an electric bill addressed to an R. L. Dobbert. There was a flyer from a supermarket, then an offer from a credit card company to a Ms. Lynn Dobbert.

"Hey!"

Startled, Gail dropped the lid with a clank. The woman waved her broom.

"Wha' you doing?"

"Just checking to see if this is the right house."

"I tol' you, she no home."

"She's expecting me." Gail reached out and knocked firmly on the door. She waited. The woman was still standing there. "Well, I'll just write her a note." She took a memo pad from her shoulder bag and scribbled a brief message—sorry I missed you, please call, important. She wrote down her mother's number.

"Lynn does live here." Gail tore off the page and stuck it in the mailbox.

"Tha' what I say." The woman shook her head and turned away mumbling, and Gail heard the word *imbécil*.

Losing her way finding the main exit, Gail spent several minutes circling, and drove past the same town house again, the woman staring at her. Gail wondered what kind of story Lynn would hear from her neighbor. It annoyed her that Lynn had been gone, but she had to admit the possibility of a misunderstanding. What annoyed her more than the waste of time was the question still unresolved: Who was the woman who had delivered the flowers?

The last of rush-hour traffic filled the expressway going west, but Gail sped along in the other direction. The buildings glittered bright orange, the reflection of the lowering sun. Irene Connor lived in a waterfront residential area near downtown. Gail called from her car to explain her tardiness, and Irene said that dinner would be waiting when she got there. Karen was in the pool with the neighbor girl, but Irene was just on her way to send the girl home and tell Karen to get cleaned up for dinner.

"Mother, if you don't stop this, you may never get rid of us," Gail said.

Laughing, Irene said she was happy to spoil them.

Gail disconnected, held the cell phone for a moment, thinking, then called Dave at his apartment. The restaurant had closed, and he could usually be found at home. Gail said she had an odd question for him. "That waitress who worked for you—Vicki. You and she were involved for a while. When was the last time you slept with her? And who broke it off, you or Vicki?"

Dave asked what in hell she needed to know that for.

"Never mind why."

He said they'd last been together in May, and he'd told her it wasn't working out. Vicki had been too young for him, and anyway, the boss shouldn't sleep with the employees. "No, she didn't get mad. We have remained pretty good friends, in fact. She wants to go to St. John with me."

"That's a bad idea, Dave."

"Are you jealous?" He laughed.

"How old is she?"

"Twenty-three."

"Like I said, a bad idea." Gail slowed at the toll booth and tossed a quarter into the basket. The gate lifted, and she hit the gas. "Did you ever tell Vicki about my sister?" When she got only a silence in reply, she said, "I don't *care* if you did or not, I just want to know if she heard about Renee."

"I think I probably told her. Yes."

"One more question? And maybe I'll have more later, but right now I'm on my way home. What were her days off?"

"Are you going to tell me what this is about, or not?"

"Later."

He exhaled, then said, "She worked Thursday through Sunday."

"She's not there with you at the moment, is she?"

"No, Gail. She is not."

Despite his demand to know what she was after, Gail said again that she would talk to him later. She put the phone back into her purse. The city came closer, then swung to her right as her car sped up the flyover to the interstate.

Wednesday. Charlie Jenkins had killed himself on a Wednesday night. Karen's cat had been slaughtered on a Wednesday. And it had also been on a Wednesday that someone had delivered flowers to Gail's office.

The screen door on her mother's front porch was original with the house, vintage 1960, a white metal silhouette of a flamingo. It banged behind Gail as she unlocked the entry door and came inside. Immediately the aroma of pie crust and savory chicken enveloped her, and she realized how hungry she was. Her mother was on a mission to fatten her up.

A game show was playing on a television farther back in the house. *Wheel of Fortune,* she thought. Karen liked to watch it.

"Mom! Karen! I'm hooo-ome." The lamps in the living room were off, and the double set of glass doors let in only the faded light of dusk.

Gail was crossing the living room toward the kitchen when someone got up from the sofa, a woman with lank blond hair.

"Hi. I've been waiting for you."

"Lynn!" Gail caught her breath. "You scared me. I was just at your house."

"I came here. I got the address from your mom on the phone."

"Well, I'm sorry for the mixup. Where is everyone?"

"In the back. I guess they're getting dressed for dinner. Your mother said you'd be home soon and I could wait." Lynn wore her usual dark slacks and a pullover. The blue and green horizontal stripes made her shoulders look square and solid. Her eyes were on the envelope. "Are the pictures of my kids in there?"

When Gail gave her the envelope, Lynn quickly unbent the prongs holding it shut. She dropped the envelope on the sofa and shuffled through the snapshots. "There they are. I was missing these. Hey, kids."

"Miriam found them under some papers in the drawer." Gail said, "Lynn, do you remember the day I got flowers at the office? Those cheap roses? A woman brought them. Could you describe her?"

Lynn lifted her gaze from the snapshots. Gail had noticed that when Lynn was asked a question that she didn't understand, her face went slack. Pale lids drooped over gray eyes, and her mouth hung open slightly. "Miriam told me she heard a woman's voice, but she didn't see her. Do you remember what she looked like?"

"You threw them away," Lynn said. "I guess cheap roses aren't good enough for you."

Gail tilted her head and frowned. "Excuse me?"

"I thought they were nice. Tom gave me some just like them for our anniversary."

"Wait a minute. *You* brought them? But what about . . . the woman? Miriam heard her voice—" Gail began to understand. "It was you."

Lynn looked back at her.

"And you . . . wrote my sister's name on the card?"

"It was kind of appropriate."

"But why . . ." Gail's head felt off balance. She blinked. "Where's Karen? Where's my mother?" Gail looked toward the hall. "Karen! Mom?" There was no answer.

"You should go check on them."

Backing up, Gail said, "Stay here!" She ran down the hall, pumps sliding over the polished wood floor as she stopped to look in Karen's room—empty—and her own—nothing amiss.

Lynn was in the hall. The little crystal light in the ceiling shone on her face, then made shadows as she passed underneath it.

"I said, stay in the living room!" The sound of the game show was louder, coming from Irene's bedroom. A clacking wheel spun around, and a burst of applause followed. Gail ran for the bedroom and grabbed the door to slam it shut. It flew into her face, and she sprawled on the carpet. Her forehead and cheek-bone throbbed.

A lamp on the night stand illuminated the room. The television flashed in brilliant colors. Gail groggily rolled over and saw her mother and Karen. They lay at the end of the bed, tied up in white cord. Eyes pleaded over the cloth that muffled their screams.

Lynn went over to turn up the volume on the television. Music blared, then applause. *Is there a W?* From the dresser she picked up a knife with a blade as long as her forearm. *I'm going to solve the puzzle.*

Scooting backward, Gail collided with the night stand, and the lamp rocked. Before she could get up, Lynn grabbed her by the hair and raised her other arm. Gail felt the pain in the back of her head like a shard of ice being driven through bone.

She awoke to intense pain in her neck and shoulders. And darkness. She heard a happy female voice. A commercial for Revlon lip color. Gail forced her eyes open. Lynn sat on the end of the bed slack-mouthed and slumped, watching television. At her feet Irene and Karen still lay tied and gagged, breathing but not moving. Gail was pinned by both wrists to the curved wooden arms of her mother's antique upholstered chair. Her ankles were tied to the chair legs.

When Gail moaned in horror and pain, Lynn looked around. "If you scream, I'll cut Karen."

Gail stifled a sob, and her voice shook. "Lynn. Why?"

Lynn stood up to set a plate of half-eaten pie on the dresser. She picked up photographs, and Gail recognized them as the ones left at the office. The television was showing a parade of Hollywood stars outside a movie premiere.

Standing in front of Gail's chair, Lynn held one photo at arm's length, changed it for another, then another. "This is why."

The lamp gave enough light for Gail clearly to see a picture of

Lynn's younger son on a pony, then the other with a birthday cake. Then both with Lynn at a beach. Gail closed her eyes.

"Look." Lynn kicked her leg sharply. Gail cried out. Lynn said, "Look at them." Through watery vision Gail saw a barefoot toddler. "This is Jason." Another photo appeared. "This is Timmy." Lynn's nails were bitten so far down that the skin puffed over the fingernails.

A single word formed on Gail's lips. "Yancey." Comprehension burst into her brain, hot as sunlight. Winter Springs, Florida. *Family tragedy: Man shoots wife, kids, self.* Simon Yancey lost his job, got drunk. Three dead. Jason . . . Timothy . . . *The wife survived.*

She took a breath. "Rita Yancey."

A smile appeared. "Rita Lynn Dobbert before I married Simon."

In the mailbox there had been a letter for R. L. Dobbert. "You made them up. The boys." Gail struggled to sit upright. "Your neighbor said you didn't have a husband. Or children. You made them up!"

"I kept them alive." Lynn shook Gail by the hair and forced her to look at the next snapshot. "Who is this?" Her fingers tightened. "Who is he?"

A big man with a smile, his hair thinning on top. Gail's voice was a breathless squeak. "Tom? Simon? I don't know!"

Lynn shoved her, and Gail's head hit the back of the chair. "Simon. He was nothing to you. You wanted to take our house and sell it. Money is all you care about, you greedy bitch."

Dear Ms. Gail Connor . . . Does it make you happy to see a decent, hard-working American family with two kids put out on the street? My wife is on medication from the stress. . . .

Gail had seen the boys' pictures taped to Lynn's cubicle. She had commented on the lack of recent photographs. *We haven't taken any pictures lately. The camera is broken.* A lie.

"You took Karen's picture! You're the one! It was your voice.

The paint!" Gail jerked her arms upward; her wrists were caught by the rope. In a blind rage, she flailed her body, bucking wildly, and the chair tipped and righted itself. Gail slid forward off the seat, landing on the floor on her knees. The rope cut into her ankles, and her arms were angled behind her.

"You killed her cat and mailed me the *head*. You're sick and twisted! Karen didn't do anything to you!"

"You did." Lynn crossed her arms and in one motion pulled her shirt off. Her blond hair hung in her face, and she stood silently in her bra, her chunky waist pinched by her dark blue slacks. She pointed to dimpled scars in the soft white skin, one near her right shoulder, the other under her left breast. "This is what you did." Lynn whispered, "I have been planning this for a long, *long* time. Coming back to this hellhole of a city. Tracking you down. Getting a job in your office, trying not to scream every time I saw you—"

"Lynn, I didn't shoot you. Or the boys. Simon did. Then he shot himself. He did it to you. I didn't. I swear to God I never hurt you or your boys." Gail strained at the cord around her wrists and felt the slender woodwork bend. If she could stand up . . . If she could get into the right position . . .

The striped top went back on over Lynn's head, and she poked her arms through. "Simon told me it wasn't my fault that I got sick and didn't send the payments. He said the mortgage company would let us catch up. You told them not to. He said the judge would help us, but *you* wouldn't let him." Lynn twitched her hips. "Go into court in your prissy-ass little suit, telling lies, acting so big. You're scum."

"What do you *want*?" By turning her wrists she could grasp the curves of wood. "I'll give you anything. Let them go. Lynn, please. I can get money for you. You could go away—"

"No. I'm the judge and you're the accused, so shut up. You don't deserve to know shit, but we have rules of procedure, don't we?" Lynn kicked Gail in the thigh then walked around her.

She circled back and kicked Gail's other leg. Gail clenched her teeth, not wanting Karen to hear her cry out. Lynn glared at her. "You fired me because I found out you stole money from your clients. That's why you fired me. Lying bitch." She kicked Gail one more time, then walked to the door and opened it.

Gail shoved outward on the arms of the chair, then pulled in until her muscles quivered, then pushed outward again, hearing the wood creak. The curtains were drawn. Irene's bedroom faced the water, and no one would hear a scream. She saw her mother's red curls and Karen's long brown hair. They were huddled together, and Irene seemed to be rocking Karen. A low humming noise came from her mother's throat. A lullaby.

"Mom! Karen! I'm here. We'll be all right!"

Lynn came back in with a red plastic, two-gallon container of gasoline and a charcoal lighter with a grip like a pistol.

"What are you going to do? What are you going to do to us?"

"Guess."

"Oh, my God. Lynn, please."

Lynn leaned down to speak to her. Her breath was foul. "I could have killed you anytime, Miss Lawyer, but you're going to watch like I did. You have a front row seat in the courtroom. My boys were asleep when it happened, so they never knew. But I knew. I saw Simon shoot them, then he put the gun in his mouth and it took the back of his head off."

"That's how Charlie died. You shot him!"

"So you'd bring Karen back. The police thought Charlie did it. I heard them talking in your office. Then when you asked if my name was Charlie Jenkins, I thought, well, why not?"

"It was you on the phone. That voice—"

Lynn laughed. "Did you like the chocolates? Kitty candy?"

Gail slowly pushed outward on the arms of the chair, feeling them give.

"I called when Miriam was in the conference room. You're so stupid. You didn't even know it was me." Lynn unscrewed the yellow cap on the container and tossed it aside. Walking around the perimeter of the room, she poured gasoline under the curtains, over the dresser, the bureau. She paused at the television and turned it off, then kept going.

"I told Charlie you needed an outlet fixed in Karen's room, and I met him there, and when he bent down to look, I used an ice pick in the back of his neck. It didn't show after what the gun did. Then I put her panties around his thing. I drove his van away and left some stuff in his house, then I brought his keys back."

The can made a deep gulping noise, and the oily stench of gasoline filled the room. Lynn poured it on the bed, soaking the comforter. On the floor, Irene was wriggling forward, shoulders and hips, scraping her cheek against the carpet. The cloth around her mouth shifted.

Gail strained at the arms of the chair, despising her weakness. "How did you get into my house?"

"Karen's key. I thought of copying the key Miriam lent me when I met Charlie at your house the first time, but Karen's was easier. You put his receipt in a drawer in the kitchen, so I used that for the signature on the note. It's like God was laying all this right out in front of me."

"God has nothing to do with it! You're evil and sick."

Lynn sloshed the can. "I guess that's enough." She set it on the dresser. Wiping her hands on her stomach, she looked down at the end of the bed. "It's time." She dragged Karen into view by an elbow. Karen's ankles and hands were tied. She thrashed, and her eyes rolled.

"Leave her alone! Don't hurt her! For God's sake, Lynn, please. Take me! Kill me a thousand times, but please don't hurt my daughter!"

"Shut up," Lynn yelled. She dragged Karen to the dresser and picked up the knife, holding the point at Karen's neck. "I'll cut her if you don't shut up."

Gail's chest heaved in silent sobs.

Lynn tossed the knife back onto the dresser. She carried Karen to the bed and dropped her, then positioned her head on a pillow. Unsatisfied with that, she rolled Karen sideways to pull back the comforter.

Gail heard the creaking of wood, and ancient joints began to loosen.

Lynn tucked Karen in. "There. That's nice." She turned around. "You're next, Grandma."

Irene's gag had slipped to her neck. She rolled toward Lynn's ankle and bit down. Lynn pulled her foot away, but Irene had the cuff of her slacks. Lynn staggered.

One arm of the chair let go with a splintering crack. Gail slid the cord off, then threw her weight on the other arm. She went for the cord at her ankles, fingers driven by desperation. "Mother! Don't let go!"

Screaming curses, Lynn drew back her other foot and kicked. She hopped, tripped over Irene, and went down. Her shoulder thudded into the dresser. The red container of gasoline went over. Lynn hit the floor. Liquid gurgled, splashing onto her shirt and into her hair. She flailed out with her hands and sat up, blinking and sputtering.

Gail leaped at her, and her hands went around Lynn's neck, digging in. Lynn swept them away. Her teeth showed, and madness flooded her eyes. She pushed Gail off her as easily as a doll, then rolled to her feet. Gail scrambled up. There was no way to win. Lynn was stronger, and fueled by her lunatic rage. Gail circled around her and grabbed the snapshots off the dresser and held the lighter under them.

Gray eyes narrowed. "Give me those pictures."

Gail backed toward the door. Still holding the lighter, her fingers slid on the doorknob. Frantically she sought a better grip. Lynn took the knife off the dresser. "Give me the pictures!"

The doorknob turned. "Come get them."

Lynn raised the knife. Gail ran down the hall. She tried the lighter. It clicked uselessly. She whirled around in the living room. "Stop or I'll burn them right now. Jason and Timothy, up in smoke. Say good-bye, Rita Lynn!"

"Give me my kids!"

Gail went sideways toward the glass doors, the nearest way out. Night had fallen—she didn't know when. She pressed the latch and slid open one of the glass panels. Her heart was slamming at her ribs.

The lighter caught, and Gail held the pictures over the flame. "Hell is waiting, you bitch!"

"No!" Lynn rushed at her, snatching them out of her hand.

The gasoline in Lynn's shirt ignited with a whoosh, and the blue and green stripes seemed to writhe. Orange tongues licked across her body, down her legs. Her eyes opened wide in agonized terror, and a scream tore from her lungs. Hair burned and crackled.

Gail stood immobilized, horrified.

The knife clanged on the terrace.

Shimmering, dancing, the flames ate into the darkness and leapt up, outlining the aluminum frame supporting the screen. The fire spun and beat at itself, mouth agape in a soundless cry. Its image flickered on the surface of the water. Then image and fire came together. Flesh hissed. Water surged upward and fell back.

Bits of curled, blackened paper floated on the surface.

TWENTY-FOUR

Irene had been complaining about the orange jasmine, which had overgrown the trellis and invaded the cassia tree. She had wanted to trim it, but her sprained back had been slow to heal. Home from work, Gail glanced through the kitchen window and saw her mother out in the backyard with a pair of clippers. Her movements were still stiff, but a pile of green tendrils, heavy with leaves, had accumulated on the grass beside the trellis.

She unlatched the screen door on the porch. "Mom! Want something to drink?"

Irene's sun hat turned toward the house, and she waved. "I have some ice water. Call Karen."

"Is she all right?"

"Sure. Just wanted to say hi."

Gail went back inside, dropped her purse on her bed, then sat down to dial the number for Dave's apartment in Cruz Bay. Karen would be in the islands with her father for the rest of the summer.

A thousand miles away, Karen picked up the phone.

"Hi, sweetie. It's me. How's it going?"

"Fine. We went to Tortola on the ferry today." Karen's high voice, piping into her ear, described the trip. The seas had been so rough that waves had crashed into the bow, and the salt spray got everybody wet.

"Weren't you scared?"

"No, it was fun." Karen told her how most of the passengers had huddled together on the lower deck, while she and her dad went to the top and hungon to the front railing, yelling like rodeo riders.

"I'd love to have seen that."

"You could come visit. I asked Dad, and he said it would be okay. Do you think you could, Mom? You could stay with me in my room."

"Well . . ."

"Say yes. Please?"

"I'll think about it."

"You always say that."

"Karen, I'm just so busy right now. Besides, you'll be home in another month. Listen. What about having your birthday party after all, when you get back?"

"I'm already eleven."

"Hmm. I don't think you can be officially eleven without a party."

"Oh, Mom."

"We could invite all your friends. Come on. It would be fun."

There was a silence on the line, then Karen said, "Do we have to have my party at Gramma's house?"

"It doesn't look the same at all, you know." Irene's bedroom has been stripped bare and repainted. The gasoline-soaked carpet was gone, and every piece of furniture had been replaced. Karen wouldn't recognize it when she got back.

Karen said, "I know, Mom, but . . . I don't want to. Okay?"

Memories. Gradually receding, but dark currents of terror still swirled through their dreams.

Gail said, "No problem. What about at Molly's house? I'll bet Molly's mother would love to play hostess for you. Then we could take everyone to the beach, or go to a movie. What do you think?"

"Okay. That would be great."

Gail heard Dave's voice in the background; then Karen said she couldn't talk much longer. She had to go to bed early. Her dad was taking her along on a charter fishing trip for some guests at the resort. "He said I could help them bait their hooks. Really, these people are so dumb you wouldn't believe it. The women make these faces and go, *ewwww*. Mom?" There was a pause. "Are you and Gramma okay? I'm worried."

"Don't worry. We're fine."

"You don't have bad dreams or anything?"

"Me? No."

"Swear."

"Well, sometimes. But not *that* bad."

"Me too, sometimes. You know what works? Pretend we were all in this, like, really scary movie. That's what I do. Try it."

For a moment Gail was surprised into silence. Karen had never seemed quite this practical before, or so grown-up in her concern. She wanted to reach out through the phone and hug her. "That's a good idea. All right, I'll try it, but really, we're fine. And so are you? Really, truly?"

"Really, truly. Mom, I have to go. You can call tomorrow if you want to."

"I will. Love you, Karen."

"Love you, too. Bye." She made a kiss into the phone and was gone.

Gail closed her eyes for a moment, then replaced the phone, leaving her hand on the receiver, reluctant to break even that connection. Karen was all right. She would be home soon. And then Gail would talk to her. Or not, depending. The decision couldn't be put off much longer. Time was running out.

Taking off the jacket to her suit, Gail felt the weight of something in the pocket and found the small box she had dropped inside as she left Ferrer & Quintana. The box was covered in black velvet and trimmed in gold. She pressed the catch and the lid slowly opened. A pair of earrings glittered on white satin, big emerald-cut aquamarines surrounded by diamonds. The color of the warm water off Varadero Beach, he had said, giving them to her. He had kissed one ear, then the other. I'll take you there one day.

This afternoon Gail had tried to return them, going first to the house on Malagueña Avenue at a time when he was least likely to be there. The last she had seen of him had been last week, a photo in the newspaper, walking with Harry Lasko into the federal courthouse. *Resort owner pleads guilty to charges of tax evasion, money laundering.*

At the Pedrosa house, Tia Fermina had reluctantly shown Gail into the living room, which seemed to echo with silence. Gail had asked if Digna was at home, but a few minutes later Elena Godoy appeared. Gail stated her purpose, but Elena refused to take the earrings for Anthony. He was no longer in Miami, and no one knew where he had gone—perhaps straight to hell, Elena added with a brittle smile. A few days after the party on the Fourth, muffled shouts had come through the door of Ernesto's study. Anthony had moved out that same night. Since then the old man had barely eaten or spoken to anyone. If he died, it would be on Anthony Quintana's conscience.

Getting back into her car, Gail glanced up at the second floor, the southwest corner where the master suite overlooked the fountain in the circular drive. She saw high windows, heavy brocade curtains, and the vacant, pale face of an old man slumped in a chair. Then a woman's arm reached over and jerked the curtain across the window.

Gail went next to Ferrer & Quintana. She'd had an appointment at four o'clock to sign some papers relating to the house on Clematis Street. Raul Ferrer was acting as trustee, handling the sale and dividing the proceeds. Gail had felt an odd shortness of breath walking through that door, even knowing that she would not see Anthony. After the papers were signed, Gail asked about Ernesto Pedrosa. Raul told her that the grandchildren, led by Elena Pedrosa Godoy, had filed an action in probate court to have the old man declared incompetent. Gail asked if Anthony knew about this. Raul gave an answer that conveyed nothing: Anthony was currently out of the country.

The house of Pedrosa was falling.

Then Gail had put the box on Raul's desk and asked if he could forward the earrings to Anthony, or at least hold them until Anthony returned. Raul sat without speaking for a moment, then shook his head. He had been instructed not to accept anything from her. No letters, no property, no messages. Nothing. Then he had risen from his desk and escorted her to the door. She had seen the regret on his face.

Gail closed the box. She had thought of sending the earrings to Anthony's daughter. Or giving them to charity. Or throwing them into the sea. But that would be foolish, and Gail had decided not to be foolish anymore. Being careful, she could live for several months on what these earrings had cost. She put the box in a drawer and changed her clothes.

A glass of lemonade in each hand, Gail went outside, walking past the pool, feeling the cool tile on the bare soles of her feet. The deck had been scrubbed and bleached, and the pool itself had been drained and refilled. New porch furniture made everything look different. She pushed open the aluminum screen door and kept to the walkway. It had rained, and the grass was soggy.

Irene looked around and smiled. "There you are. With lemonade! You read my mind."

The three-sided rectangle of posts and trellis, with slats for a roof, made a shady spot in the yard. There were uneven pavers on the ground and a wooden bench. The old cedar, silvery with age, was supported more by the jasmine vine than by its own supports, which had rotted after twenty-five years. Gail's father had built it himself, and he'd been no carpenter.

The sun winked orange light through the branches of the live oak tree. The rain had washed some of the humidity out of the air. The day was letting go like a held breath.

"Did you reach Karen?"

"She's going fishing with Dave tomorrow. She sounds so happy. I couldn't ask for more than that, could I?"

"We were all very lucky." Irene took off her hat, unneeded now that the sun was fading. As she set it and her glass down on the bench, her face tightened.

"Mom? Maybe you've done enough for today."

"No, this is good for me. Gets the kinks out." She picked up her clippers and went back to work. Her cheeks and forehead glistened with perspiration. Her eyes moved to Gail, then back to the trellis. "So. How did it go at Mr. Ferrer's office?"

"The papers are signed. All I have to do is wait for the house to be sold."

Irene squeezed her clippers with both hands through a particularly thick vine. The leaves were thin and pointed, the star-like flowers giving off a sweet fragrance. "You know what I mean."

"No, I didn't leave a letter for Anthony. Raul isn't allowed to accept my letters."

"You didn't tell Raul?" When Gail shook her head, Irene said, "But Anthony has a right to know. It's his decision too."

"It's mine. I fell in love, I was careless, and I have to accept the consequences. Mother, don't look at me that way. I'm not the first woman this has happened to."

"Are you afraid he wouldn't take responsibility? Afraid he'd reject you—"

"It's over. There is nothing between us anymore, and for the first time in my life I'm truly free. That may sound very odd, under the circumstances, but it's how I feel. Free and alive and fearless. And not confused about a damned thing."

Irene was still looking at her intently. "But still, he has a right to know."

Gail kissed her cheek. "I love you, but really, what do you expect, that everything would suddenly be all right between us? It won't. Not ever."

"Oh, darling. Everyone has troubles. You can't have a perfect life."

"Don't I even get to have *my* life, imperfect as it may be? That's all I want."

Irene said quietly, "What are you going to do?"

Gail shrugged.

"Just don't do anything . . . irreversible. I mean, without some serious thought."

"That's all I've done lately—think about it." Gail picked up the yard bag. "Let me help you finish before it gets dark. Here, hold this open."

"Darling—"

Gail dropped an armful of clippings into the bag. "I don't know what I'm going to do, Mother. That's the truth. But what I do know is that it's going to be all right. Whatever happens, I can deal with it. I've never felt that before, not so completely." She smiled at Irene, and perhaps her mother could see the effort it took, but perhaps not.

Irene's blue eyes moved slowly over her face. "All right. I don't understand you, but as long as you're happy . . ." She stepped back and looked at the trellis, brushing a hand over the foliage she had just trimmed. "This is better, isn't it? I think it's coming right along."

A breeze came off the bay and wandered through the trellis, filling the evening air with the sweet scent of jasmine.

ACKNOWLEDGMENTS

As ever, I relied on the help of others in bringing this story to life. Thank you, thank you to lawyers Adele Blackmore, Laura Fabar, Milton Hirsch, Eric Cohen, and Richard Cahan. For insight on many of my characters, I am grateful to Norman Powell, Merry Haber, Rick David, Patti Neill, and Andrea Lane. For details I could not have done without, my thanks to Jorge Milian and Mary Hoerber Milian, Dave Gilbert, Jerry Reichardt, and Harry Coleman. For my wonderful sister, Laura, another round of applause.